BLOWN
AWAY

Also by David Wiltse

NOVELS

Bone Deep

Into the Fire

The Edge of Sleep

Close to the Bone

Prayer for the Dead

Home Again

The Fifth Angel

The Serpent

The Wedding Guest

PLAYS

Triangles for Two

Crazy Horse and Three Stars

Temporary Help

Hatchetman

Dance Lesson

A Grand Romance

Doubles

Suggs

DAVID WILTSE

BLOWN AWAY

G. P. PUTNAM'S SONS / NEW YORK

G. P. Putnam's Sons
Publishers Since 1838
200 Madison Avenue
New York, NY 10016

Published simultaneously in Canada

Library of Congress Cataloging-in-Publication Data

Wiltse, David.
Blown away / David Wiltse.
p. cm.
ISBN 0-399-14208-8 (alk. paper)
1. Becker, John (Fictitious character)—Fiction. 2. Private investigators—United States—Fiction. I. Title.
PS3573.I478B56 1996 96-2387 CIP
813'.54—dc20

Printed in the United States of America
10 9 8 7 6 5 4 3 2 1

This book is printed on acid-free paper. ♾

Book design by Songhee Kim

To J. B.,

who showed up when I needed him,
strived mightily in the cause,
and ultimately fell just short.
With gratitude, rue, and relief.

BLOWN
AWAY

PROLOGUE

HE FELT HIMSELF TO BE A GOD swooping down from heaven on a mission of chastisement, Cole astride a thunderbolt hurled toward earth. His sense of power came from the thunderbolt itself, its electrical force crackling through and around him until he became one with the source. Strong enough to collapse the earth, powerful enough to conflate the globe in his fist to its nuclear essence, then blow it into a fireball larger than the sun.

There was enough explosive in his knapsack to lift the Greyhound off the highway and pop it open like a rotten fruit. He was atremble with his power and felt himself shaking like a man with an overdose of adrenaline. It would not have surprised him to see sparks jump between his fingers or for people passing in the aisle to have their hair leap upright on their heads.

He forced himself to sit very still, his hands around his mouth to disguise lips that were mumbling quietly and incessantly. He looked to some like a man in prayer. No one would have suspected he was a god on a mission. Cole in pursuit of justice.

The gorges of the rivers pouring into Cayuga Lake below Cornell University's campus are a lovely place to die. Several students take the plunge each year, hurling themselves onto the rocks some hundred feet below, although it is doubtful that aesthetics are much on their minds at the final moment. There is an abruptness to the geology of this part of Ithaca that stuns and seduces the human eye, transforming great rents in the earth and rock from cataclysms of nature to wonders of design. To the feverish imagination the verdant hillside campus looks as if it lies on land that bears the ancient mark of a giant claw whose talons have riven wounds in the rock that continue to bleed into Lake Cayuga. The streams at the bottoms of the gorges contort and twist their way to lower levels, lashing themselves into the tortured white water that humans find so fascinating, and a series of bridges span the chasms.

For some the view of the Fall Creek gorge might have inspired thoughts of art, a theory of aesthetics, or speculation about humanity's preference for scenes of violence in nature to those of the idyllic, of spectacle to calm. Jason Cole was a man of many theories, but they had nothing to do with nature. He was concerned with human nature and its infinite capacity for deceit and betrayal. His mind was absorbed by thoughts of plots and counterplots, injustice and revenge. And most specifically at the moment, he was wrapped in thoughts of destruction. The beauty of the scene made no impression on him as he climbed the paved sidewalk that ran parallel to the gorge, rising in elevation with every step. He was dressed in the casual grunge of a student and wore a knapsack that was intended to pass as a book bag to the incidental observer, but Cole was not a student and the knapsack contained eighty pounds of high explosives.

Cole was thirty and bookish by nature. The few people who noticed him on the path in the twilight—if they noticed him at all—assumed he was a student or, at the most, a postgrad. Anyone associated with a university was more than accustomed to seeing intense young men muttering to themselves and did not take them

for a danger to themselves or to society. In the case of Jason Cole that was a mortal mistake.

A former academic himself, Cole knew precisely how inconspicuous he was; he used the fact to his advantage. Except for the moment when he would actually place the charge, he would be all but invisible.

Cole slowed as he approached the footbridge over the Fall Creek gorge that was his target. It was the famous suicide bridge, the launching pad of choice for the despondent. He looked around casually, stretching his back as if taking a quick break in his climb. He saw no one on the paved path and stepped quickly onto the steps that led to the bridge, walking through the cover of trees. Only someone coming directly behind him on the trail or approaching from across the bridge would be able to see him.

The gorge was narrowest here. The bridge was a simple span supported by two cables anchored in a concrete slab buried in the hillside. The cables were held to the tieplate by a two-and-a-half-inch-thick steel rod like a pin through a ring. It was a basic system, perfectly adequate under normal circumstances, but it was not made to withstand high explosives. Cole's question was *how much* explosive to use.

He was a scientist, and a scientist needs data and a laboratory in which to experiment. They had deprived him of his laboratory, so he was forced to create his own as best he could—and new experiments to suit it. If they suffered in the process, then so be it, they had only themselves to blame. By "they" Cole meant the solons of academia, universities' elites, all of whom he knew to be in collusion. Cole had no grudge against Cornell in particular, it merely happened to have a very convenient bridge on which he could learn his craft. His malice was reserved for City College of New York and the city of New York that sponsored, shielded, and protected it. At this time in his life, however, Cole had malice enough to go around; if some spilled over onto Cornell, it was a loss he could easily afford.

Shrugging off the knapsack, he stepped from the path into the undergrowth surrounding the bridge's cable base. He removed one of the bombs from the knapsack and lifted it clumsily to the point where the rod secured cable to concrete. The bomb was wrapped in gunnysacking so that at a quick glance it looked like nothing more than a sandbag placed to shore up the cable. A closer inspection would not reveal much more unless the observer knew what he was looking for. A waterproof plastic bag held forty pounds of the high explosive ANFO, which Cole had doctored with food coloring to look like sand. The consistency was slightly coarser than sand, formed of prills, or pellets that made it feel more like crushed rice kernels, but buried within the ANFO was a radio-activated blasting cap that would convert the "sand" to heat, light, and concussive blast within microseconds. It did not look like a bomb, and strictly speaking, it was not a bomb at all, it was an explosive charge. It lacked the metallic frame of a bomb that would fracture, kill, and destroy by converting the metal to flying shrapnel. Planted in the body of a car, it would be a bomb. Planted at the base of a bridge, it was a charge. The distinction was one that Cole liked to make to himself. His one attempt at a bomb had been an embarrassing failure; this was his first try at a charge.

After placing the other gunnysack against the pin of the second cable, Cole strode down a flight of steps leading to the base of the gorge, skirting the bridge entirely. If noticed from above, he would not be seen to have entered into the woods in front of the bridge, then come out again the same way. He was still just a student taking a walk, not a man acting erratically. He followed the well-worn path along the water's edge for as long as he could bear the suspense of not turning round. The radio detonator was in a side pocket of the knapsack. He could almost feel it throbbing against his back like a living creature longing to be stroked. Only when he

had reached the base of the next bridge upstream did he begin to follow the path back up to the pavement, and only then did he allow himself a glance backward.

A young man and woman were walking toward the center of the bridge from the North Campus, the side opposite the charges. He would wait for them to clear the span. By the time he reached the second bridge itself, he could see no one else approaching. This second bridge was a wider, sturdier span designed for vehicular as well as pedestrian traffic. It would vibrate when cars were on it, he knew, but standing on it alone, he felt none of the sway and bounce that made each crossing of the footbridge a mild adventure.

The couple stopped in the middle of the footbridge. They looked over the side, holding hands. For a moment Cole wondered if they were going to leap off, linked together, like a bird of enormous wingspan; then they pulled back from the edge and the young man embraced the woman.

Cole waited impatiently for them to move on. Traffic was bound to come soon and he could not be exposed for any length of time without drawing attention to himself. His rented bicycle was in the parking lot of the campus observatory less than two hundred yards from the bridge and he could be on the bike and into the anonymity of the campus within three minutes of unhurried walking and riding after the charge was detonated. Escape was no problem. Detection at the site was.

The lovebirds lingered. He was reminded of Thornton Wilder's novel *The Bridge of San Luis Rey*, in which a number of disparate lives were joined for only a second during the collapse of the bridge over a mountain pass. Cole was no lover of literature, but he had remembered that story. There was a sense of shared destiny about it that appealed to him.

Finally the couple came out of their embrace. They separated, the woman coming toward Cole's side of the bridge, the man heading back toward the North Campus. Cole waited until both cleared the span and entered the woods. The man was gone from his sight completely but Cole knew that the girl was only temporarily out of view. She would come out of the woods only to reappear on the paved sidewalk. When it seemed to take her longer than necessary, Cole began to fear that she had discovered the charges, but then she emerged from the woods, gained the sidewalk, and walked away down the hill, her back to him.

He counted to 20 to give her plenty of space and then removed the detonator from his backpack, unlatched the safety lock, and turned the lever that initiated the radio signal. The signal would start the spark to deflagrate the tiny load of nitromannite in the blasting cap that would in turn unleash the power of the ANFO. As he did so, he saw the young man run back onto the bridge. He was calling something, probably the young woman's name, and waving his arms when the charges exploded.

At first Cole thought nothing had happened and he felt relief along with disappointment but then the sound of the blast hit him, delayed by distance, and he felt the bridge he was standing on sway in reaction. The young man on the footbridge was knocked off his feet and he fell comically, landing on his ass. He sat there for a long moment, stunned, before rising to his feet.

As clouds of smoke and debris swirled upward from the underbrush the young man on the bridge took one hesitant step toward Cole's side of the gorge, as if he would continue in pursuit of his girlfriend. But then, with the slow, inevitable motion of a dream, the bridge began to fall. The cable went limp and the span tilted gradually downward, its base still hidden in the underbrush. The young man stopped, clinging to the handrail, as the angle of the tilt grew larger, the bridge being drawn into the chasm by its own weight. He turned and tried to run up hill, scrambling desperately, but the angle steepened until the sheer bulk of the span tore its way through resisting treetops and broke free completely. The mangled steel of the bridge end fell into the chasm and swung across the gorge like a pendulum.

Cole marveled at the majesty with which the 250-foot length wheeled through space. Its size seemed to command dignity and it dropped as sedately as a crinolined Victorian dowager. It bounced once off the far cliff face amid a shower of rock and greenery and then came to rest, quivering and twisted.

The noise was too vast for Cole to hear the man scream but he saw his body plunge toward the bottom of the gorge, grasping until the last toward the bridge that had so perfidiously dropped from under him.

Cole forced himself to leave his vantage point and walk deliberately but not hurriedly toward his bicycle. The incredible image of the falling bridge was in his mind the rest of the evening and filled his dreams with imaginative variations on the event. He slept soundly and waited in the morning for the arrival of the local paper before boarding the Greyhound for the trip back to New York City.

The name of the young student who had plunged to his death was Harold Spring. Cole felt a tinge of sadness as he read about the youth's brief past and bright promise. He was allowed to be sentimental, he told himself. Spring, after all, was his first victim.

CHAPTER

PEGEEN HADDAD HAD BEEN TOLD by a jilted suitor in her teenage years that she had "legs like a fucking dray horse." Before the night was over she knew the precise meaning of "dray horse," which was more than could be said of the suitor, who finished the evening with a welt the size of a horse apple on his cheekbone where Pegeen had cracked him with her forearm. She remembered the name of the suitor and the snarl of vindictive cruelty on his face when he made the pronouncement—shortly after she had removed his paws from her breasts for the umpteenth time, and just before his expression was changed dramatically by the forearm to the face—and she was certain she would never forget the remark. She had thought of it nearly every time in the subsequent eighteen years that she shaved her legs—but somehow it had never really hurt her feelings. Even at the time, it had been more the pain of the boy's intent to hurt her than the remark itself that had bothered her. In her mind there was actually nothing wrong with her legs themselves; they were long and built rather more for power than grace, to be sure, but they were well proportioned and curved nicely at the calves. It was the ankles that were thick—which made sandals a questionable fashion choice—but in her catalogue of features about herself that she did not like, her legs were far down the list.

Although many had told her she was pretty, Pegeen herself was never convinced, primarily because of the aureole of bushy auburn hair that surrounded her head and defied control—a legacy of her Irish mother—and her fair complexion that grew fiery red when she was excited or embarrassed.

Pegeen had occasion to think of all these features as she tucked the 9 mm semiautomatic Sig Sauer in her ankle holster underneath the navy-blue trousers and checked her appearance in the mirror yet again. Becker was coming to meet her, although she didn't think he realized it would be her, and he always made her nervous. Worse than nervous, she admitted to herself. Although she had reason to be pissed at him, maybe even hate him, she knew that when she was in his presence she would be excited. Her face would glow like a stoplight and maybe even blink on and off for all she knew.

There was nothing for it, she would just have to tough it out. Becker would see through any subterfuge anyway, so she might as well get all hot and bothered and enjoy it, she told herself. The question was, would Becker also enjoy her discomfort? And if so, in which way? She would not know from watching him, that much was certain. Just as he seemed to read her like an open book, she couldn't read him at all, a problem she had with men in general, which might account for her being thirty-three and not only without any serious romantic interest but without even any adequate sex partner who was willing to feign affection in return for satiation.

Pegeen left the rest room and returned to the state police shed, just inside the George Washington Bridge tolls, that the FBI had commandeered as a temporary office for the duration of the meeting they all awaited. Hatcher—the lizard, as Pegeen thought of

him—was pacing the room, working his way between desks, stopping frequently to peer out at the toll plaza bathed in baking sunlight. A cluster of FBI agents and police from New York and New Jersey were gathered in one corner of the room, far from the window, as if shunning their peripatetic superior. Meisner, a plainclothes New York cop whom Pegeen had met for the first time minutes ago, sat on the worn sofa and mugged behind Hatcher's back for Pegeen's benefit as if they were lifelong allies. It was remarkable how quickly people could take a dislike to Hatcher, she thought. He *tried* to be liked, that was the pathetic part. Hatcher went through the motions as if he had memorized the procedures for making friends but had never grasped the spirit of the enterprise. He had the Nixon-like quality of seeming phony in everything he did—except plotting malice. Everyone knew he was genuine then.

"Now, people, let's remember Special Agent Becker is going through a difficult patch here. We might find him a little—ah—short," Hatcher said

It was the third time that Hatcher had warned them about Becker. Meisner rolled his eyes impatiently at Pegeen.

"He's not always the most—diplomatic—of men," Hatcher continued, his eyes flitting toward the toll plaza again. "At the best of times . . . at the very best of times . . ."

Lost in a sudden reverie, Hatcher drifted off, pulling the venetian blinds to one side for a better view. Meisner looked at Pegeen, shrugging his shoulders, aping some more for her entertainment. She was not sure if the cop was flirting or if he was the kind of man who could only make friends by joining forces against a third party.

Pegeen looked at him severely, giving him what she thought of as her stern look, a wordless glare intended to quell the rowdy and put a brace in the back of the slovenly. She disliked Hatcher as much as anyone but felt disloyal mocking a Bureau superior with a city cop. Cops tended to show the FBI little enough respect as it was. The feeling, of course, was mutual.

Meisner grinned at her, a goofy slide of the lips, half tough guy, half clowning boy. He was definitely not her idea of a law enforcement officer.

Pegeen realized that she had been looking at him for too long. Her chilling glare seemed to be having the opposite effect. Meisner winked at her.

"What with his wife and all," Hatcher said abruptly, as if continuing a conversation. He turned to them and gave one of his inappropriate smiles. He looked at those moments like a galvanized frog, Pegeen thought. His facial muscles twitched into a caricature of a smile, as if someone had thrown a switch and he smiled regardless of context or appropriateness.

"His wife is an associate deputy director of the Bureau," Pegeen explained to Meisner. "On medical leave."

"Quite heroic, of course," Hatcher chimed. "Quite, quite heroic."

Karen Crist suffered the lasting effects of a severe concussion administered at the hands of a maniac who had pounded her head against a porcelain bathtub in an effort to kill her. Becker had ultimately dropped the man off a cliff—or had failed to prevent him from falling, depending on the interpretation one preferred. The official version was the latter.

"Very talented woman," Hatcher continued absently. "Dreadful loss to the Bureau." He flashed his inappropriate smile.

"She'll be back to work eventually, won't she?" Pegeen asked. Her strongest recollection of Karen Crist was when she found herself fixed in the other woman's basilisk stare for a very long, uncomfortable meeting. Crist had assumed that something was going on between Pegeen and Becker, an assumption based solely on intuition—and quite accurate. Pegeen had been consumed with guilt at the time and still heard Crist mentioned with discomfort.

Due to scheduling and assignments—arrangements Crist had power to influence—Pegeen had not seen Becker since. She had no idea whether he had confessed their frantic one-night stand, but knowing Becker, she doubted it.

"We all devoutly hope she will return soon, of course," Hatcher was saying. "Can't rush these things, mustn't rush."

Formerly her superior, Hatcher had been recently demoted to a position collateral with Crist's. Pegeen could imagine how devoutly Hatcher wished her return. His ambition was as widely known as his unpopularity.

Pegeen kept her gaze on Hatcher when he talked, out of feigned deference, but she was aware of Meisner's eyes on her, sizing her up.

"He's some pisser, this guy, I heard," Meisner said.

Hatcher turned to him as if astonished that he could speak.

"Ah."

"This Becker," Meisner said. "He's a hard case?"

Hatcher turned back to the window. "Well, you know John," he said.

"I never met him. I heard some stories, mostly bullshit . . . Bullshit, right?" He looked to Pegeen for confirmation.

"What'd you hear?"

"The guy's eight feet tall."

"No," Pegeen said.

"He's got *cojones* so big he carries them in a pushcart . . ." Meisner saw an expression he took for amusement flicker across Pegeen's face. "Also bullshit, right?"

"He's actually quite sensitive," Pegeen said. She joined Hatcher by the window as if two sets of eyes might spy Becker sooner. Meisner had never seen anyone's ears turn that bright a shade of red.

"I'd be sensitive too, I carried my balls in a wheelbarrow," Meisner said. "I'd be watching out for all them bumps."

Hatcher turned from the window and faced Meisner. Some of the others in the room had been chuckling. Hatcher regarded them for a moment as if they had been speaking a foreign language.

"Becker is a special agent of the FBI," he said. It was unclear if he meant it as a demand for respect or a summation of the man's qualities.

Meisner stood and pulled at his crotch, making himself comfortable. When he thought he had stared at Hatcher long enough to establish his independence, he crossed to the window to stand by Pegeen.

"Saw a picture of a Chinaman with his nuts in a wagon once," he said in hushed tones, as if speaking an endearment. "He had whatchacallit, elephantitis. Scary."

"Charming."

"Hey, no offense."

Pegeen looked at him from the corner of her eye. He touched her elbow tentatively with the tip of his finger.

"No shit," he continued. "Just let me know if I'm out of line. I get out of hand, sometimes. I'm paper-trained and all, you know, but sometimes I just forget myself in the presence of a lady."

She turned to him and he gave her his loopy grin again. She decided he was kind of cute.

Somehow Becker arrived when no one was looking. He stood in the doorway, a dark shape in the center of a glare of midday sun, his hands on his hips in an attitude of disapproval. He didn't know I'd be here, Pegeen thought. He hates it. She was aware of a certain difficulty in breathing.

Hatcher bustled forward, bumping clumsily into the edge of a desk on his way, his hand thrust in front of him like a ship's prow.

"John," he exclaimed. "Good to see you."

Becker made no move to extend his hand, so Hatcher dived for it with both of his own, pulling it up and shaking it as if he had just caught a fish bare-handed.

"Special Agent John Becker," Hatcher announced to the room proudly.

Becker nodded into the chorus of greetings from the assembled officers but his eyes lingered on Pegeen. She felt as if her ears would burst into flame, making her the first authenticated case of human spontaneous combustion. She tried to return his serious, noncommittal gaze.

"The wife is well?" Hatcher asked, dropping into his conspiratorial tone. "Coming along all right?"

Becker ignored Hatcher, glanced briefly at the occupants of the room once more, and settled on Meisner.

"Haven't met you," he said. "John Becker."

"Arnold Meisner," said the cop, thrusting out his hand. "New York City police."

They shook hands and Pegeen noticed Meisner drawing himself up, measuring himself against Becker.

"Heard a lot about you," Meisner said.

"All bullshit," Becker said. "Don't believe any of it."

Meisner glanced at Pegeen. "That's what I figured."

"Good instincts," said Becker, smiling. He turned to Hatcher. "We waiting for someone?"

"No, no," Hatcher said. "Not at all. Let's begin. Gentlemen, if you would."

As the officers and agents gathered round him, Hatcher unfolded the situation. Pegeen glanced at Becker whenever he wasn't looking in her direction. She thought he looked thinner than she remembered. Tired. Older. Uncared for. Men went to seed very quickly without a woman to keep them cultivated, she thought. Women could not afford such a luxury, they had to maintain themselves through thick and thin, but left to their own devices men went downhill fast.

"December twenty-four of last year Sharyl Makins, a deputy mayor of New York City, received a package in the mail wrapped in

Christmas paper. When she opened it the package exploded. Ms. Makins lost her right hand and is blind in one eye as a result." Dealing with just the facts and not with people, Hatcher sounded like a different man, confident and brisk. "Four days later the mayor received a message composed of letters cut from headlines of the *New York Times.* The message said, 'To establish my credentials.' It was signed 'Spring.' The letter was postmarked from the Fordham Station in the Bronx. Ms. Makins, perhaps incidentally, or perhaps not, is black."

Becker caught Pegeen's eyes briefly but looked at her as if he didn't know her. There was no twinkle of affection, no sign of a shared remembrance, not even displeasure at her presence. He doesn't even know I'm here, she thought, then realized that of course that couldn't be true. He couldn't fail to recognize her; his reaction was far worse. He just didn't care.

"The technicians found nothing useful on the stationery or the envelope. The stamp was sealed with tap water, not saliva; so was the envelope. The individual letters were cut out of the paper with thick scissors, probably kitchen variety . . . April eighteen, the mayor received another letter, same type. I quote: 'Second warning of the Apocalypse. Conditions to follow.' And again it was signed, 'Spring.' The NYPD immediately alerted all city and state employees to beware of any unusual packages in the mail, but this time a Fed Ex package with a bomb in it was sent to Denis K. Patel, a professor of mathematics who is of Pakistani origin, at New York University. Mr. Patel, Professor Patel, did not recognize the sender's name but opened the package anyway. He died of his injuries five days later. Federal Express records show that the package was dropped in a pickup box along with the correct amount of postage—in cash. The money was clean—and I mean clean. The lab people believe it was actually steamed before it was put in the envelope. The return address on the shipping bill was H. Spring,

25001J, Grand Concourse, the Bronx. A fictitious address. The drop-off box was in an office lobby, also on the Grand Concourse."

"Spring sticks close to home," offered one of the agents.

"Thus far," Hatcher replied primly. "There's more. One week later the mayor received another letter. Composed the same as the first two. Just as clean. Quoting again, 'Makins and Patel are my bona fides. The system must change. After this I get serious. Five million dollars or I will destroy every bridge and tunnel into Manhattan. Respond via "for men" personals in *New York Post* by May fifteen or war begins.' "

The men exchanged glances. It was already late June.

"A response was posted in the personal columns in the *Post* addressed to Spring. 'Need more information. Let's be friends.' "

From the rear of the room Meisner laughed aloud. Hatcher looked up from his notes, startled. The agents closest to Meisner inched away from him. Pegeen gave him a stern look but Meisner grinned at her like the class clown, beyond rebuke. "Friends?" he mouthed, gesticulating.

As Hatcher continued, Pegeen glanced at Becker to see if he had noticed her interchange with Meisner. He stood with his arms folded over his chest, staring at some point in the middle distance, looking for all the world as if he were daydreaming. Pegeen knew he would not have missed a thing that happened in the room since his arrival.

"Which brings us to the present," Hatcher said. "At three a.m. this morning a Bridge and Tunnel Authority worker found this attached to one of the central struts of the George Washington Bridge." Hatcher donned a pair of plastic gloves and pulled a large cardboard suitcase from under one of the desks and put it on the surface. Pegeen had seen suitcases that large only in airline queues of people returning to Latin America. "The lab people have been all over this, but please don't touch it nonetheless. Inside it, in a plastic sandwich bag, was approximately two ounces of ANFO—a mixture of ammonium nitrate and fuel oil, the most commonly used high explosive in the country."

"The note?" Becker asked.

A flicker of disappointment crossed Hatcher's face as if he had been deprived of his big moment.

"There was a note, yes, very good. Obviously this is not enough explosive to seriously damage the bridge. The engineers inform us that it was attached to a non-load-bearing strut and would have done no serious structural harm if it had been filled with explosive. The point, however, is that it was there at all. That this 'Spring' had gone to the trouble to strap it on with about eighteen feet of rope, the kind of clothesline rope you can buy in any hardware store, unfortunately—the fact that he had done it at all seems to make his point that he can strike when he wants to."

Becker had moved to the window, working his way around the outskirts of the group of agents like the one student in class who refuses to pay attention. Pegeen had not seen him look directly at Hatcher since entering the building—his disrespect and dislike of the older man was part of the Becker legend within the Bureau. Hatcher, on the other hand, was acutely aware of Becker, and his eyes followed him around the room. His voice seemed to modulate from control to anxiety depending on Becker's state of motion and the distance he traveled from Hatcher.

"The note," Becker repeated. He seemed to be looking through the window without opening the blinds.

"Yes, the note, thank you, John. The note says, 'Do I have your attention? You must unlearn what you think you know. Spring.' "

Becker asked, "How long has the Bureau been on this?"

"Ah, well, sending the first bomb through the mail was a federal offense, of course, and we've been in it at a rather low level since then."

"We got in this morning, right?" Becker asked. "When this bridge was threatened."

"Well, as I say, since the first . . . With both feet, just since this morning, yes, John, that's correct, in the sense of full participation. I was given control of the case this morning. I assembled my team and naturally I thought of you . . ."

Becker walked toward the bathroom and held the door open, then crooked his finger. The associate deputy director looked around in an elaborate dumb show, seeking the object of Becker's beckoning finger. He did everything but point to himself and say "Me?" before sheepishly walking through the crowd of men toward the bathroom. The agents parted before him, stifling smirks behind grim visages. Becker stood aside when Hatcher reached him, holding the door open even wider so that Hatcher was forced to enter the bathroom. For a horrified moment Hatcher thought that Becker was going to close the door and lock him in, but then, in a motion that frightened him even more, Becker stepped into the bathroom with him and closed the door on the room outside.

It was a very small room, designed without frills for one person at a time, and when Becker moved toward him Hatcher was forced to sit on the toilet or straddle it. He sat, realizing immediately that it was a mistake because it was impossible to maintain any dignity from that position, with his nose at belt level to the man over whom he wished to maintain command control.

"Thought we should clear the air right now," Becker said, no trace of irony in his voice.

Hatcher could hear the murmur commence among the agents in the other room. Talking about him, he knew. With disrespect, with enjoyment of his humiliation. He hated them, all of them. They had mocked him all his life, had avoided him during his moments of success but were always there to gloat at his failure. He hated them all, but he hated Becker most. And unlike the others, he feared Becker. Hatcher had been forced to deal with him many times over the years and had emerged victorious every time, tolerating Becker's disdain while managing to take full credit for Becker's triumphs. He had risen up the ladder of promotion in the Bureau on Becker's back and had been forced to overcome the agent's surly contempt every rung of the way. But Hatcher was used to being disliked; he used it to fuel his rise, storing every slight and resentment and drawing energy from them. He repaid when he could do so covertly, disguising his revenge within the chain of command. His best revenge against Becker, however, was to use the agent's unusual and highly effective talents time and again to his own advantage. He would lick whatever Becker handed him, swallow and smile, then use the man to advance himself.

His career success notwithstanding, Hatcher was still uneasy about that violent, unpredictable element—physical, mental, emotional—that pulsed beneath Becker's calm, ostensibly contemplative exterior. Masked by the man's preternatural stillness was a current that made dealing with him feel like playing with a live electrical wire. Hatcher did so with extreme caution. It was lethal—but it was also the source of all that power.

"You got demoted," Becker said.

"Reassigned really, John . . ."

"So close to the top, all you had to do was poison one or two people and you would have been there. Must be very frustrating for you."

Hatcher tried to dismiss the insult with a chuckle.

"I heard you were in charge in Utah," Becker continued. "You were the jackass who gave the orders for the sharpshooter to fire and kill the bystander."

"He acted entirely on his own authority," Hatcher protested. "I gave no such order . . ."

"Didn't work this time, though, did it? You couldn't get away with blaming your subordinates for your own fuckups."

"I was set up."

Becker laughed. "*You* were set up. That would be a first. You've set up somebody to take the fall on every job you've ever handled."

"There has been a lot of malicious talk," Hatcher said, trying to maintain his dignity while tilting his head straight upward to meet Becker's eye. "I have enemies . . ."

"I know. I'm one of them."

Hatcher smiled his inappropriate smile as if Becker had just paid him a compliment. "I've never thought of you that way, John. You're not a jealous man, you're not a petty man, you would never begrudge me my advancements the way lesser men do . . ."

"I know shit when I step in it," Becker said. "I told Tyler I wouldn't work with you again. Does he know you dragooned me into this job with you?"

"Frank Tyler is a wonderful executive and a fine man, a fine man . . ."

"Does he know?"

"He took early retirement last week, John. I'm surprised he didn't call you."

"Tyler's retired?"

"He was encouraged to do so, is my understanding. He was ultimately the man in charge in Utah, not me."

Becker turned deathly still. This was the way Hatcher feared him most. He lowered his eyes so he was looking at Becker's belt buckle. He didn't mind if Becker saw him toady, even grovel, but he did not want the other man to see his fear. It might be all that was needed to trigger the infamous violence that resided within him. If Becker started to kill someone, the person ended up dead. It was part of the Becker legend.

"So you managed to set up Frank Tyler and all you got was a demotion," Becker said. The slow and measured tones made Hatcher more fearful. When he got out of this—and the one thing Hatcher depended upon in life was *always* getting out of things—

he vowed to deal with Becker only from a distance, sheltered by as many intermediaries as he could manage.

Becker raised his arm and Hatcher closed his eyes, involuntarily issuing a tiny squeak of terror. When nothing happened he opened them, looked up, and saw Becker unscrewing the overhead light bulb. There was no window in the bathroom and the room was plunged abruptly into total darkness.

What are they doing in there? Taking time out for a quickie or what?''

Pegeen turned to see Meisner at her side. The entire group of agents had drifted toward the bathroom hoping to hear something, but none of them was bold enough to actually put an ear to the door.

''I would guess that they're talking,'' said Pegeen. She gave him her stern gaze. It bothered him as little as a word of reproof to a frisky dog. ''There's not much point in speculating.''

''Who's the honcho here? It's Hatcher, right?''

Pegeen nodded assent.

''So how come this Becker seems to be in charge? Hatcher keeps looking at him for permission to fart. Becker his mother or something?''

''How'd you get assigned to this duty? What sort of cop are you, exactly?''

''You're not offended I said 'fart.' Come on. A man's got to be able to talk.''

''Not to me, he doesn't. . . . Are you in the bomb squad? Why are you here?''

''What are you, Lady Di? I thought you were a Fed. All of a sudden I can't say 'fart' to a Fed?''

''Your language doesn't bother me. I'm sure you're doing the

very best you can," said Pegeen, wondering how she had gotten embroiled in this discussion, and why she continued it.

Meisner inclined his head toward the bathroom. "So, no shit, what's the deal here? They asshole buddies, or what?"

Pegeen took a step away from Meisner. "Do you have a badge you could show me? Some kind of identification?" She felt not only her ears but her whole face aflame. She was certain she looked like a ripe tomato.

"You're blushing," Meisner said in wonder. "I don't remember last time I saw a woman blush. I think it was a nun."

Pegeen contemplated kicking him but turned away instead. Meisner was at her side in a second, leaning close to her, touching her arm.

"Hey, no offense. I like it, I think it's cute." She felt his breath on her face, smelling faintly of garlic. "Shows you're sensitive."

"Don't whisper," she hissed back at him. Several of the agents had turned to look at the two of them with knowing smiles. Pegeen wanted to fall through the floor.

In the pitch-blackness of the bathroom, Hatcher struggled for control of himself. To speak might bring forth Becker's wrath, which Hatcher could already feel as a palpable force in the dark. Without motion, without a sound of any kind, Hatcher was convinced he could sense Becker's presence pulsing in the tiny room. This must be what all those whom Becker had killed experienced at the final moment, Hatcher thought. They had all died at close range with Becker, in the dark, under confined and claustrophobic conditions. They must have known this throb of bloodlust close to them, he thought. Like a rabbit frozen by terror as the predator smelled its way toward it in the dark.

He heard a zipper being pulled down just in front of his nose.

Oh, Christ, no, he thought. Oh, Christ, no.

"Don't move," Becker said, his voice sounding loud as a cannon in the enclosed space.

"John . . ."

Hatcher felt flesh touch his face. He yelped involuntarily, then squeezed his eyes shut even though he could see nothing in the dark.

Becker gripped his jaw, holding his face immobile. Hatcher felt Becker's fingers pushing through the flesh of his cheeks and against his teeth. He tried to speak Becker's name but the sound came out as a desperate meaningless gargle.

"Be quiet," Becker said calmly. "Nothing you can say is going to help you."

Hatcher continued to moan, refusing to believe that he couldn't talk his way out of trouble, any trouble. Becker squeezed harder until Hatcher's mouth popped open and the noise ceased.

For a moment all was still within the bathroom again and the voices from the other room came through distinctly. Hatcher heard someone say "asshole" and knew they were speaking of him as a chorus of laughter spread among the men and filtered into the bathroom. There would be ways to punish them all, he thought. Given time. Time was always the key to proper revenge. There was a lifetime in which to work if one had patience enough.

"This is for Frank Tyler," Becker said. His voice was low and even. He did not sound angry in the least.

Hatcher braced himself for what he knew was coming and prayed it would be quick. He would not think of the humiliation now, there would be time enough for that. For now he would simply survive it and find a way to deal with Becker later.

The tinkle of water startled him and he was at first horrified and then relieved. Being pissed on was preferable to the alternative.

Spray hit his face and he winced, jerking away from the moisture. Becker's hand released him and, through his closed eyelids,

Hatcher was aware of the light coming on. He opened his eyes, squinting more than he needed to, instinctively trying to elicit sympathy. Becker still stood in front of him. Water ran from the faucet at the sink and Becker flicked his fingers through it again, sending another spray into Hatcher's face. He was beaming broadly.

"I feel better," Becker said. "How about you?"

Hatcher swallowed and gasped to fill his lungs. He realized he had been holding his breath for a long time.

"What did you *think* was happening?" Becker asked.

Hatcher nodded his head as if in agreement. "I trusted you, John."

"What a foolhardy thing to do."

"I knew it would be all right."

"I must be losing my touch," Becker said. "I thought for a moment you were just a tiny bit scared."

"We'll just keep this incident between ourselves," Hatcher said. "No reason to talk about it."

"The toad who would not die. No one will squash you, because they'd get slimed."

"I think we can still work together, John," Hatcher managed. "Don't you?"

Becker burst into laughter, shaking his head in amazement and admiration.

"You're the best," Becker said. "You are the fucking best asshole in the world."

"Naturally I'll spend most of my time in Washington. I know you prefer to work without too much supervision."

Hatcher stood, straddling the toilet, attempting to straighten his clothes while on his feet but not wanting to touch Becker in the process. His tie had worked its way to the side of his neck. He was clammy with sweat and his entire body tingled with the residue of fear, but he was in control of himself again.

"It's best to go out together," he said as Becker reached for the door. "We don't want anyone to get the wrong impression."

Becker stared at him incredulously.

"Ready?" Hatcher asked. "As a team now." He propelled Becker before him and through the door.

The two men stepped into the roomful of agents, Hatcher hanging half a step behind Becker and his hand hovering close to the other man's shoulder as if giving him a companionable pat. He wore just the trace of a smile, as if he were pleased with what had gone on in the bathroom but did not want to boast or gloat. When Becker stopped, Hatcher continued through the men to return to the desk.

"Sorry about that," Hatcher said. "Before I continue with the briefing you'll all be pleased to hear that this operation will be led by Special-Agent-in-Charge Becker. Unfortunately I will be primarily in Washington, but you should know that John has my greatest admiration and complete trust."

Hatcher turned toward Becker, lifting his hand and yielding the floor. This was the moment. If Becker did not walk out of the room now, he was committed to the case. Hatcher watched, scarcely daring to breathe. Becker stared at Hatcher for a moment with a mixture of awe, contempt, and amusement. It was hard to tell if he was more apt to laugh or spit. Slowly he turned his attention to the others in the room, looking at each one individually before his gaze came to rest on Pegeen and delayed for a second. Hatcher could not tell what passed between them, but he noted that when Becker turned back to the others, something had changed.

"Let's get to work," Becker said.

Hatcher took a deep breath but that was the extent of his celebration. Victories did not excite him; he expected them. It was defeat that drove him on.

CHAPTER 2

DEFONE LEE STOOD ON THE CORNER of 124th Street and Malcolm X Boulevard, waiting to meet his baby and feeling good. Defone always felt good when his baby was coming because she made him the happiest he could be. Always. Never fail. Other things let him down, other things disappointed, but not his baby. Never, never. Which was why Defone would do anything for his baby. Anything the man told him.

The life of the streets flowed around him like chunks of ice in a river, distinct clots of humanity drifting slowly, interacting only by chance. It seemed to Defone's practiced eye that nearly everyone moved in groups of two or more, for protection, for commerce, for fun. Three fat ladies headed north, moving arm in arm, taking up most of the sidewalk with their belligerent bulk, cruising through the lesser floes like an iceberg broken loose from its glacier. Men stepped aside for these ladies, shopkeepers nodded and said hello, and children scattered as if they saw a truck bearing down on them. Defone didn't know these particular ladies but he knew their type—loud, bossy, choir singers. The kind that would grab the ear of *any* miscreant youth in the vicinity as if he were their own and treat him to a lecture on manners and respect for his elders and all kinds of bullshit. Defone didn't hate that species of woman anymore, although he had in the past, but he didn't have much use for them, either. It had been a long time since one of them thought about grabbing hold of Defone's ear. You had to be old enough, for one thing, but you also had to have the look. You had to show the attitude. Defone had the look. The look that said he'd just as soon kill your motherfucking ass as not. He'd worked hard to get it, had killed a few motherfuckers just to back it up. He'd done his first with a blade, which took balls. Not one of your run-home-and-get-your-piece-when-somebody-disrespects-you-and-then-come-running-back-panicked-scared shitless-blazing-away-and-maybe-hitting-your-man-and-maybe-hitting-half-the-neighborhood-too kind of killings. There was a lot of that shit going on these days, way too much of it. A man could get shot by a ten-year-old whose hand was shaking so much he couldn't hit his target. He could be standing on the corner the way Defone was now and get blown away by complete mistake. Defone didn't believe in that shit. That was just plain slop. He killed his first with a knife through the ribs, from the front too, looking the motherfucker in the face, watching the light go out of his eyes.

Defone shook himself out of his reverie. He didn't want to be thinking like that when his baby was coming. He checked the traffic coming up Malcolm X again, but couldn't see his baby yet. A couple of workmen in uniforms came toward him looking like they just got off their shift, tired-looking and dirty, spent their day scooping somebody else's shit and stacking it up. Reminded him of his stepfather, the second one, the one who wasted about a year of both their lives trying to "make a man" out of Defone. Son of a bitch didn't know what it was to be a man in the first place. Come home every day smelling like a sewer, talk some shit about how he just did a proud day's work piling turds up six feet high or some shit, how he earned his money, strutting around with his belly lopping over his belt, act like a civic hero for about an hour, then

spend the rest of the night beating on Defone or one of the other kids or his mother. Didn't seem to care who it was long as he was beating on somebody smaller, somebody he could make cry. Defone was right on the edge of not crying anymore. Mr. Shitstacker moved out just in time or *he* would have been Defone's first killing instead of the punk he stuck.

Defone shook himself again. He didn't know why his mind kept drifting off onto that kind of unhappy shit when he could be just thinking about his baby. Still no sign of anything coming up the street he wanted to see. Six or seven gangbangers moving into view a couple blocks away. Sidewalks clearing off for them, you better believe. Even Defone watched them carefully. They wasn't none of his business and he wasn't none of theirs, but it was wise to locate yourself so you wasn't in their direct path. Didn't mean Defone was afraid of them. Meant he was smart enough to respect their numbers, their potential. Even the fucking king of beasts didn't jump into a lake full of them little fish with the razor teeth that could turn you into bones in half a minute. He forgot the name of them, he wasn't interested in that African shit the way some people was, anyway. Didn't give a shit for Africa. Wasn't going to dress like some jungle bunny, wasn't going to change his name to Azoo Aziz or some such shit. Somebody told him once that all them African names people was using was really *Arab* names in the first place. Figure that shit out. Lots of peoples was fools. Defone wasn't one of them.

Nothing else on the street besides the gangbangers worth looking at and they was taking they time coming on. Fine with him. They was on the other side of the road, too, which meant he might not have to relocate himself at all. Wouldn't want to be that PR in the car across the street, though. Luis, some shit like that. Jesus, maybe. Defone couldn't figure out where those Crisco heads got those names. Jesus. Who would call his kid Jesus? Only a Crisco, wearing five, six crosses round his neck, talking so fast you couldn't understand him, cross himself before he shoot a free throw. Who else think his kid be God, name him Jesus? Nobody else did that shit. Defone didn't see no little Jehovahs walking the street, no Allahs, no Buddhas, no whatever it was the Jews called their God. He did know a badass named Lord, but come to think of it, he was dead so he didn't count anyway.

Anyway, Defone knew this greaser, sort of, seen him around, watched him work a little drug action, not much. Fuckhead had like zero ambition, spent his whole day sleeping in the car. And what kind of car was that, anyway? Only a PR be seen dead in that car. Defone wouldn't let them bury him in a car like that, a goddamned disgrace. They was touchy little assholes, always jumping in the brothers' face and demanding respect, but in two areas they had no self-respect at all. Their names and their cars. Goddamned disgrace. Defone hoped the Crisco would attract the attention of the gangbangers, let them beat on him just for driving around a pile of shit like that.

A black-and-white came cruising up 124th Street, just mooching along, two cops staring at everybody. Defone felt the very air change. Nobody on the street moved in the same way he had been a second before. Except Luis-Jesus-greaser, who was asleep. Everybody saw the cops before the cops saw them and even the three battleship ladies seemed to cut through space a little different, a little more cautiously, like they'd just heard there might be bears in the neighborhood looking for a meal of fat choir ladies. Not scared exactly, but looking and listening and sniffing the air a little different.

Black cop, white cop, looking out the window, car doing about three miles an hour, looking everybody up and down, even the choir ladies. Daring somebody to look suspicious, begging someone to give them probable cause. Defone never seen a more innocent-acting bunch of brothers in his life. Some of them sneered and some held their chins up high, but nobody was asking them police

to get out the car and start shooting and pounding with they clubs. Seemed these days like anytime a cop got out of his car some black boy end up shot dead. Be shot six times in the back and the cop say he doing it in self-defense. Brother be filing his nails and the cop say he come at him with an ax. There was no way to win that one.

And Defone had good reason not to have no cop take a sudden shine to him. Not only 'cause his baby was coming—although Defone would waste a cop before he'd let him get between him and his baby—but because of the illegal Glock he had tucked under his shirt and the Smith and Wesson he had taped to the inside of his thigh. Hard to explain those these days. Cops getting real pissy.

Defone cast his eyes down as they passed him, but not too fast. The idea was to appear proud, but not defiant. Look away too soon and they think you acting guilty. Don't look away at all and some redneck might decide you being a little too uppity. And since they likely knew Defone anyway, likely looking for some reason to bust his ass, you didn't want to give them anything more than necessary for your own pride.

He couldn't see Dyzel anywhere, but then you wasn't *supposed* to see Dyzel, that's what he did, that's what he was good at. The brother be completely useless if you could just look around and see him. Why they called him Casper, he was a *friendly* ghost—long as he was on your side. He wasn't going to worry about Dyzel, he was around somewhere, count on it. If not, Defone would find him sometime when he wasn't acting invisible, and make him wish he was. And Dyzel knew it, too. He be around. Defone was *not* going to worry about it.

Not going to worry about *anything*. Defone set a goal for himself. He liked to do that, liked to test himself, liked to make the waiting time more interesting by seeing how much control he had over his mind, his body, his breathing, his bladder—whatever he chose to put to the proof. Defone challenged himself to not think about anything until baby came. Not anything. *Anything*. Just be brain-dead. He took his eyes out of focus and thought about not thinking about a thing in the whole world.

Slouched behind the wheel of a Chevy Caprice so battered that if it were a horse someone would have put a gun to its head out of mercy, Luis Rodriquez watched Defone Lee act as if he'd just suffered a lobotomy. One minute the man was scoping things out, taking it all in, and the next he looked about one functioning neuron away from a full-fledged coma. Like he'd just OD'd on heroin while still standing up.

Too bad. Defone was about the only interesting thing on the street that Luis had seen for the last ten minutes. If things didn't perk up, he might have to really fall asleep.

The gangbangers were suddenly there like a drop in atmospheric pressure that would becalm the Island just before a tropical storm. You knew you had a very short time to grab whatever might fly and get to shelter before the fury hit. Luis had been slouched so low that he had not seen them coming before they arrived, but they were sure as hell there now, seven or eight of them, walking that gimpy, disjointed strut like marionettes with some strings missing, bandannaed like pirates, stocking-capped, fashionably sneakered, wearing more junk gold outside their tennis warm-up suits than a Bedouin's wife. Everybody shitting green to get out of their way and disappear. They reminded Luis of the bad guys swooping into a saloon, shooting holes in the ceiling, acting mean because they were supposed to and nobody would know how to treat them if they didn't.

Luis touched the key just to remind himself it was still in the ignition. His car looked like a piece of shit, but it could *move* if it had to. Not that he thought it would have to. He didn't relish the idea of peeling away from a bunch of bangers, he had a reputation to keep. The one way you couldn't afford to look in the 'hood was

afraid. Show obvious fear and *everybody'd* be on you. He'd seen ten-year-olds run up and kick grown men with the wrong reps. Nothing wrong with appearing prudent, however. Luis held his finger on the key, kept very still, his eyes straight ahead, and acted as prudent as he knew how.

It always made Luis hate himself to behave like this. He didn't like to avert his eyes for anyone, he looked at things like he had the *right* to stare. But you couldn't always do what you wanted in life, and that was the simple fact. You didn't have to like the facts but you did have to know what they were. But still, he hated to act like this and felt even worse when it was over.

Sometimes the storms didn't touch down, they would veer off at the last minute or turn around or go over the Island so high that nothing got hurt. Luis felt the eyes of one of the gangbangers boring into the side of his head, looking for some sign of disrespect or attitude or even the glimmer of anything interesting. Luis sat as still and uninteresting as his steering wheel and the bangers moved on, the residents of the street coming to life again just the way they did on the Island when skies cleared.

Defone was still looking like a drained husk, but Luis knew he wouldn't be much longer because he could see the messenger coming up the boulevard, riding the same worthless bike, an old Schwinn, but *old,* man, like before they ever invented road bikes and dirt bikes and racing bikes and all anybody owned was the same thing the paperboy pedaled around on in James Stewart movies. Luis wondered where they found white boys like this. Man looked to be early thirties but living in some kind of time warp. He wore a surplus army fatigue jacket with the arms cut off and nothing underneath it, and Bermuda shorts and sandals. *Sandals.* The man was confused. His hair was yanked back in a ponytail so tight it made his eyes pop, and his glasses were held together by a paper clip. Hair looked dirty, too. Luis hated uncleanliness in a person. He himself was forced to dress like an impoverished pimp and wear enough pomade to lubricate a mating elephant, but underneath it all he was always clean. He found it hard to respect anyone who wasn't clean. Maybe you couldn't help all the other things in life, but in America you could always come up with some water and soap and a towel. Didn't even need a towel, if it came to that.

The messenger wheeled up to the curb and Luis watched Defone come back to life in a hurry. From nothing to full-blown as fast as an air bag in a crash. Something about that messenger turned Defone on all right. Luis wondered what but he wasn't crazy to know. None of his business, not what he was there for—there just wasn't much else to study now that the gangbangers had passed.

The messenger did a little talking, pushing his broken glasses back on his nose. With all the opportunities for white boys, Luis couldn't help but wonder how come any of them ended up like this. Pedaling something to a semisane, hopheaded thug-of-all-work like Defone Lee in the middle of Harlem. Luis wondered if the white boy even knew where he was or what he was delivering. He looked like one of those who burned his brains out on LSD long time ago—except he was a little too young for that period.

Defone seemed to be listening with more concentration than Luis thought he could muster. After a minute or so the messenger reached into that filthy jacket and pulled out a letter, business size, that Defone stuffed into his pants pocket without so much as looking at it. He was waiting for something else. The messenger talked some more, Defone shifting his weight back and forth, nodding, but getting impatient. The messenger pushed his glasses up again and stopped talking, Defone stopped talking, and they just looked at each other for a few seconds as if one or both of them was deciding about something. If anything passed between them Luis didn't catch it, but then the messenger went into that dirt-crusted jacket one more time and came out with a package. Didn't look like much: brown, about the size of a small letter envelope, looked like a pay packet. Couldn't be enough drugs to distribute and Defone had

no hand in the business anyway except as a user, as far as Luis knew. Too small for a weapon. Money maybe. It didn't take a whole lot of hundreds to amount to something interesting. Whatever it was, Defone handled it like it was both fragile and precious. He held it cupped in both hands, pretending to still be listening to the messenger, but Luis could tell his attention was now on the little brown envelope.

The messenger wheeled around and headed back toward midtown on his ancient bicycle and Defone closed his hands around the package reverently. It looked to Luis like Defone thought he had Tinker Bell cupped in his palm. Luis expected him to leave, since he had whatever he came to the corner to get, but Defone hung around, looking up and down, searching for somebody. Being casual about it, but Defone was no genius, no undercover wizard, you could tell what he was doing if you happened to be watching him.

And Luis just happened to be watching, no special interest, when Dyzel suddenly showed his scrawny ass out of a doorway and lit out on Rollerblades in the same direction as the messenger. Luis had been watching the street for over an hour and had not seen Dyzel until now, which meant the little shadow was working. Defone saw him too, and turned and walked away. Now *that* Luis found interesting.

CHAPTER 3

DEFONE SET HIMSELF A GOAL. THIS time he would make baby last for a whole week. He would ration himself, take just a little, just when he really, *really* wanted it. And right now, of course—he deserved some now. He had traveled all the way from Harlem to his apartment in the Bronx without opening the package. He had posted the man's letter for him without opening the package. He had said hello to peoples on the street in front of the project, he had behaved like a responsible man, hadn't rushed to the nearest toilet, drooling, like a junkie. That kind of restraint deserved a reward. But he wouldn't take any until he had demonstrated that he was in control of baby and not the other way around. Didn't want to act like no crackhead. He wasn't no addict—he just happened to love baby. Baby was different than anything he'd ever had, wasn't no sloppy street drug, cut up a hundred ways, mixed in with baking soda or talcum or any other shit. Baby wasn't that kind of shit at all. Baby was handmade personally, a unique chemical formula, the messenger said the man said. Nobody else in the city had it, only Defone. Except the man. The man had to be using it since he was making it. Be crazy not to, and the man wasn't crazy. And Defone got it because he was in control of himself, because he had skills, he could do things the man wanted done. Wasn't nobody in the streets doing heroin, doing coke, doing crack, doing speed, doing whatever else they be doing who could make that statement. They was all slaves to their habits, but Defone was in control. He set a goal to wait two full minutes after opening baby before having a taste. Two minutes was a good check, plenty of time to show who was the boss. He glanced at his watch and opened the brown envelope.

There they were, thirty little clear capsules, each one full of its own tiny little pellets. They looked like so many Dristans or some other time-release cold medicine, but baby didn't worry about curing no colds. Didn't matter if you had AIDS or cancer or was drowning in your own snot, you didn't care as long as you had baby. Defone loved the way the man took the trouble to empty the Dristan out of the capsules and fill them up by hand with baby. It showed he took his time, took the trouble. Showed he cared.

Defone glanced at his watch. Thirty seconds had passed. He shook the watch, put it to his ear. Without knowing what it was doing, his left hand picked out a capsule and moved it toward his mouth. By the time Defone was sure the watch was working and saw that he had more than a minute to go, the capsule was on his tongue.

He trembled with anticipation as the capsule went down, felt his heart pounding, pushing baby into his blood as fast as it could; then he heard the first of distant trumpets, like a fanfare, like a warning to everybody, an alert that the king was coming. Before long there was a roaring in his ears and Defone blinked and smiled and recognized himself as a god come to earth for a brief spell to see what he could do about setting all this troubled planet to rights.

The residents of the Alvin Blutcher projects were accustomed to seeing anger, seeing rage, belligerence, all kinds of truculent, dangerous attitude. It was part of the atmosphere, like the smell of urine and onions, the sight of rubbish and graffiti and raw garbage. They were used to all of it, knew how to accommodate themselves to it, knew how to step aside just in time without having to leap, how to pause just long enough to let it pass, even how to phrase a greeting to mollify or at least not aggravate it. But crazed was different. There was no coexisting with crazed, it took up its own space and lived by its own rules.

They saw a crazed Defone Lee emerge from his building, his eyes all but rolling in his head, the butt of a pistol sticking out of his belt, and carrying a twelve-shot, twelve-gauge sawed-off shotgun with just a contemptuous hint of concealment under the long leather jacket that was much too hot for late June. Even the boldest spread before him like sheep before a collie. Tough could talk to tough and strength to strength but there was no conversation with crazed. Defone looked like he would simply blast a hole right in the middle of anything in his path and step on through it. They could tell he wasn't even seeing them, he would pay no more attention to their deaths than to the ants on the sidewalk.

Defone the Typhoon. He liked the sound of the word, *Tyyfoooon,* loved to let it roll in his head, had no idea he was saying it out loud, too, but it didn't matter 'cause inside his head and outside his head was all the same now, all of it under his control.

"Dee-fone, Cy-clone," he said, sweeping chemical containers into the two gym bags, his arms the winds, he himself the god of the storm. "Tyy-phone Cy-clone."

The watchman of the chemical supply house lay on the floor with his head bleeding where Defone had cracked him with the barrel of the shotgun. He was certain that his assailant was insane. Anyone who'd rob such a place to begin with ought to have his head examined. Nobody kept cash in a warehouse and the chemicals themselves weren't that expensive. Like robbing a wallpaper warehouse. Why not go steal some cash from McDonald's and then *buy* the chemicals, have enough money left over to spend on yourself?

"Ty-phoon, cycloon."

The watchman lay very still and pretended he was dead. This brother was crazed, drug-mad. He pressed himself into the concrete floor, trying to become one with the cement.

"Where the nitromannite?" the madman asked suddenly, his voice clearly back to this level of reality. He bent over the watchman, prodded him in the back with the barrel of the gun. "Where you keep the nitromannite?"

The watchman tried to stop breathing altogether. Defone rolled him onto his back and pressed his thumbs against the watchman's eyeballs.

"Gon' take your *eyes*, motherfucker!"

The watchman came to life wonderfully fast.

"What you want?"

"Nitromannite! Where it at?"

The watchman looked into Defone's face, certain he was seeing the visage of death. Defone was waving the shotgun under the watchman's nose, the watchman could smell oil and something more acrid.

"I just guards it. I don't know where shit is."

"Nitromannite!" Defone repeated. He waved a piece of paper in front of the guard as if he had not understood the question, jabbing his finger at one entry on the list.

"Take whatever you wants."

"I gots to have this," Defone insisted, starting to wheedle now, trying to enlist the watchman to his cause. The man didn't seem to realize this was important. Defone banged his head against the concrete to make his point. "Gots to have it." He whopped the man's head again for emphasis. Fool just making gurgling sounds.

"Defone Cyclone," Defone said, feeling the power of the storm return to him. He was a god, didn't need no diddly-dick $4.50-an-hour night watchman to help him. "Typhoon." He pointed the shotgun at random and fired. The roaring in his ears was just right, just what he wanted. Shards of glass and fine powders and bits of cardboard flew everywhere. This was what a typhoon could do.

Defone walked into the blasted area where the finest debris still showered down on him. There, behind the wreckage, was a whole container of nitromannite, said so right on the label. Defone had known it would happen. That's how things went for a god. You just had to trust baby.

When he turned to leave, the watchman was gone from the floor, but he left a trail of blood to follow, slipping through the aisles. Defone shouldered the gym bags and wondered whether he should find the guard and remove his head or if there was something else he was supposed to do first.

At the sporting goods store Defone just took every single item in the hunting department. There was no guard there to explain the power of the typhoon to, so he simply backed the van through the window at the front of the store and loaded everything not screwed down into the vehicle, making damned sure he included what the man had asked for. The safe was right where the man had said it would be and just as easy to rip out of the wall. That would be Defone's part of the haul, lots of cash. The man wasn't interested in cash, he lived for finer things. Chemicals and such. The safe would be bulging with money, Defone was sure of that, the man never steered him wrong.

Typhoon, cyclone. The place looked like both storms had hit it at once, and just about as fast. Defone was in and out in two minutes flat.

Defone took what he wanted, which wasn't much besides the

safe, and left what the man wanted in the back of the van. He left the van on a street in Bed-Stuy where the messenger had told him to and went back home to baby.

Within seconds of Defone's departure another black man slipped into the van, grabbed the parcels the man had specified, and disappeared into the night. The more random scavengers could have the rest—and would—before sunup.

CHAPTER 4

BECKER WATCHED HELPLESSLY AS his wife struggled against the onslaught of one of her crippling headaches. Because Karen was a fighter she battled against it, as she always did in the beginning. Fought and lost. Within minutes he saw the color drain from her skin, watched her expression turn from one of defiance to pain, and finally, to submission. In the end she could not speak, could not bear even to listen. She would go to bed, lying in the darkened room, riding the pain like a life raft tossed by the sea, conserving what energy she could by not struggling. The pain became her entire environment, her sea, her sky, her horizon.

Becker would sit beside the bed, holding her hand, trying to transfer his strength to her through their joined palms. She never said so, never pulled her hand away, but Becker knew that there came a time when she wanted not to be touched, wanted him gone, wanted to be alone in her torment so that she could give herself completely to it.

He would leave quietly, drawing the door closed and tiptoeing through the house, hating himself. Eventually, when the hatred grew too strong, he would find himself going yet again to Gold.

"Not your fault," Gold said, shaking his head. "Not, not your fault. And of course you know that."

Becker seldom sat in Gold's office. He paced the room, uncomfortable with the process of psychotherapy, uncomfortable still with Gold despite their years of tortured effort together, most uncomfortable of all with the aspects of his nature that had brought him to the office of the Bureau's psychiatric department in the first place.

"It was my case, my man. I should have been there. I should have stopped him," Becker said. He moved behind Gold's desk and Gold swiveled his chair to stay with him.

"It was Karen's case, too. She was in charge, actually. Not that you want to hear the facts, I suppose."

"I'll tell you the facts, Gold." Becker looked out the lone window in Gold's office. On the street below two cabbies emerged from their cars and began raining blows on each other. Becker never used Gold's title of doctor, an omission that chafed the psychologist but one he had long since accepted. "The facts are, I'm a dangerous man to be around. People close to me end up getting hurt . . ."

"Bad guys get hurt, John."

"She's my wife!"

"I didn't mean Karen, you know I didn't mean her."

"She hasn't left the house except for therapy for six months," Becker said. "Bright lights hurt her. Flashing lights set off the headaches. She's afraid an ambulance will drive by and she'll have an attack. This is a woman who had more courage than any of the men who served under her."

Becker was by the door, twisting the leaves on the potted ficus plant. After his visits Gold had found some of the leaves as tattered as fringe.

"How are your intimate relations?"

"Private. How about yours, Gold? How often do you fuck the wife, and who does she fantasize about when you do?"

"Why do you bother to come to me, John? You don't respect my profession and you never have."

"Because the only alternative to talking to you is talking to myself. I can call you a shithead without damaging my self-esteem."

"It's natural if she's a little slow to resume normal relations after what she's been through," Gold said. The great trick was to remember that Becker really wanted to be there, because no one could ever force him to come.

"You mean after a madman tried to rape her, strangle her, and beat her head to a pulp in our bathtub? Yeah, I'd say a certain reluctance to sleep with the man who didn't prevent it from happening is natural. In fact, I'd say it was advisable. I'd say if she never let me put a finger on her again she'd be justified."

"Do you know your problem, John?"

"Are we going to pick just one?"

"Everyone else thinks you're Superman, so you've started thinking you are too. Of course you think you're to blame for not preventing what happened to Karen. Superman wouldn't have let that happen, would he? He would have used his X-ray vision and seen through walls."

"Is it true that only people with deep psychological problems themselves take up shrinkage for a career?"

"I've heard that said. I've heard a few insinuations about career law enforcement officers, too," said Gold.

"I think I am to blame because I am *responsible,*" said Becker. "I am *responsible* for my actions and for the consequences of those actions. That's not a concept you endorse, I realize. Everybody is the victim of historical, familial, societal forces, according to you. To know all is to forgive all, right, Gold? Well, bullshit. I know as much about myself as anyone ever will, and I don't forgive. I am *responsible.*"

The two men lapsed into silence and Becker finally returned to the chair in front of Gold's desk.

"Sorry about that," Becker said. "I don't mean to be disrespectful to you, particularly. It's just the whole process that seems so futile."

Gold nodded, making meaningless marks on his notepad.

"I often feel that way myself," he admitted.

"Do you think you've ever cured anybody of anything this way?"

Gold arched his eyebrows. "Cured? I hope I've helped a few people. My ambitions don't go much beyond that anymore. I've been at it too long."

"There's got to be a better way," Becker said.

"Find it and you'll make millions."

"It would make me feel guilty if I had millions," Becker said. Gold was relieved to see Becker smiling. Progress was something to be measured in very small increments.

CHAPTER 5

DEFONE DIDN'T WEAR HIS NORMAL street clothes when he traveled to Manhattan's Upper West Side. He donned a suit and tie, same as he would for a funeral. Looked just like a businessman, he told himself. Looked like he could stroll into a Madison Avenue law firm, have peoples think he was a partner. Clothes don't make the man, clothes *disguise* the man. He was the same Defone Lee, had the same Glock tucked into the back of his belt, but the peoples on Riverside Drive would never know that.

Dyzel had given him the address on West Eighty-seventh Street just off Riverside where he saw the messenger go into the basement apartment. Dyzel had said the messenger wasn't worried about being followed, he hadn't bothered to look behind him the whole trip back from Harlem. Messenger had gone into the basement apartment and hadn't come out for the three hours that Dyzel waited. Defone had hoped the bicyclist would return to the man himself, tell him he'd done the job, get paid, something like that, and was disappointed that all he had learned was where the messenger lived. Still, there were ways to get the messenger to tell him what he knew about the man. Where to find him if he needed him.

As he had stared at his dwindling supply of baby a few weeks earlier, practicing his self-control, Defone had had a revelation of startling clarity. Although he was in control of himself, he realized, and although he was in some control of his environment through his reputation and willingness to do whatever was necessary, he had no control whatsoever over the man. The man could just stop doing business. He could retire. The police could get him. He could get caught in the cross fire of some lunatic gangbangers out to prove their manhood. And if the man lost touch with Defone, baby was gone too. Defone didn't care to imagine life without baby. So he thought he would put himself in touch with the man. Nothing stupid, nothing to anger the man. Just enough to allow Defone to find him if he needed him.

Defone got himself into the basement apartment without too much trouble. Nothing that couldn't be fixed. The ratty old Schwinn was chained to the radiator, as if someone was dying to break in and steal it. It was the best-looking thing in the room. Messenger looked like he collected furniture off the street after other peoples threw it away—out the tenth-floor window. Damned TV set had rabbit ears. Fool didn't have cable. People in the Bronx who couldn't afford decent *sneakers* had cable.

Defone thought about sitting down, until he got close enough to smell the mildew wafting from the blanket on top of the recliner. He wasn't about to soil his butt sitting in that mess. Damn recliner was somebody's thrown-away *lawn* furniture. No telling what they got up to on it.

The door to the bedroom was locked, which piqued Defone's interest. If it was anything like the living room, there wouldn't be but a bare mattress on the floor in there. Defone had seen the messenger's wardrobe. Wouldn't need a hanger, just let it stand up by itself. But the bedroom was locked and locked hard.

Something valuable in there, a man bothers to lock it like that. Could be the messenger kept his own baby in there. He told Defone the man said Defone was the onliest one in the world to have baby, but you never knew. The messenger could be was lying to Defone. Have to be a fool to lie to Defone about anything, but you never knew.

It took him ten minutes of concentrated work to get into the bedroom. Wouldn't have taken much longer to get into a bank vault. Had to be *something* mighty good in there. When the door finally swung open Defone took one look around and smiled hugely. Jackpot.

Cole stood in the bottom of the ravine, his ankles immersed in water that felt icy cold all year round. The temperature seemed never to vary, only the depth. If he came after a heavy rain, the water could be chest-high. He had even seen it over his head. Now it was scarcely a trickle but it still ran fast and it still would freeze his feet if he didn't have the foresight to bring boots. Patches of sunlight filtered through the canopy far overhead, but never much, never for long, which was why the stream remained so frigid.

The ravine and the surrounding cliffs were useless as farmland, too steep and dangerous to hunt, the waters too variable to maintain a fish supply worth the trouble of fishing for. The locals considered it junk land, even too far from the road to serve as a dump.

To Cole it was invaluable. He could do things here that would be impossible in the city. For instance, where in all of Manhattan could he go to master the properties of the crossbow Defone had stolen from the sporting goods store? Nowhere. For that matter, where in the country could he find the combination of isolation and habitat he required to perfect his skills in the various areas he needed to master? This ravine was the only place he knew about. That in itself was worth the taxes on the land.

Cole aimed at the chosen branch two hundred feet above him, the arm of a pin oak that jutted from the side of the cliff. He settled

the rifle stock of the crossbow into his shoulder and looked through the telescopic sight that was standard equipment on the modern version of the ancient weapon. The bowstring snapped with its distinctive metallic twang and the bolt sailed up and over the limb, arcing its way into the tangle of rock, earth, and foliage that lay beyond. It was his tenth successful shot in a row and Cole decided it was enough for the preliminary work. He was confident that he understood his weapon.

He had painted the bolts an iridescent orange so that he could recover them without difficulty. For his next shot he would attach a line to the bolt and see how much the added weight and drag affected the equation. He would not stop until he was certain that he could put a length of lightweight nylon line over the branch two hundred feet above him. At night. Every time.

He walked along the ravine bottom searching for the bolts. As he had from the moment he first touched the crossbow, he wore disposable plastic gloves. There would be no need to remove his fingerprints because they would never be on either the bow or the bolts or the line.

He returned to the city at night to discover that his home had been invaded. Worse still, the intruder was still there.

There was not much Cole could do. The police were out of the question. Even though he held the crossbow in its case it did not occur to him to use it. It was not an option. Cole loathed violence. He disdained it philosophically—and he feared it physically. He was a coward and knew it and felt no shame. He could only go in, confront whoever had jimmied the door, brazen it out, deal with it.

The door to his workroom was still ajar. He pushed it open.

"I'm coming in now," he said, hanging back, not exposing himself.

" 'Bout time," a voice replied.

"I'm not armed," Cole said.

"I is."

Cole paused, trying to stop his jaw from shaking so violently. He tried to swallow but couldn't force his throat to move. In the next moment his life would be changed drastically—if he was still alive.

He stepped into his workroom and saw a black man seated in the swivel chair, holding a gun in his lap, the barrel pointed negligently toward Cole's midsection. The man was dressed like a funeral director and it took Cole a moment to recognize him as Defone Lee.

"How you doing?" Defone asked.

"What are you doing here?"

"I came to see you," Defone said. "You glad?"

"I have nothing for you," said Cole. "He didn't give me any more messages for you, yet."

Defone smiled broadly. "Who *he* be?"

"I don't know his name," said Cole. "He contacts me when he wants me to deliver something."

"Look different today. No ponytail. Got yourself a shirt, not wearing that army thing. No glasses."

"My glasses are in the other room."

"Look like a different man."

"What are you doing here?"

"Already told you. Came for a visit."

"Why? I don't have anything I can give you."

"Never seen a man look like two different mens so easy. Why you want to do that?" Defone was grinning, being clever.

"I have no money."

"You got better than that," Defone said. He waved his hand at the workshop that surrounded him.

Test tubes, beakers, retorts lined one wall atop a Formica counter. A large marble mortar and pestle and a smaller cousin sat on either side of a chemist's balance and a pair of burners on the

back wall. The third arm of the counter was occupied with the miniaturized electronic spectrometer and centrifuge. Not that Defone could appreciate these high-tech wonders. Above the counters were shelves of books, nearly all of them unintelligible to Defone, and covering the floor under the countertops were bottles, baskets, and bags of chemicals and piles of equipment, some of which Defone recognized, some of which looked as if it was intended for use on Mars.

"It's my hobby," Cole said.

"Sit down, let's talk," Defone offered. There was no other furniture in the room; Defone occupied the only chair. He waved toward the floor, barely aware the gun was still in his hand. He certainly wasn't going to need it against the messenger, who was sweating and shaking like he had a fever. Defone had mugged old women—cracked them over the head and stuck a gun barrel between their eyes—who wasn't as scared as this one.

Cole sank onto the floor with an air of relief.

"You gots to think of me as your friend," Defone said. He didn't want the messenger to fear him any more than he already did. Didn't want him to freeze up and paralyze. Be no use to Defone that way.

"All right," Cole said.

"Just relax yourself."

"If I just knew what you wanted from me . . ."

"Want to help you."

"Help me do what?"

"Help you do whatever you do." Defone beamed. "I'm a good helper."

"All I do is deliver things for the man."

"You be the man," said Defone, still smiling.

"No, no . . ."

Defone nodded slowly. "You *be* the man. This the place you make my baby, ain't it?"

Cole stopped speaking. He turned mute as suddenly and definitively as a child turning an imaginary key to seal his lips.

"This the place, ain't it? Right here. You could make as much as you want."

Cole laced his fingers together.

"Make as much as *I* want . . . How long it take you to make some?"

Cole stared blankly in front of him.

Defone set himself a goal. He would not bash the motherfucker in the teeth no matter how long he didn't talk. He would not hurt him no matter what. The man would be his friend whether the man wanted it nor not. Defone was going to *charm* him or put a bullet in his head, but he wasn't going to hurt him, that was his goal.

"What you got to say?" Defone asked. "You want me to be your friend? . . . A man with all this equipment living in a dump like this, hiding hisself, disguising hisself as a messenger . . . man like that could use a friend."

Cole straightened. He looked more confident now, not so scared. Watch out now, Defone told himself. Motherfucker look like he's up to something.

"How about being my partner?" Cole asked.

CHAPTER 6

LUIS RODRIQUEZ HAPPENED TO meet Arnold Meisner in the locker room as he was leaving his shift and Meisner was coming on. Together the two of them comprised one third of the manpower of the NYPD unit dedicated to illegal-firearms trafficking and terrorism, activities invariably linked. What one knew the other eventually learned.

"I was staked out on Lenox today," Luis said. "Waiting for the Irish to make a buy."

"Anything?"

"Never saw them," Luis admitted. "Fucking harps are getting too careful."

"Supposed to be peace over there in Ireland," Meisner said. "Maybe they canceled the buy."

"Supposed to be peace in this country, too," said Luis. "That don't stop nobody from buying guns."

"This is a nation with inalienable rights. You got a constitutional duty to keep a rocket launcher in the bedroom, case you hadn't heard."

"I heard you got the hots for some FBI lady," Luis said. "That's what I heard. What's she look like?"

"Who told you this shit?"

"She a skank like your last lady?"

Meisner decided the best thing was to smile. Being forty and single and shaped like a dockside capstan, he took a lot of ribbing about his social life. He had long since decided that he was not going to waste his energy fighting it. They tired of it soon enough if he didn't respond.

"Oh, and I saw Defone Lee today," Luis added when he saw he could not get a rise out of Meisner.

"That must have made your day."

"You know the little spook Dyzel?"

"The one they call Casper?"

Luis nodded. "Defone got something from a white messenger on a bike, then sicced Dyzel on the messenger."

"I've seen Defone talking to a white guy on a bike before," said Meisner. "What do you make of it?"

Luis shrugged. "Drugs? A buy? Who knows?"

Defone had a record of dealing in stolen weapons in a small and basically uninteresting way. It was one of his many sidelines. Meisner and Luis were primarily concerned with the larger stuff, not the illegal handguns in which Defone dealt, and he had occupied only a peripheral position in their attentions. They both knew Defone was the kind of man who would eventually screw up in a very large way, but until he did, he would continue to get arrested, avoid indictment, escape hard scrutiny.

"What was interesting was he used Dyzel," Luis continued. "Just thought I'd tell you."

It was one of a thousand bits of information that were passed on informally from cop to cop and never officially reported. It might be important someday but most likely not. Like most police work, it more closely resembled rumor than investigation. Who was doing what to whom and where and when. Observing the streets daily was like watching a soap opera, and friends filled each other in on what they missed.

However, since Meisner was looking for an excuse to talk to Pegeen again, he chose to give it weight.

I don't understand the significance," Pegeen said. Meisner had come to visit her in the partitioned cubicle the Bureau called her office. Somehow his presence made it crowded, and Pegeen felt him pressing in on her even though there was a desk between them.

"Well, I thought you might want to come check it out with me," he said.

"But why?"

"I think we'd make a good team. You're smart and I'm obedient."

Pegeen's stern look had no effect. Meisner continued to give her his loopy grin and lean in on her.

"Explain the significance of this event," she said. "What's so interesting about this Defone Lee?"

"Ah. I thought we were talking about us."

"When I am talking about us, I will refer to us by name," said Pegeen. "That will clear up any confusion."

"You can call me Arnie," Meisner said.

"Defone Lee," she said.

"He's a kind of utility bad guy," Meisner said. "He's on the fringes of trouble all the time: drugs, guns, armed assault, you name it. Nothing big enough to do any serious time, but probably not for want of trying on his part. He's ambitious, dangerous, and can be hired. We've had him as a suspect on two weapons heists in the last six months but not enough to nail him. His rep on the street is that he's a true badass, not to be messed with, may have iced a couple people. That's a rep that's out of line with his official sheet, so I'd say he's doing more than we know. So somebody comes to see him in Harlem—Defone doesn't live in Harlem—the messenger is white and riding a bike. Kind of strange right there. Then Defone sends a professional shadow after him, a kid named Dyzel who trails people for a living. Interesting? Finally, we get word that on the night that the chemical warehouse in New Jersey was hit, Defone was seen leaving the projects armed like a Mexican bandito and wired for sight, sound, and three-d. Nothing else happened that night that sounds like Defone's work. Spring needs chemicals, right? He needs someone to mail his letters from the Bronx. Defone lives in the Bronx . . ."

"Why not assume Spring lives in the Bronx?"

"A white man drives into the projects to mail his letters? That wouldn't attract much attention, would it?"

"You know that Spring is white?" Pegeen asked.

"The last brown bomber I ever heard of was Joe Louis. This is not a thing black people do."

Pegeen was silent. The latest profile from the Bureau's psychologists had described Spring as probably white, probably educated, certainly intelligent, and with delusions of grandeur and contempt for authority. It had not taken a genius to figure any of that out but it annoyed her that Meisner had done so without waiting for the report.

"So you want to talk to this Defone?"

"Not Defone. There's no point in letting him know we're onto him. I thought *we* should talk to Dyzel."

"Why do you need me?"

"The woman's touch," said Meisner, grinning. "You'll be able to get him talking easier than I can."

"Do you always use this much imagination when working on a case?"

"I don't always get the opportunity," he said.

As special-agent-in-charge, Becker was entitled to an office with four real walls. The total space was not much greater than Pegeen's cubicle, but the privacy was. She found him on the telephone but he signaled for her to wait as he said his last goodbye and hung up. He put his face in his hands.

"Just give me a minute," he said, his voice muffled.

"I can come back," said Pegeen.

He groaned something, his face still covered, and Pegeen went to him instinctively. She put her hand on his shoulder to ease his pain.

"She's still bad," she said.

"She might always be bad," he said, as if the notion surprised him. "She might never come out of it."

"Sure she will. She just needs time."

Becker made another sound, a humorless chuckle. Not a cry, but as close as Pegeen ever expected to hear from him.

He turned to face her and took her hand in his own.

"It's awful for you," she said. She was intensely aware of his skin on hers. This was how they had started before; she had taken his hand while they sat in the car, trying to ease his pain. His hands were always so warm. They were healer's hands. Lover's hands.

His face looked so bleak, so devastated, that she stepped forward and cradled his head to her bosom.

It was like holding wood. He did not pull away, but the muscles of his neck were stiff and unyielding and his arms did not slip around her. Pegeen released him and stepped quickly away, her face burning.

"I'm going out on an interview with Meisner," she said hurriedly, not looking at him. "It's an unlikely lead but might be worth investigating."

"Fine," said Becker. "Use your best judgment."

"I'll go with Meisner then," she said, nodding as if the point had been at issue. She had sent Meisner away brusquely. She hoped she could catch him before he left the building.

Becker stopped her before she was out the door. "Pegeen," he said, "we'll have to talk."

"Sure. Whenever you want."

"As soon as I can," he said.

"No rush," she said, hoping she sounded as cool as she was trying to.

"You look nice," Meisner said. He drove Pegeen toward a children's playground on the Upper West Side.

"Thank you."

"What do you call that color? Buff?"

"Fawn."

"That's a good color for you. You ever wear green?"

"Where are we going?"

"To find Dyzel."

"Where are we going with this conversation?"

"I thought you'd probably look great in green, what with the red hair and that skin and those eyes and everything."

"Are you making fun of me, Meisner?"

"What? What'd I say? I thought redheads liked to wear green."

"Redheads would like to be blond," Pegeen said sourly. "Or brunette. Or bald. Anything but hair the color of iodine."

"I think you look great," Meisner said weakly. "Sue me."

"I'm not that easy, anyway. It takes more than a lame compliment."

"What? Who said anything? Did I say anything? It was just a comment . . ."

"Forget it. Let's find this little creep."

"Okay. Pretend I never said anything." He drove in silence for a moment. As they parked within view of the playground, he said, "So what does it take?"

"Couldn't resist, could you?"

The playground was brick and cement surrounded by a chain-link fence. Designed for small children, it had been commandeered by Rollerblade skaters who used the steps and railings and curved surfaces for their stunts. In one of the few places in the famously diverse city of New York where the races actually mixed, young whites and blacks and Asians and Hispanics all took their turns at the athletic, dangerous tricks.

"There's Dyzel," Meisner said, pointing at a skinny youth who sat next to the fence, his sneakers tied by their laces and dangling from his neck. "He's probably just watching. In his line of work he can't afford to get injured."

"How effective can he be on roller skates?" Pegeen asked.

"In this city? He can get most places faster than a car. Remember, he doesn't worry about stoplights, he can go on the sidewalk if he needs to, the wrong way on one-way streets. As long as his target doesn't take to the thruway, Dyzel can keep up with them, believe me. If he takes off now, for instance, I won't be able to stay with him if he doesn't want me to."

"We'd better not let him take off then," said Pegeen. "One look at you and he will."

"That's why I wanted the woman's touch."

"Uh-huh. Among other things."

"Jesus, I didn't say *anything* . . ."

"Panting counts," she said, reaching for the door.

"Hold it." Meisner reached into the back seat and produced a camera. "Try it with this. It's even got film."

"Convenient," she said.

"Be prepared. I'm always ready."

"See, it's that kind of remark," Pegeen said, getting out of the car.

"What? What did I say? What?"

As Pegeen walked toward the playground she wondered why it was that she always got the Meisners of the world. Why the short, squat ones? Why the overeager, the uncouth, the insensitive? Why were the men who were attracted to her not the men to whom she was attracted? Her previous relationship had been an out-of-work actor who spent most of his time hanging around the apartment, waiting for her to come home so he could bitch about being out of work. Weren't actors *always* out of work? Especially in Tennessee? Why did she attract the lame, the dysfunctional, the desperate?

The answer is simple, stupid, she told herself. The good ones are already taken. Becker is *married*.

The Rollerbladers saw the woman in a business suit with a camera and pulled up their socks and straightened their knee and elbow pads and began to perform for her. Pegeen aimed and snapped and aimed and snapped, working her way around the playground, never once looking at Dyzel until she was right beside him.

"Hello," she said, smiling at him. "Mind if I take your picture?" She aimed the camera at him and stood so close that he could not get to his feet without bumping into her. The shutter snapped and Dyzel opened his mouth to speak, revealing a golden bicuspid.

"I usually charge for that," he said.

"I usually charge for this," Pegeen replied. She moved her legs together, locking his knees. "I'm a federal agent, Dyzel. If you stand up now you'll knock me over and that would be interfering with a federal agent during an investigation, which is a federal crime."

"I ain't stood up."

"Duly noted," she said. "Now why don't you say cheese so your friends think I'm taking your picture?"

"They look at the way you standing on top of me, they think I be eating your pussy."

"New York is not a pretty town, is it? Do people really have thoughts like that?"

"No, I just made that up. Man would never think like that."

"I knew it," said Pegeen. "Do you want to come along with me in a peaceable manner, Dyzel?"

"I ain't done nothing."

"See that man over there?" Pegeen indicated Meisner with an incline of her head. "He keeps saying he hasn't done anything either, but we know what he's thinking about, don't we?"

"What's he thinking about?"

"Same as you, Dyzel, but he's not half so honest about it."

As they walked toward Meisner's car, Dyzel asked, "What *you* be thinking about, cop lady? You so good at reading minds, you must be thinking about the same thing."

"I am a woman, Dyzel. I very seldom think about eating pussy."

Dyzel laughed. "You the best cop I met yet," he said.

Pegeen smiled at him. "That's because I'm not finished with you yet."

Dyzel caught Meisner's eye as he slipped into the back seat of the car with Pegeen and winked.

Meisner stepped out of the interrogation room and met Pegeen in the hall.

"You got a pin of some kind?" he asked.

"What kind of pin?"

"Any kind. Hat pin, maybe? Safety pin?"

"Has anyone worn a hat pin in the last thirty years? How about this?" She touched the red metal ribbon of AIDS awareness in her lapel. Meisner carefully pulled it so that the silver pin showed clearly against the cloth of her suit.

"Perfect," he said. "Now touch it once in a while. Kind of twirl it around. Dyzel's going to like that."

"What did you tell him?"

"I said you had a way of sticking it into a man's—uh—penis, sorry—so that it wouldn't show up in a medical exam and he couldn't claim police brutality because there would be no marks."

"What's the matter with you? Is this how you treat everybody you interview? He's just a boy."

"You don't have to use it," Meisner said sheepishly.

"I certainly won't . . . . Is that even possible?"

"God, I hope not."

"Where do you even get such ideas?"

Meisner shrugged. "I'm so ashamed."

"Did you get anywhere with him with your bully tactics?"

"He keeps grinning at me like we share a secret. I asked him what's that about and he just tells me, 'We thinking on the same wavelength.' What's that all about?"

Dyzel drew back as Pegeen sat in the chair opposite him.

"It true what he say?" Dyzel asked.

"What did he say?"

"He say you a bull dyke and don't like mens."

"That's what a lot of men say when they can't accept that we don't like *them.* They used to call us frigid. Now they say we're lesbians. Do you know what he told me about *you,* Dyzel?"

"He don't know shit about me."

"He said you wouldn't tell him about the man you were following for Defone Lee."

"Wasn't following nobody for Defone Lee. That's how come."

"We know you were. We have a witness."

"Ain't no crime."

"That's right, it's not a crime . . . so why not tell us who you were following? No harm will come to you."

"That's what you say," Dyzel said.

"That's right, that's what I say. I'm a federal agent, Dyzel. If I tell you that you won't be prosecuted, then you won't be."

"I ain't talking about *prosecution,* shiiit."

"I realize that, too, Dyzel. I know what you're afraid of. You're afraid of what Defone will do if you tell us. I understand that. Defone Lee is not a nice person."

"He's a crazy motherfucker."

"That's another way of putting it. Defone is dangerous and you're afraid of him and I understand. I'll tell you what, Dyzel. Tell me what you think of this idea."

Pegeen leaned forward slightly and touched the AIDS pin on her lapel. Dyzel squirmed.

"What would you say if after you tell us who you were trailing and where he went, I personally will have a talk with Defone Lee and assure him that you didn't tell us anything prejudicial to him?"

"You crazy, lady? I don't want you to talk to Defone about me."

Pegeen fingered the pin, twisting it slowly in the fabric, keeping her gaze on Dyzel as he moved about uncomfortably in his chair.

"How about if we drive you right up to Defone's door and all of us sit there together and talk things through until he agrees not to be angry with you? Would that work for you?"

"Out of your fucking mind."

"Then how about if you don't cooperate at all, don't tell us a thing, but I drop you at Defone's door anyway and act like you did."

"You a hard bitch."

"I thought I was your favorite cop."

"It's true what he said. You don't like mens."

Pegeen withdrew the pin from her lapel, opened it, held the pointed end in front of her.

"Sometimes I get angry with the way they behave," she said. "But I've learned ways to deal with that."

"How about I talk to you and you just let me out the door and I find my own way home."

"Dyzel," Pegeen said, "you've got a deal."

When the name of Jason Cole was traced through the files, nothing of interest was found. He had no history of crimes, small or large, and the state computer showed him with only one traffic violation, a fender bender with just over the reportable minimum damage of a thousand dollars. The car was a rental—there was no record that he had ever owned one. There were no prior arrests, no outstanding warrants—nothing, in fact, to link him with someone like Defone at all.

Meisner shrugged at the lack of success. He had really only wanted an excuse to spend some time with Pegeen, anyway. Successful law enforcement was like commercial orchard management. You didn't just pick one apple, you shook the tree and saw what fell. This time nothing fell. Either Dyzel had followed the wrong man—which didn't seem likely—or he had lied to them and given them the wrong name—which seemed a strong probability. He had since vanished, to no one's surprise, and would be a good deal harder to locate next time. Not that the situation warranted any further investigation. The fruit on the tree simply wasn't ripe—or it was the wrong tree.

CHAPTER 7

FROM THE POINT OF VIEW OF drivers moving along the FDR Drive as fast as traffic will allow—which is frequently very slow indeed—the East River looks dirty and uninviting, but from the walkway along the stone embankment, two feet above water level, it looks absolutely filthy and smells worse. Escaped oil, floating in a series of extended slicks that at times appear to be a continuous film from shore to shore, reflects light and converts it to the primary colors, but there is no confusing this spectacle with a rainbow. The water is dark at the best of times and at night it is pitch-black except for the surface sheen that catches the city lights. Floating atop or within this turbid flow are the corpses of a surprising variety of animals, including not only the predictable household pets and local rodents but a sampling of the medium to large mammals of North and South America. Monkeys have been seen, and pigs and civet cats and even live alligators grown too large to remain in a city dweller's bathtub and sent forth to fend for themselves. Because of the intemperate climate the southern reptiles have no more chance of survival than the tropical fish that are "freed" into the river with regularity.

As he stood at the water's edge Cole thought he saw the form of a dead and bloated horse lying on its back, feet in the air, floating past in midstream. The horse was caught momentarily in a shaft of moonlight through a cloud as surely as an actor in a spotlight; then it toppled slowly to one side and passed into the darkness. Cole allowed himself no curiosity about the horse and how it came to be there. He had work on his mind and it required all of his concentration.

A watch cap was pulled low over his eyebrows and his face was smudged with the grease and grit of the walkway. Barring a face-to-face confrontation, he would be impossible to identify later. Given the lighting—and the cap—he might even be remembered as a black man—if he was seen at all.

He had the crossbow with him in its original box, which was now covered with plain brown paper. From a distance it would appear that he was carrying a mirror or picture frame.

He stopped in an area that was reached by neither moon nor streetlight and crouched down in the darkness. With the sound of traffic humming and honking overhead and the river hissing beside him, he unpacked the bow and the line and laid them out carefully in front of him. Placing his foot in the stirrup, he cocked the bow to its full 150 pounds of draw weight. He tied the fishing line to a twenty-inch bolt with plastic fletches, then opened his fatigue jacket and unrolled the explosive that had been wrapped around his middle like a twenty-foot sausage. By itself the explosive was harmless. Cole could have hurled himself out a window and it would not have ignited. It was his own concoction, a mix of nitroglycerin, ammonium nitrate for stability, kieselguhr clay, and guar gum, borax, and water to form a gel that he had encased in plastic sheeting so that it could be twisted and formed as he desired. He had created the nitroglycerin and ammonium nitrate himself in his workshop, reveling in the danger and the technical proficiency involved in making the nitro. Along the entire surface of the plastic sausage was glued a strip of piezoelectric material that converted

pressure into electricity, the same material used to make children's sneakers glow with every step. Defone had acquired it for him on one of his "shopping" trips.

The tiny electric charge he would have created had he bumped into anything also presented no danger of igniting the explosive. The sausage became a deadly snake only with the addition of the detonators. Cole took three of them now from his pocket. He had built them himself, packing the cases of ballpoint pens with the volatile nitromannite and wiring it to allow for the very low voltage of the piezoelectric strip. There were other ways to do the job, but Cole had chosen this method because it appealed to him. He liked the intricacy of it, the need for attention to detail—the difficulty. He had time, there was no rush, no timetable other than the one he created as he went along, so there was no need for superefficiency. And there was something very appealing to him about the fact that he was doing it all himself, his own, handcrafted way. With Defone's help he might have acquired a handheld missile and blown up the tramway with it, but where was the fun in that?

As he inserted the three detonators along the body of his bomb and gently wired them to the piezo strip, he felt the rush of godlike power again. The mail bombs had been necessary and had done their job, so he took a pride in his craftsmanship, but they had not given him the thrill of expectation that he felt now. He would destroy on a large scale now. He would wreak havoc with the same wanton, whimsical power of a deity. Once again he was Cole astride a thunderbolt, a sensation he had not felt since his expedition to Cornell several years ago.

A tug chugged noisily past and Cole hugged the dark crevice where he stood. There were frequent drunks and derelicts along the water's edge and he knew he would attract unusual attention only at the moment when he fired his shot, but there was no point in being careless. When the tug had gone, he stepped onto the walkway and looked up at his target. In the distance was the Queensboro Bridge, the Fifty-ninth Street bridge where Simon and Garfunkel had felt so groovy. Its lights and enormous span served as a backdrop for the tramway to Roosevelt Island that loomed in the darkness above Cole. He could make out the cable occasionally in the inadequate lighting, but it was a hard target under these conditions. Cole would wait for the tram itself to put things into perspective.

He heard the grinding and the whir and knew that a tram car was already setting out from the terminal on Second Avenue. The tram covered more than half the length of its trip over Manhattan pavement before it reached the river. Roosevelt Island with its once trendy high-rises lay closer to Cole's hiding place than did the terminal, which was beneficial to Cole. He would have that much longer to escape.

The tram car swung into view overhead, people visible behind the glass, looking like so many executives in business suits on their way up the Alps in a funicular.

Cole could feel the pulse in his eyeballs throbbing, his mouth was parched, and the familiar roar of power sounded in his ears as he raised the crossbow in his gloved hands and sighted just behind the car where the cable was now clearly visible. He aimed well above the cable, as he had practiced so many times with the tree limb, and fired. The bolt, painted matte black, soared into the darkness and disappeared. Cole heard the line hissing smoothly after it from its coil at his feet and then he saw the plastic-encased serpent lift smoothly upward. His bomb was launched.

Cole hurled the crossbow and the extra bolts into the river, crumpled up the packing case and paper and kicked them over the edge too. He glanced back once as he walked away, hoping to see the twenty feet of explosive dangling over the cable, but it was too dark and too dangerous to hang around. If it had worked, if his calculations were right, the sausage would be draped over the cable like a hose over a wash line, waiting for the heavy crunch of the

tram itself to ignite it. If it worked, he would know soon enough and he could not afford to be near by when it did. If it did not work, then he would abandon the method and try something else. It had worked on the tree limb. It *should* work on the tram—but if it didn't, something else would.

On its return from Roosevelt Island the overhead wheels of the tram car nudged against the length of explosive and pushed it before them along the cable. The piezoelectric strip was facing away from the wheels and received none of the shock. The tram car continued on its way, propelling the serpent bomb in front of it as if it were pushing a python off a limb. One of the passengers in the car noticed the length of dun-colored rope dangling in front of the window and wondered idly what it was. She did not remember having seen it on any other trip.

Cole was on the corner of Second Avenue and Sixty-sixth Street, seven blocks away, when the wheels pushed the bomb into the gearbox at the terminal. The pressure created an electric current that traveled to the detonators, which exploded and triggered the vastly larger explosion that severed the cable and mangled the steel stanchions of the terminal. The car crashed to the ground and the cable, suddenly freed of tension, whipped like a scythe through the air, killing whoever it touched in the next three blocks, before it came to rest at last in the river.

Cole heard the roar and could just catch a glimpse of the turmoil as it erupted into the street seven hundred yards away. He did not stay to watch but mounted his bicycle and pedaled home, feeling like a god every inch of the way.

CHAPTER

FOLLOWING THE BOMBING OF THE Roosevelt Island tram, and the subsequent deaths of seventeen people, they shook the tree in earnest. At Becker's instigation, his unit—augmented by five dozen city cops—hauled in for questioning every petty and serious criminal who ever had been or presently could be associated with anything even remotely connected with illegal arms, terrorism, extortion, or bombings. With a shaking that vigorous, a great deal of fruit fell from the tree.

Defone heard them at his door at four a.m. and for a brief moment thought of reaching for the shotgun and the Glock and making a fight of it. He had a fully automatic Tec-9 with a clip holding thirty rounds in the other room, but by the time he thought of going for it he heard the door break in and saw shapes of a SWAT team race past the bedroom door. He would take his chances against most people but he wasn't about to tackle trigger-happy cops with bulletproof vests and tear gas. Defone was prepared to fight a skirmish, not a war.

"I'm in here buck naked with my hands in the air!" he called out loudly.

"Move an inch and you're a dead motherfucker," growled a

voice from the other room. Defone heard all kinds of weapons cocking and safeties switched off and rounds ratcheted into place.

"That's what I'm saying," Defone replied. "I ain't moving, I ain't fighting, I sure as hell ain't resisting . . . Come on in."

He heard more movement, whispered voices. He could smell the scent of oil on gun metal from the other room almost as strong as his own sweat. There was so much fear-induced energy on the other side of the wall, just waiting to blast his ass into a tea strainer, that Defone was scared as shit.

"Keep your fucking hands *up,* motherfucker."

Defone, who had never thought of lowering them, stretched his hands toward the ceiling. He wished crazily that he was married so that he could have someone in bed with him that he could use as a shield. They just naturally *wanted* to kill his ass, no question about it.

"Come on in," Defone repeated. "The light switch right around the corner."

"We'll come in when we feel like it," the voice responded, and Defone heard other voices saying that the light switch was a trick and still other voices suggesting they just shoot the son of a bitch and be done with it.

"Get on your face on the floor," said the voice, and Defone did it without hesitation. The beam of a powerful flashlight was turned on him and there was a rush as many feet leaped into the room all at once. Defone was almost happy to feel the first kick. That meant they weren't going to shoot him after all. He curled into a ball and endured.

How's your wife?" the technician asked.

Becker forced himself to smile and sound cheerful. "Fine, she's just fine."

"We all look forward to having her back at work soon," the

technician continued. His name was Coates. He was a very tall, goofy-looking man with a receding chin and eyes that seemed to freewheel in their sockets, and it was easy to see why he had chosen to spend his life in a laboratory.

"Thank you," said Becker, still smiling. "I'll tell her that, she'll be glad to hear it."

"She's a hell of a woman . . . and a terrific agent."

Becker nodded, feeling the smile begin to weaken at the edges. Coates didn't seem to know when he had said enough and Becker did not want to appear to cut him off prematurely. It's because they do care about Karen, he reminded himself. Not because they're trying to make you feel worse.

It was only when Coates turned his attention to the documents in his hands and looked for a way to change the subject that Becker spoke of business.

"Tell me about Spring," he said. "How good is he?"

"It was clever," Coates said, still looking at his papers. "Yes, it was clever. In fact, I'm not quite certain just yet how it was done, something attached to the cable itself, apparently. The engineers say that's the only way to account for the blast pattern. There may be fragments of the bomb itself yet to be found—there may be, although we don't have anything yet. But I can tell you something about the explosive that was used. According to the results from the mass spectrometer, this was not a commercially available explosive."

"Where did he get it?"

"Well, there's the thing. And this is bad news, I'm afraid, but the nitroglycerin and the ammonium nitrate were both of slightly different chemical balances than you would find commercially. Their mix together was not quite the normal proportion, either. Close, but not quite. And here's something very surprising. He used a kind of clay called kieselguhr as a dope—that is, a kind of absorbent filler. Well, no one has doped with guhr for years. Probably not in

this century. Alfred Nobel used it in his first dynamite in the 1860s and even he gave it up after a few years. There are a lot better materials to use now. It's not just old-fashioned, it's antique."

"And this is bad news because . . . ?"

"Because the bomb was entirely homemade," said Coates. "Spring knows what he's doing. He may have access only to old texts or he has a sense of history, I don't know which, but the end result is that he knows how to make a bomb, all by himself."

"And a good bomb too," Becker added.

"Oh, yes, a very effective bomb . . . an imaginative bomb."

"A fucking homemade genius," Becker said. "But you're wrong about its being bad news. Bad news would be if he's buying his bombs off the shelf. He could be anybody. If he's rolling his own, that's good news. That limits the field very fast."

When Defone was released by the police, he had three priorities. The first was to find a newspaper, the second was to get himself a weapon—the police had not only confiscated the Glock, the shotgun, and the Tec-9, but they even found the Smith and Wesson hidden in the lining of his sofa—and the third was to make a phone call to his friend and partner.

His partner sounded surprised to hear from him.

"Where are you?" Cole asked.

"On the street. What you want to know is where I *been.*"

"Where have you been?" Cole said slowly, humoring him. Don't condescend to me, motherfucker, Defone thought. Keep up that shit and pretty soon Defone going to descend on *you.*

"I been in the *po*-lice station. They kept asking me what do I know about Spring, when do I see Spring next. Shiiit, I thought they was talking about April and May. Turns out Spring is a man. How do I know that? I looked in the paper and there he is on the front page. Man named Spring blew up a train or something.

Wrote a letter, asking for five million dollars or he's going to blow everything up. Turns out they asking *every* last brother they could catch about this Spring. I seen brothers in there I thought was dead for ten years. Even *I* asked them what does they know about Spring. You know what they all told me? They don't know shit about Spring. Never heard of him until they saw the papers or heard it on the TV. I got to think Spring ain't a brother."

"Why are you telling me this? I said I'd get in touch with you when baby arrives."

"Thought you'd be interested what's going on in Defone's life. Since I's your friend—and partner."

"Yes, well, of course I'm interested."

"I'm sure as hell interested in *you*. I'm so interested that you know what I done after I met you at your apartment? I went to the library. You know what I had the woman who works there look up for me? Nitromannite. Mercury fulminate. A little potassium chlorate."

"What do you want, Defone?" His voice was low now, angry. Defone grinned to himself. Gotcha, motherfucker.

"Those are some of the things I saw in your workroom, partner. You know what they do? They explode. They blow up. They go boom. And they all sitting right there in your room. Some of them sitting there because I got them for you. You know what else, Mr. Spring? They ain't expensive. They ain't hard to get. You can walk in and buy them chemicals yourself. If you didn't mind somebody knowing you bought them. If you didn't mind a witness."

"I got your point, Defone. What do you want? I have no baby yet."

"Now, what kind of deal is that? You going to get five million dollars and I get another bag of baby? How about I get a truckload of baby and four million dollars? That leaves you with a million dollars and you can still call your asshole your own."

"I think we should talk about this."

"What do you think I'm doing, motherfucker? You think I'm just farting over the phone? I *am* talking about it."

"Let's be calm. We should meet. We'll have lunch, we'll talk."

"Don't take that tone of voice with me. Don't be telling me what we'll be doing."

"Sorry."

"I be telling *you,* Mr. Spring-blow-up-the-city-motherfucker."

"It's best not to call me Spring, Defone. Someone might hear you."

"Whole bunch of peoples going to hear me pretty damned soon if you don't cut out this *calm* shit and start asking what can you do for me. You go to talking all *calm* and I know your white ass is up to something."

"I'm not calm. I'm scared to death."

"Your ass better be."

"What can I do for you?"

"You can start by getting me some money. They going to haul my ass in on a weapons charge. Illegal search and seizure, too. The police motherfuckers didn't knock, just beat the door down. My attorney's going to be outraged." Defone laughed. "That's how the son bitch talks. 'I is outraged on your behalf,' " he piped in a high, squeaky tone, dissolving at the end in laughter at his own wit. Defone was having a good time. "So get me ten thousand dollars I can pay this bastard, let him get all outraged."

"I don't have ten thousand, I don't have anything close to that."

"You going to have five million dollars."

"That's not real, Defone. That's play money. There's no way to collect it. They'd have that money treated with dye so that if you touched it your hands would glow purple. They'd have radio transmitters in the bag, they'd be watching from helicopters and every window in the city, they could put a device in the bills that sends a message to a satellite so they could track you anyplace on the planet. I have no intention of ever seeing any of that money."

"Why you asking for it?"

"Because it's what they understand. I'm not interested in money—they could never understand that."

"What are you interested in?"

"Justice."

Motherfucker's crazy for sure, thought Defone. Worse than I thought. If there was anything a black man knew for sure in this world, it was that there was no such thing as justice. Might as well say he was doing it for Santa Claus. At least folks knew what Santa looked like. Justice didn't even have a face in Defone's mind.

"You blowing up things for justice," Defone repeated.

"They took away something I should have had, something that I deserved. They can't be allowed to get away with that."

"Uh-huh." Defone had no idea what the man was talking about but he recognized the sound of paranoia when he heard it. And he knew that he had set it off.

"I was due for tenure. Do you know what tenure means in the life of an academic?"

Defone didn't know what tenure meant, period. He grunted sympathetically.

"It means life and death, that's what it means. Life and death. Well, I had earned life but they took it away from me in the name of affirmative action. Well, pardon me, no offense, Defone, but affirmative action is a crock. They took my life, the city took my life and gave it to somebody else. They can do that to an individual, you know. There's nothing to stop them. They can look at you and decide, 'You win, you lose.' An individual can't fight them, they just mouth their platitudes about the greater good, redressing ancient wrongs, blah, blah, blah. It's my *life* they're talking about, but they don't even know it. Well, there are greater powers than the individual, Defone. There are greater powers than the university administration, there are greater powers than the city of New

York, and those powers can rise up, and those powers can strike, and they can render the whole city a cripple— Oh, excuse me, they can render the city 'access-challenged' . . ."

"Ten thousand dollars," said Defone, who had heard enough to know he didn't want to hear any more.

"I don't have ten thousand—"

"By tomorrow. I'm going to call my attorney. I love to see that man get outraged on my behalf. He acts like he believes half the shit he says. He be better than Johnnie Cochran at making you laugh and feeling sorry for me and shit. But he always wants his money first. I got to have that ten thousand up front or he be outraged I even showed up in his office. You understand? By tomorrow, or I got to cut some kind of deal with the police, and when I cut a deal, I going to use whatever I got to help me out."

"I can give you more baby. A lot more baby."

"Lawyer don't accept no baby. Don't take no chickens, neither. Sucker's got a heart like a stone unless you give him cash—then it's bleeding all over you. Ten thousand dollars. By tomorrow. You know how to reach me."

Defone hung up and dug in his pocket for change for another phone call. He would have to check with Auntie Berthine to make sure she was receiving calls for him this month. He could not remember if he had paid her for the last two months or not—he had not needed her services once he got his supply of baby and the messenger gave him instructions about the next meeting. Auntie Berthine was old and blind and never left her apartment, so she was pretty sure to be available to answer her calls. On the other hand her memory wasn't the best, so the messages were sometimes garbled, sometimes forgotten. Still, she was better than an answering machine because that meant a telephone line that could be traced to an address. And after the ease with which the police SWAT team had found him, Defone had no intention of returning to his old apartment.

Defone seized a passerby by the throat and demanded a quarter. The man fumbled for his wallet. "A quarter, just a quarter. This ain't no holdup," Defone said impatiently. After the fool got the idea and came up with the change, Defone checked in with Auntie Berthine. After being promised twice her usual payment, she agreed to receive any calls for Defone for the next month.

CHAPTER

BECKER WAS APOLOGIZING AS HE reached the door, his mind filled with concern and excuses on his lips.

"The traffic in and out of the city is slower than a crawl," he said.

"I knew that, I expected that," said Karen. She was in the kitchen, dressed in sweat clothes as if she had been exercising, but Becker knew that they were the only garments she could trouble herself to put on these days.

"The city's got every cop they could scrape together checking all the bridges and tunnels. *I* couldn't get past the inspection. You'd need a helicopter to get in or out without a two-hour backup."

"I knew that, John. I've been watching the news."

"You must be starving. I'll fix something quick," he said, moving toward the refrigerator. "I'm sorry I'm so late."

"John, I *understand,*" Karen said impatiently. "I already ate. I made myself an omelette."

To Becker's knowledge, Karen had cooked nothing in six months. "I'm sorry."

"It wasn't that bad an omelette. Do you want me to make one for you?"

"You shouldn't have had to do that," Becker said. "I should have called someone to come over . . ."

"Don't be silly."

"You should be resting . . ."

"That's all I do is rest. I rest so much I'm exhausted. I got woozy just beating the eggs."

"I'll help you to bed," Becker said, taking her arm.

Gently but firmly she removed her arm from his grasp. "John, listen to me, please. I am not sick. I have an injury. It is my injury. Not yours. No matter how sympathetic, no matter how guilty you feel, it is still *my* injury. You cannot make it yours. I even resent that you *try* to make it yours. You are not injured. I don't want you to be injured. You have pain enough in your life without taking on mine—"

"What is all this?" Becker interrupted. "Where is this coming from?"

"I've been meaning to say it to you for a while now," she said. "It's how I feel. I want you to let me deal with this in my own way, on my own. No one else can help me, anyway, and if I think I'm hampering you or your work in any way, it only makes it harder for me."

"What are you talking about? I don't get it."

"Just do your job, John. You've got a unit full of people depending on you, you've got the city blowing apart at the seams, you've got a lunatic on the loose—quit worrying about me."

Becker took her hands in his and looked at her closely, studying her face.

"Who called?" he asked. "Who talked to you?"

"Nobody."

"Somebody's been talking to you."

She shrugged with her eyebrows, then pulled her hands away.

"Don't give me that investigative look," she said. "Technically

I'm still your boss, you know. My orders are to get your mind back in your work."

"Did Gold call? That meddling old nanny, he doesn't know anything about anything. Pay no attention to him."

"You like Gold, as a matter of fact. You just hate it that you need him now and then."

"The only one I need is you," said Becker.

"Is that true?"

"Truest thing in my life," he said.

This time she took his hand. "Then you can put me to bed after all. It's been a long time."

At first Becker felt that he was engaged in a prescriptive coupling, a little medicinal cure ordered up by Dr. Gold to renew the marital bonds, demonstrate the wife's good health, and send the warrior revitalized back into the fray. He handled her gingerly, as if it were all of her nerve endings that were frayed and raw, not just the pain centers of her brain. He kissed her as gently as a breath, caressed her skin with the wonderment of a man greeting his newborn for the first time. As they proceeded he realized that the cure was working, at least for him. Initial doubts about whether or not they would remember how to do it, voiced half in jest, half in concern, were quickly forgotten. He made love to Karen as he had always made love to her—as if he loved her.

It was the way he usually made love, Karen thought, only more so. He was the most tender of lovers, and every time, he made her feel—at least in the preliminary minutes—as if what moved him most of all, more than lust, more than excitement, was a sense of awe and gratitude that such a precious thing as a woman had been delivered into his hands. It was like being loved by a feather and it drove her wild.

Afterwards, as they usually did, they lay in each other's arms and discussed the miracle of their sex life. Unlike many others who in panting enthusiasm did the same, they were both experienced enough and wise enough to know it was true.

Later still, she asked him about the case.

"Time is on his side," Becker said. "No one in his right mind would attack any of the bridges right now, not after the uproar he caused with the tram—but that kind of security will lapse, it has to. All he has to do is wait a few months or so and he can strike again. There's really no way to prevent him—Manhattan is an island, not a fortress. There's no good way to defend it for very long. If he keeps his head down, he can wait this period out, then hit us again whenever he feels like it, and there's nothing we can do about it."

"Except catch him first."

"Any bright ideas how?"

"What does he want to stop?"

"Money, he says. It seems an extreme way to go about it. I think he has some other motive, some private lunacy that drives him. He talks about unlearning things and changing the system."

"Do you think you can find out what it is?"

"How?"

"Ask him?"

Becker sat upright in the bed. "There's an idea." He was out of bed and on the phone before Karen said she was joking.

"I know. But you were right." On the telephone he asked to speak with the duty officer. "I want to hold a press conference tomorrow. I want a big splash in the papers and the local TV. It's about the tramway bombing, so you should have no problem getting complete coverage . . . Get on it, get all over it. And I want to meet with Gold and the rest of the unit first thing . . . And you'd better send a chopper for me to the White Plains airport or I'll never get in."

Becker slept soundly for the first time in weeks, unaware of his wife's waking state beside him. He never knew when the attack hit her and she sat up, pulling her knees to her chest to struggle

against the pain. He never knew about the tears that coursed silently down her cheeks, or about the tiny moans in her throat like imprisoned birds, straining to break out.

He woke once, briefly, not certain what had disturbed him. Karen lay stretched out beside him, a pillow over her head. Under the cover of the sheet it was impossible to see that she was rigid as a board, every muscle fighting the pain. He went quickly back to sleep.

In the morning when she said she felt fine, she felt much better, he believed her—as they both wanted him to do.

Karen watched from the kitchen as he left the house. She had pulled on a pair of jeans and a T-shirt for the occasion, and she managed a smile whenever he was looking. When he went to meet the helicopter and she slumped back to bed, beaten and exhausted by her efforts to make him feel better, she was proudest not of all the things she said and the little lies she told, but of the one question she didn't ask. The only thing she really wanted to know. But she never mentioned Pegeen Haddad's name

CHAPTER

TONY BUONO, KNOWN AS TONY the Good, wore his refuse hauler's work pants and work shirt to the meeting with Mr. Case because he had another meeting of the carters union afterwards. As an officer of the union—officially sergeant at arms—Tony wore the uniform to display his unity with the workingmen. In reality Tony had never lifted a garbage can in his life except to dump it over the head of some gabon' who decided to be uncooperative.

"I think some of the future has gone out of hauling," Tony said by way of introduction to Mr. Case. From Tony's point of view, it was a mild statement of cruel facts. The city, state, and federal authorities had broken the grip of organized crime on the commercial garbage business and Tony's company, like all the others, was now forced to actually *compete* for trade. Since the only competition they had ever participated in previously had been to see who could twist their customers' arms the hardest, they were ill equipped to survive under the altered conditions. Tony's sinecure and livelihood were in peril. Membership in the Mafia was no longer a guarantee of prosperity. A man had to hustle these days, just to get by. In ways that he could not quite articulate even to himself, Tony blamed the Republicans in Congress, but he kept this opinion to himself. Messing in politics was always a dangerous business.

"So I'm looking for a new line of work. I'm branching out. I find your proposal very interesting, Mr. Case."

"I haven't made a proposal."

"Understood," said Tony. He folded his hands on the table in front of him and looked intently, but politely, at the man across from him. Already Tony could see that there were problems in dealing with civilians that he wasn't going to like.

"I just have a problem. I wanted to discuss my problem with someone who might be able to help me."

"You got the right man," Tony said.

"I was hoping for someone with experience."

"I been solving problems all my life," Tony said.

"You just said it was a new line of work."

"New on a free-lance basis," Tony explained. "I solved my first problem when I was fifteen, but that was a personal thing. After that I solved maybe ten, twelve problems for—uh—on an organizational basis. This would be my first free-lance problem. But believe me, Mr. Case, you couldn't have come to a better man. I'm discreet, I'm quick, I'm untraceable, and if it comes to it, I'm a stand-up guy. Nothing would ever come back to you, no matter what. There's a problem, I do the time, you go on about your business—not that there's going to be a problem . . . And I happen to be free right now."

Tony watched the man think. A scrawny, washed-out type, English, maybe Swedish, certainly no paisan. Stringy hair, glasses, probably older than he looked. The kind of guy you'd see in the Village, or picketing for peace. Not a fagola, but a kindred spirit. He was having trouble making up his mind.

"I can see you have your doubts," Tony said. "Fair enough. You don't know me and my problem solving has all been in the private sector so my name is not known to you. You want to commit but you're just not sure. Let me make you a proposal. Since this is the first for me under these conditions, and since it's the first for you—This *is* your first problem?"

Case nodded.

"So you're a virgin, and I—I ain't no virgin, I been around, I covered that already, let's just say I'm not a brand name to you just yet. Because of all this, I'm going to make you a offer. I will get rid of your problem for only fifteen thousand dollars. Believe me, that's a big savings."

Case stared at him.

"Let me explain what that includes," Tony continued. "One, I get rid of your problem. That goes without saying. Quick, efficient, no mess for you. Two, I'm a family man, I have expenses—I know that's not your problem, but you should know it. I got a lovely wife and three great kids, all daughters, but hey, they cost more than the boys. You know the expense of private education these days? . . . Okay, just so you know. And three, that price includes any legal expenses on my part should that be necessary. I'm not saying it will. It won't. But just in case, that's already built into the price. Anything happens, nobody comes back to you and says, what about Tony's family, what about Tony's bail, what about Tony's lawyer. That could happen, with other people, that could happen. For fifteen thousand, you got no problem with that sort of thing. Ever. So there you go, mission accomplished, insurance paid, silence guaranteed, and you got the gratitude of my family, all for the same price."

"I can't afford fifteen thousand," Case said.

Tony buried his face in his hands and breathed deeply. There was a limit to the uses of reason. He saw that he wasn't going to like the free market.

"What can you afford?"

"I can raise five thousand."

"Five thousand," Tony repeated dully.

"If I had ten thousand I wouldn't have such a problem in the first place."

Tony wondered how such a cheap gabon' made his way in the world. Why didn't somebody just break him in two out of principle? Tony hated cheap. Everybody he knew hated cheap. One of the purposes of money was to display it, to spend it freely. That's what kept the economy working. Spread the shit around, for God's sake. Wear it, ride in it, put it on your fingers and around your neck and on your woman. What were you going to do, die with it? This cheap shit, this savings bullshit, was a WASP attitude. Tony wanted to ram his beer glass down the little turd's throat.

"You catch me at a bad time," Tony said. Five thousand? The ring on his little finger cost more than five thousand. "I'm eager to get started in my new career, but let's not be totally ridiculous." He was bargaining with this asshole. He could not believe it. What would Donny the Snake say if he knew? The Snake got twenty-five thousand a pop. No dickering, no discounts, no bargains. Twenty-five thousand. Tony had asked him in person before taking the meeting.

"Mr. Case, talk to me," Tony said, wiggling his fingers in encouragement. "Work with me here."

They agreed on sixty-two fifty and then Case asked Tony to step into the men's room with him.

"I wonder if you'd mind taking off all your clothes," Case said, evenly enough considering what he was asking. He leaned against the door like some punk holding up a light post.

Tony decided he'd been wrong about the fagola thing, but still, he was the calmest fag Tony'd ever seen.

"Just to demonstrate that you're not wired," Case continued. "Personally, I believe you are who you say, but one reads about these things in the paper all the time. Undercover policemen being solicited to do this and that."

Tony glared at the skinny, miserly son of a bitch, trying to decide whether to kill him or just incapacitate him for life.

"If you think about it, you'll see that it's a reasonable request," Case was saying. "I'm afraid I can't explain the nature of my problem to you if I'm not completely comfortable that you're not with a law enforcement agency. It would be too bad because I've come to trust you otherwise."

"You can't believe what my fucking wife spends on clothes," said Tony. He removed his shirt and hung it on the door of the stall. "I tell her times are changing, pull in your horns, so what does she do? She goes out and buys another outfit, then looks me in the face and dares me to say something."

For the kind of chump change he used to blow in an evening in Atlantic City, Tony the Good was stripping in a public john in front of some possible fag he'd met fifteen minutes ago. Fucking could not believe it. If Donny the Snake saw this, Tony would die of shame. If *anybody* he knew saw it he would die.

"I know why she does it. It's psychological. She needs those clothes to make up for her face. It's a funny thing, she looks great from behind. She's got the nice hair, the body, great ass on her. I see her from behind, I know she's got to be beautiful, know what I'm saying? I watch her like that on purpose sometimes, just walk behind her, look at her legs, her arms, her ass, watching the way it stretches the cloth, jeans, skirt, shorts, it don't matter, she looks like a fucking piece and a half—and all the time I'm enjoying the view, I'm hoping she don't turn around and spoil it. A body like that and she's—what's the word—homely. She's not ugly, it's not painful to look at her, it's more—disappointing. I don't know how I come to be married to a homely woman." Slipping out of his pants, hopping on one foot to get them over the shoe, and wondering what the fuck he was telling this gabon' all of this for. He'd never told anybody this much in his whole life. He couldn't seem to stop talking.

Tony stood with his pants dangling in front of him, offering partial protection.

"Would you mind hanging them up?" Case said.

What the fuck am I worried about? Tony asked himself. He knew he was a good-looking guy, well built, getting just a little heavy in the middle, but nothing to be ashamed of. He had a good body, Franca told him that all the time. He hung his pants atop the shirt.

"The rest, please," said Case.

Some subtle shift of power had taken place, as if Tony had handed his dominance over to Case along with his clothes. Tony felt it, couldn't define it, but knew that Case was now in charge.

"You don't need that," Tony protested, indicating his bikini underwear.

"I don't know how large a transmitter or a tape recorder is these days," said Case. Tony did not know either. "I'd feel more comfortable."

Tony looped his thumbs under the elastic of his shorts. He wished that he had saved some of that money when he had it; he wouldn't be in this position today. Not that he had anything to be ashamed of in *this* area, either, he reminded himself, but he was now aware of something that surprised him entirely. As he lowered his shorts he realized that he was swelling rapidly. He held his hands in front of him to cover his inexplicable semierection.

"Turn, please," Case said, seemingly unaware of Tony's distress.

Tony turned in a slow circle, deliberate as a runway model, and Case noted the swirls of dark hair on his back, like nascent wings. Tony was without wire or diode or electronics of any description.

The door pushed into Case's back as someone tried to enter the men's room.

"Get out of here or I'll kill you!" Tony screamed, grabbing for his shorts while still trying to hide his erection. "Come in that door and you're dead!" They heard the sound of someone in full retreat.

Case waited until Tony was fully dressed and some of the blood had drained from his face before announcing, "The name of my problem is Defone Lee. I don't know where he lives, but I have a telephone number."

"Up front," Tony said angrily. "I want that money up front, all of it. All sixty-two fifty, and no argument, or you can keep your fucking problem."

"Of course," said Case.

"In fact, if I don't see that money, you got a new problem. Me. Understand?"

"You're upset."

"And let me tell you something else. I ain't doing this again. One time is it."

"I understand," said Case.

"So okay," Tony said, stretching elaborately, as if he had just awakened from a long sleep. His dignity restored along with his clothing, he demanded, "Forget what I said about the wife, I don't know what that was."

"Of course."

"So when you want me to get rid of your problem?"

"Would today be too soon? I could have put something in his baby but I couldn't be sure when that would work. If you wait until tomorrow, it would be very messy."

"Put something in his baby? Hey, I draw the line—"

"No, no, you misunderstood. I wouldn't hurt a child."

"I got kids of my own."

"No, no. Just Defone. Can you do it today?"

"Today's fine with me," said Tony, who was in the perfect mood to kill somebody.

CHAPTER

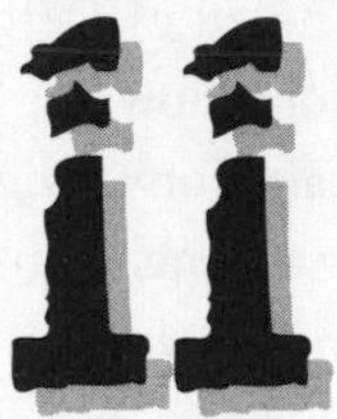

BY THE TIME THE OLD LADY HAD shuffled to her entrance, Tony the Good had decided to just shoot Defone as soon as he cracked the door. Just pop him in the head two, three times and walk away, not even wait until he unlatched the chain. Sudden violent deaths were nothing out of the ordinary in the River Towers project, no one was going to get too excited about this one.

Tony was not prepared for the querulous voice asking, "Who dere?"

"Federal Express," he said, standing clear of the fish-eye peephole. "You got to sign for it."

He was even less prepared for the old woman's face peering out of the crack in the door.

"I didn't send for nothing," the woman said.

Mr. Case had said nothing about an old woman, but he pointed the Smith and Wesson between her eyes anyway. She stared back at him through her dark glasses as if everyone greeted her this way.

"It's for Defone Lee," said Tony.

"I don't know him," said the old woman. "Why you bringing it to me?"

"Is this 417 River Towers?"

"Yes."

"Defone Lee lives here."

"I tell you I never heard of Defone Lee. Don't want to hear of him neither. Go on along now."

"Open the door," said Tony, wiggling the gun. "Let me in."

"You got something for me, just slip it through the crack." Tony waved the gun up and down in front of her face. "But I ain't opening the door for nobody, certainly not no white folks."

"I'm going to blow you away, old lady. Open up."

A telephone rang in the room behind her and the old woman turned to answer it.

"You git along now," she said to Tony, closing the door in his face. "You got the wrong place."

Tony stared for a moment at the door, then stared blankly down the hallway that led to the stairs. The walls were so covered with graffiti they were almost solid with paint. It was hard to know what to do with someone who had no respect for a Smith and Wesson aimed between the eyes from twelve inches away.

As he walked down the three flights of littered steps, ignoring the hostile stares of all he encountered, Tony tried to figure out where he had gone wrong. Case had provided him with the phone number for Lee, and he had looked up the accompanying address in the reverse phone book just the way Donny the Snake had shown him. The old woman had verified the address herself, which meant either she was lying and Defone Lee lived there, or Case gave him the wrong information to begin with. Since there didn't seem to be any chance of intimidating the old woman into letting him in, Tony decided the fault lay with Case.

He came into the night air and with his first deep breath he realized that he had been trying not to inhale the whole time he was in the project building. The place reeked of cooking smells and urine and body odor and worse. It reminded Tony of a trip he once

made to an animal shelter to get his daughters a kitten. All that contained energy crammed together in tiny cages, barking and meowing and chirping and living an existence amid the stench. People spent a lifetime that way, never knew the difference. Tony thought of the space and privacy of his house and lawn and fenced-in backyard in Queens and shook his head in amazement.

When he reached his car it was surrounded by a swarm of children who acted more curious about his arrival than threatened, as if they wanted to see his reaction to the fact that the Cadillac was already missing hubcaps and radio and cassette player. Tony stared at it, stupefied. Nobody in his Queens neighborhood or lower Manhattan would dare to touch his car. They wouldn't dare to *think* about touching his car.

He touched the Smith and Wesson reflexively, then noticed the crowd gathering on the corner. Gangbangers, half a dozen of them with more hurrying toward the corner as if a signal had been sent. They watched him from the distance of half a block like a pack of wolves gathering.

Tony got into the car quickly, grateful that it still worked, and drove to Manhattan where a made man still commanded the respect to which he was entitled.

For just a moment he contemplated driving on home to Queens, forget the inconvenience of a three-hour wait to get over the bridge, just drive on home, play with the kids, maybe fuck the wife later, and forget about Defone Lee. He already had Case's money in his pocket and Case wasn't the kind of man—if he was any kind of man at all—to come looking for him. The thought passed, however. For one thing, it was not a promising way to get started in a new line of work. There were plenty of others to take Tony's spot if he backed out. Times were getting hard within the brotherhood and work was very scarce. For another, Donny the Snake would kill him personally if he cheated the job. Donny had stood for him to get the opportunity in the first place and Donny was a man of exceptional honor. If everybody had Donny's sense of honor and didn't cooperate with every district attorney and crime commission that came along just to save their own asses, Tony and the rest of the people wouldn't be in such a mess in the first place.

He drove to the bar where he had met Mr. Case earlier in the day.

When Defone called, Auntie Berthine told him he had two messages. One was to meet the messenger at the usual spot tomorrow morning at ten.

"The other wasn't a phone call," she said. "A man come looking for you."

"What kind of man? What'd he look like?"

"Honey, you knows I can't see."

"Sorry, Auntie."

"He say he be a Federal Express, but he don' sound like one. Not polite."

"What else he sound like?"

"White. Nervous. Mad. I say he be Italian by the sound of him. Got an accent like that."

"What a Wop want with me?"

"Say he have a package for you. I say I don't know you, don't want to know you. And Defone, honey, any more mens come around here looking for you, that be the truth. I don't want to know you. All I do is answer the phone. Don't need no Italians calling at my door."

"I take care of it," said Defone.

"See that you do," she said sternly, hanging up.

Defone pondered the significance of a visit by a Wop pretending to be a Fed Ex man. A cop could be a Guinea, of course, but in that case Auntie Berthine would say he be a cop, not he be a Wop. And cops liked to advertise theyselves, *tell* you they was cops in case

you was brain-dead and couldn't see it or smell it. They always be waving badges and calling out "Police officer" and all that shit, like it was going to make you hurry up and do what they wanted. Unless they was busting Defone's door down. Didn't hear no announcement about *that* ahead of time. "Hello, Defone, we your friendly neighborhood SWAT team, kindly open up and let us in." Defone didn't recall hearing *that* announcement.

So, if it wasn't a cop and it wasn't no pizza deliveryman, there wasn't a whole lot left for an angry Guinea to be. Defone didn't deal in drugs in any significant way, he didn't run no ho's, he didn't even play the numbers. There was no reason for the Wops to be looking for him.

He thought of the messenger and corrected himself. He thought of the *man*—Jason Cole, according to his mail. Spring, according to Defone and the newspapers and the TV. Defone had *thought* the man agreed to the ten thousand pretty damned quick. He had thought he was just a little too calm from the moment Defone met him in his workroom to the last conversation on the phone. Defone always suspected the scrawny little motherfucker had something up his sleeve. Didn't want the money? Didn't want five million dollars? My ass, thought Defone. Greedy little bomber wanted *all* the money, didn't want to share a nickel with Defone. Had some motherfucking Wop up his sleeve the whole time.

Defone was depressed by the perfidy of human nature and genuinely distressed about the prospective loss of baby, but such was life. The thing that really annoyed him about the man was that he seemed to think Defone was stupid.

Defone checked his supply of baby. He had enough to get him through his meeting with the man tomorrow and about a month after that besides. Hell, in a month he could find someone else to make it for him.

CHAPTER

HATCHER ARRIVED IN TIME FOR the press conference. "Just to show the flag," he assured Becker. "Just for moral support. I'll stand up with you during the conference—I think it's important that everyone knows I'm a hundred percent behind you here, in whatever you do, whatever it is, I'm there for you, you can count on me. We'll send that message out. Subliminally. I'll just be standing behind you at the dais, then I'll just turn around and go back to Washington."

"Who told you there was going to be a press conference?" Becker asked, wondering if someone in his unit was reporting to Hatcher.

"I heard it on CNN," Hatcher said, flashing the inappropriate smile that made Becker suspect him of lying. But then Becker thought he was lying all the time. Hatcher put him in mind of a living example of a classic problem in logic that he remembered from college: All Greeks tell nothing but lies. All Cretans tell only the truth. . . . He forgot the rest of the problem, which was designed to discover who was telling the truth, but had no difficulty putting Hatcher in the proper category.

"This is your baby," Hatcher continued. "I won't say a word."

But of course he did, taking the microphone before Becker spoke and filling the airwaves with meaningless hokum about the hard-working and dedicated public servants who would not rest until the perpetrator was found, et cetera, to the point that Becker contemplated just walking away and leaving Hatcher to finish the mess he had started. He did not do it because the conference was far too important. It was the beginning of the way to get to Spring.

Donny the Snake Sabela positioned himself in a protective doorway and watched his cousin Tony confer with a man on a bike and wondered what the world was coming to. Now they were taking orders from punks on bicycles? In his time Donny had done business with a lot of people, living and dead; there had been some mighty men among them, and there had been a variety of weasels and lowlifes and scum, the same cross section of humanity that anyone in any walk of life might encounter. Some of them were brave and some were sniveling whiners and some confronted Donny by soiling themselves, or throwing up on their shoes, or clutching his knees and weeping. He had even had a man die in his arms of a heart attack once he realized who Donny was and why he had come. But every one of those people, both the ones who paid him and those he paid off, had something in common. They went around the city in a car, or they went by public transportation, or they took cabs, or they went afoot. But none of them, until now, had ever ridden a bicycle. How could you take such a man seriously? This was a serious business that Tony had entered into—how could he expect to do well if he couldn't take his employer seriously? This punk on the bike wasn't even the target, he was the *customer*. Incredible.

Tony was sawing the air with his arms, explaining his earlier failure to Bicycle Boy, Donny surmised. Tony had told the whole story to Donny just an hour ago, excusing himself, alibiing, even hinting that in some measure it was Donny's fault for giving him the wrong advice about how to find his target. Donny had stiffened at that and suggested that if Tony had ripped the fucking door off and walked over the old woman like he should have, he would have found his fucking target hiding under the bed.

The problem with Tony was he talked too much. He never *said* anything as far as Donny could tell, but he certainly heated up a lot of air in the process. When you went to cap somebody, you weren't supposed to engage in *conversation,* for Christ's sake. At the most, if you felt like it, if you were close enough and things were secure enough, and you *felt* like it, you might whisper "Goodbye" in the target's ear before you slipped in the ice pick or looped the garrote or pulled the trigger. Not that you'd want to be that close if you shot him, not unless you wanted his brains on your face. Sometimes the employer had messages he wanted you to deliver before you capped the guy. "This is from Frankie, you asshole," that kind of thing. They'd seen too many movies. You didn't do that kind of thing—why give the victim the advantage of knowing what was happening if you didn't have to? So you kept your mouth shut and did your job and later you told the employer that yes, you had delivered the message, and yes, you had seen the terrible realization cross the victim's face so he died thinking of Frankie and of what a terrible mistake he had made to ever cross him. Where in reality you had shot him from behind so he wouldn't see you and, equally important, so you didn't have to watch his face. Who wanted to see that? Sometimes, conditions permitting, you delivered the message after the target was dead. If you believed that the soul hung around for a while after death, you could consider the message delivered. Donny didn't want to cheat anybody.

Bicycle Boy was talking now and Tony was looking sheepish. Donny could see that his cousin was just building up to some bluster, which was usually the way he tried to get out of whatever mess he'd put himself in.

Actually, Cole was asking for his money back.

"You didn't do the job. I realize you say it wasn't your fault, I'll accept that, I don't question you there, but since the job wasn't done—for whatever reason—I think that I'd prefer to have the cash back rather than have you try again."

Tony looked at him as if he was insane. "The money back? Wait . . . wait . . . wait . . . The money back? There's no money back. What are you thinking? I'm going to do the job."

"But that's what I'm saying, Mr. Buono. Don't bother. I no longer need you to do the job."

"Bother? It's no bother. It's what you paid me for. It's what I do. I'm going to do it. I just came to you—like a stand-up guy—and told you there's been a delay. I didn't have to tell you this. I did it out of honor. You would never have known."

"Actually, Defone called me and told me. So I already knew."

"Told you what? What'd he tell you?"

"I have to go now, Mr. Buono. I have to meet Defone and take care of things myself." He put his hand atop the brown-paper-wrapped shoebox in the basket of his bicycle. "I've decided to pay him. So I'd appreciate it if you'd return the money, please."

Cole held out his hand as if he actually expected Tony to put the money in it.

Tony was aghast. "Listen, there's *no . . . money . . . back.*"

Cole didn't move, his hand still out. "I think it's only fair."

"Fair?" Tony wondered what Donny would do if he killed his first employer. Nothing that Tony would like. "Listen, Mr. Case, I don't have the money anymore."

"I gave it to you yesterday."

"I have bills, I have debts. My oldest daughter has got teeth coming in at right angles to her gums, she looks like she swallowed a fence—it's her fucking mother's genes—and you wouldn't believe the bills for the orthodontia."

"That's not really my problem, if you think about it."

I'll tell you what your fucking problem is, Tony thought in rage. Your problem is you got to swallow my Smith and Wesson right here on the sidewalk, you fucking cheap little creep.

"All right, Mr. Case, I'm going to level with you. You remember I told you about the wife and her—uh—facial situation? I found a guy says he can fix her up. He'll do a little something with her nose, something with the teeth, quite a bit of electrolysis—there's not much you can do with the eyes, did you know that? If they're that close together, they just got to stay that way . . ."

"You're not going to pay me back, are you?"

"I don't *need* to pay you back, I'm going to do the job."

"No, *I'm* going to take care of it right now."

"Just tell me where I can find him."

"I'm going to meet him in twenty-five minutes." Cole pushed off on the bike and pedaled swiftly away. Tony was amazed at how quietly the bicycle moved. It looked as if it would rattle and creak and fall apart. Case must have it oiled and lubed like a race car. "I expect my money back," Cole called back over his shoulder.

As Cole approached the corner it finally dawned on Tony that the little creep must have had ten thousand dollars in the shoebox and he was going right then to give it to Defone Lee. The lying little bastard had jewed Tony down to sixty-two fifty because he swore that was all he had. Tony sprinted for his car.

When Tony was gone, Donny the Snake stepped out of the doorway and retraced the path to the building from which Bicycle Boy had emerged. There was no one named Case on any of the mailboxes. Donny wrote down all the names, then rang each buzzer in turn and asked to speak with the man who owned the bicycle, until he got the information he wanted.

CHAPTER 13

AT THE CORNER OF MALCOLM X and 124th Street, Luis Rodriquez sat at a table by the window in Blue Philly's coffee shop, his hands wrapped around a chipped mug of coffee, doing his best impersonation of a druggie trying not to nod off. Every few minutes he would allow his head to sag to his chest, then rebound only to fall again, then finally to bounce all the way up, eyes wide, looking around to see if he had been observed. The rest of the time Luis kept his attention on the street. The potatohead Irish were supposed to be meeting Red Ingram to set up a buy on this corner, unless his informant was wrong, which Luis was beginning to suspect he was. He'd seen a few white people who might or might not have been Irish—there were a surprising number of whites who passed through Harlem if you waited long enough to notice, showing up like ghosts in time-lapse photography—but he had seen nothing of Red Ingram in weeks. Red was a small black man, very dark and not red in any way. You would have to know him to recognize him. He was also very seldom sighted and had been absent from public view altogether since jumping bail on a major gun-trafficking charge, which was why it was worth Luis's somewhat speculative time to sit and wait. If he tilted his head just a bit, he could see past the apostrophe in *Philly's* painted on the window and cover all of the intersection and three of the corners of the square where the streets met. He could have covered more if he were in his car, but he had done that twice already and didn't want to draw attention to himself.

Luis sat fully upright, forgetting his cover for the moment, and stared at the white guy who was ambling up Lenox like he was walking in the park. That was not the way whites walked this deep in Harlem. They scurried, they hunched over, they assumed a very low profile. They did not stroll, stopping to look in shop windows, tying their shoes, gawking like a tourist the way this guy was doing. Luis could think of three possibilities. One, the guy was insane. Two, the guy was a foreigner and didn't know where he'd wandered to. Or three, he was trying to check to see if he was being tailed. A fourth possibility was that he was all three together, a crazy potatohead coming to meet Red Ingram and checking out the territory first.

A Cadillac with a busted side window cruised slowly by, also driven by a white guy. Luis felt his scrotum tingle the way it did when something was going to happen. They were scouting the area, something was going down. The potatoheads were moving in.

The Cadillac nosed into a space where it didn't fit, leaving its ass sticking out into traffic, and the driver got out without locking the door—another thing a sane American was not apt to do in the middle of Harlem, or anywhere else in New York City. It appeared to Luis that he hadn't even pocketed the keys. He looked to Luis more like an Italian than an Irish but you couldn't ever be sure about these things, there was a lot of mixed blood among the Europeans. He also looked very steamed about something. So fucking steamed—or crazy—that he didn't notice the gangbangers moving in the direction of his car.

Defone Lee was suddenly there on the corner, the same place where Luis had seen him last time, but in a very different mood.

Last time he had been holding up the building, languid as old pasta, but today Defone was wired for sight, sound, and motion pictures. Walking in tight little circles like dust devils inside a hurricane. High as a fucking cloud and his lips moving like he was singing—or talking to himself. Not talking, more like giving a fucking speech.

If Defone was mixed up in the IRA gun deal after all, he was moving up in the world. Luis wondered how to play this. There were too many bad guys for him to get directly involved. He wished he had backup, but there was no way to get that surreptitiously yet instantaneously. He wished Meisner were around. He wasn't the smartest cop in the world, but he didn't seem to be afraid of anything. Luis thought that showed a certain lack of intelligence, not to mention enlightened self-interest, but there were times when it was comforting to have a pit bull by your side, smart or not. Luis decided to observe and nothing but observe, and when Red Ingram showed up, try to get a fix on him in some way. Maybe through Defone. In the meantime, he ignored the tingling that told him to act and pretended to nod off again, all the while keeping the street in sight.

When the messenger on the bike showed up he forgot all about his cover again. This was getting complicated. He was going to have to take notes.

Defone was a motherfucking Typhoon, he was riding in the eye of it, all that roaring going on all around him, but he could fucking *see,* motherfucker. Perched up here in his command seat in the middle of the Typhoon he could see everything, he could see all the peoples, he could see what they was thinking. Thinking they was smarter than Defone, thinking he didn't notice them, like they was invisible or some shit. White man gets out of his Caddy like the machine is on fire on this side. Closer, on the other side, another white man comes toward him, toward the storm, moving like he's in motherfucking White City, looking all around like he's actually going to *buy* something in one of the stores. Man going to buy hisself some pimp clothes, all of a sudden? That's why he likes that window? Going to put on some high-rise clogs? What's he think, Defone is blind? Think Defone is stupid?

Behind the Caddy white man come the gangbangers. Fucking trouble wherever he looks, but Defone is afraid of none of it. There's enough storm for all of them. Typhoon Dyfoon can blow them all away.

Now, what's this? Coming toward him from across the street is old Red Ingram with a couple of thugs. Red is one dangerous black motherfucker, but he ain't no match for Hurricane Defone, not today. Defone had heard that Red was dead or arrested, one or the other, and the son bitch was going to wish he was if he got in the way of the storm. Didn't care if he had a whole troop of apes with him, whole jungle full.

Terence Nealy was suffering a bit of culture shock during his stroll through Harlem. He had never seen so many black people, so many black *things* in his life. In Belfast he had known a total of zero blacks. Not American blacks. None. He had met a few Paki blacks, but that was different. He meant blacks from Africa via America. In Dublin he had known one, but not to speak to him. He had heard the man talk, however, and he spoke proper English, same as Terence, although with a Dublin accent. You could tell he hadn't grown up in Belfast.

Now this. Black people, black stores, black babies. It was amazin'. Fascinatin'. Brilliant. A happy sidelight to his main mission, which was to tell Red Ingram that it looked like they wouldn't be needin' the arms, after all. They would like to just put the whole thing on hold until after the talks with the fookin' Brits, Saint Patrick curse their hearts in eternal damnation.

It felt funny being in this foreign country inside the much bigger foreign country of the States, and without having to carry a weapon or be on the lookout for his backside. It was a holiday, like. Just deliver the message to Red Ingram—if he could find him, if the man showed up, which apparently sometimes he did not—and then he thought sample some of the soul food. Strange it was, and probably unclean, but Terence thought he'd fancy some all the same.

He saw the man on the corner where he was supposed to meet Ingram, and quickened his pace. He could sightsee later.

A man on a bike passed Terence and stopped in front of Red Ingram. Terence suddenly realized that was one of the things that was missing from America. You never saw grownups on bicycles.

The man on the bicycle handed Ingram a package and pedaled off and Terence stepped up to Ingram and said, "Would you be after being Red Ingram then?"

The man he thought was Ingram pulled out a pistol and shot Terence Nealy twice in the chest.

And that was when Luis saw the world start to come apart. After Defone Lee shot the first white guy, the second white guy, the one who abandoned his Caddy, pulled out a piece and started firing at Defone from about thirty yards away. It was like World War III had been declared. Red Ingram and his thugs were suddenly holding automatic pistols and spraying the area with bullets like troops landing on a beach, not knowing who they were shooting at, just pointing in the same general direction as Defone and the white guy. Then thundering down from the north came this posse of gangbangers waving the motliest collection of cheap pieces, Saturday Night specials, and retooled silver plates, guaranteed to jam or blow up in your hand, and they were all firing at the major source of firepower, Red Ingram and his thugs. The thugs returned fire and by now everyone on the street who didn't have a gun was lying flat on the sidewalk and screaming.

Luis got his own nine in his hand and crouched down so only his eyes peered over the window. The other customers were on the floor or heading out the back door, several with weapons in hand, and Blue Philly himself had vanished behind the cookstove. As far as Luis could tell, no one in the street was actually hitting anyone they were aiming at, but the surrounding real estate was taking a serious ventilation. Defone had sought shelter in a doorway and was firing away at the white guy, who was hunkered down beside a car and blazing away at Defone. The thugs and the gangbangers had lost interest in Defone and the white guy and were shooting at each other.

Luis knew that he should call for backup on a serious scale, but the scene was so riveting he could not make himself crawl to a telephone. From the looks of it, if any one of the combatants got killed it would only serve the general cause of law and order anyway.

The white guy was the first to break, though whether from prudence, cowardice, or lack of ammunition Luis could not tell. He dashed toward his Cadillac looking like the pictures of civilians crossing Sniper Alley in Sarajevo, bent over and going like hell. He was forced to skirt the gangbangers who had taken up position in midstreet, and one of them fired a couple of perfunctory shots at him—probably just because he was moving. The white guy leaped once in the air and Luis thought he was hit, but he kept running and made it to the car. Defone came tearing after him, blazing away, pausing momentarily to change clips while gripping the package under his arm, then blazing some more. Something about him excited Red and his group and they turned their fire on Defone suddenly. He went down; the package flew out from his grasp and landed in the street.

Seeing this, the white guy leaped out of the car and ran toward

the package, shooting at Defone, who got to his knees, returning fire. They fired point-blank from twenty yards, each trying to inch toward the package while shooting at the other. Defone had his head scrunched down as he shot and the white guy held an arm in front of his face as if warding off blows—which might account for the fact that neither of them seemed to hit the other.

The white guy gave ground and ran back to his car and Defone fell flat on the sidewalk as a fresh volley from Red Ingram came his way. The gangbangers, now under no immediate threat, watched the show involving Defone and the white guy, dumbfounded. Defone whipped off a couple of shots at Red and his thugs, then crawled toward the package. The Cadillac, its rear window shot out by Defone in an earlier fusillade, came screaming backward in reverse, heading toward a spot between Defone and the package. The white guy leaned out the door and grabbed at the package like a stunt rider at a rodeo, holding on to the wheel with one hand and tilting through the open door at a dangerous angle. He could reach the pavement that way but he couldn't steer and the car swerved off course as he missed the package. Defone was on his feet again, howling with rage, and he ran around the rear end of the car, trying to fire at the driver and scoop up the package at the same time, so that he was ineffective at both. The car drove forward, changed its angle, then came tearing backward again, trying to run Defone down. Defone leaped out of the way and tripped and rolled up against the gutter. The car missed him and the driver pulled forward, making another stab at the package, but by this time the curiosity about the package was too much for the gangbangers and one of them darted forward and grabbed it. The white guy slammed on the brakes and started to get out of the car and give chase, until the gangbangers turned their firepower on him and the car. He sped away to the sound of lead ripping into metal like rain on a tin roof.

Red Ingram and his men took advantage of the gangbangers'

diverted attention and came running toward them, firing. Their progress carried them past Blue Philly's and Red paused, recognizing Luis's face in the window. Luis shot Red in the right shoulder and the left hip, missed once entirely, then knicked his ear and hit him in the chest and the throat and killed him, all in the space of three seconds.

About the time that Red's body hit the sidewalk, one of the gangbangers ripped open the package that had seemed so valuable to Defone Lee and the white guy. The package exploded, sending fragments of lead pipe and fourpenny nails that had been glued to the bomb to increase the shrapnel effect into him and several others nearby.

In the sudden silence that followed the explosion Luis heard the first siren. He lifted himself from the floor where he had instinctively fallen and surveyed the damage in the street. Defone Lee was wobbling down the street and away, his hands out to the front as if he was dizzy or blind or disoriented. The Cadillac was long gone. Red Ingram was dead. The first white guy that Defone had shot was lying very still, probably dead. One of Red's men had dropped his weapon and was looking stupidly at his arm, which was pumping blood onto the sidewalk. Luis figured him for dead soon enough. One of the gangbangers seemed to have been blown almost in half, one was writhing, another lay on his back, one arm in the air, not moving at all. The others were in various states of disrepair and just beginning to stir.

The unwashed white bicycle messenger who had delivered the bomb to Defone had pedaled off before the shooting started.

Luis was untouched but shivering badly with the onset of shock.

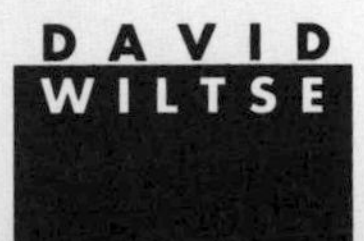

CHAPTER

COLE LISTENED TO THE NEWS ON television as he prepared his security system. There would be no repeats of Defone's break-in. Any future intruder would not live to taunt Cole, or blackmail him, or decide to become a partner. Cole could not be sure who Defone had told about him; another might come in his place now that he was dead. But the next intruder would be the last.

His VCR was running in case there was anything he wanted to see again—a very real possibility now that he was a major source of news in the city.

The press conference with the FBI investigators came on immediately following some shenanigans of the newly elected Congress and their tart-tongued leader, who was making a career of baiting the President. That sort of political story ordinarily would send Cole into an internal tirade against the system, working him up to such a lather of indignation that he would spend the rest of the night calling in to radio talk shows, trying to vent his spleen. Occasionally he would write angry letters to newspaper editors, setting them right about the issues of the day. Even less occasionally those letters would be printed and Cole would then save the yellowing newsprint clippings in a scrapbook, feeling every bit as much pride of authorship as any published author. He thought of them as "my writings," and imagined himself one day placing the whole scrapbook in the lap of a deserving reader—although who that reader might be he had no idea, since he had no friends and very few acquaintances. He knew more about the private and emotional life of Tony Buono than he did about almost anyone else in the world besides his mother. And in turn Tony Buono, who knew nothing whatsoever about Cole, still knew as much about his private and emotional life as almost anyone else in the world besides Cole's mother. Cole detested his mother and had not communicated with her in years.

But tonight the political news drew from him no more than a dismissive sneer. He was waiting for the meat. The switch for the overhead light in the workroom was on the living room wall and Cole used it now as the means for turning his security system off and on. He ran a wire from the light fixture to an electrode he had secured to the wall just inside the door. If the door was opened a quarter of an inch when the switch was on, an electrode on the door itself would contact the one protruding from the wall, closing the electrical circuit. He tested it several times, swinging the door open and closed so that the two electrodes brushed briefly against each other. On the other end of the circuit, just for testing purposes, he had secured a flashlight bulb instead of a bomb. It blinked off and on like a firefly as the door moved. The circuit was activated for only a fraction of a second as the electrodes kissed, but for a bomb that would be sufficient.

He stepped into the living room as the story of the press conference came on the air. Later, replaying it again and again, he would snarl with rage, cursing the perfidy of the FBI and the city and this agent John Becker in particular. The first time through, however, he simply listened in amazement as John Becker, special-agent-in-charge, a man he had never seen or heard of previously, maligned his name, called him weak and cowardly and emotionally dysfunctional, and made up words to put in his mouth. He had been misquoted. His carefully crafted messages had been twisted out of shape.

Cole was still stunned and seething when the news item about a shoot-out and explosion in Harlem came on after a commercial. They spoke of a gang of armed youths and gunrunners and the IRA. There was a reference to the heroism of an undercover policeman, mention of the estimated number of shots that were fired, of the power of the bomb, of a terrorized citizenry, of three wounded bystanders in addition to those who had been shooting at each other—but not a word about Defone Lee. Cole had turned around on his bike at the sound of the first gunshot and had seen the white man fall at Defone's feet. He had no idea who the man was or where he had come from and, given the circumstances, no real curiosity to find out. He had put his head down and pedaled as fast as he could until the sound of the firing was no more threatening than the noise of firecrackers on the Fourth of July.

He had hoped Defone was on the receiving end of some of that firing; he had hoped that he opened the package that was supposed to contain ten thousand dollars but held black powder in a sealed steel pipe instead. He had hoped he was dead. That would solve many problems, but it was not necessary. Cole would be gone soon enough and Defone Lee would be no more able to find Jason Cole than Tony Buono seemed to be able to find Defone.

Late into the night, after he had planted the charges in his workroom that would destroy any intruder who did not first throw the switch in the living room, he watched the tape of the news conference again and again. Cole dismissed the first FBI speaker as a fatuous fool and the overweight city chief of police as an affirmative-action incompetent, and focused all of his attention on the one called Becker. He memorized the lean, drawn face, the hard eyes, the cast of features that made him look to Cole on the fifth viewing like a cowboy out of place in time. Like a gunslinger. Unlike the others, who were merely posturing outrage, Becker seemed to be speaking directly to Cole. His determination was real, his anger was real, his thinly veiled ferocity.

By the tenth viewing, when his own indignation had leveled off, Cole saw and heard nothing but Becker, as if the man were sitting in the room, leaning toward him, threatening to tear his throat out. He felt a chill of fear and realized that for the first time since he began his crusade for justice he was genuinely afraid. Here was a man who wished him ill, genuine physical harm. Defone had frightened him during their confrontation in the workroom, but not for long. He knew he could outsmart Defone. Buono had at first intimidated him with his seeming self-assurance, his hard sell, but Cole had quickly seen through it. And neither of them had any motivation for wanting to hurt him. But this man, this Becker, was different. He seemed to be taking the bombings personally. There was nothing personal about them, Cole wanted to tell him. They were being done in the framework of a larger issue, an attempt to bring about social justice. There's no point in being angry at *me,* he longed to say to Becker, you should be angry at the system.

Finally, weary from watching, Cole turned off the television and stepped into his workroom. A beeper sounded and he stopped, momentarily baffled by the noise. Directly across from the doorsill where he stood was a large bull's-eye painted in concentric circles of red and black. It was therc to remind him . . . the noise was to remind him . . . the bomb was *armed.* Cole leaped back into the living room and threw the light switch, then stood, panting, barely comprehending what he had almost done. There was a fifteen-second delay built into the bomb's electronic fuse to prevent just such a mistake by Cole, but he had never really thought he would need it. He could not believe it. He had nearly blown himself up.

Tony dropped the Cadillac at a body shop owned by Steve Baggiatello, a hanger-on and wannabe tough guy who measured his success by the number of favors he could do for made men like Tony. There would be no questions asked as to just why Tony had converted an expensive automobile into a sieve, and if any of the workers got curious Baggiatello would tell them to shut up if they knew what was good for them, and then nod knowingly as if he himself had the lowdown but was too important a man to share it with them. Some people believed him. Just as his reputation depended upon hanging out with the made men, there were lesser hopefuls who gathered cachet by being a friend of his. And so on down the ladder. It was the way things worked in Tony's world, where who you knew was far more important than what you knew. In that regard it was very like most other worlds.

Unlike his car, Tony had emerged from the shoot-out unscathed. He remembered from a movie about Wyatt Earp that Wyatt had never been hit during a long career in which all of his friends and brothers got riddled more than once. He wasn't even knicked at the O.K. Corral. Tony felt like that. Triumphant. Somehow better than those who did get shot. And fucking lucky, man. He had plugged Defone, he was almost sure of it, and had left him lying in the gutter. The sucker had to be dead, Tony must have pumped at least a full clip into him, couldn't have missed.

For a moment Tony had thought he had been hit himself. He had felt a shock and something had propelled him into the air, but he had kept running. Later he discovered that the heel had been shot off his shoe. Must have been a thousand spooks shooting at him and all they could hit was the heel of his shoe . . . and his car. They were pretty good at hitting the car. Tony wondered if he could claim insurance.

Tony watched the news that night proudly, knowing he was part of it. He was annoyed that there was no direct mention of him, a white guy shooting it out with half of Harlem and winning, but then realized it was just as well. *He* knew and he'd make sure some other people who mattered knew, and that would be good enough. The explosion interested him. He had been at least a block away and going fast when he heard it. He had looked in his mirrors but both of them had been shot out so he never really saw the result. He wondered which of those spades was stupid enough to get into a firefight while carrying a bomb. It occurred to him briefly that it had been in the package for which he had risked his life, but he dismissed the thought.

After the news, feeling heroic, Tony came up behind his wife where she was working at the kitchen sink and slipped his arms around her waist. She tried to turn to face him but he buried his lips in her neck and kept her turned so he could see only her neck and her gorgeous head of hair. As he slid his hands up to squeeze her breasts he noticed the headlights of a car coming to a rest outside his house. The lights went off but Tony did not hear the sound of a door closing. Franca reached back to caress his cheek with the rubber gloves she used when doing the dishes, but Tony slipped away from her and peered out at the street from the side window next to the door, sliding the white lace curtain aside with a finger.

He wasn't expecting anybody but it never hurt to be careful. He could see the car in the streetlight. It was a baby-blue VW Golf. Only Donny the Snake drove such a car.

Tony threw open the door, expecting to find Donny on the doorstep.

"Hey, Donny, I know you from your car," he called happily. Donny the Snake was not on the doorstep. Tony saw his shadow standing beside the kitchen window, looking in. Tony wondered

uneasily what that was all about. He hoped it was just Donny's naturally stealthy nature.

"What's wrong with the car?" Donny asked, stepping into the light.

"Not a thing," Tony said hastily. "It's just you're the only guy I know drives one." He assumed Donny drove something else when working.

"I'm the only one got sense enough not to waste my money on a twenty-ton tank. You know what kind of mileage you get?"

"Do I give a shit?"

"Where is your car?"

"I left it with suck-up Stevie. It's got a few holes in it." Tony was feeling very cocky. Let Donny ask how he got the holes. Hold off until he was asked, then let him have the story of how he rubbed out Defone and probably several others.

"You alone in the house?"

"Franca and the kids," said Tony.

"So why we standing out in the dark?"

Tony took him to his den in the converted basement. He plopped in his favorite leather recliner and regally waved Donny to a seat. Donny stood.

"You use some cover like I told you?" Donny asked.

"Cover?"

"You go into Harlem alone, the only white guy on the street, how smart is that? I told you to hire a couple, three guys, have them walk past the target first, just walk past, don't even look at him, get the guy used to seeing white people, he's not so wary about you."

"Donny, I'm only getting sixty-two fifty for the job. I can't be hiring extra people."

"You told me ten."

"That's all he give me."

"He welshed on you? You shouldn't have taken the job, throw the money in his face. He owes you ten, you get ten or don't go on the job."

"I'll get it from him, I'll get the difference . . ."

"Best give it to me."

"Give what to you?"

"The sixty-two fifty."

"Hey, Donny, what I have is yours, you know that. But the thing is, I don't have it . . . I can scare up about a thou for you, things are tight."

"What do you mean you don't got it? He gave it to you yesterday. Where is it?"

"I give it to this face guy. I swear to God, Don, I got to get rid of her mustache at least. How can you kiss that?" Tony stopped, wondering if he had stepped onto infirm ground. Donny was suspected of liking mustaches on his lovers, although not necessarily on women. This was not something ever said aloud in Donny's presence.

"The money don't stay in your hands twenty-four hours?"

Tony glanced toward the stairway. "Donny, I love Franca, you know that. She's a great person, a beautiful woman in many ways, and I ain't asking her to change her personality at all . . ."

"Well, maybe you should take Franca and give her to the guy."

"What guy?"

"The guy that hired you to kill Defone Lee."

"He ought to give me a bonus. I had to kill half of Harlem just to get at him. I'm not shitting you, Don, I was doing the city a favor today, I must have popped ten if I popped one—"

"You didn't kill Defone Lee."

"Donny, listen to what I'm saying. I left him lying there in the gutter."

"Then he rose again. Defone Lee ain't dead."

"How do you know this?"

"I asked the cops. One of them seen him walking away."

"The cops told you this?"

"I got friends. Simple as that. You think it's more complicated? He walked away. You missed him."

"Donny, I swear on my mother, I swear on my children . . ."

"Don't do that."

"I was standing close to him as I am to you. I hit him three times at least, maybe more. He must have been wearing one of them vests. You think that's it? A vest?"

"You was always a little different, Tony. Me, I don't mind, you're my cousin, but some guys it makes nervous, a guy is a little different."

"I ain't different. I swear on my mother . . ."

"I said don't do that, don't be swearing on Aunt Teresa, show some respect. You know what's your problem? You think too much, Tony."

"I don't think very much."

"I know that—but you think too much anyway."

"I see. Okay. What should I do about it?"

"Shut up, Tony."

"Okay, Donny, I see your point, I appreciate your telling me this—"

"Shut *up*, Tony. . . . Now we got to figure what's the honorable thing to do about the guy who hired you."

As Cole slept his mind was ablaze with demons. His dreams' twisted imagery haunted him with reminders of his confrontation with Becker, of the bloodbath that he had escaped in Harlem, of his near disaster in the workroom. He woke with startled relief to find himself sweating and the creaking of the lawn furniture chaise that served as his bed still echoing in the room.

It took him a moment to realize that it was the sound at the outer door that had awakened him. It came again, a gentle knock as from a diffident caller. After a pause there was a third knocking, just as quiet and restrained as the first. Cole looked at his watch. It was four o'clock in the morning. It was too polite for the police, too patient for Defone, Jehovah's Witnesses did not come to call at this hour—and no one else came to his apartment, ever. For a moment Cole thought of retreating to the workroom and locking himself in, but then he realized that an inadvertent flip of the switch by any intruder would kill Cole within fifteen frantic seconds.

He held his breath and listened, not daring to move for fear the flimsy chaise would scrape against the floor and give away his presence. There came a gentle rustling, like a mouse in the wall, and then a scratching sound, very brief, as the tumblers in his lock were tested. The outer door swung in slightly, letting in a flood of light from the hallway.

Cole watched a pair of powerful bolt cutters push through the gap and snip the chain. The door eased open all the way and a dark figure stood silhouetted against the hallway light.

"Mr. Cole?" the silhouette intoned. "Don't alarm yourself. I'm a friend."

Cole saw the bolt cutters hanging from one hand. The other held a pistol with the bulbous end of a silencer pointing toward the floor.

The figure in the doorway stepped toward Cole and turned on the overhead light, then closed the door. He looked briefly at the squalor in the room.

"You live alone, Mr. Cole?" he asked, unnecessarily.

"I don't believe you have the right to come in here like this," Cole said. He moved backward on the chaise so that his shoulders were touching the wall. His feet were drawn up on the chaise in front of him. It was as far away from the intruder as he could get.

"I apologize."

"I have a right to my own space," Cole said. He found that he

was close to tears. He felt violated as well as frightened, he felt small and weak and young and powerless. It came out as petulance. It was the same sense of trespass that he had suffered when his mother read his private journals.

"You can't just come in here," he said, his voice rising. "I am an individual. You have to ask my permission to come in."

"I knocked."

"I didn't say you could come in."

"Settle down, Mr. Cole."

"This is my room, you have no right to come in here without my permission and I didn't give you my permission and I don't want you in here and I don't even know who you are—" he said, slipping into hysteria.

Donny the Snake slapped him, aiming for his cheek. He misjudged his distance slightly and caught Cole's nose with his fingers.

"Stop that now," Donny said. "That's no way to do. Don't do that anymore."

"You hit my nose," Cole said.

"That's okay."

"No, it's not. It hurts."

"It doesn't hurt. You're a grown man, now behave yourself."

To Donny's embarrassment, Cole began to weep. He had encountered weepers before, but he wasn't here to kill this one, he was going to assist him. He watched helplessly for a moment, then sat on the rickety bed and awkwardly put an arm around Cole's shoulders.

"That's okay," Donny said. "You're all right. You're all right. I'm not going to hit you again." His voice was low and soothing.

"I don't know why you're here," Cole said, sniffing.

"I'm here to help you. Think of me as a friend. You don't have to be afraid."

"What kind of friend?"

"I'm here to clean up after Tony. What is this you're sleeping on? You're lucky it doesn't fall down. If you can afford ten thousand for Tony to kill somebody, you can afford a real bed."

"I only paid him sixty-two fifty."

"You owe him the rest."

"That's what he agreed to do it for. Besides, he owes me, he didn't do the job." Cole sniffed again and took a long, shuddering breath.

Donny smoothed Cole's hair and rubbed his shoulder. He was beginning to feel more comfortable with his arm around the man. It was not an unfamiliar position, just an unusual circumstance. The gun lay in his lap, the bolt cutters across his feet.

Donny spoke soothingly, as if details and specifics would be calming to Cole. "Let me explain to you. You can't shoot straight if you're jerking around. You see in the movies when the cowboys are riding their horses as fast as they can go and shooting at each other and the hero picks off five, six guys this way? This is bad propaganda. More people have been misled by this kind of thing. You can't hit anything when you're moving. You can't do it when you're walking. Try it riding and you're lucky you don't hit the horse in the head. You have a guy like Tony trying to fire when he's running and ducking and afraid of getting popped, he's not going to hit what he's aiming at. It's that simple. That don't mean he isn't trying, he's doing it in good faith, you understand. Soldiers in the war, somebody's shooting back at them? What do they do? What do you think? They hide, they squint, they jump around anytime a bullet comes near them, they try to save their own ass. This is normal. More people in the war get killed by planes and bombs and shells than by another guy with a gun. You see what I'm talking about?"

Cole was only half aware of what the man was saying but he found that something in his voice took away the sense of violation. There was a warmth to the man that seemed to issue not only from his voice but his hands and body as well.

"Bombs are better," Cole said.

"I was meaning to talk to you about that," said Donny. He put his hand on Cole's neck and gently massaged. He could feel Cole relax under his touch.

Cole looked at the gun in the Snake's lap. He could reach out and touch it if he wanted to. He did not want to. He closed his eyes and concentrated on the other man's fingers on his neck. It was the first time another human being had touched him or spoken to him with any warmth in years. The scent of powerful cologne made his head swim. Cole had not noticed perfume on a man since dances in the gym in high school.

"You know anything about the bomb went off up there in Harlem?"

"I don't have to tell you," Cole said. "I have my rights."

"I'm not a cop. Did you think I was a cop?"

"Doesn't matter."

"You only have rights if I'm a cop. I'm just a private citizen like yourself. So who was that bomb for? Defone Lee?"

"I didn't say anything about a bomb."

Donny paused. He was not accustomed to others treating him with this kind of defiance, passive though it seemed. A reputation did you no good if people didn't know who you were, he realized. Besides, there was something about this man that appealed to him. Some helpless, childlike quality. Cole was one of the few men Donny had encountered in years who made no pretense of being brave or acting macho. Donny had an impulse to protect him.

"Don't worry about it," Donny said, patting Cole's head. "I'm going to take care of everything for you, you won't have no complaint."

Cole looked Donny in the face. He had the same killer's eyes as John Becker, but this was not Becker, he had memorized that face.

Donny smiled with a shyness that surprised Cole. He cast his eyes down, then back at Cole, and some of the fierceness had gone out of them. Cole regarded him uncertainly.

"What are you going to do?"

"Get rid of this Defone Lee for you." Donny surveyed the room. "You should have someone in here to clean up once in a while. It's not good to live like this."

"I don't like other people in my room."

"Even so. You're a good-looking man. You shouldn't live like this."

Cole was surprised by the compliment. He didn't think of himself as good-looking or bad-looking or any kind of looking. Most of the time he regarded himself as a spiritual force.

"I don't care about Defone so much anymore," he said. "I've decided to leave. I don't think he can find me."

"Tony can't give the money back."

"Can you kill somebody else for me instead?"

Donny hesitated. "That's unusual."

"I already paid for it. What's the difference?"

"I don't know. It's just not normal practice. I'm not sure about it."

"Then I have to have my money back."

"There's no money back. There's no question of that. I'm afraid the money's been spent."

"I thought I could trust you people," Cole said. "That's your reputation, you can be trusted, you're dependable. Now you've cheated me."

"Listen, listen . . . who is it you want taken care of?"

"You mean it?"

"I'm willing to listen to you. I want to do right by you."

"Would you mind taking your clothes off?" Cole asked.

Donny was surprised. "Just like that? Don't you think we ought to get to know each other better first?"

"Tony did."

Donny's cousin, his own blood, and Donny had never had a clue. He was astounded.

"You want to take them off for me?" Donny asked, knowing he was wrong. This was not a professional way to proceed.

"No. I want you to do it."

"Let's finish with the business," Donny said. "Afterwards, you still want my clothes off, we'll find a way."

Cole realized he was not going to be able to talk his visitor into disrobing as easily as he had his predecessor. But he was also convinced that this man was not a cop. Entrapment was one thing, breaking and entering in the middle of the night to solicit business was something else and rather beyond the machinations of the cops.

"I want to show you somebody," Cole said.

As Donny watched, dumbfounded, Cole played the tape of the press conference with John Becker. Cole froze the tape and pointed at Becker's stern, threatening face.

"Him," Cole said.

"That's a federal agent," Donny said.

"I know."

Donny realized he had gone far enough on too little information and too much speculation.

"Mr. Cole, I think we better start at the beginning. Suppose you tell me everything."

When Cole had finished his tale Donny asked to see the workroom. With difficulty he conceded to himself that Cole's story was true. It was hard to imagine that this naif, this petulant, socially retarded innocent, was holding up the city for five million dollars—and had a good chance of getting away with it.

CHAPTER

KAREN CRIST RECEIVED THE PHONE call in the morning, and by noon she had sufficiently overcome her reaction of anger at the caller, sorrow at the message, and self-pity at the result to make a call of her own to her husband's office.

He was immediately solicitous. "How are you feeling? Is everything all right?"

"I feel fine," she said. "Really good."

"Great."

She lay on the bed in the darkness of her bedroom and lied to him. "I'm in the kitchen, sorting the laundry."

"I can do the laundry when I get home," he said.

"I've already done it. I feel terrific. Listen, John, I think you ought to stay in the city. It's such a hassle getting in and out now with this Spring operating . . ."

"I can take the copter," he said.

"I don't think we can justify that on a regular basis. It's too expensive and there's no need for you to come to Connecticut now that I feel all right. I still work for the Bureau too, don't forget, and I don't want to be responsible for any budget drain that can be avoided. It will be so much easier on you to just stay there and you'll be able to walk to and from work, especially now that you're so busy."

"I want to come back to you," he protested. "I want to see you."

"Well, that's sweet of you," she said. She spoke to him in the tones of politeness with which she might repel an unwanted suitor. "But I think I could use some time on my own, anyway. I have a good deal of rethinking to do—about work, whether I want to come back or not, that sort of thing. It will be easier for both of us if you just stay in the city for a while."

When she had finally wrested a reluctant agreement from him Karen hung up with a sense of relief that surprised her. She might owe the meddlesome caller a vote of gratitude after all. Now, at least, she could suffer on her own. She could drop the charade of being game and plucky, she would not have to worry about keeping his spirits up by elevating her own. And she would not have to deal with his guilt, a struggle that had become almost as burdensome as her fight against the pain. She had energy enough to nurse only one of them at a time, and right now she had to choose herself.

After the call Becker was baffled and depressed. Karen had sounded like a person he did not know. The voice wasn't hers, the logic wasn't hers. He wondered who had been talking to her, who had put the idea into her mind.

The only one he could think of was Gold. Before returning to work he spent a few moments thinking of how to deal with the meddlesome shrink without breaking his neck.

Meisner brought his friend Luis Rodriquez to Pegeen and Pegeen took them both to talk to Becker, who had just had the disturbing phone call from his wife. Pegeen thought he seemed distracted by their presence, as if he had better things to think about.

Luis, however, was impressed. Unlike Meisner, he felt no need to thrust himself next to heroes to see how he compared or to tread upon their feet to check for clay. Luis wanted to believe in heroes. The notion that there were none, that all of life was handled by men no larger or braver or better than himself, was too frightening to contemplate. The fact that he had never actually met such men after ten years on the force did nothing to disturb his faith; he believed because he wanted to and wanted to because he needed to. It was part of his Catholic training.

"This is such a big pleasure," he said, pumping Becker's hand. "I have heard so much about you. Great, great things."

Becker shrugged dismissively. Even though it had dogged him for years, he had never gotten comfortable with adulation. Flattery made him uneasy.

"Most of it's probably not true," he said.

"I've heard it from Agent Haddad," Luis said, smiling at Pegeen.

"Ah," said Becker, wondering just how much Pegeen had been saying about him—and how much of it would get back to Karen. Pegeen's face was unreadable but her ears had gone suddenly red.

"Sit down, Luis," Meisner grumbled, trying to end the fuss over Becker. Meisner had decided he didn't like the special-agent-in-charge the moment he realized that Pegeen did. Nothing had happened to change his mind.

"Luis thinks that this guy Cole, the one whose name we got from Dyzel, was the one who delivered the bomb that went off in Harlem."

"Definitely looked like him."

"You checked Cole out before, didn't you?" Becker asked, looking at Pegeen.

"We checked him for a criminal record and didn't find anything, but Luis is sure it was the same man on a bike—"

"Pretty much definitely," Luis interrupted.

"—who gave a package to Defone Lee just prior to the shoot-out and explosion."

"And you're sure it was the package that exploded?"

"It was hard to be sure of anything," Luis admitted. "There must have been a dozen weapons going at the same time. Red Ingram was shooting at me and I was shooting at him—"

"Luis is a hero," Meisner interjected. "He's going to get a medal for wasting Ingram."

"No, no, I'm not a hero," Luis protested.

"He put Ingram away single-handedly, something the whole force hasn't been able to do for years. A fucking gold-plated hero."

"I'm no hero," Luis said.

"Capital *H*," Meisner said, watching Becker to see how he felt having another hero in the room. Watching Pegeen.

"Don't call me that," Luis said. "I ain't a hero."

Becker smiled thinly. "I believe you," he said. "It will be harder to convince others. They have to pin their medals on somebody."

"I just shot him, you know?" Luis said.

Becker nodded. "Yeah, I know."

"There wasn't anything else I could do."

Pegeen regarded Becker, and Meisner looked at her. Becker was looking within himself although his eyes were on Luis.

"There's always something else you can do," Becker said darkly, seemingly to himself, before looking at Luis again. Luis squirmed uneasily under Becker's gaze. This was a man who cut you little slack. He had the feeling that Becker knew exactly how Red Ingram's death had happened, and just because he understood Luis's actions he didn't necessarily applaud them the way everyone else seemed eager to do. Luis remembered that killing people was the foundation on which Becker's reputation was based. It was something he knew about.

"So you don't know if the package was a bomb or not?" Becker continued, finally looking away from Luis.

"It was the only thing I saw that might have been. Maybe somebody had a bomb strapped to him. Maybe it wasn't even a bomb.

You're dealing with Red Ingram and the Irish, it could have been a mortar shell, a rocket launcher. Who knows? Ingram was into very heavy stuff."

"It was a pipe bomb," Becker said. "I just got the lab report this morning. An eight-inch steel pipe, scored to increase fragmentation with finishing nails secured to it with rubber bands to make more shrapnel."

"That doesn't sound like one of Red's items," Meisner said.

"It was homemade," Becker said flatly.

"Not Red's then. Red deals—used to deal—only in bulk."

"Not Red's," Becker agreed. "It sounds like Spring to me. Spring was sending a message to somebody, would be my guess."

"You think this bike messenger is working for the Irish?" Luis asked. "Or Red Ingram?"

"I don't know what the connection is," Becker admitted. "I don't know who the message was for. I don't know if the bomb was intended for Defone or if he was supposed to pass it on to someone else or if he was supposed to use it in the street the way he did. Is Defone Lee part of Ingram's group?"

"Not unless he recently stepped up," Meisner said. "Maybe Red took him on, but I don't see it. Defone isn't your basic organizational type. He's not stable enough."

"Defone works alone, far as I know," Luis confirmed. "Besides, Red was shooting at him right after Defone popped the Irish."

Becker turned to Pegeen again. "What do we have on the Irishman?"

"Terry Heany. Suspected IRA courier, very low-level kind of guy. CIA thinks it's unlikely he was here to do any heavy buying. Maybe just setting up a meeting, delivering a message, something on that order. Our Terrorism Branch agrees."

"So why would anyone shoot a messenger from the IRA? You're sure he was the first to go?" Becker asked Luis.

"Absolutely. Defone dropped him, Red started shooting at

Defone, and this white guy—not the Irish, a white guy in a Caddy—starts shooting at Defone. After that it got kind of confusing, everybody shooting at everybody."

"White guy in a Cadillac? Are we talking about a wiseguy here?"

Luis shrugged. "He looked like a Wop to me, but I don't want to call nobody no names."

"Excuse me," said Pegeen. "I'm a little lost here. The first report was it was a gang war."

"There was gangbangers there too," Luis said.

"It was an active day," said Becker.

Pegeen asked, "So do we think Spring has something to do with the Irish?"

"He may just be providing bombs for anyone who pays the price, I don't know."

"He gave the bomb to Defone," said Meisner. "What would Defone be needing with a bomb?"

"The Italian looked like he wanted it pretty bad," Luis contributed. "In addition to killing Defone, I mean. He wanted both. But what did Defone think he was going to do with it? He nearly got killed himself when it blew up."

"Defone killed the Irish and tried to kill Red Ingram, too, right? Maybe he was trying to take all the action for himself."

"What action? If he killed both sides of a deal, what's left for him?"

"And what does Spring have to do with it?"

"How hard did you try to find Cole the last time?" Becker asked.

Meisner said, "We were just checking out his record."

"He hadn't done anything at that point except give something to Defone Lee," said Pegeen. "That's all he's done this time as far as I know."

"But this time the 'something' may have killed several people. I'd like to know how Spring got the package into Cole's hands in the first place. If he gave it to him directly, which I doubt, then Cole can ID Spring. Did you talk to Cole about his customers when you interviewed him?"

"We didn't actually talk to him," Pegeen said hesitantly.

"You didn't even interview him?"

"What about?" Meisner asked. "There was no bomb involved at the time. No reason to think he had anything to do with Spring. We were just curious about him and Defone."

"I gave you our report," Pegeen said defensively. "You didn't seem interested."

Becker stared at her for a moment and Pegeen felt her face ignite.

"Well, then that was my fault," Becker said at last. "I'm interested now. Go find this Cole."

"Oh, we know where he is," Meisner said. "Dyzel told us."

"Well, for Christ's sake," Becker said. "We could have been having this conversation on the way to the judge to pick up a warrant."

He led them out of the room.

"I don't think he likes me," Luis confided to Meisner as they followed Pegeen and Becker.

"Sure he likes you, why wouldn't he?"

"I just don't think so. You think so?"

"Who gives a fuck, anyway? Who is this guy supposed to be in the first place?"

"You kidding? He's John Becker."

"Big fucking deal. That don't mean a thing."

"It does to your FBI lady. You see the way she looks at him?"

"He's her boss."

"I don't look at *my* boss that way. He'd kick my ass."

"She ain't looking at him in any special way."

"She ever look at *me* that way, I'd throw her on the desk and fuck her till she couldn't stand up."

"You're getting on my nerves, Luis."

"She don't like you, huh? Too bad, she's hot—if you go for redheads."

"She don't like anybody. She's a bull dyke," Meisner said.

Luis laughed. "You sure can pick 'em . . . but tell me this. If she's a dyke, how come she wants to fuck Becker so bad?"

They had reached the street. Meisner let the door flap back into Luis's face but it didn't stop Luis's laughter.

Armed with a search warrant, Becker, Pegeen, and Meisner knocked on Cole's basement door. When no one answered, Meisner tried the knob and to his surprise the door opened. After announcing themselves to the silence of the apartment and declaring the presence of a warrant, they cautiously entered. As the others examined the squalor of the living room, Becker noticed the chain dangling in two pieces.

"Someone's been here first," Becker said. "Without a warrant."

Meisner tried the door to the bedroom and found it securely locked. "Something worth protecting in here," he said, applying himself to the lock with a set of locksmith's picks.

Pegeen examined the marks along the frame where Defone had forced the door days earlier. "Someone's been here, too," she said.

"Sounds like the Three Bears," Becker said as Meisner stopped fiddling with the picks and turned the knob. The door swung slowly open and Pegeen stepped into the workroom to the sound of a persistent beeping. She was reminded at first of the noise of a truck backing up. Meisner stepped in behind her, bumping into her slightly as she stopped at the sight of the bull's-eye target.

"Look at this shit," Meisner said, emitting a low whistle. "It's a fucking chemistry lab."

Pegeen turned her face back toward the living room with a questioning look. Something was wrong, she knew, but just what . . . Becker flew at her and tossed her through the door, using her arm for leverage, slinging her onto her face.

"Down!" he barked, and grabbed Meisner, propelling him toward the door also. Instinctively, Meisner resisted and Becker lifted him bodily and charged through the door, then dropped him as he dived for the floor himself.

The blast slammed the door closed before breaking it into pieces and showering the living room with its shards. Pegeen came to her senses with the room filled with dark smoke and an incredible ringing in her ears and Meisner lying atop her. He was blinking his eyes repeatedly as if trying to bring the world into focus. Becker was already crawling toward them. A foot-long splinter of door rose out of his back beneath the shoulder blade like a banderilla from a bull.

"Out," Becker said, pulling at both of them. "Out of here."

"Your back," Pegeen said, realizing that she was not concentrating on the main issue, whatever that might be. She wondered about Becker's urgency, about the noise in her ears, about the smoke.

Becker tugged at them, tried to stand and fell back to his hands and knees, but kept tugging. "Got to get out," he said. "It will all go."

Pegeen tried to get up to help Becker. She wanted to remove the splinter from his back but she could not rise because of Meisner's bulk. She felt a surge of anger at him, lying stupidly atop her, blinking dazedly.

"Would you get off?" she asked. Meisner opened and closed his mouth like a man with water in his ear. "Get the fuck *off*. You look like a fish."

Becker took Meisner by the collar and dragged him toward the hallway, working his way backward on his butt. "Come on," he said to Pegeen, panting with exertion. "Hurry."

"Why don't you stand up?" Pegeen asked querulously. The men

were beginning to annoy her. She liked it on the floor, she was quite comfortable now that Meisner's bulk was off of her. She hoped they would both go to the hallway and stay there.

"Pegeen," Becker called. "Help me, for Christ's sake."

Wanting him to shut up, Pegeen rolled over and felt the room suddenly swim before her. She saw the carpet move sideways, lifted her head and watched the stick that emerged from Becker's back wobble back and forth from his exertions like the nascent wing of a giant insect.

"You can't fly," she said impatiently. How silly of him to try. "That's ridiculous." The carpet stopped moving from side to side and started to rise toward her. Something was wrong about that, but Pegeen was not certain what it could be.

Becker was coming toward her now, still crawling. She saw his mouth moving but could not make out the words. He put his face next to hers and she hoped he would kiss her, but instead he put his lips to her ear and said, "Crawl." Pegeen did not want to crawl, she wanted to get that unsightly stick out of his back. She reached for it and saw him react in pain and fall to the floor, the stick still in place. She thought maybe she would kiss him since he was too shy to initiate things, but when he looked at her now his face was clouded with anger. She wondered what could be wrong with him.

Becker put his arm across her back and under her arm and pulled her alongside him. It was so nice to feel his touch again. Pegeen leaned against him and let him tug her toward the doorway. Strange shadows danced on the wall in front of her and she looked back and saw flames in the bedroom. That seemed interesting and she told Becker about it but he acted as if he already knew and just kept pulling her until they were in the hallway and then outside the house.

People she did not know with frantic faces took hold of her and lifted her and carried her away from Becker and finally put her down next to Meisner, who was now sitting up, holding his head as if it were in danger of falling off. He was turned slightly away from her so that she could see his back. Meisner had many more splinters than Becker did and his whole back was red with blood. He looked like a dartboard, Pegeen thought, puzzling why both men had become like that.

A woman squatted in front of her and repeatedly asked if she was all right and then Pegeen heard a siren wailing ever closer and then the whole front of the house which she had just left erupted into the street as though chased by the great fireball that leaped out after it.

After recovering from the effects of the blast and the disorientation, Pegeen visited Meisner in his hospital room. His back was covered with bandages but he was sitting up in bed and he gave her his loopy grin when she walked in.

"Hi . . . is this a personal visit, or an official one?" he asked.

"I came to see how you're doing," she said, puzzled.

"That sounds personal. Then, hi, gorgeous."

"What if I had been here on official business?"

"Hi, gorgeous special agent." He patted the bed beside him. Pegeen sat in the chair.

"We were nearly killed. Why are you so cheerful?"

Meisner looked surprised. "Because we were *nearly* killed. If we had been *actually* killed I'd be really pissed off."

Pegeen started to cross her legs, then thought better of it.

"Listen," she said. "I want to thank you. You may have saved my life."

He looked at her blankly.

"You may not remember," she said. "I don't remember much of what happened myself, but I do know that you covered me with your body when the first explosion happened. I would have taken

all of that stuff you got in your back right in the face. That was very . . . Thank you."

"Did you talk to Becker about this?" Meisner asked.

"I asked him what happened because I don't remember anything except coming to and finding you on top of me, then being on the sidewalk, and I think I passed out when the whole house blew so I wasn't really clear about anything until I woke up here in the hospital."

"And he told you I jumped on you to save you?"

"He said it looked that way to him."

"And I'd do it again," Meisner said, trying this time not to grin. He turned slightly on the bed and winced with more pain than he felt. He saw Pegeen compress her lips in sympathy so he winced a bit more.

"Can I just ask you one question?" she inquired.

"Anything."

"Why did you do it?"

"Cover you and save your life, you mean?"

Pegeen nodded.

Meisner paused, wondering what would work. Right at the moment, he guessed that just about anything would do, but he didn't want to overplay his hand and have her think about what he said in a less confused or sympathetic moment. His own recollection of what had happened was also a bit hazy. He thought he remembered Becker lifting him, removing him from the room, then dropping him as he dived for the floor, but who could say for certain? If Becker remembered it as a heroic act on Meisner's part and Pegeen thought so, too, then who was Meisner to argue? He might well have done it. As he thought about it, he decided that he was capable of making such a gesture, he had it in him, so why not assume that he had done so?

"I guess I did it instinctively," he said finally.

"I see," Pegeen said. She stared at the wall for a moment. "So you would have done it for anybody then."

"Nooo, I don't know that that's true."

"If it was an instinct . . ."

"A semi-instinct. I had time to think. I knew it was *you* lying there."

"Well . . . thank you again."

"Not necessary," he said nobly. He moved and winced once more but remained stoically quiet.

"One more question?"

"You bet."

"How did I get on the floor in the first place? You said you saw me lying there, so I was already there before you covered me, right?"

"Didn't Becker tell you?"

"He didn't seem to want to talk about it."

"Probably still shaken up," Meisner said. "To be honest it's kind of a blur for me, too. All that I remember clearly is that I knew I had to get you out of there. The rest was sort of instinctive, like I said."

Meisner lapsed into silence and decided that was his best play for the moment. He kept his eyes on her, casting them downward in manly humility, then back up at her face. After a moment Pegeen stood and moved to the side of the bed. She slipped her hand into his and held on. Meisner never said a word.

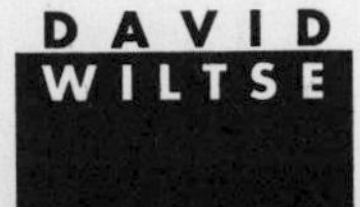

CHAPTER 16

BECKER ASSEMBLED HIS UNIT IN the FBI headquarters and narrowed the search for their needle now that the haystack had been blown away.

"We're after a man named Jason Cole," Becker told them. "We had a clue about him earlier but due to my inefficiency, we didn't follow up. We'll get him this time. We don't know that Cole is actually Spring. It's possible that Spring rigged Cole's apartment to get rid of him, and we happened to stumble in before he did—but I doubt it. In any event, he certainly knows about Spring if he's not Spring himself. Whether he's Spring or just scared shitless after his apartment blew up, he's vanished. The bad news is that the only Jason Cole who shows up in Motor Vehicles and voter registration and library card holders is eighty-six years old . . . and dead. He lives, or used to live, in the apartment that just exploded on us but he's been buried in Forest Lawn for the last seven years. So whoever we're looking for has appropriated Cole's name and apartment. We're trying to locate the owner of the apartment building to see if he has some other name on the lease, but there's some suggestion that the owner is an illegal immigrant who probably figures that right now is not the time to be talking to the authorities. At any rate, we haven't found him yet. NYPD will keep up with computer searches and the rest of the routine stuff and meanwhile we're going to spread our net wider."

"*Is* there any good news?" Pegeen asked.

"The good news is that Detective Rodriquez of NYPD has provided a description and we have a police artist's drawing that Rodriquez says is pretty good. It's been distributed to every checkpoint at every bridge and tunnel leaving Manhattan. If he tries to get out of Manhattan, we should have him, but I don't intend to wait for that. If he's smart—and he gives every indication that he is—he'll just stay here and keep his head down until the public screams so much that we have to take surveillance off the bridges. That's assuming he wants to leave the city at all—which I suspect he does from time to time."

"Why?" Meisner asked. "He's managed to get his explosives up till now by hiring somebody like Defone to do the work. It seems a pretty effective way to me."

"He can *get* the explosives while just sitting in place," Becker admitted. "But he can't *test* them here. The bombs do him no good unless they work, and they have to be tested first. This man is a very careful craftsman. Even a very *proud* one, the technicians tell me. He's inventive, he creates a new bomb appropriate for each explosion—I don't think he's going to take the chance that one of them wouldn't go off. I think he'd be embarrassed. So he needs a space large enough, remote enough, and isolated enough to set off an explosion and not have the cops come running. We're going to expand our search to Connecticut, Massachusetts, New York State, Pennsylvania, and New Jersey to begin with. If we have to we'll look farther out, but we'll start within a three-hour drive from the city. I want to know about anyplace in any of those states where anyone has even a vague recollection of hearing a loud noise in the last year. I want to know from every quarry if there has ever been any unauthorized blasting that they reported—or didn't bother to

report. I want you to check the ownership of every farm or subdivision or undeveloped piece of property that is at least half a mile from a town or city. We're looking particularly for the name of Cole or Spring but don't limit yourselves to that. I want to know about every potential site, regardless of the owner. We will also check every chemist, every chemistry instructor, every postgraduate student in chemistry, every current or retired military man with a history of ordinance or explosives within this five-state area. We will check every newspaper in the same area to see if there have been any fires started by explosion, any property damage of a possible explosive nature, any unexplained deaths that might conceivably have to do with explosives over the last five years."

"That will take forever," Meisner said.

Becker continued, ignoring him. "If that doesn't turn up anything we'll go back another five years. Spring didn't just emerge full-blown knowing how to do this. He had to have been practicing somewhere, sometime, before he opened his act in the big city. Also find out if a car has been rented to anyone named Cole or Spring from any outlet in the entire city. Go back five years on this, too. If you find anything get the mileage and we'll know how far he went and that just might take us to his practice range." Becker paused, waiting until the note takers had stopped scribbling. "Meanwhile, get a copy of this picture of Cole to every cop in the city. If he's still around, maybe we'll get lucky and stumble over him. . . . Any questions?"

Again, it was Meisner who spoke. The others seemed to take the massive workload for granted.

"I don't want to sound negative, but with this many people, it's going to take about six months to check all this shit out."

Becker paused. "Yes? Is there a question?"

"Have we got six months? What did the latest note from Spring say? Two days to respond or he blows something else?"

Becker lifted the paper from his desk. " 'Next incident within forty-eight hours barring positive response.' End quote."

"Sounds like two days to me."

"That depends when he started counting. However long it is, it isn't long enough. Do you have any suggestions as to how we can work faster, Meisner?"

"No, but can't we slow him down? How about a positive response in the newspaper. Another one of those 'let's talk' messages in the singles ads or something."

"We've already placed it," Becker said. "It's running in today's edition. I doubt that it's enough to placate Spring, he's going to want real communication about the money by now, but it's all the mayor was willing to go for."

Meisner snorted and shook his head in disbelief. "How much damage has Spring done already with the tramway blown? How much is it costing the city to check every car coming in and out? Why not just pay the asshole and be done with it?"

"You know the answer to that as well as we do," said Pegeen. "We don't deal with terrorists."

"Oh, yeah. Silly me. I guess I don't think of Spring as a terrorist so much as an entrepreneur."

"Something like Donald Trump?"

"In that category, but the Donald makes more profit," Meisner said. He looked around at the dour faces of the other agents. "It's a *joke. A joke.*"

CHAPTER

DEFONE LEE SAT AT THE FORMICA table in his one-room apartment and tried to get comfortable as he ate his breakfast of Pop-Tarts. Part of the time he ate standing up because the burning in his leg got worse when it rubbed against the chair. A bullet had gone cleanly through his thigh, just below the right buttock, and it had felt like a hammer blow when it hit him. But J'André Wambeau, who had been a medic in the army before becoming an addict in the Bronx, had declared that it was a simple wound without complication and had poured half a bottle of disinfectant on it before applying several neat stitches on both the entry and exit holes and slapping on a bandage. According to J'André, Defone was a lucky man because the bullet had struck nothing of importance but muscle. Defone had offered to blow a hole in J'André's ass and see how lucky *he* felt.

J'André had nothing useful to offer for the ringing in Defone's ears that had not subsided since the bomb went off. He suggested seeing a doctor, which was not something Defone considered an option. Then he suggested heroin, which Defone was not stupid enough to do either. Defone thought a dose of baby would probably take care of it but he was determined to ration his baby until he could figure out how to get a future supply. Baby had seen him through the shoot-out in Harlem, he was certain of that. Baby just wouldn't *let* him get shot—except for the one time in the leg—and Defone might well need protection of that sort in the days to come. He couldn't be wasting his supply just to get rid of a noise.

Of course, his supply probably wouldn't be coming from Cole/Spring. Defone would have to kill Cole/Spring, or maybe capture him and keep him as a slave in a chemical laboratory. No, he would have to kill him. He couldn't trust anything more that came from Cole's hand, it might well be poison instead of a bomb next time.

Almost worse than the fact that Cole had tried to blow him up—other people had tried to kill Defone, he could understand the impulse—was the obvious implication that Cole thought Defone was stupid. That would have to be punished. Cole would have to be shown that Defone was not stupid before Defone killed him. A man had to look after his reputation. If word got round that you could blow Defone up or send some Wop to shoot him and get away with it, Defone would cease to be feared as Defone Typhoon and might as well go back down to South Carolina and live with his great-grandma. Old bitch always act like he was stupid too. Whupping on him with her switches, trying to smack him upside the head when he walked past. Might's well go back down there and be treated like a six-year-old again as let *anybody* get the idea that Defone Lee was stupid.

Cole sat in the breakfast nook of Donny the Snake's Greenwich Village apartment and read the papers that Donny had acquired for him. The late-afternoon sun struck the second-story window on Christopher Street and bathed him in warmth and light as he read the vilification that was printed about him. Seated side-

ways on the window seat with the view of two enfenced locust trees on the street below and of the birds that came to the feeder suctioned onto Snake's windowpane, out of sight of stoplights or significant traffic, Cole found it easy to think that he really was living in a village. The odious trash in the *Daily News* brought him back all too quickly to reality.

"They just don't understand what I'm after," he said bitterly.

Donny was across the room in the kitchenette preparing squid for their dinner. He expertly cut off the head and eyes and removed the pen, and eviscerated the cavity with a practiced thumb before rinsing the body and tentacles, adding each little cephalopod to a growing pile draining in a colander.

"No, they don't understand," Donny agreed. Donny didn't understand him either, but he had gotten used to hearing him carry on. He talked as much as Tony Buono but it was not nearly so embarrassing. Cole didn't elaborate on personal matters best left unspoken the way Tony did. Cole—Jason, as Donny thought of him now—dealt in theories. Persecution theories, scientific theories, psuedoscientific theories, civil rights theories, racial theories, political theories. Theories of government, society, art, and literature. Theories of design and traffic flow and social advancement and skin pigmentation and anarchy and the likelihood of extraterrestrial life. He had a theory for everything, and nothing else. Donny had not heard him say anything of a practical nature since he had met him, even though he had not stopped talking the whole time. Jason talked as if he had a lifetime of theories to get out and into somebody's ear and a limited time to do it. He talked like a man who had just discovered his voice after thirty-five years of silence. The only thing he didn't have a theory about was cuisine. Jason didn't know shit about food.

"Maybe I should write a letter to the *Times* and tell them why their editorials are so—so horribly wrong about me."

"I don't think that's a great idea," Donny said. "Is there a message from the city to you in there?"

Cole put his thumb atop the city's response in the personals as if Donny might see it from across the room. There was no point in explaining to Donny that he did not want to negotiate, nor did he want the money. He wanted to continue doing the job. Justice would not be served until he had done what he set out to do. Like Defone, Donny was not overly concerned with justice—he, too, wanted the money.

"What are they waiting for? You blew up *my* tramway and I'd be asking where to send the money," said Donny.

"Would you really?"

"Well, not really. I'd be looking to blow your head off, but I'd be *saying* I was going to pay you, at least." He wiped his hands on his apron after cleaning the last of the squid. Donny gave the colander a final shake, then transfered the squid to the cutting board. Jason looked up from his newspapers and stared at Donny as if noticing him for the first time.

"What is that?" he asked in a horrified tone.

"Calamari. Squid."

"I don't eat that."

"Why not?" Donny asked, expecting a theory.

Jason shook his head. His hair flowed freely around his shoulders now that Donny had told him to shampoo it.

"I don't like it."

"You've never had it," Donny said.

"I still don't like it."

"You'll like it," Donny said, meaning, "You'll eat it" and ending the conversation in his mind. To his surprise Jason did not keep yammering on about it. Donny looked up to see him immersed in the papers again. And this time he looked happy about it.

"*She* gets it," Jason said. "She understands."

"Who?"

"Robin Sheehan. Robin is a woman's name, isn't it?"

"Can be." Donny shrugged. He had known a couple of Robins who weren't women, but didn't want to go into that at the moment.

"It sounds like a woman," said Jason. "There's a certain identifiable tone to a woman's writing, you can always tell, it has to do with issues of deference."

"Uh-huh."

"Or sometimes a stridency. It varies."

"Gotcha."

"This is a woman. A wonderful woman."

Jason read him a letter to the editor of the *Daily News.*

> *Dear Editor,*
>
> *Galileo, Martin Luther King, the Lord Christ himself. How many others will we ignore? How many minds have not been appreciated until it is too late? Although I don't understand his methods, either, shouldn't we at least listen to the man who calls himself Spring? If he speaks to us in his way with such an urgency, isn't it possible that his message is urgent, too? Or is the establishment so very sure that it is right that it can't consider another point of view? Are things so right in our society and our city that they can't be improved? Shouldn't we listen? I don't know all the answers but I'm not too proud to listen to someone who might have them.*
>
> *Robin Sheehan*

"She *got* it," Jason exclaimed. "That's it exactly."

"We'll eat in about half an hour," Donny said. "You want some Campari?"

"Why do you suppose she got it and nobody else does?"

"She's an enlightened spirit," said Donny, pouring two Camparis.

"I'd like to talk to her."

"No."

"Maybe just write her a letter."

"Absolutely not." Donny placed a coaster on the window seat and put Jason's drink on it. *"Salud."*

"I don't like it," Jason said, looking into the glass as if he saw something swimming within.

"Taste it."

"Alcohol is a depressant. Every drop kills millions of brain cells."

"You got plenty to spare. Drink it."

Cole raised the glass to eye level and looked at Donny over the liquid. He knew what was going on. Donny the Snake was trying to control him for his own uses just as Defone had tried to do. The only difference was that Donny was nicer about it. But Cole was not going to be controlled. He would give the *appearance* of being controlled, but he was much too smart for any of them, really. He lifted the glass slightly in a toast and sipped the bitter liquid. At the same time he decided to write a letter to Robin Sheehan at his first opportunity.

Donny the Snake walked past the New York City headquarters of the Federal Bureau of Investigation and looked south for any line-of-sight positions where he could wait without being noticed and still keep a view of the headquarters entrance. Fifteen minutes later he strolled past again, going the other way, checking out all possible positions to the north. Eventually he settled on the lobby of an office building across the street and halfway up the block. The lobby had been designed as an indoor mini-park where

weary pedestrians—presumably tenants of the building or their clients—could sit and rest for a minute or two while admiring the sculpture, the giant frescoes, and the fake waterfall. Donny took up residence on one of the marble benches, unfolded his newspaper, and began his surveillance.

After an hour and a half his patience was rewarded. Becker emerged from the FBI building in the company of a redheaded woman and two other men. Donny hurried from his lobby lookout and fell in step behind Becker and the others at a distance of forty yards.

To the Snake's surprise, they kept walking. This first reconnoiter was intended just to give Donny an idea of Becker's schedule—he had expected the target to hop in a car or a cab and whisk away. After a block, the two men went their separate ways and Becker and the woman continued to walk south. Donny continued to follow them from the same distance and when they turned west he crossed the street and kept watch from the other side.

His friend with the police had told Donny that this Becker was something special, some kind of bigger-than-life jack-off hero, and Jason went into a mumbling terror just thinking about him, but to Donny he looked as mortal and vulnerable as anyone else. If Jason hadn't made such a stink about it, if he hadn't insisted that Donny get rid of Becker as a condition for sharing the money—if he hadn't made an *honor* thing about it all, Donny wouldn't even be bothering with it. The best way to deal with cops was to ignore them. If you did your job right they never came into the picture in the first place—and if they did, you could deal with them then. There was no point in stirring the rest of them up by offing one of them.

But it would be easy—it was often easy. Most people didn't expect Donny to come up and put a bullet in their ear. You lived your life with certain assumptions, Donny knew, and one of them was that no one was trying immediately and directly to kill you, that you could walk on a city street and not expect to get hit by a professional—although you took your chances with the random muggers and druggies and crazies. Some of his targets were watching out for him, of course, because they had been tipped or they realized who they had offended, and some were always on the lookout in a general way because of their walk of life. Most, however, took their safety on faith and Becker seemed to be no different from most.

Donny could almost catch up with him and put him away right now. *Almost.* A careless man might try that. One pop for Becker, one for the lady if she seemed to need it, then just walk away. In that kind of situation nobody was going to give a positive ID on the shooter. Especially not with the kind of attorneys working for him that Donny knew how to get hold of. But it was sloppy and reckless and a smart man always eliminated as much uncertainty as he could. There might be an ex-footballer among the business suits who decided to put a tackle on him. There might be some tourist with a camera pointed in the right direction at the wrong time. Donny might sprain an ankle stepping off the curb.

Killing was best done in private where there was margin for error.

Becker and the woman entered a hotel and Donny told himself not to get too excited yet. If the man was staying in the hotel, then this was a cakewalk. There was no place easier than a hotel, the place was crawling with strangers and security was laughable. On the other hand, there were other reasons a man and woman might go into a hotel. Donny waited a few moments, then followed them in. He was wearing his dark blue business suit, very conservative. He could go anywhere.

Donny found them in the bar, where Becker was carrying a drink to the redhead, who sat at a tiny table in the corner. They must have just lucked into the table, Donny thought, because the bar was crowded and the few places to sit would have been at a premium. Donny took a position as far away from their table as he could get and elbowed his way to a space at the bar. He ordered a beer and moved his mouth now and then so that Becker, if he happened to look, would think he was talking to the man next to him.

There were about three men to every woman in the place, but it didn't seem to matter because they were all cut from the same bolt. From what Donny could overhear, everybody was talking about business. It made a pleasant change from Jason's torrent of theories.

Becker and the woman were talking, with Becker doing most of it, it looked like. The woman leaned close to him and did a lot of sympathetic nodding. He understood that, he'd been doing a lot of that to Jason himself. It didn't necessarily mean you agreed, or even that you were sympathetic.

He saw the woman put her hand atop Becker's and thought, Oh ho, so that's how it is. They might be taking a room upstairs at any minute. Now there was a situation Donny really liked. Talk about a man being distracted. If he timed it right, Donny could probably drive a truck through the door and not get noticed. Send the target out happy, for that matter. He'd done that before, crept up behind some guy when he was moaning and groaning and pumping away. He had been requested to do them both since the woman was the employer's wife and Donny's solution had seemed a whole lot cheaper and easier than divorce—which was problematical in the first place seeing as both employer and wife were good Catholics. The man had been the employer's bodyguard—probably a Catholic as well although no one seemed interested in *his* religious affiliation—which meant he was being punished for dereliction of duty as well as an alarming display of disrespect for his employer. The woman had opened her eyes just as Donny put the gun to the man's head, so he had been obliged to zap her first. The guy didn't seem to notice she was dead. He might even have thought that last little buck on her part was from excitement. Which meant he was a very inattentive lover as well as a lousy bodyguard. He might have heard the silenced whisper of the shot, though, because he grunted, "What?" as if she had spoken, but he didn't slow down the pumping. Not until Donny shot him in the ear, that is.

If Donny had the opportunity to dispatch Becker with the same happy thoughts in mind, he didn't begrudge it to him. What was important was that Donny could see that this was not going to be a very difficult job, Jason's little problem wasn't going to amount to much. No matter how much John Becker might frighten Jason, Donny could report that he was very human after all.

"I don't know if she was being noble, or unselfish, or if she doesn't really want me to come home or what," Becker said. "Her voice was so cool."

Pegeen nodded sympathetically. She had heard Karen Crist's voice be cool to the point of frigidity. But that was when Karen thought Pegeen was a rival for Becker's affection. That was when Pegeen had thought that too.

"I think Gold put her up to it," Becker said. He had been looking at a spot on the table in front of Pegeen. It was a good angle for a confession. He was looking *toward* her but not directly *at* her. Now, out of long habit, he lifted his eyes and scanned the room, checking for anything or anyone out of place. Becker had tailed too many people over the years not to have acquired some of the wary habits of one who is aware how prevalent and surreptitious surveillance can be.

"Did you ask Gold about it?" asked Pegeen.

"Not yet." A man and a woman who had been standing nearby, covetously regarding Becker's table, were leaving the bar. The woman gave one last backward glance, glaring at Becker as if he had been unchivalrous. Three businessmen who had gotten into an argument had settled down and were drinking morosely. A single woman in a business suit assumed her third position at the bar in the last twenty minutes. Becker wondered if she was trolling for a partner. She insinuated herself next to the dark, thin man with the heavy eyebrows at the end of the bar. He had been in the bar as long as Pegeen and Becker.

Pegeen slipped her hand over Becker's and he stifled the instinct to jerk away.

"It must be terribly hard for you," Pegeen said. "I know how much you love her . . ." She paused deliberately, giving him an opportunity to confirm or deny or modify her remark. Becker said nothing but inclined his head toward the tabletop again.

"But it's probably for the best," Pegeen continued, uncertain how to read the signals—if indeed there were any signals. "Your staying in the city for a while, I mean. It's certainly easier on you."

"That doesn't matter."

"You've always been very hard on yourself, John," she said softly. The use of his first name seemed to Pegeen to resonate between them like a struck glass. The tone was suddenly personal, direct, suggestive. Pegeen slipped her hand away, thinking she had overstepped.

"I'm hard on everyone around me," Becker said.

"Sometimes, maybe."

"I've been rotten with you."

Pegeen brought her hands together in front of her on the table and sat very still. At least he was going to talk about their episode together. She had been afraid he would never mention it again, as if it had never happened.

"You weren't rotten," she said quietly. "I was hurt. I was confused. But I never felt you were malicious."

Becker looked away from the table, glanced at her wide, expectant eyes, then quickly away and into the room again. The peripatetic woman was saying something to the thin man with the eyebrows but getting very little satisfaction. He treated her as if she were interrupting him. A bar was a strange place to come to commune with oneself in solitude, Becker thought. At least this bar at this time of day.

"Pegeen . . . I never told you, there didn't seem to be a time to tell you—and afterwards—I mean the next day—there didn't seem to be a *way* to tell you. First we were on the job, in the cave . . . and then in Washington, with Hatcher and Karen . . ."

Just don't say you're sorry, Pegeen thought. Say anything else, just don't apologize. Don't regret that most incredible night.

"It was a very hectic time," she offered.

Becker chuckled humorlessly. "Yes. Insane, maybe."

"In a way." Pegeen held very still, trying not to disturb his train of thought. She wanted very badly to talk about it and she knew that he did not, that he was doing so only from a sense of duty, and that he could be distracted from it in a second.

"Listen, Pegeen . . . this is hard for me to explain. But I want to try. When we were after Swann, when we knew he had the young woman in the cavern, the night before we found him—the night you and I—the night I lost control with you in the motel—I was so . . ." He stopped and eyed the room again.

For a moment Pegeen thought she had lost him.

"You were so . . . ?"

"I'm trying to think of a way to explain it so that it will make sense to you. . . . Something happens to me . . ."

"It happens to all of us. It happened to me."

He shook his head. "No . . . no. When I am that close . . . to a man I've been chasing . . . when I feel that I have him within my reach but I haven't quite got him yet . . . What's the saying? Browning, is it? 'Man's reach must exceed his grasp, or what's a heaven for?' Something like that. I don't know about the heaven

part, but that night with you . . . I was like that, I was so close to having Swann I felt I could reach out and touch him but I couldn't quite close my hand on him yet. It made me so excited, so tense, I thought I was going to go crazy. Literally. I thought if I didn't do something . . . to relieve that tension—I would do something crazy. Something dangerous."

Pegeen stared, stunned, as she began to realize what he meant.

Becker watched one of the arguing businessmen leave. The other two—who had been drinking in silence—immediately began talking animatedly to one another. The woman in the business suit gave up on the tall, thin man and moved next to them at the bar. Another couple had come and were standing close to the table Becker shared with Pegeen like a pair of vultures, looking for an encouraging sign of listlessness.

"I'm not sure I understand," Pegeen said, hoping that was true. "Are you saying you slept with me—to ease your tension?"

Becker thought of the violent passion of their coming together. He had made love to her with wild, desperate ferocity and a stamina and muscularity that had astounded both of them. His mind had been numb throughout what had seemed to be an endless, night-long struggle of carnality as his body refused release and sought more and more and more of her. Later he had been appalled at what he had done, the way he had come at her like a beast. Normally the most patient and gentle of lovers, he had acted so out of character that he was certain that Pegeen must have been equally horrified.

"I'm saying . . . I'm trying to explain my state of mind at the time." But he thought, Yes, exactly, if I hadn't spent those two hours with you in that way, I might have . . . He knew what he might have done even though he could not tell Pegeen, and he had committed a far less serious transgression to avoid it. No one had died as a result of his night with Pegeen, and that was the difference.

Although the incident had been two years ago Pegeen remembered it vividly. She had yearned for Becker from the moment she met him, but he had seemed unattainable: happily married, older, her superior in the Bureau and on the case, vastly more experienced in both work and life, often melancholically, mysteriously—and romantically—distant about some vague curse that he felt stalked him. He had shown no interest in Pegeen except as an agent and, typically she thought, even predictably given her penchant for sailing in amorously impassable waters, all of this had only made her desire him more. When he had suddenly swept her up like the torrent bursting through a dam, she had succumbed with a passion that matched his own. It was not only Becker she had responded to but the wild urgency of his need. No one had ever wanted her that badly in her life, before or since. No man had ever needed her so utterly and the hurricane of his compulsion was all the aphrodisiac she would ever require. It did not matter that at moments she was certain that he hadn't known who she was—there were times in the evening when Pegeen did not know what name to give this body that possessed her, either. Nor, at times, did she care.

That one night had defined for her the structure of possibility. Becker had provided her with a view of life and passion that she had known, even as it happened, would inform her view of the world for the rest of her nights.

And now he was threatening to destroy it.

Pegeen got to her feet. The couple waiting for the table stirred expectantly. She felt her face and ears to be aflame. She wanted only to find a way to leave without making a scene but she was not certain she had enough equilibrium to manage that.

"You're a shit," she said in tones audible only to Becker and the waiting couple.

Becker nodded agreement in such a sorry way that Pegeen wanted to slap him.

"I am not something to be used," she said in a whisper. "I am not around just for your convenience. How dare you. How *dare* you."

"I would have killed someone," Becker muttered.

She sat back down again, ignoring the sighs of exasperation of the waiting couple.

"What did you say?"

"I would have killed someone," he repeated. "If I hadn't . . . if we hadn't . . ."

"If you hadn't fucked me?" she said, impatient with his groping propriety.

". . . I would have killed someone that night."

"What are you saying? What bullshit is this? You were so excited about catching Swann that it was either kill somebody or fuck poor stupid Pegeen?"

Becker did not deny it.

"Am I supposed to believe that? What are you saying, you're some kind of werewolf? Please."

Becker studied the spot on the table.

"No wonder your wife doesn't want you at home," she continued. "At least have the balls to admit you don't care about me, don't ask me to believe some horseshit you come up with to let yourself off the hook."

The waiting couple leaned in closer, the better to eavesdrop on a conversation that was getting interesting. The thin man with the eyebrows left the bar, and the woman in the business suit was finally getting some attention from the businessmen.

"I didn't think you'd understand," Becker said. No one understood, which was one of the reasons he never talked about it. Gold had struggled to come to some comprehension but his was an understanding hedged with carefully maintained professional detachment, a willfully imposed distance. Gold did not want to come too close to the condition he had sporadically tried to change. Karen knew of it and was frightened by it because it echoed too closely some of the feelings she had experienced herself. There was no point in trying to explain it to others. They did not understand, did not want to understand, and could deal with it only in derisive terms of exaggeration, as Pegeen had done in calling him a werewolf. Becker was no mythical monster, he knew, but rather a human who knew all too well what lured the men he pursued to kill and kill again.

"Oooh, you're misunderstooood," Pegeen cooed. "You poor thing."

"I'm not misunderstood," Becker said, suddenly grinning, tired of being punched. "I'm not understood at all."

"Surely you can do better."

He looked her in the eyes and held her gaze. Even now Pegeen felt the powerful attraction of the man when he gave her his full attention. His eyes managed to be simultaneously serious and amused. For Pegeen it was as if another being had suddenly entered Becker's body and was looking out at her through his eyes, winking mischievously at her while maintaining a straight face. When he engaged her this way, Pegeen knew why she had been so ardently mad for him. He was a different man than the one who stared at the table and absorbed her punishment.

"What would you like me to do, Pegeen?"

"I don't care what you do," she said, suddenly flustered.

"That gives me a pretty wide range." His grin broadened wickedly.

Pegeen felt a familiar sensation of frustration. He had suddenly, quixotically, become so cocksure of himself, so unjustifiably self-satisfied, so ineffably and completely *male*. Ultimately they didn't care what was being said, she realized—not for the first time—as long as it was about *them*. They fed on abuse and disapproval nearly as much as praise because it indicated that you were think-

ing about *them.* In the long run men all thought they were just as cute as hell.

"Go fuck yourself," she said, pleased with her courage. She stomped out of the bar, not caring that her face and ears looked like a fiery beacon. And that was it, she vowed to herself. She had had it with men. When a tall man with heavy eyebrows looked up from his newspaper with a quizzical expression as she passed she gave him a look that would curdle milk.

Becker waited for a moment to give Pegeen time to clear the hotel before he moved, ignoring the restless buzzing of the anxious couple. He had handled the confrontation badly, he knew, although he was not sure how he might have handled it differently without giving Pegeen false hope. He was aggrieved that it had gone so sourly, sorry that Pegeen now probably hated him, but most of all relieved that it was over.

He recognized the man seeking refuge behind the newspaper as the tall man who had just left the bar, and walked past without looking directly at him. He got his key from the desk, took the elevator to the fifth floor, and walked quickly to the stairwell, where he waited, the door cracked, to see who got off the next elevator. The elevator did not come and after a few minutes Becker returned to the lobby.

The man with the newspaper was gone. Becker approached the clerk.

"Room 537," Becker said. "Was anyone asking about me?"

"As a matter of fact, a man was just here," the clerk said, surprised. "He said he wanted to leave a message in your box and asked for your room number and I told him."

"Is there a message?"

"I gave him paper and a pen and he just crumpled it up and said he'd changed his mind."

Becker nodded as if expecting as much. "A tall man, dark complexion, heavy eyebrows?"

"That's him, sir. Maybe he'll call later," the clerk offered.

"I wouldn't be at all surprised," Becker said. "In the meantime, I'd like to change rooms, please."

"Is there something wrong with your room, sir?"

"I'm superstitious." Becker smiled. "I never sleep in the same room twice."

The clerk studied him a moment, not certain if he was being ribbed. Becker's smile was not reassuring.

"Of course, sir," he said at last, choosing the noncommittal approach.

In his new room Becker arranged blankets and pillows on the floor and slept with his feet against the door. Anyone entering would have no chance of slipping in without disturbing him. He could have arranged for a Bureau watchdog agent as he slept, of course, but Becker did not think that a display of paranoia from its chief was what his unit needed right now. There were dozens of perfectly valid explanations for the behavior of the tall thin man with the heavy eyebrows and Becker thought it might make for a good idle-time entertainment to list them, but in the meantime he would stick with the only one that came along with his line of work.

In the morning, as quietly as he could and given any free time, he would study mug shots of the type of people who might find it interesting to tail a federal agent. Becker knew he had made hundreds of enemies in his career, starting with the men and women he had put in jail and the relatives of the several whom he had killed. Interagency spying was not unheard of either, although recently that had become mostly a matter of vying for the actively growing segment of corporate security violations and corporate espionage, an area in which Becker had neither interest nor expertise. Still, many things were possible. Becker could only prepare for those he thought likely.

He slept lightly and dreamed of a woman who was sometimes

his wife and sometimes Pegeen and in either case hostile and frightening in the unspecified way of dreams. There was also a black basketball player named Chaney and the women seemed to have it in for him, too. When he awoke Becker realized that a former NBA pro called Don Chaney was very close in name to the actor Lon Chaney, who had played the werewolf in movies that Becker had watched as a youth. The sleeping mind was weird, he reflected, but not nearly as dangerous as when it was awake.

CHAPTER 18

WHEN DONNY THE SNAKE LEFT the apartment Cole wrote his letter to Robin Sheehan in care of the newspaper. He had never before corresponded with someone who might actually write back and he was surprised to find himself suffering the excitement and anticipation of a man in love. His heart raced faster as he composed his words and he felt stirrings in his groin just thinking about this woman reading his words, sharing his thoughts, being moved by his reason and his eloquence. Unbidden, an image of Robin Sheehan came to his mind based on nothing other than her name and his wishes. She was a typical Irish lass with auburn hair and blue eyes and—since she had come to his aid in the newspaper—the look of courage and wisdom in her features. He saw her as thirty years old, someone slightly his junior whom he could instruct in the ways of life yet rely upon as a fellow adult. He saw her dressed in a peasant skirt with a scoop-neck blouse and an expanse of cleavage of creamy white skin dusted with freckles. Then he mentally removed the freckles. He was not certain of her height, nor did he think it mattered as long as she was not taller than he was.

Excited and impatient, he hurried to mail the letter, taking it directly to the post office rather than a more convenient letter drop, and then, too wound up to return to the apartment, he started to walk the streets. He had been strolling aimlessly for half an hour, enjoying the sights of the Village and the balmy summer evening air, before he realized that he had been heading all along toward the warehouse where Donny had stored his equipment. Inexplicably to Cole, Donny the Snake, a man who brandished a pistol with the careless ease that others did a pencil, was terrified at the prospect of having explosives in his apartment. Cole did not like having them too far from him; Donny would not have them around at all. They would compromise, Cole thought. He would retrieve his necessities and he would not tell Donny about it. They weren't dangerous, after all, until Cole made them so. Laymen were so slow to understand.

Officer Glenn Herndon had been a cop for eighteen years and for the last twelve of those he had been an alcoholic, but it was only for the last three of those foggy dozen that he had taken to sleeping on the job. His partners—and there had been a series of them—had been aware of his tendency to doze for a half hour or so in midshift but Herndon was an amiable, nonthreatening man, the kind of cop who had never even removed his gun from its holster while on duty, and one after another they had elected to go along with his ways rather than try to change them. He was a senior man within a few years of retirement and very few cops on the NYPD or any other force would interfere with a man in such a position.

Some of his partners accommodated Herndon by turning the radio down and keeping quiet during his naps. Some of them joined him. It was easy enough to do in the early-morning hours on a patrol that covered the warehouse district of Manhattan's West

Side. Once Herndon had drifted off, the partner would just lean his head back against the seat and relax quietly. Nature would take care of the rest—which wasn't like *trying* to go to sleep.

Herndon's current partner had joined him. Neither of them saw the skinny man slip into the warehouse, even though their squad car was parked in the darkness less than forty yards away with a full view of the building; but Herndon saw him slip out again. Or he thought he did. He had just awakened, startled by his own openmouthed snore, and the figure of a man climbing from the warehouse window was one of the things against which he blinked his eyes as he struggled to remember where he was. Herndon had seen a few things of late that he knew weren't there and consequently he was a bit chary of believing everything that seemed to be unfolding before his eyes. He certainly didn't tell anyone else until he was certain that his vision hadn't just crawled out of one of his empty bottles.

But he was still a cop. Herndon watched the man walk toward him carrying an armful of bags, seemingly unaware of the cop car lurking in the shadow. He took a short draft from one of the small bottles of vodka that helped him get through his working day. There was something vaguely familiar about the man's angular features, the stringy hair, the nerdy eyeglasses, but Herndon could not place them precisely. The first drink after his nap brought water to his eyes and he wiped them clear as the man approached. His motion caught the man's attention and he started with surprise.

"Hello," the man said.

"How ya doing?" Herndon asked, his voice still thick with sleep. He had felt wonderful before he dozed off, floating on a high that he had managed to sustain for several hours, but now he was struggling against the grip of a hangover. His head hurt, his eyes scratched despite the tears, and the taste in his mouth was disgusting. He could get out of the car and hassle the man. Or he could

not. If he was quiet enough, his partner might not wake up yet and Herndon could steal a few more vital minutes in which to recover.

"I'm fine. How are you?" The man spoke in articulate, middle-class tones. He looked like the son of a banker who was still struggling to find his way in the world.

Herndon nodded in answer, feeling the pincers travel up his neck and grab his skull. If he did not speak again, the man might move along. He looked away from the man as if he were someone with more important things to do. The man took the hint and walked away. Herndon took another nip and tried to pull himself together.

Cole walked back to Donny the Snake's apartment from the warehouse, carrying with him the paper grocery bags that he had rescued from the sidewalk refuse basket to use as containers for the treasures he had taken from the warehouse. In the apartment he stashed the bags underneath the living room sofa that he was using as a bed.

He made one quick phone call and heard a sleepy voice answer unintelligibly.

"Is this Marvell?"

"Who you, motherfucker?"

"I'm your friend," said Cole.

The change in the speaker's tone was immediate. "Oh, how you do, friend? This Marvell."

"Hello, Marvell."

"Yeah, hello. Didn't mean to sound all nasty, I didn't realize it was you. You need me?"

"Could you meet me Wednesday at the corner of Ninety-sixth and Lexington at ten o'clock in the morning?"

"I be there."

"Good, I'll see you then."

"I ain't heard from you in a while." Marvell's last job for his friend had been to deliver the items left in the van after Defone's robbery of the sporting goods store and the chemical warehouse. He had never done anything but act as a cut-off man who waited in the darkness until Defone arrived with whatever goods he had been sent for. Marvell would have been very surprised if Defone even knew of his existence. He certainly never would become aware of him through any voluntary action of Marvell's. Marvell did not wish to come to the attention of someone like Defone Lee. "You all right?"

"I've been rather busy. Dismantling an entrenched social system is not an easy business."

"No, uh-uh, that's right."

"People are basically conservative. They cling to that which they know, no matter how outdated or inefficient or deleterious it might be."

"That sure the truth."

"It requires a rude shock to make them release their hold on the outmoded," said Cole, who had been practicing some of the things he would say to Robin Sheehan when he met her.

"I know what you mean," said Marvell, who did not. The woman beside him in bed opened her eyes and glared at Marvell.

"Good night, Marvell."

"You take care of yourself, friend."

Cole lay back on the sofa to scheme awhile and in the Bronx Marvell's woman propped herself up on one elbow and looked at him derisively.

"Just what friend that be?" she demanded. "Call you up in the middle of the night, got you agreeing like some kind of puppet?"

Marvell wished to God the woman would cut him some kind of slack once in a while. Just once in a while, give a man enough room to turn around without bumping into her.

"You don't know him, Phistra. He just a friend."

"I know your kind of *friend,*" she said, shaking her head in

disapproval with a motion that started her double chins wobbling. "You keep your ass *clean,* Marvell Samson, or you haul your sorry ass out of *my* bed. You hear me?"

"Hope I can pick my own friends at least," Marvell muttered, with more defiance than he felt.

"You pick your own friends and I'll pick my own man," Phistra said. The vehemence of her utterance set off another shock wave of quivering flesh.

Woman was so fat that conversation set her to shaking, Marvell thought. Marvell traditionally favored womens with meat on the bones. Everyone said the skinny ones was the meanest ones, but sometimes he had his doubts. Phistra was so fat she might have passed the happy stage right on by and come around the corner back to mean again.

She turned her back to him and he waited for the bed to stop shaking, then fell asleep, dreaming dreams of baby.

The following day at role call, as the sergeant was reminding them of the search for Spring and showing them the artist's rendering of Jason Cole—a copy of which had been in Herndon's squad car the entirety of the previous day—Herndon remembered the man he had seen coming out of the warehouse. He conferred first with his conscience, and then he conferred with his partner to make sure they had their stories straight before contacting his superiors. They whisked him into the presence of the FBI before he had time to take another surreptitious drink.

CHAPTER

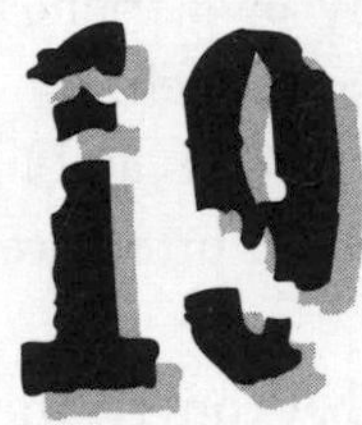

WITHIN A FEW HOURS IN THE morning, Becker's unit had three major breakthroughs dumped into its lap. It was an embarrassment of riches but no one at the Bureau was disposed to give any of it back.

"First, we think we may have had a sighting of Cole. A patrol officer says he got a pretty good look at him around two in the morning in the warehouse district along the Hudson River below Greenwich Village," Becker told the unit.

"Why didn't he grab him?" Meisner asked.

"The reporting officer was having an attack of diarrhea," Becker said.

"So how'd he see the suspect? He came into the toilet and stood around?"

"I'll leave it to you to get the details on that, Meisner. The thing is, he was seen. New York City has a dozen of its finest knocking on doors in the area right now. We should have a search warrant for the warehouse within an hour. That's number one. Number two, we planted a letter in the paper under the name of Robin Sheehan, purporting to be sympathetic to at least listening to Spring's case. He keeps referring to our "learning and listening"—whatever paranoid delusion his message might be—so I thought we should go proactive, see if we could prod him, make him react to us for a change instead of the other way around. A number of letters arrived at the paper addressed to Robin Sheehan. Most of them accused her of being an idiot or worse, giving aid and comfort to the enemy, how dare she, that kind of thing. One offered to sit on her face—or his face, for that matter. We called the writer Robin in case Spring is interested in either, or both, sexes. He can take his pick. One offered to let her sit on *his* face. And then we got a letter from someone claiming he's Spring. He wants to meet her—and the psych ed boys are certain he's writing to a woman."

"And she wants to meet him," Pegeen said. "He set up a rendezvous and I'm going to keep it."

"When?" Meisner asked.

"This afternoon," Becker said. "Half of you will be assigned to surveillance for her."

"I volunteer for that," said Meisner.

Although pleased, Pegeen did not look at Meisner.

"The boys in the psych department doubt that it's really Spring, by the way. More likely some opportunist trying to score with a girl—or a potential copycat. But we're treating it very seriously anyway."

"What are the other half of us going to be doing if we're not watching for Pegeen?" asked Agent Vanhooven, a former college tight end who still looked ready to charge through a line of tacklers without a helmet.

"Helping to coordinate things for tomorrow. That's number three. We got a message from him half an hour ago. Addressed to the FBI in block letters drawn with a Magic Marker."

Becker lifted a copy of the message from his desk and read, " 'You still need education. Here's your next lesson. Put five million in fifties in black photo portfolio. Deliver by black agent in good suit and tie. Randalls Island. On foot. Alone. Message third bench. Four p.m. 7/23. No cops.' "

"Right, no cops, you bet," said Vanhooven.

Becker looked at his unit as if noticing their race for the first time. A black man rose to his feet.

"I guess I'm your black delivery boy by default," said the black agent. He was the only African-American in the room.

"We can get others," Becker said.

"And you're going to need them all for backup," the man said. "Randalls Island Park is next to Harlem."

"Okay, Mac. The job's yours."

"Any idea why this nutcase wants a black man in the first place?"

"Do you want my first guess?" Becker asked.

"Any guess at all," said the agent.

"He doesn't like blacks."

The black agent grinned ruefully. "Glad to know I'm dealing with a typical fellow American."

"You'll be covered all the way."

"I know it," he said skeptically. "But by who?"

Cole woke to find Donny the Snake bustling around the kitchen, whistling annoyingly between his teeth in a distracted manner. The apartment had a stinging, unpleasant odor and Cole vowed to himself not to eat it, whatever it was and no matter how much his host insisted.

As it turned out, the smell came from a bottle of hair dye. Without ceremony or explanation Donny cut Cole's hair, changed his part, then dyed it all black.

"Can you grow a mustache?" Donny asked.

"Of course."

"Do it."

"What's going on?"

"The police have a picture of you," Donny said. He wiped his hands on a towel, then unwrapped some new clothes while Cole stared at himself in a hand mirror.

"How do you know?"

"I got a friend or two," Donny said. He removed the pins from a purple poplin golf shirt with an animal on the breast.

"I look . . . awful," Cole said. He had almost said that Donny had made him look Italian but decided not to be quite so specific.

"You look great. I mean it. It shows off your face better, that way."

Cole tilted his head, viewing himself from an angle.

"Eh."

"You have a very handsome face," Donny told him. "There's a sweet quality there that you should let come out more." He held the golf shirt out to Cole.

"I can't wear this," Cole said.

Donny sighed, keeping the shirt in front of Cole.

"Why not?"

"Look at the color. It'd make me look queer."

Donny regarded him coolly, taking his time before answering. He had to remember the man had been living in a cocoon for the last couple of decades.

"The preferred terminology is 'gay.' Are you gay?" Donny asked finally, keeping his tone uninflected.

"Of course not."

Donny smiled wanly. "Then it will be a good disguise, won't it?"

"I don't need a disguise. No one ever remembers me. I have that kind of face."

"I'm going to remember you."

"Well . . ." Cole didn't know how to take a great many things that Donny said. Some of them made him uncomfortable. Some of them made him feel warm. Sometimes they did both.

Cole moved backward instinctively when Donny reached toward his face.

"Ay," said Donny. He removed Cole's glasses. "How bad do you need these?"

"I don't know. I got them so I could see the blackboard from the back of the room."

"When was this?"

"High school."

"You been wearing these since high school? The same glasses?"

"They still work."

"Must be made of titanium. Can you see across the room all right without them?"

"Yes."

"Can you see how many fingers I'm holding up?"

"Of course."

Donny folded the glasses and gingerly laid them on the end table beside the sofa. The table was a reproduction of a Georgian antique that Donny had stripped and refinished himself, staining it a black walnut and then distressing it with care. The glasses were probably older than the table.

"You look really good that way," Donny said. "Don't wear them, they give you away. They're just that little bit out of style. You look much better this way anyway."

"Really? I thought they made me look kind of distinguished."

They made you look like an asshole, Donny thought. He said, "They weren't really you. You look a lot cuter this way. The cops aren't looking for anybody this cute."

Cole smiled uncertainly. "You're sure?"

"The only cops who will notice you now will be the gay ones."

"Are there queer cops?" Cole asked, astounded.

Donny tried not to let the contempt show in his face. The man had been living not only in a cocoon but under a rock as well.

"So I've been told," he said. "And the word is *gay*."

CHAPTER 20

THE CAFÉ SOIXANTE-NEUF SITS AT the junction of Sixty-ninth Street and Columbus Avenue with its outdoor tables wrapping around the corner onto both streets. A waist-high red-and-blue-striped canvas stretched across a railing serves to divide the café from the sidewalk but in reality the only thing that prevents passing pedestrians from snatching food and drink from the plates of diners is social civility. In New York City, a town not noted for the restraint of its citizens, the proprietors of the café are taking a risk.

Pegeen arrived ten minutes early for her rendezvous, wearing a green scarf around her neck as the letter had stipulated, and wishing she could take it off. The day was hot, she was sitting in the sun, and her body temperature was up enough already because of tension without adding any extra clothing. She also hated the color green. Her mother had dressed her in green, thinking it set off her eyes, which were a light hazel, and Pegeen's recollections of childhood included too many memories of showing up at parties looking like a carrottop growing out of a stalk of broccoli. It was one of many issues Pegeen had with her mother's idea of child rearing.

She gave her order for a beer to a waiter who informed her that his name was Bryant, and settled back to wait, trying to appear calm. She assumed she was being watched by Spring, or whoever her correspondent might really be, and she knew she was being watched by Meisner. The last thing she wanted to do was to let Meisner see her anxiety. She allowed her gaze to wander over the scene around her in what she hoped was a natural way, trying to locate him. Meisner was nowhere to be seen, which was as it should be. Pegeen didn't really want to know where he was, so that she wouldn't instinctively be glancing too often in his direction—particularly in case of trouble—and thus give him away. If she encountered any trouble she was determined to deal with it herself. The last thing she wanted was to be bailed out by a sexist like Meisner. He would never let her forget it.

Bryant the waiter returned and asked if she was Robin Sheehan. Pegeen followed him to the telephone at the reception desk inside the restaurant. She noticed Meisner clearing tables and busing the dishes into the kitchen and wondered how long he had been doing that. He did not look at her, did not acknowledge her presence.

"Hello," she said into the phone, turning her back to Meisner and looking out toward the street. "This is Robin Sheehan."

There was silence for a moment.

"Hello? Who's this?"

"You know me as Spring," said a tentative voice.

"Oh . . . hello." Try to treat him as a date, she had been advised. To Robin Sheehan, Spring would be a correspondent, an exciting man who had unexpectedly appeared in her life. An opportunity. Gold and the psych department, as Becker called them, had constructed not only an identity but an entire inner life for her. Pegeen had been given less than twenty-four hours to assume the persona of a single woman, no longer truly young, an idealist, naive, disillusioned by her experiences with men but willing to keep trying to find one. None of the psychologists had used the word "desperate" to describe her character but Pegeen had heard it

hanging in the air. Fitting into the role had not been much of a stretch, she thought ruefully.

Act a little annoyed, a little disappointed, she thought. Not yet certain she was being stood up, but wary. Yet still hopeful.

"I thought we were going to meet," she said.

"Well, yes, that was the plan." There was something uncertain about his voice, as if the speaker were just trying it out for the first time.

"Please don't misconstrue the fact that I have not yet arrived."

Be friendly, accommodating, she thought.

"No, that's all right. I haven't been waiting long."

"Obviously I would like to meet you. That goes without saying."

Not in my experience, Pegeen thought. It was never said often enough.

"I'd like to meet you, too . . . I mean, if it's convenient. If you can't do it today, I certainly understand. I know you're . . . busy." Had she gone too far? She had expressed a certain sympathy in the newspaper. That didn't make her a fan who thought his work came first—considering the nature of his work.

"I have to take certain precautions, you understand. I—uh—I was touched by your letter to the editor. Do you write often to the newspapers?"

"This was my first time," said Pegeen. "I've thought about it before but I've just never quite done it. Some things make me so angry that I feel I have to *say* something. Do you know what I mean? I have tried to call some of the radio talk shows but their numbers are always busy and I—I'm shy. I express myself better in writing."

"You're expressing yourself very well right now," the man's voice purred into her ear.

Well, aren't you smooth, Pegeen thought.

"Thank you," she said. "I feel comfortable. I don't know why."

There was a slight pause. "You should write more. This country is so dominated by received opinion. Whose voices do we hear? The same ones over and over. They have strangled the rest of us."

"I know."

"Democrats, Republicans, it's all the same thing. They just want our votes, but who cares about *us?* People with real opinions like yours, people with a different point of view have got to speak up."

Pegeen said, "I know. That's why I finally got up the courage to write about you. I mean, they weren't even *listening* to what you had to say, it was like there was all this hysteria but nobody really *cared* what your true message was. It made me so mad and so, so—frustrated for you."

Again a pause before he responded. Come on, you sucker, Pegeen thought, keep talking. Give me something more to work with.

"Have you written to the papers much yourself?" she asked, speaking into his silence.

"Oh, yes," he said proudly. "I've been published a great deal . . . I may come out with a book."

"Really! A book. That's wonderful. Congratulations."

She allowed herself a glimpse around the restaurant, letting her eyes flit without interest over the patrons, wondering if any of them were watching her performance with more than idle curiosity. Meisner was setting up a table at the end of the room, laying out napkins and silver with a practiced hand. She wondered where he would have learned such a skill. She thought of Meisner as barely domesticated at all.

"I thought I'd compile all my letters and add a sort of manifesto that I've been working on."

"A manifesto? That's interesting."

"A thesis, really. About the corruption of education in this country."

"Oh, yes?"

"You're aware of it, of course."

"Well . . . in a way."

"Do you know what's the really curious thing about it all? No one has commented on this at all, as far as I know. My work will be the first to point out that every truly intelligent man in the history of this country has been self-educated. If you want to learn, *you have to teach yourself.* Why? Because of the teachers, of course. And what's wrong with the teachers? Why aren't they any good? Because the system weeds out the gifted ones, that's why. It gets rid of the ones who really know their subject. The authorities are not interested in people who can *teach,* they only want people who follow their simpleminded rules. Excellence is punished in the educational system. If you're a student who is bright, I mean really has something on the ball, don't you dare argue with a teacher. You know what happens then, don't you? You Get Expelled! And if you're a teacher who disagrees with the powers that be? What happens? You Get Expelled Again!"

"I never thought of it that way."

"No one has. It's never been said. And why? Because the system is supported by government, courts, journalism, you name it. The entire establishment is living a lie. *Reinforcing* a lie. Well, it's ruining everything. The country is disintegrating because everyone listens to authority and authority is *stupid.* You can't get educated by going to school, it's as simple as that. Well, I say it's gone on too long. It's time it stopped . . . Anyway, that's the gist of my thesis. I phrase it in a more scholarly fashion in my paper, of course."

"Uh-huh. I certainly see what you mean."

She heard him take a deep breath and sigh. "Well, anyway, I just think it's important to get that word out," he said. "I think I can find a publisher pretty easily now."

"I'm sure you will," said Pegeen, thinking, To get published, is that what this is all about? To get *published?* Impulsively, she took a chance. "I'm in publishing, actually."

"You are?" Pegeen heard him rise to her improvised bait like a trout ready to leap out of the water. "That's terrific. What house?"

"Well . . ." What house indeed? She had said it spontaneously, seizing an opportunity. The cover story the Bureau had prepared had her working for the state Department of Motor Vehicles, a position that would seem to require no special skills or knowledge yet would give her firsthand reasons for discontent with the system. "I'm not actually working there *now*, but I used to be with Random House. We had a sort of—dispute."

"Random House. That's a good house—isn't it?"

"My boss wasn't so great. He seemed to think I was his property, not just his employee, if you know what I mean."

Spring was clearly not interested in her personal injustice. "What was your job?"

"I was an editor," Pegeen lied. What other jobs were there in publishing? She had no idea. "I'm looking for a position at a smaller press now. Something more scholarly, more academic."

"But you still have friends at Random House? You didn't cut yourself off completely?"

"Oh, I have a lot of friends in the business," she said. "It's a pretty clubby industry."

"Yes," he said darkly. "It's not how good you are, it's who you know. That old story. You wonder how some of this slop gets printed while the really worthy manuscripts never even get read if you've got the wrong name."

"It always helps to know someone," she agreed.

"So, listen," he said, his tone becoming businesslike suddenly. "I imagine they want you to get off the phone there."

"No, I think—"

"I'd like to talk to you again. Can I call you sometime?"

"Why, yes, of course . . . but I was hoping we might meet . . ."

"In time. I have to be cautious . . . You're not in the phone book."

"I have an unlisted number. A woman has to be careful in the city."

"I knew you were a woman right away," he said, sounding proud.

"Well, thanks very much. I don't look that bad."

"No, you look very nice. You're pretty. I meant I could tell from your letter. Robin can be a man's name, too."

"Oh . . . I wore the scarf you asked for."

"Yes, I thought it would go well on you. I just sensed it, somehow."

"It's my favorite color."

"Would you feel all right giving me your phone number? I won't abuse it, I won't give it to anyone else."

Like that's the problem, Pegeen thought. She told him the phone number that the FBI had established for her last night. She assumed that by now they had located a suitable address to go with it in case Spring wanted to come calling.

"I have a roommate," Pegeen said. "If she answers or if you want to leave a message, who will you say you are?"

"Can't very well tell her that I'm Spring, can I?" He chuckled, then thought for a moment. "I'll say that I'm Nels Kjelsen."

"Nels . . . ?"

"Kjelsen."

"All right," said Pegeen. "If Nels Kjelsen calls, I'll know it's you. . . . Is there any way I can get in touch with you?"

"Write another letter to the editor," he said. The line went dead in Pegeen's ear.

When she left the restaurant her mind was spinning with thoughts of the conversation. She would soon be grilled on Spring's side of it since the recorder taped to her bra would have picked up only her words. Her eye saw but her mind did not register the black man who stood across the street, snapping photographs of Café Soixante-Neuf and its patrons. She did not notice that he remained focused on her, continuing to shoot as she walked quickly away from the restaurant.

Meisner shed his apron and fled through the kitchen entrance, coming out onto Columbus Avenue half a block behind Pegeen. He noticed the photographer and wondered mildly about the incongruity. Black men dressed for the ghetto did not normally stalk the gentrified area of this part of Columbus Avenue, photographing people on the street. But as long as he was not threatening or following Pegeen, Meisner had no time to worry about him further.

Two hours later the pictures that Marvell took of Pegeen were in Cole's hands. Although blurry and with Pegeen's image inexpertly framed in the shot, they were preferable to the long-range view Cole had gotten of her through his binoculars three blocks away. His hands had shaken too much, for one thing, and a minor tremor was woefully magnified at a distance of three hundred yards. He had been able to identify her by her location and the green around her neck but all the rest was guesswork by his imagination. Now, with the photos, he was not disappointed. If she was not exactly a beautiful woman, he could make her attractive by filling in some of the blurs with details he preferred. He chose the most flattering—and least typical—angle and decided she was in-

deed pretty. And more amazingly, she looked very like the image he had conjured using only her name for a guide.

Cole took his favorite photograph and folded it to fit into his wallet. He would have preferred to frame it and place it beside his bed but he did not want to have to explain its sudden appearance to Donny the Snake.

CHAPTER 21

THEY GRILLED PEGEEN FOR SEVERAL hours, trying to wring every last nuance from her conversation with the man on the phone. Many were still uncertain if the caller was Spring or not. They played the tape again and again, pausing after every comment by Pegeen to get her recollection of what Spring said next, striving for a verbatim account. When her memory didn't provide enough words to fill the silence on the tape, they goaded her for more. With each replay she remembered slightly more and when they felt that they had as many of the actual words as they would get, they started to work on his tone.

"Was he angry during this talk about changing society?"

"When he said you were pretty, did you wonder how he knew? Was there anything in his voice to indicate he had actually seen you?"

"His wording is very formal. Do you think he knows many women? Has he dated before?"

"Did you get any sexual feelings from him?"

"How old a man did he sound?"

"Was he disguising his voice in any way?"

"What sort of accent did he have?"

"When he told you to write another letter to the editor, was he serious?"

"He ended abruptly—did you piss him off?"

"When he said you weren't in the phone book, was it an accusation? Was he suspicious?"

When the psych department was temporarily sated, Pegeen was sent to the language department. Becker accompanied her through the halls.

"First of all, great job," he said. "Telling him that you work in publishing was very quick thinking."

"The psych boys were upset that I departed from their script."

"The psych department has never actually caught anyone yet that I know of. You showed great initiative and imagination. I'm proud of you."

Pegeen felt her ears light up. She nodded in what she hoped was modest acceptance of the praise.

"Thank you."

"Now forget the technical details for the moment, Pegeen," he continued. "Just gut reaction. If this guy called you up because some friend gave him your number, if it was that kind of call, what would you think?"

"Do you mean would I go out with him? A woman of my standards?"

"Yeah."

"It depends. How long has it been since I've had a satisfying time with a man?"

"I don't know, how long?"

"I'm speaking theoretically. You asked a relative question."

"Let's say you haven't had a satisfying time with a man for several months."

"Oh, is that all? Hell, no. I wait that long to see if they're going to call back after the first date. If it had been a couple of *years*, on the other hand, would I go out with him then? That's another question. At that point it might depend on whether he had a body temperature or not."

"Should I be worrying about you, Pegeen?"

"Me? Why? This is life in America for the single girl, it's the way it's supposed to be."

"Maybe I asked the question at a bad time."

"No, I'm sorry. It was a fair question."

"The transcript makes him sound like a stuffed-shirt bore, but maybe he's not," Becker said.

"In my opinion, he's a wet fish."

"Meaning?"

"I think he's a false alarm. I think he's some asshole who can't get a date and can't look a woman in the eye and ask for her phone number. He got a bright idea when he saw the letter in the paper and once he set up the rendezvous didn't have balls enough to go through with it. I don't think he's Spring, but maybe I give Spring too much credit. Somehow I expect somebody who's managed to do what he's done and not get caught to be more of a man than this guy. But then I may be wrong." She caught Becker's eye. "I frequently am when it comes to men."

"Just in case you're wrong again, we're going to have to have you be Robin Sheehan for a while. Housing has found you an apartment and your phone line will be covered by a female operator at all times who can act as your roommate. You can get some of your personal stuff together tonight and move in. Housing will have provided you with everything else you'll need by now. They also bought you some green skirts and blouses and such. We can't rule out the possibility that he'll be watching you."

"I fucking *hate* green."

"You looked good in that scarf," Becker said. "It brings out your eyes."

"Thank you, Mother dearest."

"And . . . as a bonus . . . I'm assigning Meisner to stay with you as backup until this is over."

"Oh, Christ."

"Courage, Agent Haddad. We must all make sacrifices."

"Stop grinning at me. Sir."

"I'm happy for you. I can't repress it."

"Sure you can. Sir. See how well *I'm* doing it?"

They reached the language department and Becker stopped her with a light touch to her elbow.

"Be careful," he said.

"I can handle Meisner."

"I mean Spring. You're probably right, it was some opportunist on the phone, but until we're sure, take every precaution."

"I will."

"No heroics. He may or may not be your idea of a real man, but Spring is very smart. And that means very dangerous."

Pegeen nodded, her eyes on his face. For the moment he looked as if he really cared about her, she thought. As a person as well as an agent. When he walked away she remembered herself. "Fuckhead," she muttered.

In the language lab she told them what her caller's accent was *not* and they played her tapes of every regional accent left. She selected the intonations of upstate New York and northern Pennsylvania, stopping well south of the Yankee accents of Vermont and New Hampshire and the Canadian influence of the border.

After six hours of discussion and argument, Gold brought the results of the committee to Becker.

"I'll put this in proper psych-speak in my official report, but I'm kind of tired right now. Is it all right if I just tell you?"

"I'd prefer it," Becker said.

Gold rubbed his eyes. His normal day was ten to four, he wasn't accustomed to emergency meetings and six-hour sessions without a break. "We think he's an academic. Somebody who's led a very sheltered life in a college or some other quasi-intellectual situation. My guess, our guess, is that he didn't get tenure or was fired or laid off and blames the system. He is clearly educated. Doesn't know bupkiss about women . . ."

"And who does?"

Gold shrugged agreement and continued: ". . . but would like to find out, if he could do it in a totally safe environment. I don't mean no cops, I mean no touching, no chance of rejection, no reality in general. He'd probably be quite contented with a telephone relationship."

"Phone sex?"

"I doubt that sex enters into it. Not on a conscious level, at any rate. He's probably spent most of his life without sex—sex with another person, that is—and won't be apt to change things now. . . ."

Gold talked for a good deal longer and Becker listened with a growing sense of despair. All the theoretical speculation in the world wouldn't help much; didn't, in fact, bring them any closer than Pegeen's gut reaction that the man was a wet fish.

Finally a weary Becker held up his hand to interrupt the flow of speculation.

"I get the general picture. It's not a great improvement on what we already thought, but it might clarify things for somebody else when they read it. Just give me the short strokes now. Is the guy really Spring?"

Gold hesitated. He looked embarrassed. "To be honest, John, we don't know. We can't tell by listening to him—not that we were actually able to *hear* him anyway. Society is full of people like this, bearing a grievance, antisocial or at least asocial, maladjusted, full of resentments and ill will—but very few of them actually step

over the line and plant bombs or go on a shooting spree in the shopping mall. Even if we met him face-to-face we couldn't tell you on the basis of the conversation he had with Pegeen. He didn't say anything only Spring would know, did he? He didn't betray himself in any real way. The best we can do is tell you whether or not he has the *potential.* I say he does, some of the others don't agree. Grandiosity and paranoia don't make you a criminal—hell, they aren't even uncommon. People *vote* for clowns like this these days. It's becoming respectable." Gold shrugged, ultimately absolving himself of responsibility. "It's an inexact science, John. I don't have to tell you that. You know it."

"I agree with the 'inexact' part," Becker said. "All right, that's about all I can take for now. Too much intellectualizing about dysfunctional assholes makes my foot itch. I want to kick somebody in the butt."

"I assume you mean Spring."

"If he were here . . . But as he's not." He looked at Gold darkly, no sign of a joke in his eyes or his voice.

"You seem a little more annoyed with me than usual," Gold said uneasily. "Anything other than the stress of this business . . . and my general proximity?"

"Since you noticed, yes, there is. I don't appreciate your calling my wife and telling her to keep me in the city."

Becker saw that Gold was genuinely surprised. "I didn't do that."

"Did you call her at home?"

"Not in months. We spoke after she was attacked, you knew that, but not since then. I'm not treating her."

"I know that. Okay."

"What is it?"

"Forget it. Thanks for the report."

"I'll have a written version for you tomorrow. Christ, it's already tomorrow, isn't it. This afternoon."

"No rush," Becker said dismissively. "I think I can remember the gist of it."

"I know it doesn't help . . . but is there anything I *can* do for you?"

"Like what?"

"Do you want to talk?"

"To you? Gold . . ." He sighed heavily, struggling to control his impatience. "No. I want to find Spring and rip him a new asshole."

"Does that mean . . ."

"What?"

Gold proceeded cautiously, as if offering his hand to a very large and hungry animal. "Are you feeling that old obsession?"

"Obsessed? Me? Doc, how you talk."

"So, all right, you don't want to discuss it."

"I believe I told you that in the beginning. Talking to you just makes me feel—what?—sarcastic, more than anything else. It is just too easy to be sarcastic when talking to you. I don't much like sarcasm as a rule. It's fun with you, though, Gold. Why is that?"

"I'm an easy target. You're not the only one." Gold rose to his feet. "Well, I must say it's always interesting talking to you, John."

"Good that one of us feels that way."

"Remember, if there's any way at all that I can help you . . ."

Becker regarded Gold for a long moment, an ironic smile playing on his face. "There so seldom is."

When Gold was gone Becker berated himself for his attitude. You're becoming a genuine shithead, he thought. Not only does it not help to belittle your associates—it's not nice, either. He promised himself that he would apologize to Gold in some calmer time. Right now he needed all the emotional energy he could muster to apply to the case.

Finally, by early morning, as the sun was rising over the beleaguered island of Manhattan, Becker reassembled his unit.

"First, we find a Nels Kjelsen somewhere in this country. There can't be that many of them. It's not his real name, but it's probably *somebody's* name, which means it's somebody he knew or knew of at some time."

"I think there's a cookie made by Kjelsen . . . butter cookies," said Pegeen.

Becker shrugged. "Maybe he was looking at a box of them . . ."

"They come in a tin."

"Maybe he was looking at a *tin* of them when he was on the phone, I don't know. Let's find out. At least we'll know what he eats."

When he dismissed the unit, Becker locked his door and lay down on the floor for a nap. In two hours he would begin final preparations to trap Spring when he came for the ransom money. If he came. Becker admitted to himself as he dropped off to sleep that he would be surprised if Spring showed up. It was hard to figure just what exactly Spring wanted. To get published? To blow up the city, bit by bit? Five million dollars? Or maybe just to get laid. He wouldn't be the first to wreak havoc to sublimate his thwarted sexual drive.

When he slept he dreamed of Pegeen, with whom he had indulged his sexual drive to thwart the havoc he would have wreaked otherwise.

CHAPTER 22

DONNY THE SNAKE CALLED THE hotel switchboard from a pay phone in the lobby and asked to speak with John Becker.

"That's room 437, I believe," he said.

"That would be room 531," the operator said. "I'll connect you, sir."

Becker had changed rooms for some reason, Donny realized, but the significance was uncertain. When the operator informed him that there was no answer and asked if he would like to leave a message, Donny hung up. He crossed the lobby carrying his gym bag and giving the registration desk a wide berth.

After stepping off the elevator on the fifth floor, Donny located the alcove that held the soda and ice machines. In less than a minute he was out of his suit and shoes and into his terry cloth bathrobe with the navy-blue piping. He folded the suit neatly and put it into the gym bag, which he then locked and stowed atop the soda machine.

Donny stepped out of the elevator, pausing just long enough to be certain that he would get the full effect of his entrance into the lobby in his bathrobe and bare feet. He kept his eyes on the registration desk now, willing them to look at him. The longer they had to be uneasy about his appearance, the more pliable they would be.

"I've just locked myself out of room 531," he said, sounding both embarrassed and angry.

"I'll have the bellman let you in," said the clerk.

"This wouldn't have happened if my wife hadn't taken the key. All I did was step out to get a bucket of ice and forgot to leave it unlocked. Why don't you just make me another key so it doesn't happen again."

"Of course, sir. I'll send one up."

"I'll wait."

The clerk's eyes flitted around the room at the other patrons looking in amusement at the man in the bathrobe. He was not inclined to argue. "Room 531. Just a moment."

The clerk was gone less than a minute. "Here you are, Mr. Becker," said the clerk, handing Donny the electronic key. "Sorry for any inconvenience."

"Not your fault," said Donny, striding back toward the elevator with the key to Becker's room in his hand.

In the room Donny unfolded his suit, shaking it gently to be sure it did not wrinkle before putting it on again. He stood in the bathroom to knot his tie, a wide strip of silk with leaping speckled green trout breaching deep blue water seriatim and snapping at invisible flies that they would never catch. His Aunt Cosima had given him the tie last Christmas and Donny was partial to it.

Donny adjusted the shower curtain, making sure he could step in and out of the tub without being heard, then took his paperback book from the gym bag and sat on the edge of the tub to read. When Becker entered the living room Donny would have plenty of time to put the book in his pocket and pull the long-barreled Browning .22 from his shoulder holster, where it now sat awkwardly because of the silencer screwed onto the barrel. He was happy to return to the book. Donny loved a good thriller.

He waited behind the curtain while the maid came in and turned down the bed. An hour later he relieved himself in the toilet and stepped back into the tub without flushing in case Becker came in and heard the noise. He tried to read for several minutes, distracted, then finally stepped out of the tub and flushed the toilet.

Around one o'clock in the morning Donny felt ravenously hungry. He tried not to think about it but the gnawing in his stomach got worse and worse. After a while he convinced himself that stomach grumbling could betray him at the vital moment. He walked into the bedroom with the pistol in his hand and took the chocolate that the maid had left on the pillow. Still unsatisfied, he opened the mini-fridge and ate the peanuts and the cheese crackers and drank a bottle of spring water. He placed the empty bottle and the wrappers in the gym bag and returned to his lair in the tub to wait some more.

By four in the morning he was convinced that Becker would not return that night. He unscrewed the silencer, put it in the bag, and left the room. The next time he came he would need to wear a disguise to cross the lobby. He could not afford to become a familiar figure to the desk clerk.

Jason was asleep on the sofa when Donny returned, curled up like a baby. He looked like a little boy when he slept, Donny thought. A cute, angelic little boy. Sleep removed the pinched aspect, the guarded paranoid look, and left only the innocence and naiveté that managed somehow to live alongside the suspicion and distrust. Donny picked up the blanket that Cole had kicked off in his sleep and covered him again, pulling the cloth all the way to his chin.

He noticed the plantains on the kitchen counter and wondered what on earth had prompted Jason to buy them. The Bicycle Boy continued to surprise him. What Donny could not know was that his houseguest had riffled through his Rolodex, read all of his bills, and looked through his checkbook. Naiveté was one thing, innocence quite another.

CHAPTER 23

EXTREME SECURITY MEASURES work for two reasons. The first, and more obvious, is that they foil attempts at sabotage by detecting hidden weapons, explosives, and so on. The second reason for their efficacy is more a matter of image making. They deter attempts because the would-be perpetrators *think* the methods are effective and are reluctant to try. The reality is that all security systems are breachable given sufficient imagination and courage. And the larger the system, and the wider the area it seeks to protect, the more porous it becomes.

Protecting all of the bridges and tunnels into Manhattan was an impossibly wide area and Jason Cole possessed more than enough imagination. Although a physical coward when actually threatened with violence, he was literally without fear in all other circumstances. Cole had a complete—and thus far warranted—faith in his ability to deal with any circumstances that arose. He simply and totally believed that he was cleverer than anyone else he would encounter.

On the Thursday afternoon at 3:55 he stood in the bodega on the corner of 103rd and Second Ave in East Harlem examining plantains when Special Agent Arthur McArthur, Jr., arrived in the dark blue Chevy Caprice and double-parked. Agent McArthur was an African-American and alone, as instructed. He wore a dark blue suit by Bill Blass and a muted tie and looked as out of place in the Latino neighborhood as would a policeman on a horse. After placing a card with the letters of the FBI writ large in the front window to avoid getting a parking ticket, Agent McArthur got out of the car carrying a large leather photograph portfolio and started walking briskly toward the bridge two blocks away.

McArthur assumed that he was being watched by Spring. He *knew* he was being watched by at least half a dozen FBI agents and undercover cops. One would be a sniper on a nearby rooftop but McArthur did not look upward to locate him. He had served in that capacity himself earlier in his career and knew the type of position the sniper would have, knew the feel of the sniper's Remington rifle, even the heat of the roof's asphalt sealant on his knees and butt. Two more would be in front of him, maybe the shop clerk with the apron sweeping the sidewalk in front of a bakery or the derelict in the doorway or the young man sticking his tongue down a young woman's throat at the street corner in front of him. In that case the young woman would be an agent as well, although more likely a New York cop. Young Latino women were in short supply in the Bureau.

There would also be at least two more agents falling into place a discreet distance behind him. They would follow casually and circumspectly, covering his back. In Randalls Island Park there would be several more agents who had been positioned for hours. Some of those would be disguised as Parks Department employees, an easy costume to come by.

Overseeing them all, either by telescope or radio, would be John Becker, special-agent-in-charge. And hovering in the background would be Associate Deputy Hatcher who, McArthur had heard, had arrived in town earlier in the morning from Washington.

Two uniformed policemen with an explosives-sniffing dog barred the entrance to the footbridge that leads from Manhattan to Randalls Island Park. The only footbridge into Manhattan, it is of no commercial importance but it does provide access by foot to the tower leg supports of the Triborough Bridge, a major connector with Manhattan to both the Bronx and Queens.

A few pedestrians were being sniffed and electronically scanned for firearms before stepping onto the bridge, but McArthur was allowed through without pause by the well-briefed guards.

His first destination was the park bench where he had been instructed to find a message. Although they had known about the message for a full day, the authorities had not disturbed it for fear that *they* were being watched.

McArthur strode rapidly but easily over the bridge and toward the third bench. His demeanor betrayed none of the tension he felt and he allowed the portfolio to swing naturally at his side without treating it as if it contained the valuable cargo that it held. Inside the portfolio were packets of fifty-dollar bills, all neatly wrapped with genuine bills on the top and bottom and the remainder bad counterfeits that the Bureau had borrowed from Treasury, which had confiscated them a few months earlier. Although ineptly bogus from a professional point of view, they looked real enough to pass the kind of cursory inspection Spring was apt to give them if he riffled through the packs. Concealed in one of the packs was a radio transmitter the size of a watch battery that could send a signal capable of being tracked from a distance of four city blocks. Sewn with great care into the false bottom of the portfolio was a larger transmitter that was capable of communicating with the loran satellite, a modern marvel that could track the case to within six meters anywhere on the surface of the earth. Becker did not really expect Spring to keep the portfolio, but if he did he would have trouble finding a hole anywhere on the planet deep enough to hide in.

The portfolio didn't really carry five million dollars, of course, not even in counterfeit bills. There was no way to tuck a hundred thousand pieces of paper of that thickness in the case, no matter what was written on them. It had puzzled Becker and the others that Spring had not seemed to realize the impossibility of his request. They could not have stuffed five million dollars in the case if it had been in five-hundred-dollar denominations instead of the fifties that Spring had requested.

Not that the amount of money he was or was not going to give over to Spring was of any immediate interest to McArthur. He wanted to deliver the portfolio and be done with it. With everyone's eyes and the sniper's rifle on him, he felt like a goat being staked out for a tiger. If Spring showed up in person, McArthur would take him down, but that seemed highly unlikely. The man might not be able to count to large numbers very effectively, but he had given no indication that he was foolhardy.

McArthur sat on the bench and breathed deeply for a moment, then reached under the seat and felt for whatever awaited him there. He found an envelope secured by tape, pulled it out and opened it. The message read: "Go to Triboro, first Bronx exit. Be there by 4:30."

McArthur looked at his watch. It was 4:05. He had to shake his ass. McArthur headed back toward his car on the run, speaking loudly so that the radio taped to his chest could pick up his words clearly.

"Message says to drive to the first Bronx exit off the Triborough. I got to four-thirty. Tell them to clear a path for me." He ran a few steps, expecting an answer, before remembering that the earpiece was tucked under his collar in order not to alarm Spring if he actually showed up. He grabbed it with his free hand and plugged it into his ear in time to hear Becker say, "You've got plenty of time. Cruisers will clear a lane until you get to the bridge itself. Once you're on it take your time. Do not, repeat, do *not* take that exit until you hear from me that we're set up ahead of you. Got it?"

McArthur was beginning to pant as he passed the guards at the entrance to the bridge. "Got it," he said.

"Good man. And don't worry, we're still with you."

The two cops on the bridge gave him a razzing cheer as he chugged past them. McArthur had put on a good deal of weight since his running days and his lungs seemed to have shrunk. He could imagine the turmoil going on ahead of him as the cops and the Bureau tried to scramble men into place without alerting Spring to their presence. Assuming he was there, of course. More likely just another message to keep McArthur humping. Keep me moving all day long, sucker, he thought, we're still going to be there when day is done.

He reached his car and leaped in, dropping the portfolio on the seat beside him. His hands were shaking from the exercise as he turned the key and headed toward the FDR Drive and the Triborough Bridge.

McArthur was waved around the line of impatient drivers waiting to get through the security check at the beginning of the Triborough Bridge. He drove past the dogs, the officers searching cars, the wheeled mirrors that were slid underneath the chassis to reveal the whole undercarriage. He fell in line behind the thin string of traffic on the bridge itself and checked his watch for the tenth time since running from the park. He had five minutes left and was less than two minutes from the exit.

"Slow down," Becker counseled through the earpiece.

"I can't go any slower."

"Stop, if you have to. You're not covered on the other end quite yet. We need three more minutes."

McArthur slowed the car still further. He was halfway across the bridge and wondering how to fake a flat tire when his Chevy Caprice exploded. The ruptured fuel tank was ignited by the heat of the pipe bomb fragments and it went up in a secondary explosion stronger than the first. The van immediately behind McArthur collided with the burning Caprice and within moments was enveloped in flames. Three cars back a driver in the adjoining lane was killed by flying shrapnel from the pipe and as he slumped forward he dragged the steering wheel to the left. His car cut across traffic and slammed into the left-hand guardrails in front of oncoming traffic, which could not stop in time. Within seconds a chain of cars spanning the width of the bridge were involved in the crash and as the drivers and passengers scrambled free as best they could, the fire spread from one car to the next, setting off a series of explosions until the span was filled with flying, twisted metal and rocking to the concussion of detonating gasoline.

By the time Cole reached Donny the Snake's apartment in the Village, the Triborough Bridge was closed.

CHAPTER 24

BECKER AWOKE WITH MUSCLES sore from sleeping on his office floor for the second night in a row. His eyes were burning after only two hours of rest, and a persistent pain had settled in along both temples. He called his wife and they lied to each other that they felt fine and everything was going well. Each heard the lie in the other's voice and opted not to act upon it. It was much easier for both to accept the lie, not to challenge it. After a few minutes during which neither inquired closely about the other's activities, they declared they loved each other—which was true enough—and hung up. And both of them, in their separate ways, felt slightly soiled by the dishonesty of the conversation.

Hatcher had flown into town the day before the bombing on the Triborough and he orbited around Becker now, staying just out of range but imparting his panic to everyone else. If things were out of control, it was Hatcher's primary goal to make it seem as if it was Becker's fault. He was notably absent during the next press conference. He no longer wanted to be publicly associated with the unit.

Becker approached the press conference with a dual purpose. He wanted to reassure the public that everything that could be done *was* being done and that the authorities were in control—a large chore since they were so manifestly *not* in control—and to provoke Spring. Becker wanted to prod him, pressure him, keep him worried instead of calmly sitting back and destroying the city at his own pace and pleasure. Proactive techniques had become a staple of Bureau methodology in the past decade and they worked because the sociopath was fascinated with the results of his crimes. Most of them would read and watch everything pertaining to their acts and more than one had been known to respond directly to intentional FBI misquotes or character analysis. Becker had decided that Spring's vulnerability was just a variation on the weak spot of all serial killers, serial arsonists, or serial bombers—an overpowering sense of personal inadequacy. The individual twist on that had something to do with instruction although no one knew quite what. Becker would put his thumb on that weak spot and bear down and twist.

"We'll have him soon," Becker announced to the assembled reporters and microphones and cameras. "I can't give you details for the obvious reasons, but I can say this: Spring is making lots of mistakes. He probably knows what some of them are himself—but we know the rest. The fact is, the man is not up to it. He's a failure, he's always been a failure, and the reason is simple—he's not good enough. He knows it and we know it. We'll catch him. Every step he takes is a misstep and it only brings him closer to us. He's not good enough to pull this off."

The reporters went wild with curiosity. What did he mean? How was Becker getting closer? Was Spring betraying himself? How?

Becker avoided specifics but leaned closer to the camera, glowering directly at it.

"I'll say just one more thing, and I'm saying it to you, Spring. I know you're watching. You're a poor, pathetic, miserable little underachiever. You think we're not learning? It's because you aren't good enough to teach. You want us to 'learn' so that we will understand you, because when I catch you—and you know I will—you're hoping that if we know about your sexual failures and your emotional failures and your rotten parents and your awful childhood and all the injustices you're suffered since you were born—you're hoping if we understand all that, we'll understand *you.* And if we understand you, we'll forgive you. Listen carefully, Spring. I know it all—and I don't forgive. I *don't* forgive."

Becker stepped away from the dais amid a hail of questions and exited the room, leaving the chief of police and the mayor to say the politic and evasive phrases they had mastered long ago. They had not been prepared for either the personal tone or the intensity of Becker's message.

It had all come out of Behavioral Sciences I, A Refresher, as delivered by Gold in a twenty-minute coaching session. The charges and descriptions were generic enough to apply to just about any sociopath, but to Spring, who was certain to be feeling ecstatic about his success, it would sound as if Becker had been reading his personal file. Or such was the hope. It was as inclusive as a horoscope for the criminal personality, but millions believed in those, too.

In Donny the Snake's apartment Cole watched the press conference with awe. Becker's eyes had seemed to glow and Cole was certain they were looking through the camera and the screen directly at him.

"What is that shit?" Donny scoffed. "Not forgiven? Who does he think he is, a priest?"

Cole rewound the tape and played it again. Cole knew what Becker meant.

"He's a fucking cop," Donny said angrily. "That's all he is. He thinks he's a psychic? He's getting closer? If he was getting closer

we'd hear his flat feet tripping over themselves. They don't know shit about you, they don't know what you're doing."

In fact, Donny had not known either. He had found out about the Triborough Bridge explosion in the newspaper and had listened with amazement to Cole's explanation of how it had been done. It was so difficult to believe that Jason was responsible. Donny considered himself a student of human nature—his job required it—and like most people who hold that opinion of themselves, he did not understand the difference between being a student and being a master. It wasn't that Donny was surprised to learn that evil could lurk behind baby faces, or that malice could masquerade as innocence. It was that he couldn't bring himself to accept the fact that this bookish, theorizing, naive wimp of a man who was glued to the TV set was *capable* of demolishing a bridge while shopping for plantains and beans.

"He knows me," Cole said with a sinking feeling. The replay confirmed what he had feared on first watching.

"He don't know shit. If I didn't know, how in the hell is he supposed to know? He's just blowing smoke for the reporters. Did you see how crazy they went?"

"He wasn't talking to the reporters," Cole said. He rewound the tape and started it for a third run but this time with the sound off.

"Who was he talking to?"

"Me. He was talking directly to me. Didn't you hear him say that *he* was going to catch me? He didn't say 'they,' he said 'he.' " Donny looked at Cole with concern. The man seemed to be coming unwound. He was acting as if he had just seen a ghost on the television—or some kind of prophet.

Cole froze the tape on a close-up of Becker's face as the agent glared at the camera. "His eyes are on fire. Can you see that?"

"He hasn't slept in his bed for two nights running," Donny said contemptuously. "They're bloodshot. He's going loopy from lack of sleep. That's why he's talking out his asshole. 'Forgiven.' What the fuck is that? Who does he think he is, Bishop Becker?"

Cole shook his head. "He's the god of destruction."

Donny stared at him. He was definitely coming unglued. "What?"

Cole had not told Donny that he, Jason, was the god of vengeance and thus could recognize a fellow deity when he saw him. It had not seemed the best tack to take this early in their relationship. Although there were many qualities about Donny that he liked, he did not feel that his grasp of personal theology was vast. Catholics tended to be doctrinaire about such matters.

"I thought you were going to take care of him for me," Cole cried.

"I am. You can't rush these things."

"Everyone was quick enough to take my six thousand two hundred and fifty dollars, but as for *earning* it, nobody's in any rush."

Donny wanted so badly to slap him.

"In the first place, I never saw your money. You gave it to Tony the Good, not me. In the second place, do not ever put me in the same category with a gamaguch' like Tony. He's my cousin but the guy is an amateur."

"He took my money!" Jason was getting hysterical.

"Shut up about your money! Where's the real money? When are you going to go for the five million?"

"When are you going to get rid of him?" Cole gestured at Becker's angry face on the screen.

"As soon as I can. All right? You want me to walk into FBI headquarters and do it? As soon as I can."

"That sixty-two fifty was all the money I had." He looked like he was going to cry. It's like dealing with a temperamental child, Donny thought. Up, down, round in circles. A cop looks at him cross-eyed and he's going nuts. Like the fed has a pipeline to his soul. And what's this 'god of destruction' stuff?

"And don't *sulk* about it," Donny said impatiently. "If you want money, then let's set about getting it."

"I'm not ready."

"You want me to do it? I can set it up."

"*I* want to do it," Cole said petulantly. "It's *my* idea, *I've* done all the work, I don't want you to do it, it's *mine.*"

"Okay. Do it."

"You're always taking things away just when I get to the point where I really, really like them. You don't want me to have anything fun."

"I never took anything away from you. What are you talking about?"

Cole clammed up abruptly, turning his back on Donny.

"Or should I ask, who are you talking to? You did this once before, you know. When we first met. You think I'm your mother or something?"

After a moment, when Cole still did not answer, Donny sat beside him on the sofa and put an arm around his shoulders.

"I hate it when we quarrel," Donny said. "We shouldn't fight, we should be the best of friends."

"I know," Cole said dully.

"It's my fault. Sometimes I forget that I'm not you. That I can't always understand you because I'm not living inside of you . . . You're not always easy to understand, Jason. You're a very complex person."

"I know."

"And so am I. So I think we both have to keep making that extra effort to understand each other . . . all right?"

"All right."

Donny stroked Jason's neck for a moment, then let his fingers stray to the other man's ear.

"The main thing is to keep communicating. And to remember that I care for you very much." He traced the outside of Jason's ear with his finger. "And I think you care for me a little bit, too, don't you . . . ?"

Cole did not respond. Donny allowed his finger to stray into the bowl of the ear. He felt Jason's body stiffen and removed his finger.

He got to his feet, checked his weapon, moved toward the door. "I'll take care of Becker *now*," he said. His voice was angry with rejection. "Then we'll get the big money."

After Donny left, Cole felt his ear still tingling where it had been touched. It made him think of Robin Sheehan. He exited the apartment, looking for a public telephone.

Following the press conference, Becker decided he needed to change his clothes. He had slept in these two nights in a row and they looked like it. His face was gummy with fatigue and he knew that he was beginning to smell. There was so much more work to do, so much more time to spend thinking, but concessions needed to be made to the body or it would force the mind to shut down on its own. Reluctantly, Becker left the office and returned to his hotel to take a shower and change.

CHAPTER 25

DONNY SAT ON THE EDGE OF THE tub and finished his paperback with a sense of disappointment. He liked characterization and he liked romance and he liked humor in his stories as well as plot and excitement and there were not very many writers who delivered all of those qualities. Especially not the best-sellers. They gave him either tons of plot and marginal writing or good writing and no plot. The few who really gave him all he wanted did not seem to sell very well. It looked to Donny as if writing novels was a mug's game and he was glad he was not in it.

He was sorry he had not brought along another book, however. Becker was not present for the third night in a row. If it weren't for the few items of clothing and the toilet articles still in place Donny might have thought he had checked out. Maybe he was shacking up with the woman Donny had seen with him in the bar. When she walked out she looked more like she wanted to spit on Becker than sleep with him, but who knew about women?

Donny had trouble enough understanding men. He was confused about Jason. Sometimes the man looked at Donny so sweetly that he was weak with desire. But whenever Donny touched him Jason curled in on himself like a turtle yanking back into its shell.

Donny didn't know what to think except that it was dangerous to let himself care for the man so much. He was putting his heart at risk and it looked as if there was little chance for reward. It was hard enough finding the right person without choosing a guy who didn't know what he wanted.

Donny knew what *he* wanted. He wasn't like his moron cousin Tony, he didn't demand a great beauty. The pretty faces never stuck around, he had discovered that painfully enough. What he needed in his life was some softness, some sweetness, some loyalty. Some innocence. A little romance. A little excitement. Someone with a good character. Not unlike what he looked for in a book. It didn't seem too much to ask for—why was it so hard to find?

His reverie ended when he heard the outer door open. Donny stood and pulled the Browning from the holster, lifting his elbow high and moving with exaggerated care to accommodate the length of the silencer.

Becker unlocked his hotel room and stood to one side as the door swung slowly open. After a moment he stepped inside, immediately moving out of the hallway light, and paused with his back to the wall, listening. He did not expect to find anyone waiting for him, but he had not forgotten the man asking about him two nights ago, either. He had survived an adult lifetime of hunting killers by being wary when caution was called for, and it was a habit that stuck.

As he entered the bedroom he noticed an odor lingering in the air as if someone had stood where he stood now and left a trace of themselves behind. Becker would never use scent himself, was opposed to it on cultural grounds, linking it in his mind with breeds and creeds and manners foreign to his own, but he recognized it well enough. It smelled partly of barbershops, partly of department

stores. Partly of fraternities and men who moussed their hair and dressed too carefully, and also of men who kept their shoes too clean and overtipped as a matter of style rather than largesse. It was a smell that Becker found often associated with cigar smoke, although there was no hint of tobacco here.

Without pause he walked around the bed and picked up the telephone.

"Send security to room 531. Immediately. Five three one . . ." He heard the sound of movement in the bathroom and dropped to his haunches beside the bed.

Donny did not know how the gabon' knew he was there, but he wouldn't be calling security just for fun. He stepped into the bedroom with the .22 held in front of him with both hands. He couldn't find the target immediately; then the mattress on the bed rose up before him. Donny fired twice into the mattress, doubting if the weak velocity of the .22 would penetrate well enough. It was a weapon Donny never intended to use from more than two feet away. The silencer drained still more power and affected the accuracy as well.

The mattress, tall as a man, raced toward him, trying to pin him in the bathroom. Donny fired once more, heard the gun cough ineffectively, then launched himself against the mattress to force a pathway to the hotel room door. The mattress fell and Donny popped another slug into it while running for the door. A hand snaked out from under the mattress and grabbed his ankle and Donny fell headlong into the living room. He kicked with his free foot and tried to shoot while writhing on his back but saw the bullet smash a lamp on a side table instead.

Scrambling to his feet, he shot down but the hand pulled back under the mattress before Donny could pull the trigger. Security was on the way, it was already too late to spend any more time killing the guy. Donny yanked the door open and fled.

Becker had stayed in a crouch while carrying the mattress, so all of the shots had gone over his head. They found the holes later, several errant but three of them surely lethal if Becker had been standing. It had required strength he knew he could not duplicate without the adrenaline that came of a fight for survival, and his back ached now as if he had just lifted a car into the air.

In the bathroom he found a discarded paperback novel and in time they would discover fingerprints of maids and bellboys and dozens of hotel guests, including Becker's own. Someday, when time permitted, Becker knew he would have to go through those prints and the identities they provided and try to find the man who wanted him dead. There were so many—men he had killed, men he caught, their families, the gangs and friends and rentable accomplices they might have hired. The result and residue of a talent for sliding into the holes where the wild things lived and emerging again with them in his jaws. Sometimes alive. More popularly dead.

He knew he should be worrying about it more than he was, but for now he was simply too tired. When the police arrived Becker got another room in the hotel so that the technicians could pore over his, and slept.

CHAPTER 26

COLE CALLED ROBIN SHEEHAN AND her "roommate" answered.

"Robin's in the shower," said the roommate from her office in FBI headquarters where all calls to Robin's telephone were forwarded. "Can you wait, or do you want her to call you back?"

"I'll call her back."

"Can I say who called?"

"Tell her Nels Kjelsen."

"Oh, I know she wants to talk to you," said the roommate, who had been selected for the job in part because of the quality of her voice. Happy, enthusiastic, confiding, and with just a hint of sexual availability, it was the type of voice that men would linger to listen to. "She'll be disappointed that she missed your call," the roommate continued. "I can get her out of the shower pretty fast."

Cole was tempted. He wanted to talk to Robin. He wanted to talk to this woman, too.

"What's your name?" he asked.

"Cheryl." The name had been selected by the experts for its euphoniousness after a random sampling of agents had preferred it to several other candidates. The roommate's real name was Deirdre, which the agents found hard to pronounce.

"I'll call back, Cheryl," Cole said reluctantly.

"I'll tell her you called."

Cole was disappointed. He had not realized how badly he had wanted to speak to Robin until he found out that he could not. He walked two blocks, watching the passersby to see if they were regarding him with anything more than normal indifference. In a city in which people wisely avoided eye contact, it was a relatively easy manner to spot real scrutiny. Anonymity was not difficult—even with a likeness of one's face on the screen and in the paper—in a city in which most people never really looked at anyone eyeball to eyeball unless they were on the other side of a security peephole.

When he found another working pay phone he called Defone Lee's answering service. After leaving his message for Defone, he called Robin Sheehan again.

This time Robin was out of the shower. Pegeen had been located and she sat in her office cubicle with a running tape machine and Meisner listening on one extension and a Bureau psychologist on another.

"Hello, how are you?" she said cheerfully. "I was hoping you'd call."

"Why?"

"Well . . . I wanted to talk to you again. I enjoyed our conversation last time."

"Oh. So did I. . . . There aren't many people who understand what I have to say."

"I'm not sure I understand everything," she said. "I'd like to hear more, though."

The psychologist gave her a thumbs-up sign of approval.

"You have such an interesting mind," she added. There was no great trick to dealing with a psychotic bomber, she reflected. Just treat him like any other man and flatter the hell out of him. She'd never met one who wouldn't respond—except Becker.

Cole talked about himself for ninety seconds, the time he had allotted to the conversation before the call could be traced. Not that he thought it *was* being traced, but there was no point in taking unnecessary chances until he knew her better.

"Are you going to be home the rest of the evening?"

Pegeen laughed lightly. "I suppose I should say that I'm going out on a date . . ."

"Why?"

"But no, I'm not. I'll be here alone the rest of the night." Meisner waved frantically.

"What about Cheryl?"

"Cheryl? . . . Cheryl's going out," Pegeen said, catching herself just in time.

"I'll call you back," Cole said, and hung up the phone.

He took a subway, standing well back from the platform until the train had stopped, rode for five stops uptown, then found another pay phone.

He spoke to Robin eight times before returning to the apartment in the Village. No call was more than two minutes in duration, and none were traceable to a specific location. No information of immediate assistance to the Bureau was transmitted. Mostly Cole talked about himself, or rather his ideas and theories, and Pegeen was sympathetic and supportive and interested.

"What a dickhead," Meisner said between calls.

"He sounds pretty average to me," said Pegeen.

"He hasn't even asked you what you're wearing."

The psychologist was puzzled. "Would most men ask what she was wearing?"

"She just stepped out of the shower? I would."

"I take it back," Pegeen said. "This schmuck is above average."

Cole concluded his final call by asking if she would be willing to meet him sometime.

It was the question they had been waiting for and this time both Meisner and the psychologist gave her excited thumbs-ups, but Pegeen hesitated for effect. "Well . . . last time . . ."

"I'll be there this time," Cole said urgently. "I promise."

"You really promise?"

Meisner tossed his head with impatience.

"I do. I'll be there. . . . You trust me, don't you?"

"Yes," Pegeen said. "Yes, I do."

"I trust you, too," he said. "Do you have a car?"

"A car?" She looked wildly to Meisner and the psychologist, neither of whom knew if Robin Sheehan had a car or not. "I can borrow one if I need it," she said finally.

"Great," said Cole.

In the way that these things work, Cole asked no questions about Robin, elicited her opinions on nothing, shared no emotion that was not his own, yet came away from the telephone calls convinced that an intimacy was growing between them. He rode the subway home feeling like a prince. For a moment he even forgot himself so far as to smile at a girl on the subway. She looked away as horrified by personal contact as if he had revealed fangs and a bloody mouth.

CHAPTER 27

TONY THE GOOD'S WIFE HAD CUT her hair and Tony was devastated by the result. In his opinion she had removed her most visible sexual characteristic. Now she looked like a man with breasts, he thought. He could no longer fantasize about her even from the rear.

Franca was pleased with the result. "It's so much easier to manage," she pointed out. "Easier to wash, I don't have to brush it forever, and it's so much cooler in the summer. Do you like it?"

Tony stared at her. She ran her fingers through her hair and it immediately fell back into place. She tossed her head and it bounced lightly.

"Tony says it gives me that gamin quality." Tony was the hairdresser, not her husband.

"The fuck's a gamin?"

"I don't know exactly," she admitted. "I think it means boyish. Audrey Hepburn had that gamin quality."

Tony stared at his wife incredulously. Did this woman look in the mirror and see any similarity to Audrey Hepburn? One of them was crazy, or blind.

"Do you like it?" she repeated, in the tone that told him there was only one answer.

"Great," he said.

Franca thought her husband seemed a little down, but then Tony had been depressed since the mob lost control of the carting industry.

Tony took a cab to the River Towers projects in Harlem. The cabdriver did not want to take him at first but Tony gave him a fifty and the driver turned into a very jovial sort, for an Israeli. After a time Tony had to tell him to shut up, he had things to think about.

At the project Tony told Avri to wait for him and flashed another fifty. Avri still looked nervous. Tony wondered how a foreigner got so scared so fast. What about ignorance being bliss and that shit?

"They won't bother you as long as you stay in the car," Tony said. "I wouldn't advise getting out and leaving it alone, but you stay put and you're okay. I won't be five minutes. Okay . . . Avri?"

"Okay," the driver said, not sounding very convinced.

Tony marched through the air of hostility that rose up before him as soon as people saw him, and entered the building defiantly. He had come to seriously regret his decision to branch out from the carting industry and its associated thuggery and into professional homicide. Nobody had warned him it would be such hard work, not to mention the people he would be dealing with. If it hadn't been for the need for his cousin Donny's respect, a nagging sense of professional honor—and the money—Tony would not be here at all. But since he was, he would do what he had to do.

This time when Auntie Berthine opened the door he shot his hand through the gap and grabbed her by the throat.

"Unlock the door, woman," he said. "I don't want to hurt you unless I have to."

"You hurtin' me now," Berthine said. But she unlatched the chain.

Tony swept through the tiny apartment in seconds. There weren't that many places to hide.

"Where's Defone?" he demanded, returning to the blind woman. She stood by the refrigerator where he had left her, her arms crossed over her chest in a posture of defiance.

"I ain't keep him here, fool. Why you think he here, anyway? You think I *live* with that bad man? I take his messages, that's all."

"You know where he is. Where is he?"

"Ain't going to repeat myself all day long. Don't know where he is, don't care where he is, never *did* know where he was. I ain't studyin' no Defone Lee. Let his own mama look out for him, ain't my worry."

"You see this gun I'm pointing at you, Mama?"

"Ain't you mama."

"You see the fucking gun or don't you?"

"No. But I believes you has one. You sound like the kind of man be threatening an old blind woman with a gun."

Tony had not realized until that moment that she was blind. He felt foolish, almost remorseful.

"Well, I'm sorry about that, but I'm going to shoot you if you don't tell me where I can find Defone Lee."

"I believes you would," she said. She took a step toward him and Tony backed up. He could see that she was blind by the way she moved with the questing turn of her head, but she kept her arms folded across her chest. He thought that was strange. She moved again and he backed up some more. It was like being approached by a witch. He wasn't *afraid* of her, but he didn't want to be touched by her, either.

"Just hold still now," he said.

"It's my apartment."

"Sit down then. Sit." She sat, her arms still folded. Tony wondered if it was because she was cold. Old people got cold no matter what the season.

"Give me something I can use here, Mama, or I'm going to have to get mean. What messages have you got for Defone?"

The old woman didn't say a word. When he moved, she moved her head to follow the sound, just a beat slower than a sighted person would do. Tony found it eerie.

"Talk to me," Tony demanded. What made an old blind black woman so stubborn?

"All that is privilege'," said the old woman.

"Privileged? Privileged? Like attorney-client?"

"Das it."

"You give me no choice. I'm going to have to rough you up. You don't want that, do you?"

"I give you a choice," she said, breaking her silence. "Get the fuck out of my apartment. How's that for a choice? Get out or I scream."

"You could yell your head off around here, I don't think anybody would care."

"They will I holler 'White man,'" she said, and began to scream.

Tony lunged for the old woman's mouth and never saw the kitchen knife that she had concealed beneath her folded arms until she slashed at him. He took the first blow on the forearm that was extended to clamp off her scream, saw the second strike coming but was only able to avert his face before the blade caught him on the scalp. In grabbing for the knife Tony released her mouth and she emitted another yelp before he could stop her.

"White man killing me!"

Tony put his left hand on her face while grappling for the knife with his right and Auntie Berthine managed to bite him so hard she loosened her dentures. Screaming himself this time, Tony moved his wounded hand to her throat and squeezed.

She was wiry but without stamina. He took the knife away from her and applied both hands to her throat. When her eyes flickered

toward unconsciousness he eased his grip and allowed her to take a shuddering breath.

"Now, Mama, I'm going to give you one more chance to talk to me." The blood from his scalp wound oozed through his hair and onto his face in a warm flood. She's killed me, he thought, feeling the great quantity of his own blood. He felt like fainting but fought it back, more fearful of the damage his reputation would suffer if he died at the hands of an old blind black woman than of the death itself. He had to get what he came for and get out of there. At least let him die in the streets, not in this musty little hole in Harlem.

Drops of blood dripped from his face to Auntie Berthine's and splashed on her cheeks and forehead. Berthine had managed to get through a life surrounded by dangerous, abusive, violent men by bluster. There was something about the sight of a woman standing on her own feet and scrapping back that amused, or cowed, or shamed most men in her experience. A combination of pluck and moral superiority was usually enough to win the day. However, she had not lived to her ripe old age by being stupid. There was a time to concede to superior force.

"That's enough, honey," she croaked. "You win."

"You going to tell me where he is?"

"Know where he's going to be," she gasped. "He supposed to meet somebody."

Tony emerged from the projects with so much blood flowing from his head wound and onto his upper body that he looked to some as if he had been decapitated. At the first sight of him Avri, the cabdriver, who had been feeling anxious in the extreme at being parked where he was, took off and drove away with a squeal of tires. Tony stood in the street impugning his ancestry as a crowd of people gathered like spectators to an arson—fascinated but removed a safe distance.

Tony pulled back his jacket so they could see his gun, but he need not have bothered. They parted before him as if he were breathing plague. He walked three blocks, caught a gypsy cab letting out a passenger, and hopped in the back before the driver realized who, or what, his fare was.

Tony gave an address in lower Manhattan where the carters union had a doctor who never asked any questions about anything and stitched and sewed and medicated and took payment only in cash.

"You ain't goin' to bleed on my seat covers now," the driver said after getting over the shock of seeing Tony.

"Nah," said Tony, who was already doing just that.

"I think you want a hospital, man."

"What I want is for you to shut your mouth and drive," said Tony. Now that he was over the initial shock he realized from having administered many in his time that head wounds bled far out of proportion to their severity. The cut in his arm was troublesome but the bite bothered him more than any of it. The old woman's dentures had not broken the skin, but they had left their impression, two crescents of sunken flesh on either side of his hand. Tony wondered if he could get infected by something lethal if the skin was still intact. He shuddered to think what might be in that crazy old woman's mouth.

It seemed to Tony that he was paying a very high price just to get started in a new career and to keep the respect of his cousin, Donny the Snake. On the other hand, he now knew where and when to kill Defone Lee.

CHAPTER 28

DEFONE LEE WORE HIS LEATHER coat despite the warm weather, because it offered him more protection than anything else he owned. What he really wanted was one of those bulletproof Kevlar vests the cops wore on their chests and another to wrap around his head. He didn't *think* the little shit Cole would have another bomb waiting for him at the telephone, but he wasn't altogether convinced that he *wouldn't,* either. Not that a vest or anything else short of a concrete wall would be much good against a bomb if it was like the one in the package that blew half the gangbangers into dog scraps. Still, there was such a thing as psychological armor, and the leather coat provided him with a measure of that. As did the wraparound sunglasses. And the porkpie hat. If he looked rather like a jazz musician of a somewhat earlier time, so what. He felt *protected* and that's what mattered.

Defone paused for a moment outside Tenny's Bar, trying to whip up some feeling of invulnerability. He wanted to go into this—whatever it was going to be—as Defone Typhoon but mustering the strength of a hurricane was hard with just his own resources. Despite the goal he had set for himself, Defone had somehow used up his supply of baby. It was difficult doing without baby once you got accustomed to being able to rely on her. Not that he was *addicted.* That was for fucking dopeheads, not someone like Defone. It was more like missing a really good friend.

Cole's message to Auntie Berthine had promised Defone half of the five million if he took a phone call in Tenny's. A man would acquire a few friends pretty fast with that kind of money. Defone still didn't trust the little honky but Cole had taken him by surprise with the package bomb. Defone hadn't even realized Cole was mad at him until then. Now that he knew what was up, Defone saw no reason he couldn't deal with him. He wasn't about to be caught off guard again.

The first thing he saw in Tenny's was the green harp painted on the mirror behind the bar. The next was the people. The fucking place was an *Irish* bar. Faces as pale as a fish's asshole turned to look at him from the stools. None of them appeared happy to see him. Leave it to Cole to find a functioning telephone in a place loaded with out-of-work Micks with hereditary drinking problems. They regarded Defone as if they just couldn't understand why all of his bones weren't broken the moment he stepped through the door.

The bartender scowled at him. "Help you?" he said, sounding as if he'd like to measure Defone for a box.

"Gimme a beer, yo," said Defone.

"Yo?" A chorus of "yo's" went down the bar, each sounding more incredulous than the one before. What was the matter with these fucking Irish?

"What kind . . . yo?" the bartender said. Some of the assholes snickered.

"You mean 'bro,' " contributed a wit. Defone ignored him.

"Do I give a shit?" Defone asked. He wasn't scared of six pink-eared, blue-eyed Irish. He didn't care if they each had a brick in their pocket. Defone had more firepower under the leather coat than your average posse. "Just don't give me what *they* be drink-

ing,'' he said, indicating the men with a contemptuous nod of his head. Fuck 'em. He didn't plan to sit around and drink with them. Let 'em get excited. He didn't mind blowing somebody away if it came to that, long as he got his phone call first. He hadn't killed a honky in almost a week.

As he walked toward the men's room and the pay phone, Defone noticed a man sitting in the booth closest to the phone. He looked like a Wop to Defone, and almost as out of place in here as he was himself. The man was studying his beer like there was something written in the foam but Defone thought he looked kind of familiar. He couldn't place him right away, but he didn't know all that many white men. It would come to him.

The phone rang just as Defone checked his watch. On the button. One of the bar boys looked as if he was inclined to answer it but Defone held up his hand.

''It for me,'' he said.

''It for you, yo?'' That got a chorus of laughs.

''Defone,'' he said into the phone, keeping his eyes on the assholes.

''Hello, Defone,'' said the familiar voice. ''It's nice to talk to you again.''

''What you be giving me a bomb for, you little motherfucker? I ought to kill your ass.''

''I didn't realize it was a bomb,'' said Cole.

Son of a bitch couldn't lie worth a shit. Sounded like some lame excuse for why he didn't have his homework—except he didn't even bother with an *excuse.*

''Whatchoo think it was, ten thousand dollars? You a *nasty* little motherfucker, ain't you? And after all I done for you. Makes a man think you ungrateful, you try to blow him up after all the favors and shit he do for you, you understand what I'm saying?''

The men at the bar had lost interest in him but the Wop was still reading the bubbles in his glass. I be in his place, sitting in a black bar, a white man comes in and gets a phone call right away on a public phone, I be wondering what the fuck, Defone thought. I sure as hell look up from my beer once in a while and check him out. You got no more curiosity than this Italian, you be brain-dead. And he don't look brain-dead. He look like he straining every nerve in his body to eavesdrop without actually moving. I watch carefully, I probably see his ear growing in my direction, Defone thought.

"I don't see any point in reliving old times," said Cole. "The past is merely prologue."

"Maybe it prologue to you, motherfucker, but I almost didn't live it. Almost had my head removed by your little brown package, supposed to be money."

"Since you mentioned money, I've figured out a way to get the five million dollars safely. I'd like to give you half of it."

Defone thought of a dozen things to say but finally said nothing.

"Are you listening, Defone?"

"You don't hear no dial tone, do you?"

"Are you interested?"

"Am I interested in five million dollars? That kind of a stupid question for a man as smart as you, ain't it?"

There you go. Saw the Guinea's ear grow about half an inch when he heard five million dollars. Don't blame him, thought Defone, it make my dick grow too.

"All right, good. We can't talk on this phone any longer," said Cole.

"You tell me where you at, I come visit you."

"Go to the lobby of the Farnham Building, Forty-fourth and Madison. There's a bank of pay phones in there. Pick up the one that rings. You can be there in twenty minutes."

"Don't fuck with me no more. Don't slip me no more exploding packages, Spring, or I'll have your guts for chitlins, you understand what I'm saying?"

Cole had already hung up on him. Defone paid for the beer,

because he didn't need no pissed-off Irish bartender chasing him down the street just now, and left the bar.

Tony Buono watched him go, looking up from his beer for the first time since he saw Defone enter. He was amazed that the spade had not recognized him. Maybe because all he saw of Tony at their first meeting was the barrel of a gun. Maybe he wasn't too concerned about face recognition at the time.

Tony had arrived a half hour too early. Maybe the old black bitch lied to him about the time, but he had been sitting in the bar far too long not to let everyone have a good look at his face. The plan had been to walk in, pop Defone while he was on the phone, and then leave in the panic and confusion following the shot. The plan was *not* to sit around and get chummy with the bartender and half the Mick customers, who kept looking at him because he was the only guy in the place without a face full of freckles.

He hurried onto the street and saw Defone walking away, heading south, taking his time. He didn't look to be in any hurry and he was doing the ghetto ramble, too, putting on that phony walk that was supposed to mean something to somebody. A half-limping, arm-swinging strut. He won't go anywhere fast walking like that, Tony thought. Which was fine. Tony could catch up with him whenever he wanted, and in the meantime, it allowed Tony time to plan his next move. He had come with the intention of capping Defone and thus doing the honorable thing to earn his money from Mr. Case. And to reverse the disapproval he had felt from Donny the Snake when he last spoke to him. Donny had called and asked Tony to set up a little favor with a collection truck, which Tony was happy to do for him. No questions. In fact, Tony never asked Donny any questions unless you considered comments like "How's it going?" a question. There was no point; Donny would never tell you anything anyway. Still, Tony knew Donny would be proud when he learned that he had completed the Defone Lee hit successfully. Tony needed Donny on his side if he was going to make a go of this business. And, of course, this thing with Defone had taken on a personal meaning, whether that was a professional attitude or not. The black bastard had shot at Tony with intent to kill—which was personal right there. And there was the matter of the blot on his reputation that failing to kill Defone would mean. If anyone ever found out that he had been outwitted or outshot by somebody like Defone Lee . . . Tony just couldn't leave him alive, that was all there was to it.

But that was what Tony had thought before he overheard Defone's conversation in the bar. Five million for Defone? The figure of five million was in the news all the time these days. That was what the bomber was demanding from the city. And Defone was carrying a package that contained a bomb—not the ten thousand Case had said was in there. Defone had even said "Spring" on the phone. The coincidence was so obvious that Tony would be a fool to ignore it. There might be a better way to handle things after all. There might be a whole lot more money involved than sixty-two fifty. He would always want Donny the Snake on his side of course—who needed a hit man for an enemy?—but it could well be that Tony would not require his active support in his new career. Tony just might retire altogether. A man could just about do that on five million dollars these days. Old Defone looked like he might all of a sudden be worth more alive than dead.

CHAPTER

LAW ENFORCEMENT IS SELDOM akin to searching for a needle in a haystack. That is too simplistic. Given enough people and enough time, every needle would be found. Unfortunately for the searchers, the medium is never as bland and uniform as hay. A better metaphor is sifting through the garbage to find one rotten egg among the ordure. Frequently the difficulty lies more in selecting from too much information than too little.

After several days of seeking out information, the machinery of the FBI began to spew it back onto Becker's desk. Within hours he knew that some 367 people thus far had laid claim to the $250,000 reward for information leading to Spring's arrest. The number could be expected to grow exponentially as good citizens turned in their bosses, co-workers, neighbors, landlords, relatives, and spouses with unaccustomed righteousness and in record numbers. All the leads would be checked out, none would prove useful. Becker was fairly certain of the results before the winnowing began but the slow sifting would continue anyway.

More information of a beneficial nature also started to come in. A check of all the telephone subscribers in the nation revealed just under two hundred males named Nels Kjelsen. More than half of them lived in Minnesota; the rest were scattered more or less randomly across the country. The closest lived in upstate New York, a drive of several hours from the city.

The quest for Coles yielded thousands.

The number of Springs was unmanageable.

The search for Becker's hypothetical bomb-testing site had produced several dozen isolated areas in the five-state region. A search of county records found that none of them belonged to a Spring, a Cole, or a Kjelsen.

Agent Vanhooven suggested to Becker that the test site was just a theory. Perhaps there was no such place in reality.

"Maybe. But I still can't believe he learned to set off bombs of this magnitude without trying one first. I want the records checked to find out the maiden name of the wife of the registered owner of each of these possible sites. Or the husband's name if the land is registered to a woman. If that doesn't turn up a Cole or a Spring or a Kjelsen, then go back to the records and find out the names of both sets of grandparents, all four of them, maiden names there, too. Start with the sites in New York State, we already have some Kjelsens there. Then run through the Springs again and look for any that have had any connection whatsoever to explosives whether through employment or education or accident. Maybe one of them lost a relative to an explosion and this is his revenge."

"What you're asking for won't show up on computers," said Vanhooven.

"So? You had other plans?

CHAPTER 30

THE LOBBY OF THE FARNHAM Building contained a convenience counter that sold magazines and candy, a bank of elevators, and a cluster of telephones removed a discreet distance from both. A uniformed functionary hovered around the registry of the building's occupants, walking occasionally to the elevators and gazing at the flashing floor buttons before strolling over to the candy counter and gossiping with the emaciated clerk there. As far as Defone could tell, the man served no useful function whatever. But one thing was certain. He was too old, too fat, too spavined, too altogether pathetic in his ancient brown uniform to be a member of the police force. In Defone's opinion, you didn't have to be very smart to be a cop, but at least you had to be certifiably alive. You had to be able to take a piss without dousing your shoes. You had to have a hand that didn't shake too much to take a bribe.

At the moment, there was no one else in the lobby. The telephones were in tiny three-quarter cubicles resting on a waist-high platform of perforated metal. Defone sank to his knees and looked under the platform for bombs. He checked the telephones themselves, not certain what he was seeking other than some wires that didn't belong. Or maybe something ticking. The old man in the uniform was watching him so Defone slapped him with the "fuck with me and die" stare, which was even more effective with the shades on. The old man quickly turned to a detailed scrutiny of the tenant listings.

The phone that was farthest from the doors and closest to the elevators rang and Defone wondered what the little shit would have done if the line was busy. He probably had the numbers for every phone in the bank and just started with the best first. By stretching the cord all the way, Defone could step around the bank and use it to shield him from most of the lobby. With his back to the functionary, there was no way the old fool or anyone else could overhear his conversation.

"Uh-huh," he said into the phone.

"Is that you, Defone?"

"No, I be the man answers pay phones."

"Hello, Defone."

"You done greeted me enough today. I want to hear some serious shit from you now."

And then he listened with interest until some fool smacked him upside the head.

Tony entered the lobby behind a delivery boy and a man in a suit and followed them past the functionary and the candy stand toward the elevators. As first the man in the business suit and then the delivery boy, not trusting the other's competence, pushed the elevator button, Tony removed the Smith and Wesson from his shoulder holster, turned it butt first, and hit Defone on the head as hard as he could.

Defone staggered a step, then turned angrily. "Fuck's the matter with you, man?" he demanded, then realized he had just been hit by the Wop from the Irish bar. Just before the gun butt crashed

against his skull again, Defone remembered where he had seen the man before today—and in somewhat similar circumstances.

The second blow dropped Defone to his knees. The third managed to render him unconscious. The businessman and the delivery boy were gawking at the scene but when Tony looked at them they both hastily looked away. The functionary was staring, mouth agape. It was a flagrant assault, even by New York standards.

"Citizen's arrest," Tony said. "This man is my prisoner . . . That okay by you?"

"Okay by me," said the functionary. "I thought he was pretty suspicious. I was thinking of doing the same thing."

The emaciated man behind the candy counter had disappeared completely.

When an elevator door opened the businessman and the delivery boy stepped inside hurriedly, being careful not to even glance in Tony's direction as they waited for the doors to close again. The people who got off peeked, then hurried past. It occurred to several that something was wrong; none felt constrained to call the police.

Tony made a very brief phone call, then took the next elevator himself. Two women arrived and were about to enter before Tony dragged Defone's body into the car. They quickly exited, then waited for the next available car as calmly as if Tony had been a service worker loading a piano.

Tony rode to the basement, dragged Defone to a dark corner by the water pipes, and frisked him. After removing what seemed to be a small arsenal of weapons he waited for help to arrive. Whenever Defone stirred and seemed to be returning to consciousness, Tony hit him on the head again. It was the kind of work that Tony was used to. He was good at swinging heavy objects against skulls and knees and forearms and had a somewhat better aim than he did when firing a pistol. Especially when no one was swinging anything back at him.

Within a few minutes three dark, dour men in sanitation workers' uniforms appeared carrying a rubbish can. They doubled Defone like a lump of dough and dumped him into the can and put on the lid. When he groaned, his voice sounding faint and cavernous through the metal bin, Tony ripped off the lid and screamed, "Shut your fucking mouth!" and Defone took his advice and made the rest of the trip out of the basement and into the street and into the back of a truck in perfect silence.

Still wearing his delivery boy disguise of bicycle clips, helmet, and satchel, Marvell got on the phone and called the number his friend had given him.

"Hello?"

"You be my friend?"

"I'm your friend, Marvell."

"How you be?"

"Was he followed?"

"Yes, sir, that sure right. Defone not only followed, he be *caught.*"

"Caught? Oh my God, caught?"

"Yes sir, friend. I seen it."

"What did they arrest him *for?*"

"For to beat his head off, looked like. The man hit him seven, eight times upside the head. Look to me like Rodney King all over again, white folks oppressing the brothers."

"Oh, spare me," said Cole impatiently.

"Don't see the *po*-licc arresting no white peoples by pistol-whippin' they heads. Only the brothers."

"Where did they take him? What precinct?"

"I had to leave, you understand. A white man beatin' on a black man, arresting him, you a smart brother you get the hell out of there, you don't stand around and watch. The police going to think you an accomplice, you understand what I'm saying? They arrest you and kick you around and show you to they dogs just because you be black and *close.* So I don't know where they took Defone Lee, 'cept down. That man sure took him down."

"You people are so paranoid."

"Ain't paranoid when someone hitting you on the head," said Marvell. What kind of shit his friend talking all of a sudden? He hadn't heard shit like this from him before, paranoia and "spare me" and disrespectful attitude. No, it was always, Marvell, can you do me a little favor, Marvell come meet me, Marvell do this for me. It was one thing to take attitude from Phistra but they wasn't no reason to take it from his friend—except for baby.

"I be wondering where at is my baby," Marvell said. "You be promising me some baby for the last job, taking them pictures. I be taking your pictures, but I ain't seen no baby yet."

"I'm out of baby just now."

"*I* be out of baby."

"We're both out of baby, Marvell. There's no point in whining about it. We have a current shortfall. I'm temporarily separated from the means of manufacture—"

"What kind of shit you talking now? You promised me my baby. I done *two* jobs now and ain't seen no baby, ain't even seen no cash money."

"You think only of yourself. What about me? I'm in the midst of a very complicated situation right now. I'm doing nothing less than trying to change society, I'm shaking it at its very roots, I'm tearing this system *apart,* Marvell . . ."

"Don't know nothing about that."

"Read your newspaper, Marvell. I'm blowing all the entrenched and codified establishment rules away. I'm letting some *air* into the political argument."

"Well, ain't you some fine shit piled up a mountain high. What about *paying* me, motherfucker? Maybe you can live on your own gas, but I ain't going to."

"I don't know if you're stupid or just ignorant, but you seem to be incapable of understanding a concept bigger than your immediate carnal pleasures."

Cole hung up, leaving Marvell to stare furiously at the telephone. He had been dissed many times before, most of his childhood because of his quiet, noncombative nature—he was a coward—and all of his adulthood, because of his childhood. But it was always by someone bigger, stronger, meaner. Phistra fell into all three categories. But he had never been dissed by telephone, certainly not by a pale-faced, weaselly, dirty-haired, half-assed, deadbeat, no-pay little honky.

CHAPTER 31

JASON COLE MADE HIS OWN entrance into a garbage truck with vastly more comfort and ceremony than had Defone. Under Donny's direction the men whom Tony had loaned to him made a sheltered cubicle with metal cans and plywood sheets deep within a bed of refuse in the back of a compactor truck. Despite their assurances that it was safer than a bus and more comfortable than the sofa at home, Cole refused to get in unless Donny joined him. Sighing with exasperation, Donny the Snake climbed into the recess first.

"These guys are experts, Jason," he said.

"I'll feel better," said Cole.

Donny settled down tailor-fashion and held out a hand to assist Cole. When the two were ready, the men from Tony's union tossed in several more cans of garbage reserved for the purpose, then very slowly compacted the men and garbage so that one was snug upon the other. In the total blackness, hearing the whir of the engine close upon them, Donny said, "They've done this before. They know what they're doing."

Cole squeezed Donny's hand and Donny squeezed back, trying to exude more confidence than he felt. He had wanted to think of a more elegant way to leave the city but with every cop at every exit armed with pictures of Jason, and with time at a premium, it was the best he could come up with. After the explosion of the FBI man on the Triborough, the police were opening crates, checking trunks, peering into boxes. Inelegant measures were called for and Donny took a philosophical view. It had been hard enough to convince Jason to leave Manhattan in the first place.

The truck headed toward the Holland Tunnel and the long line that inched toward the police checkpoint. In the blackness of their cubicle, Cole moved closer to Donny.

"I'm a little claustrophobic," Cole said.

Donny remembered the cramped hovel of an apartment in which Donny had first found him.

"There's nothing to it," Donny said in whisper. "It's just like sitting in a chair. You don't need more space when you're in a chair, do you? The chair is plenty. This is plenty."

Donny put his arm around Cole. He felt the other man shivering with fright.

"It's all right," he said gently. "You're okay."

"I don't like it," Cole said in his childish voice.

"You're okay." Donny sniffed.

"I don't like it." They felt the truck lurch and move forward slightly, then come again to a halt. "I want out."

"Shh."

"I want *out*."

"Keep your voice down."

"Let me out of here. Let me out! I want out!"

"Shut up," Donny hissed, groping in the dark, trying to get a proper hold on Cole who was now pulling away. Donny heard him striking the plywood wall of their enclosure.

"Please! Let me out! Please!"

Donny wrapped both arms around him but Cole was struggling

wildly, scratching at the boards, flailing with his head. If he managed to knock down the wall, Donny feared they would be buried in garbage.

"Cut it out. Cut it *out.*"

"I have to get out! I have to get out!"

"You're all right, I've got you, you're okay."

"Please! Please!"

One of the carters got out of the truck and banged on the side to quiet the occupants. The police were only a few car lengths away. The blow resonated in the cubicle like a tap on the side of a submarine. Donny clamped a hand over Cole's mouth and pushed him down. He spread his body atop Cole's, wrapping his legs around the other man's to keep them from thrashing. The further restriction made Cole more frantic and he struggled desperately, twisting his body, trying to throw Donny off, and continuing to scream through the muffling hand.

"You're going to give us away," Donny hissed into his ear. "Now shut the fuck up."

Cole bucked beneath him, thrashing as best he could. Donny squeezed Cole's legs between his own, bearing down with all his weight on the other man's body. He clamped his hand so firmly that he could feel Cole's teeth.

"If you don't stop I'm going to hurt you."

The threat of pain made Cole hysterical. He thrust and bounced and twisted maniacally beneath Donny's weight. Whimpers rose from the back of his throat. Donny clutched and scrabbled for purchase with his toes and pressed his cheek against Cole's face, trying to stop the thrashing.

The truck moved forward and the police were there, speaking to the drivers, checking license, registration, carting permit. Mirrors were run under the vehicle to check for bombs and the dogs were encouraged to sniff. At the order, the hydraulic press was opened and the police, clearly daunted, viewed the compressed pile of garbage. With a nod of distaste the okay was given and the driver's assistant carefully closed the press once more.

Hearing the whir of the big machine, Cole went completely crazy. Only the noise of the machinery drowned out his cries, which sounded to Donny like open roars.

Cole felt the rap of cold metal against his temple and froze immediately. He did not need to see to know that Donny had the pistol pressed against his head. His hysteria dissolved into the cold sweat of mortal fear.

"Good," Donny whispered, and then the truck was moving forward, not crawling or lurching this time but driving smoothly and at speed. They were past the roadblock, in the tunnel and on their way out of Manhattan.

With the struggle over and the rhythmic bouncing of the truck propelling him up and down atop Cole, Donny realized he had an erection. This was not professional, he thought. He wondered if Jason felt it—but how could he not?

"You okay now?" Donny asked.

Cole murmured something softly and Donny removed his hand from Cole's mouth at last. Cole breathed as deeply as he could, in a shuttering gasp. Donnie realized his fingers were sore from gripping so hard. He could only imagine what Jason's face felt like.

"I'm okay," Cole finally managed to say.

Donny made no haste to get off.

The compactor truck let them off in an alley behind a restaurant in Union City, New Jersey. The two union men helped Donny and Cole out of their improvised shelter amid the garbage as if they were elderly royalty. Although they had no idea who Cole was—

and would not have cared much if they did—they knew that Donny was Snake Sabela. If there was any indignity involved in traveling in the business end of a garbage truck, it did not occur to them to imagine it as tainting Donny the Snake. Donny was not a thug or strong-arm or tough guy. Anybody could wield a baseball bat against a victim, and most of the people they worked with had indeed done so at some time or other, but few could pass through solid walls the way it was said the Snake could do. Few could penetrate electronic security systems as easily as bad air or make themselves invisible to bodyguards or silence sentry dogs with a single look as could the Snake. Donny had killed a Colombian drug lord holed up in a Manhattan hotel room filled with trigger-happy, Uzi-toting spics. He'd left the hotel and returned home before the spics even realized their boss was dead. They just thought he was taking a long time deliberating his next move in the card game, the story went.

In the future, if they spoke at all of their trip with Donny the Snake, it would be with pride, they thought. They would not speak of the stench of rotting food or of the shrimp shells clinging to the Snake's back or of the browning lettuce glued to his shoes by smashed tomato. But, in fact, they would not live long enough to speak of any of it to anyone except each other.

Donny was extracted first and then he helped the others pull Cole out of the truck and into the alley. Donny said a quick word of thanks and the men backed out of the alley and headed back to the long wait to reenter the tunnel and return to New York.

Only after the truck had gone did Donny notice that Cole had left his bag of belongings behind.

Cole shrugged. "It doesn't matter. The only things I have that are important are up here." He tapped his skull in the spot where Donny had touched him with the barrel of his pistol. "Materialism is part of the abiding problem in this nation. If everyone made do with half of what they now possess—which is a hundred times more than the rest of the world has—our environmental problem would shrink to a manageable problem overnight . . ."

Fearing an onslaught of theories, Donny led him into the restaurant where a friend was waiting.

"There are a couple of things I'd like to pick up, though," Cole said as Donny led him to a booth where a singularly anemic-looking man was sucking on a breadstick as though it were a surrogate cigar. "Just a few chemicals."

Defone had been awake for some time but chose to act unconscious. It was the only time they weren't killing him. If it was up to him he'd play dead for days until they got tired of beating on him and shit. They wouldn't permit that, of course.

He heard one of them walking across the room toward him, the footsteps echoing in the empty room, heard him stop a step away.

"You're breathing different, Defone." Defone recognized the voice of the one the others called Tony. The asshole from the bar, the asshole from Harlem, from the lobby of the Farnham Building. The asshole who had done most of the killing so far. Others helped out when he got tired, but mostly it was Tony holding Defone's head underwater until Defone was sure his chest would explode.

"You have a different way of breathing when you're really unconscious. Did you know that?"

How the hell was Defone supposed to know that? He couldn't hear himself breathe if he was unconscious.

Tony slapped him and Defone's eyes popped open. What did he see but the Wop motherfucker smiling at him like it was all some fun game. Some game he must be winning because Defone sure as hell wasn't. Defone had yet to score a point. He didn't even know

the rules. He had volunteered to cooperate with Tony and the others as soon as they dumped him from the garbage can onto the bare concrete floor of the enormous garage. Tony hadn't even bothered to tell him what he wanted but set right out to try to drown him, plunging Defone face first into a vat of something that was at least part water. Part oil, part grease, part shit for all Defone could tell. He wasn't no chemist, all he knew is you couldn't breathe the stuff, not more than one lungful at any rate. Tony had yanked him up by the hair, Defone sputtering and promising to tell, to do, to be whatever Tony wanted. Wop pushed his head right back under, held it there for longer than Defone believed possible. Same thing the third time and the fourth. After that Defone stopped trying to talk when his head was up, just spent all his energy sucking in the air before he was thrust under again or until he passed out. This was the third time he had come back to consciousness and he was beginning to wonder why he bothered.

"How you feeling about now, Defone?" Tony smiling at him. Like it was some kind of Guinea joke.

"There be something you like me to do for you?" Defone asked. " 'Cause you got me convinced."

"How about sucking my cock, Defone? You be willing to do that now?"

"If that's what you're used to," Defone said, regretting it immediately. They had his head underwater so fast Defone didn't remember them even crossing the room.

"I do it!" he sputtered as they brought him up.

"Do what?"

"Suck your dick."

"How about rimming my asshole? You like to do that to all of us, Defone?" asked another voice.

"You bet!"

"You want to be our pussy now, Defone?" The second voice. Motherfucker looked just like Tony, far as Defone could tell. Dark hair, too many eyebrows, nose like a chunk of rock.

"I be your pussy. Whatever you say."

"You ready to lie down and spread 'em?" asked a third voice. Defone caught a glimpse of this one out of the corner of his eye. Looked to Defone like if you hit Tony hard enough a chip would fly off and it would look like the third guy.

"I do that," Defone said, his eyes rolling wildly. To his own amazement he realized he was crying. "Whatever, just tell me, just tell me."

"He's done," Tony said, as if Defone was a piece of meat on the barbecue. Tony knew when a man was broken. It was his business to take them to the breaking point. He had done it many times, like this with the water, with baseball bats, with pliers, with as many ways as imagination and time permitted. The water was best, it left no marks, didn't even cause real pain. Just unmitigated terror. Occasionally he had gone too far in his persuasions and had been unable to pull the victim back, but not often. It happened, but it was not the purpose of the exercise. Cooperation was what the union required. Heartfelt, sincere cooperation. It was what Tony wanted from Defone.

They returned Defone to his chair and strapped his arms and legs once more. Tony pulled up another chair and faced Defone from three feet away.

"You want to talk to me now, Defone?"

"I tol' you I talk the minute you bring me in. Didn't have to keep killing me."

"I wanted to get your complete attention. I don't want you to say one thing and be thinking another. I want your heart and your head and your tongue all in sync. You understand me there, Defone?"

"Got my complete attention. Who you want me to kill?"

"I don't want you to kill anyone, Defone. I happen to do that sort of thing myself. What I want you to do is tell me everything about Spring and the five million dollars."

"Spring?"

"Don't do that, Defone."

"No, sir. I see what you mean. That just a bad habit. I'm going to tell you *everything* about Spring."

And he did.

CHAPTER

32

VANHOOVEN BURST INTO BECKER'S office as if he were crashing through the line for extra yardage. His face was flushed with excitement and he was working hard to suppress a triumphant smile that he did not think was professional.

"We got a live one," he said, braking abruptly to keep from colliding with Becker's desk.

Becker considered him calmly. In the last few hours the case had begun to pick up speed as all the diligent digging and screening started to pay off. He knew it was a dangerous time for the unit's morale. If they became too hopeful now, it would make any setback seem worse. If possible, Becker wanted to maintain an atmosphere of positive skepticism. Expect the worst but keep plowing ahead. For ninety percent of the time in ninety-nine percent of the cases it was the only sensible way to proceed. The roller-coaster swoop downward—that final exhilarating ride they worked doggedly toward and would remember when the case was long dead—would take up the remaining fraction, but it could not be anticipated too much or they would never make the long climb to the top of the track.

"What's your live one?"

"Somebody claiming the reward says he has Spring's phone number."

"Who is this one turning in? His mother-in-law? The local parson?"

"I know, I know," said Vanhooven, "but this one is different."

"How different?"

"He mentioned Defone Lee."

Becker rose from his chair.

"Fill me in on the way," he said, leading Vanhooven from the room. Anyone who had connected Defone Lee to Spring or Cole was to be taken with utmost seriousness. Theirs was not a connection that had been in the news or anywhere else outside of law enforcement circles.

Vanhooven looked at his notes as he hurried to keep pace with his superior. "A man named Marvell Samson. He says he knows Defone worked for Spring. He says he saw Defone get arrested, too, and he wanted to claim the reward before Lee does."

"Who arrested Lee? When did that happen? I haven't heard about it."

"I don't know. I couldn't find anyone who has him. But this Samson says he saw the cop take him down."

"Where is Spring now?"

"He didn't know. He only had a phone number. He said he spoke to him yesterday."

"You've got the address to go with that phone number," Becker said. It was not a question.

"Of course. It's in Greenwich Village. We can be there in fifteen minutes."

"Have you alerted anyone else?"

"No, sir."

"Good, I don't want a bunch of sirens scaring him off. We'll seal him off first. And notify a bomb squad to stand by. We're not going to walk into a trap again, either. Meanwhile, get somebody to track down Defone Lee. If he's been arrested, we want to talk to him. In fact, freeze him. Make sure he talks to *no one*, including—especially—the NYPD until we're finished with him."

The process of evacuating all the neighbors and then entering and securing the apartment at which Marvell had called his friend took two hours. The forensic people required three more for their work in the apartment. Becker's personal involvement had ended when it was determined that no one was at home in the apartment. He returned as the forensic people compiled their survey, plucking fibers and hairs and dust motes and placing each of them in its own plastic evidence bag. It was meticulous labor that could provide information that was useful in court but it was seldom of much value to the men who were actively seeking a suspect.

Vanhooven followed Becker through the rooms of the apartment, conferring with his notepad. Becker toured the apartment once quickly and then strolled through it slowly, stopping to study things that caught his eye.

"The apartment is registered to a Donald Sabela," Vanhooven informed him. "He doesn't have much of a record. He was brought in nine years ago as a material witness on the felonious death of one Remo Scarfani. He was charged briefly with manslaughter and the charges were dropped for lack of evidence."

Becker paused by the sofa where an investigator's legs squirmed as the man wriggled underneath. A pillow and a light blanket were crumpled on the sofa.

Vanhooven had stopped. "I'm listening," Becker said, still watching the investigator's legs.

"The deceased was a known homosexual and suspected of having peripheral mob connections through a cousin. There was speculation at the time that he was hit because the bosses found out about his homosexuality. There was also speculation that Donald Sabela

was a spurned lover. Apparently there was no solid evidence for any of it and Sabela walked. He has had no dealings with the police since."

"You said hit. What makes them think so? How did Scarfani die?"

Vanhooven looked at his notes. "A twenty-two slug through the ear, another between the eyes . . . and two through the testicles."

"The twenty-two sounds like a hit, all right. But shot in the nuts? That's the spurned-lover theory?"

"Apparently. Not the sort of thing a pro would normally bother to do."

"Doesn't sound to me like the work of a talented amateur, either."

"Pardon me?"

"Not quite a joke, it didn't reach that level. Just a wiseass remark."

"Yes, sir. Got it."

"So we're looking at a mob connection here? I'm amazed. It didn't look like their work at all. . . . Are the arresting officers still around? Maybe they can tell us more about Sabela. And how he knew we were coming to see him."

"Are you sure he knew?"

"Did you see his bedroom? Neat as a hospital room, not a sock out of place, the bed was made with hospital corners. The guy is completely anal. Would a man like that leave the house with two coffee cups on the counter, half full? There's a spoon on the floor by the sofa, the newspaper's on the floor, the bathroom sink has toothpaste in it, there are dirty dishes in the kitchen sink. The sofa is a mess. Either our man Sabela underwent a very rapid personality transformation, or he left *immediately*."

The investigator wriggled out from under the sofa. He looked like a college student to Becker. A fraternity brother condemned to live under the furniture as part of his initiation.

"Next time you can tip the sofa," Becker said gently.

"I didn't want to rearrange anything," said the youthful agent.

"What did you find?"

"Some fibers, sir. I can't say what they are just yet and a—uh—well, it's not evidence . . ."

"What?"

"There's a smell under there and the carpet is pressed down as if something fairly heavy was resting on it."

"What's the smell?"

"It's not real strong and I may be wrong . . ."

"Go ahead."

The young agent held his fingers to his nose and sniffed again to be sure. "Well, it smells like gunpowder."

Becker bent and delicately sniffed the man's fingers, as if he were offering a flower.

"Black powder," Becker said. "You're right, son, that's what it is. That's what he uses in his pipe bombs."

"You think Sabela is Spring?" Vanhooven asked.

"No, I think Spring was sleeping on the sofa and keeping his stash underneath. Sabela was his host unless Spring drinks out of two coffee cups at the same time. Have you contacted the arresting officers yet? We need to know more about Sabela."

Vanhooven glanced again at his notes. "One is dead . . ."

"How?"

"I don't know."

"The arrest was only nine years ago? It shouldn't have been from natural causes. Find out."

"Right."

"Where's the other officer?"

"He's a detective now. Working undercover for the NYPD terrorist squad. His name is Luis Rodriquez."

"I met him. Let's talk to him. Meanwhile find out everyone who was present when this Marvell Samson gave the phone number

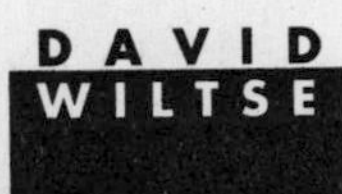

where he called his *friend.* Somebody recognized that phone number and called to give a warning. Or maybe they were trying a little free-lance sleuthing and just called the number to see who was here and gave things away—I don't know. Find out. And talk to Luis Rodriquez. See if he can tell you anything more about Donald Sabela."

The telephone rang and the agents in the apartment froze in place, all of them looking at the instrument as intently as if it were a man with a gun.

"Is there an answering machine connected to this?" Becker asked the room in general after the third ring.

"Not in here," said a voice from the bedroom.

"Not in here, sir," said the agent who had come from under the sofa.

After the fourth ring Becker took an evidence bag from a forensic man, put it on his hand like a mitten, and picked up the receiver.

"Yeah?" he said gruffly.

"Who's this?" said a man's voice.

"You're calling me. Who are *you?*" Becker said.

"Is Donny there?"

"He's in the shower. You want me to get him?"

"Yeah."

"I ain't going to disturb him unless I can tell him who's calling," Becker said.

The agents watched Becker's performance in absolute silence.

"Tell him it's Tony."

"Tony who? There's hundreds of Tonys."

"Just tell him Tony. Who the fuck are you, anyway?"

"Hang on, I'll tell him."

Vanhooven turned on the water in the kitchen sink and Becker pointed the phone in that direction. As verisimilitude went it wasn't great, but would have to do.

"He says he'll call you back. Where are you?"

"I'm in the garage."

"What garage is that?" Becker asked.

"*My* garage, jack-off. He's got the number. Tell him I wanted to know if those guys showed up with the truck like he asked for. I ain't heard back from anybody yet."

"Just a sec." Becker indicated to Vanhooven to turn the water back on. Becker waved the telephone toward the sound again. "He says you sent the wrong kind of truck."

"What you mean, the wrong kind? What kind did he want?"

"What kind did you send?"

"A regular compactor. What kind did he want?"

"What the fuck's a compactor?" Becker demanded, sounding annoyed.

"Who are you?"

"I'm the guy who's fucking your sister, all right? You expect me to tell him you sent a compactor and I don't even know what that is?"

Vanhooven stifled a laugh and the young agent listened in amazement. It seemed a strange way to conduct a probing conversation with an unknown subject. Certainly not the way it was taught at the academy. On the other hand, the other party was staying on the line.

"Donny knows what it is, asshole. You know who you're talking to with shit like that about my sister?"

"No. Who am I talking to? Tony the Phony? Bony Tony? Tony Baloney? Tony the hard-on who gets on the phone like a tough guy tries to make me run errands like I'm his servant. Let me tell you something, asshole, before you go making any more threats. You don't got any idea who I am. For all you know I'm Gino Scalese, all right? I could have some people come to your garage and use that telephone for your suppository, you understand, big mouth? Show some fucking manners."

Tony was silent for a long time and Becker feared that he had lost him.

"He wants a number where he can call you," Becker said in a calmer tone after a pause. "He says he wants to talk to you."

"Well, I want to talk to him. And one of the things I'm going to talk to him about is you, dickhead."

"I warned you about that. You show some respect or I hang up right now. Now what's your number he can call you right back?"

"He's got my number."

"You going to make him get out of the shower? He's pissed enough as it is. You know how he gets when he's mad."

"Who the fuck *are* you?"

"I'm the guy answering the fucking phone. Who the fuck are *you?*"

The line went dead in Becker's ear. He shrugged and hung up the receiver.

"Mr. Sabela has one friend, at least," Becker said. "Tony who has a phone in his garage." He turned to Vanhooven. "Get in touch with the NYPD Organized Crime people. See if that means anything to them. Tony who has a garage and a connection with Sabela and can send men with a compactor truck. Also, get on the phone company and get a list of all the numbers that rang through to this number today."

"They don't normally keep a list of *incoming* calls," Vanhooven said, scribbling at his pad.

"I know they don't and if any calls were long-distance from different carriers they may not be able to get the information at all, but you can tell them that the FBI and the NYPD and the mayor and the governor and every citizen of this city will be very grateful if they oblige. If we're extremely lucky we might find out who tipped off Sabela and Spring a few hours ago and maybe even who sent the truck to drive them away."

A beeper sounded and five men reached for theirs. It was Becker's. Using his improvised mitten again, he called the office and listened silently for a minute.

"Which way was it going?" he asked, then nodded sadly at the response.

When he was finished with the telephone he turned to the men in the room with ashen face. "A garbage truck just exploded in the Holland Tunnel. Seven people are dead. The tunnel is closed."

When the murmur of dismay died down, Becker asked, "Would a garbage truck be a compactor?"

"You think he had an accident transporting some of his bombs?" Vanhooven asked hopefully.

"We wish," said Becker glumly. "I'm afraid the news is worse. The truck was heading *into* Manhattan. Assuming Spring was sending the bomb to us deliberately—and we have to assume he was—then it means he's escaped. He's safe. He's gotten out of Manhattan."

CHAPTER 33

PEGEEN WOKE TO THE SOUND OF a desperate struggle for life, a soul-deep gasp for breath and the crash of a body breaking through the wooden box that imprisoned it. She realized that the gasp was her own and that she had left her weapon across the room. She had to get to it, there was someone else in the darkened room. The horrible noise of splintering wood came again and she knew that the someone else was not only in the room but naked in bed beside her.

"Holy Christ," she muttered as full memory of the night before flooded back to her. She needed to get to her weapon to shoot herself.

Meisner emitted another wrenching snore, like a penful of hogs snorting in unison. Like two boars fighting, she thought. Or worse, like two hogs rutting. She wondered what had possessed her, what deranged instinct could have so completely overcome her common sense, not to mention her taste, her rudimentary faculty for proper judgment, and her heretofore strongly developed aversion to Meisner as a sex partner.

It was that stupid grin, she told herself. She had been vulnerable because of the stress of the case, the anxiety about Becker's episode with the attempted assassin, the nights with insufficient sleep. They had drunk a couple of beers together, only two for her, nothing irresponsible, and she had wept a little—something she did from time to time for reasons emotional or hormonal or tidal, she was never certain which—and Meisner had comforted her by putting his arm around her and that had felt nice enough, in itself, as a disembodied arm having nothing to do with the man himself, and she had looked up at him from time to time to apologize and each time he had given her that loopy, lopsided, half-demented, *understanding* grin and for some reason that had made her weep even more and when he kissed the tears off her cheeks there had suddenly seemed no compelling reason not to let him continue. He had muttered something inaudible that had sounded like a sweet sentiment at the time and when he got around to unbuttoning her blouse Pegeen—God help her—had *wanted* him to do it and to do more and to keep on doing it until she screamed with release that seemed about six months overdue and then, amazingly, he had just kept going and going like the battery-powered bunny and Pegeen had forgotten the worry about seeming selfish that usually plagued her right about that time and besides she didn't think she could have stopped him if she'd wanted to—and she didn't really want to—and damned if she didn't scream again and then, in a tribute to chivalry that wasn't dead after all, a third and fourth time before she really *did* begin to feel selfish and tried to do something for him but as it turned out he was doing just fine on his own, thank you, which he gasped to her, so she gave up her brief attempt at charity and lay back to accept this remarkable gift from this surprising man and screamed a final time for good measure as he collapsed at last, groaning and shivering and panting. They had both laughed as soon as they caught their breath because although it didn't seem especially funny it did have the feel of something amazing about it. When he tried to roll off of her she wrapped her arms around him and wouldn't let him go and he really relaxed

then, putting more of his weight on her and grunting "yeah" as if he was in agreement with her, as if something beyond the physical had just passed between them, which Pegeen wasn't ready to concede, not at all, and then she was crying again, that damned leakage problem, but this time it had nothing to do with Becker, and once more he kissed her tears and stroked her hair and said sweet, inaudible mumbles that were much more affecting than real words could have been. In fact she hoped he wouldn't talk, not for days, because she knew that when he did he would louse things up, he would say the wrong things, he would put his foot in it for sure—and besides, what was there to say anyway? It was a stupid thing to do with the wrong person at the wrong time and she had needed it with ravenous desperation and maybe so had he unless he was just a steam engine by nature and did it this way every time, which it occurred to Pegeen was probably the case because why would he treat her any differently than he did everyone else and that made her realize that this was just another lay for him, which infuriated her even though she felt fully justified in making it just another lay for *herself* which seemed to her to be an entirely different matter although she could not explain why. But then she didn't have to explain a thing, especially if they both kept their mouths shut, which suited her just fine as she was beginning to get really pissed off about his treating her like just any off-the-rack fuck, not to mention ashamed of herself and, in retrospect, maybe a little embarrassed at all that noise and the weeping and the general vulnerability that she had displayed with such a wonderful sense of liberation only minutes before. He was apparently thinking the same thing because he was not saying anything although Pegeen realized that in his case it could have been because of a certain oxen obtuseness rather than misgivings and then he twitched and she realized it was because the fucking ape was falling asleep and she eased out from under him not wanting him to wake up, God knows, and it looked as if he might so she lay very still beside him and when he put his arm across her body she let it stay there and maybe, to keep him comfortably asleep, she even snuggled in against him a little bit, feeling the great heat of his body and not being quite as angry as she had been a moment earlier because . . . and she had forgotten why because . . . and she fell asleep while his breath was ruffling her hair and whispering softly and soothingly past her ear—until hours later when he made the explosive porcine sounds that woke her with a start and an enveloping sense of guilt.

The phone rang and Pegeen grabbed it, as if by getting it quickly enough she could prevent the caller from actually looking into her bedroom.

"Good morning." It was Spring's voice, brighter, cheerier than usual.

"Morning," she managed, trying to shift shapes into her other persona. For a panicked second she could not even remember her other name.

"Did I wake you up?"

She looked at the clock. It was five in the morning. Of course he woke her up, or should have.

"Yes," she said. Meisner was awake now, staring at her with soulful, if groggy, intensity.

Oh, no, she thought. He looks like he wants to take up where he left off. Not in the light of day. Not cold sober. Not so goddamned *early*. She turned her back to him. She couldn't deal with both men at once.

Spring was asking her to take the day off. "Just call in sick," he urged. "You can do that, can't you?"

"I suppose," said Pegeen. Robin could be sick if she had to, why not? "But why?"

"You trust me, don't you?"

Men always said that. Pegeen had trusted none of them after the

first two had proven to be liars on a grand, that is to say typically masculine, scale.

"I trust you . . . but I don't understand," she said. She heard Meisner get out of the bed behind her.

"I have a surprise for you today," said Spring.

"What kind of surprise?"

"I can't tell you, that would give it away."

Jack-off, she thought. Jerk the poor girl around, keep her in the dark, expect her to jump through fucking hoops for you while you commit to nothing. She wanted to yell into the phone, to tell the scumbag to come visit her, she had a little surprise for him as well.

"Well . . . okay—if it's important."

"It's important," he said. "I'll call you later when everything is set up."

He rang off just as the toilet flushed. She turned to see Meisner coming out of the bathroom. He had put on his green bikini underpants, which made Pegeen feel even more naked than she already was. Short of grabbing a sheet to cover her body like some virgin in an old movie, there was nothing for it but to sit there buck naked and pretend she wasn't self-conscious.

"Look . . ." she started to say as he took her arms and lifted her to her feet.

He embraced her, holding her tightly, pressing his cheek next to hers for he was no taller than she. He held her for so long that Pegeen began to relax and to actually feel him against her, the whole length of him. As time passed without his saying anything and he continued to hold her in his arms with a kind of vibrant intensity, she began to feel as if he was actually communicating something to her and whatever it was it wasn't all that bad and she ceased to resist and felt her body give in to him at last as if she had taken a small leap, nothing grand, nothing more than a hop, but it seemed to take her out of a quagmire and onto dry land and even as she thought it she didn't fully understand what it meant, either what *it* meant or what *she* meant by making it a metaphor in her mind. Not that she cared very much.

Finally he moved, shaking his head as if stupefied, and still holding her, he said, "Never in my life." But he said it very low and reverentially and Pegeen wasn't sure she had heard him correctly even though the words were clear enough.

"Not in my whole life," he said, with the same awe, and there was no mistaking him this time.

"Look," she said once more, wanting to forestall any exuberant or pro forma and dishonest protestations of affection—or partly wanting to but still willing to be dissuaded. As before he did not let her finish but put his lips on hers, just brushed them really. She smelled the toothpaste on his breath and realized he had done that for her and felt for a moment rather discourteous for she had not done as much for him but then he put his lips on hers fully and she soon forgot her general inclination to disapprove of him and herself.

He made love differently in the morning, slower, more gently, but with the same attention to detail and the same elephantine stamina that had her writhing and making noises again. She was grateful that he did not introduce any gymnastics or contortions or lotions and creams the second time around but handled her as if the basic thing was the best of all and not as if he needed novelty right away or as if he was into some kind of performance and she a trained seal to put through its paces.

She never lost control the way she did the night before, which was to say that she never approached the point of blacking out or of not being aware of where she was—and for a few moments even *who* she was—but which was *not* to say that she didn't have all the pleasure she wanted because she did, she had a good deal more than she was used to, but when he rolled over and put her on top as if to say go for it, she wondered just what he thought there was left to

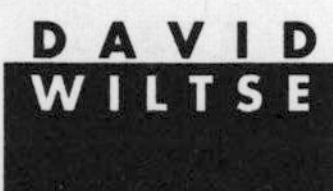

go *for.* And then she found out and thought oh my goodness, how did *he* know? She looked down at his face once while she was above him. He had his eyes closed, which was fine, but then he opened them and made contact with hers and just sort of sucked her into them, somehow, as if he had a huge dark hole in there behind his eyes just waiting to be filled by her and Pegeen blinked because that was not what she wanted to see, or even know about, because he was still in all ways terribly unsuitable—or at least in all ways but this one—and when she glanced at him again the hole was closed over and he was giving her that silly grin which was a lot easier for her to handle. She looked away from him anyway, lifted her head and closed her eyes and turned up the velocity and goddamned *went* for it. She heard him moan, but it seemed far in the distance and she was not about to stop or even slow down for she was taking no prisoners and showing no mercy and then the top of her head came off and her body turned to flame and streaks of lightning zipped back and forth behind her eyes and she *had* to stop or die.

Afterwards, but *immediately* afterwards so that he wouldn't start kissing her tears again, she told him about the phone call from Spring. They both quickly decided that they still had some time left since Spring obviously wasn't going to do anything in the way of contacting her until her working day started, which was still close to four hours away. The more pressing problem was to figure out how to fill those four hours.

But they managed.

CHAPTER 34

BECKER POSTPONED HIS HELICOPTER takeoff for his meeting with the Nels Kjelsen who lived in upstate New York for the second day in a row after the mail arrived. He had been scheduled to leave the first time when Marvell Samson surfaced with the tip on Spring's phone number. His second departure was scheduled for first thing in the morning following the explosion in the Holland Tunnel. The letter arrived before then. The post office in the FBI's zip code zone had been alerted to notify the Bureau of the arrival of *any* mail addressed to the New York offices of the FBI as soon as it arrived in the building. Considering the possibility that any packages sent to the Bureau during the duration of the Spring case might well be explosive, the post office managers were most happy to oblige. Members of the bomb unit whisked everything that arrived into specially shielded vans and transported it to a lead-lined vault where it was subjected to X rays, sonograms, and other tests before being passed on to the addressee.

This procedure meant that mail trickled into the office throughout the day and night regardless of the hour. Becker, who had finally given in to reality and had a cot installed in his office, was awakened by a nervous clerk at five-thirty in the morning, an hour and a half before his scheduled departure.

Becker squinted blearily at the clerk, who held an envelope addressed to "Becker, FBI."

He recognized the block letters printed in Magic Marker and sat up, reaching for it.

"You said whenever it came in," said the clerk.

"Right," he said, clearing his throat. "Thank you."

The latest message made another demand for ransom. That same afternoon.

Two hours later Becker emerged from an extraordinary conference in which he had heard both the mayor of the city of New York and the governor of the state of New York urge the FBI to pay the five-million-dollar ransom, in full, to a terrorist.

The sole dissenting voice had belonged to Becker's boss, Hatcher.

"It's a matter of principle," Hatcher argued.

The mayor, a Democrat, said it was a matter of lives, and the Republican governor added that it was also a matter of property. No one seemed to think that it was a matter of money. Five million, in the grand scheme of things involving entities as large as the city and state, was of very little consequence at all. The city had been paying off the mob, in one way or another, for decades.

Finding himself outnumbered and outranked, Hatcher quickly tempered his stance, pointing out that he could only advise the elected officials what to do.

"It's not as if I could state unequivocally that we would catch this man Spring, is it?" Hatcher said accusingly to Becker following the meeting.

"Certainly not in front of the mayor and the governor," Becker said. "If you did they might hold you responsible for something."

"You have my full support, John, you know that. But this is very much your show. You've made it clear you want it that way. . . . And we've lost a tramway, a bridge, and a tunnel. It's understandable that people are getting impatient."

"And an agent," Becker said. "We lost an agent, too. Or did you forget about McArthur?"

"Of course not. A terrible loss."

"I didn't see you at the funeral."

"My plane was delayed. The important thing is, I'm here now and I'm prepared to offer you any assistance you need."

"Why don't you take it upon yourself to stop the leak? Someone has tipped him off that we were coming. Twice."

"The Bureau is looking rather foolish, John."

"Meaning Washington wants to know what you're doing."

"Actually, Washington wants to know what *you're* doing, John. I'm trying to take the heat for you, of course. I'll shield you as best I can."

Becker laughed. "I'm already roasted in that case. I assume you're here just to baste me now and then."

Hatcher glided to the window, too dignified to engage Becker's bitterness directly. The secret to leadership was to inspire by example. "How's your wife, John? Mending quickly, I hope."

Becker realized guiltily that he had not thought of Karen in at least twenty-four hours.

"She's fine," he said, wondering how she could have slipped his mind so completely. What kind of a man was he? What kind of husband?

"We can't have her back soon enough," Hatcher said unctuously. "But we mustn't hurry the healing process. Better safe than sorry. Give her my best regards, won't you?"

"You probably have the phone number in your files," said Becker.

"I'll give her a call the first chance I get," Hatcher said brightly, as if Becker had suggested a radical new means of communication. "Is there anything you'd like me to tell her from you?"

Hatcher delivered the line while looking out the window. Becker stared at his back, wondering how it was that the man always seemed to know precisely where to push to make Becker want to murder him. He was grateful that he did not have any more time to waste talking to him.

CHAPTER 35

PEGEEN MANAGED TO GET IN TOUCH with Becker as he surveyed Van Cortland Park by air. She could barely hear him over the crump of the copter's prop.

"He wants me to meet him in New Jersey," she said, raising her voice against the background noise. "He says to use the George Washington Bridge and take the exit to Fort Lee."

"Pegeen . . . I can't back you up," said Becker. Below him the vastness of the park skimmed quickly by as the pilot made his first pass.

"Okay," she said.

"I have every man I can find on the ransom drop."

"Uh-huh."

"Did he say anything—did you get any better sense this time as to whether he *is* Spring?"

"He didn't say anything he wouldn't already know from the papers—I don't know. It probably isn't him, but I don't know."

"The current thinking is this is a mob operation. The garbage men blown up in the tunnel were mob-related through their union. Your man sounds like a loner, I really don't think he's the one."

"Okay."

Becker motioned to the pilot and the helicopter moved into position over an outdoor basketball court surrounded by bleachers. The drop was to take place there in three hours. Becker tried to imagine what was in Spring's mind, how the traffic would flow, how the whole thing would take place. There didn't seem to be any good place to hide and no way to flee.

"What do you want me to do?" Pegeen asked.

Becker hesitated. "The thing is, I can't give you cover."

"Meisner is here," Pegeen said, feeling herself blush. The cop was still in her bed, where they had been actively engaged when Cole's second call came.

"Two of you isn't enough," Becker said. "It would take at least three cars and half a dozen men to cover you in the open like that. I can't spare them."

"What?" The noise of the blades had drowned him out completely.

Becker made his decision. "Don't do it, Pegeen. Let it pass. If it *is* Spring it's much too dangerous to go in alone. Or even with Meisner. If it isn't Spring you're wasting your time anyway."

"But if it *is* Spring . . . how can we pass on the chance?"

"I can . . . not . . . cover . . . you," Becker said angrily. "I've lost one agent, I'm not going to risk another one unnecessarily. Let it go. We'll get him another way. Right now we have to concentrate on the ransom drop. We're using real money this time."

"How about using the New Jersey State Patrol? Or even the Fort Lee police?"

"There's no time to set it up properly. If it is Spring and he thinks you're part of a trap . . . if he even suspects that you're an agent . . . We have a leak, Pegeen. It may be mob-related, I don't know yet, but I'm sure as hell not going through any police force I haven't checked out first. Forget about it, Pegeen. We're not going to do it. You're not going to do it."

"It's probably not Spring, you just said so."

"Don't do it."

"Is it because I'm a woman?"

"What? I can't hear you."

"You're trying to protect me because I'm a woman. If it was Meisner, for instance, you'd tell him to go ahead."

"I don't give a flying fuck about Meisner, you're right about that part. You're not doing it because you're an agent under my command."

"You're not treating me like one. You're making me a special case."

She listened to the air being sliced and slammed by the helicopter's huge rotor.

"You *are* special, Pegeen," he said at last. "Take the day off but stay away from Jersey."

"Shouldn't we be helping you?"

"Stay there. If you don't show he'll call you. Tell him something came up, you're desperate to see him, you'll do it tomorrow."

"I don't want to be treated differently," she lied. "Just because of . . . for any reason."

"I can't deal with this right now, Pegeen. Not now."

Pegeen held the receiver to her ear after Becker had gone, struggling with her emotions, not wanting Meisner to see. Why had he said that now? Why call her special on a day when Meisner was in her bed, her body still warm from his?

"What did he say when you mentioned me?" Meisner asked.

"Hum?"

"You said he'd send me but not you."

"He said he prizes you as highly as any of his agents," said Pegeen.

"Yeah?" Meisner said, pleased. Then he added, "I still think he's an asshole."

"He's a very complicated man," Pegeen said. "And he has a great deal on his mind. He is not an asshole."

"I'm entitled to my opinion."

Meisner put his hand on her neck and gently massaged it while kissing the bumps on her spine. It had surprised Pegeen to learn that he was such an affectionate man. He brought a degree of touching and caressing that she was not accustomed to.

"He said not to go to Jersey, right?"

Pegeen did not answer. She touched the hand on her neck to still it while she tried to remember if she had heard a catch in Becker's voice when he called her special. How had he meant it? Was he just parroting her word back to her, or did he really mean that he held a unique feeling for her?

"If we don't go, what should we do for the rest of the day?" Meisner pulled aside the sheet, which covered the lower half of her body. He put his hand on her thigh.

"You've got great legs," he said.

"Legs like a dray horse," Pegeen replied, the phrase leaping unbidden to her tongue.

"What the hell is a dray horse?"

"A draft horse," Pegeen replied. "A workhorse. A horse that's been bred and trained to work."

"And you work awfully good," said he.

"I *do* work well," she said, getting suddenly to her feet. "I do good work. As good as anybody."

"Don't have to convince me."

"No, not you."

To Meisner's disappointment she located her underwear and put it on.

"Let's go if you're coming," she said briskly. "Get your gear on."

"Where are we going?"

"I'm going to work," she said. She opened the closet and surveyed the outfits the Bureau had supplied for Robin Sheehan.

"What should I wear?" she asked, not hoping for an answer.

"You'll make anything you put on look beautiful," said Meisner.

She turned to him with a smile and saw him dancing on one foot while drawing on his shorts. Hairs bristled on his shoulders, sparse and vulnerable-looking as new growth from a Chia pet. With his head bent she could see he was losing it faster on top than he was gaining it elsewhere. He appeared to have caught his toe in the elastic of his shorts. He noticed her looking at him and he beamed at her, fighting for his balance. A man who can't quite dress himself, she thought. And he's crazy about me.

"I suppose I'd better wear the green since it's Spring's favorite color."

Meisner had managed to hop to the edge of the bed, where he now sat, drawing on his trousers.

"Spring? . . . Hey, gorgeous, I don't think I can let you go to Jersey to see that son of a bitch."

"And I don't think you can stop me."

Meisner tilted his head to one side, contemplating how to take the challenge.

"Not without seriously damaging our relationship," Pegeen added. "And my guess is you don't want to do that just yet."

"Not ever," he said with great seriousness.

Pegeen sighed.

CHAPTER 36

DEFONE AND TONY ARRIVED AT the tournament early in order to stake out the prime viewing seats in the top row of the bleachers. From that position they could watch the approach of the money, the disposition of the money, the dispersal of the money. At the moment the final *reunion* of the money was being taken more or less on faith. And while they waited, they could watch the basketball that was taking place on the outdoor courts below them. Although most of the audience and nearly all of the players would be black, there were enough white agents and scouts and fans in attendance that Tony's skin would not be too conspicuous. Or at least so he hoped. For Tony it felt somewhat like the advice occasionally given to those entering bear country: Stand very still and they won't notice you. Or was it to play dead and they won't eat you? Either way made no sense to Tony, but then relying on Defone Lee as a partner was beginning to make less and less sense the farther they got from Tony's garage and the vat of drowning water.

Shorn of weapons so that he had nothing to conceal, Defone was free to strip to the waist as so many others were doing in the blazing sun. Tony sat next to him, sweating and uncomfortable in a sports coat—but heavily armed.

An hour before tip-off time of the first game the stands were packed. Hundreds more sat and stood along the fences, fingers laced in the chain link. The annual summer basketball festival provided an opportunity to see big-name professionals compete with semipros and schoolyard legends and no basketball fan or curiosity seeker worthy of the name missed it. The park swelled and seethed with vendors, hustlers, promoters, and merchants trying to sell to the overflow crowds, and pickpockets, thieves and muggers to take whatever was left over. Picnickers, strollers, frolickers, the Frisbee-tossing, dog-walking, kite-flying regulars added to the surge and flood of humanity of the park on a summer weekend.

At the top of the bleachers Defone and Tony had the vantage point to see it all.

"Lots of peoples," Defone said approvingly. "That's good."

"People. Just say lots of *people.*"

Defone looked at him as if he was crazy, which Tony thought he probably was for having brought it up in the first place. This was hardly the place to correct a black man's speech.

"That's what I just *said,*" said Defone.

"Right. Forget it."

Tony looked distinctly uncomfortable. "What the matter with you?" Defone inquired. "Look like you got your ass on an anthill."

"I'm fine," Tony said, scanning his immediate neighbors. Some of them glanced at him occasionally; most of them ignored him once they had recognized his presence.

"Anybody say anything to you?" Defone asked. "Anybody do anything?"

"No."

"Anybody looking at you?"

"No."

"Well, shit, they ought to be. Look at you. White man sitting

here in the sun, sweating like a pig, wearing a black jacket, black shirt, black pants. Know what you look like? Look like you're in the fucking mob."

"Keep your voice down."

"How come you people dress like that? Somebody make a rule, it ain't enough to be a Wop, you gotta dress like one, too?"

"Shut your mouth, Defone."

"Or what, motherfucker? What you gon' do? Gon' drown me up here? I don' see no water, do you?"

"I can shoot your ass."

"You already done shot my ass. You know that? You shot me in the ass in Harlem, bet you didn't even know that, did you?"

"Should have shot you in the dick. Maybe I ought to do that now."

"How you gon' shoot me and walk away? You can't even get out this bleacher 'thout crawling over a hundred peoples. How far you think you gon' get you shoot a brother here?"

"I wouldn't have to leave. Just shoot you in the dick and sit here and watch the game."

As the two of them glared at each other, Defone wondered if the stupid Guinea was crazy enough to do it. Tony wondered the very same thing.

"Shiiit," Defone said contemptuously, turning away. It was then he saw the ransom money being wheeled into the park.

Meisner left the apartment building fifteen minutes before Pegeen. He walked two blocks to his car and drove to upper Manhattan, positioning himself on a side street so that when he wished he could join the line of autos waiting to take the George Washington Bridge to New Jersey.

After an impatient quarter of an hour Pegeen got the car the Bureau had provided for Robin to "borrow" from the parking garage beneath the building. As she pulled into the street she did not register the workman eating a sandwich in his utility truck that was illegally parked by the corner. The workman registered Pegeen's departure, however, and duly made his way to a pay phone from which he called the restaurant in Fort Lee. From the restaurant the message describing Pegeen's car and time of departure was relayed to Donny the Snake.

Meisner fell into line four cars behind Pegeen, ignoring the angry honks of motorists he had cut in front of. He watched to be certain that the officers made a thorough inspection of her car, then got out to help in the scrutiny of his own.

Once over the bridge Meisner overtook Pegeen, who was dawdling in the right lane, and pulled off at the Fort Lee exit. He noticed the old Chrysler with its distress lights flashing that was pulled onto the shoulder off the exit ramp. A blue Volkswagen was sitting at the stop sign at the end of the ramp. In his mirror Meisner watched the man standing next to the Chrysler. He could have been positioned there waiting for help. Or he could have been taking in the afternoon sun for all the distress he displayed. Meisner realized that the car in front of him was still waiting at the stop sign. He honked his horn and the driver of the VW waved him around. Meisner pulled abreast of the VW, mouthing a New York courtesy at the driver, then pulled into traffic.

The instructions were to drive for two and a half miles on the speedometer and begin to look for a signal from Spring some time thereafter. Meisner drove slowly for several blocks, watching his mirror for a sign of Pegeen. Puzzled, he pulled into a service station and waited for a measured minute before driving back toward the thruway exit.

When Pegeen drove onto the exit ramp the Chrysler backed up abruptly as soon as she passed, crossing the ramp and stopping

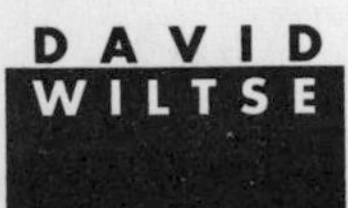

lengthwise across the pavement, blocking the roadway behind her. Pegeen did not see the impromptu sealing of the exit to her rear, nor did she see the driver sprinting toward the stop sign at the end of the ramp.

Pegeen was at the stop sign first, falling in line behind the baby-blue VW Golf in front of her. The driver got out and approached her. Pegeen saw a man with dyed hair and mustache who looked faintly familiar. He was smiling as he tugged at the locked passenger door, then tapped on the window.

"Robin, it's me," he said, smiling away.

"Who are you?"

"Jason," he said, then corrected himself. "Spring, you know me as Spring. Let me in."

Said the fly to the spider, thought Pegeen. She unlocked the door and Spring climbed into the front seat beside her.

"Turn left and get back on the thruway," he said. She heard the blare of horns coming from the thruway end of the ramp where traffic was now piling up.

"I thought we were meeting farther down the road."

Spring tapped his forehead to indicate his cleverness and grinned at her.

"Turn left," he said, pointing. "We'll go back onto the thruway."

"Where are we going?" she asked.

"Someplace we can talk," said Spring. "You'd like that, wouldn't you?"

"Yes, I would. . . . What about your car?"

"A friend of mine will pick it up for me," he said. "Turn here."

Pegeen drove onto the thruway heading west. Meisner was not in her mirror. Then fuck it, she thought. I'll handle it myself. The man calling himself Spring and sitting beside her, anxiously watching the traffic as if he were driving himself, did not look as if he would be hard to handle. Pegeen felt a surge of disappointment.

She was not certain what she had expected her new boyfriend to look like, but it was more imposing than this. Really, she had hoped for horns on the son of a bitch, she admitted. She had hoped he would be big and evil and she would bag him herself and drag his carcass and drop it on Becker's desk. She had not expected a wimp who was too shy to look her in the eye, even now.

Once he gave her some proof that she could use to convince everyone else that he was a phony, she would dump him and drive home. Meisner could take care of himself.

"Pull in here," Spring said, gesturing as if she could not see the service-station rest stop herself.

"Where are we going?" Pegeen asked again, already annoyed with the man.

"Trust me," he said. It seemed an unlikely leap of faith to Pegeen. Any man who would dye his hair that badly was not to be trusted with anything. "I'm really very good at these things."

"What things?"

The powder-blue VW pulled alongside them and a lean man with the face of an undertaker got out and slid into the back seat behind Pegeen.

"This is my friend Donny," Spring said. "Donny, this is Robin Sheehan."

The man looked at her frostily. There was no searching in his gaze, no appraisal. No interest. Gay, thought Pegeen.

"Let's go," Donny said.

"We transfer cars now," Spring said apologetically.

"What?"

"We'll go the rest of thc way in our car. We'll leave yours here."

"I'm not going to leave my car here. It's not even mine. It's a girlfriend's."

"It will be all right," said Spring. He glanced nervously at the man in the back seat.

"It'll be all right," Donny echoed flatly. He saw little point in the reasoned approach, they were just wasting time.

"In New Jersey? It will be stripped or stolen within hours," said Pegeen. "You drive and I'll follow you in my car."

"All of New Jersey isn't like that," said Spring. "Besides, we can't take your car."

"Why not?"

Spring looked once more to the man in the back seat. Pegeen couldn't determine if it was to solicit help or ward it off.

"Please, Robin," Spring said, with desperation creeping into his voice. "Just do it my way. Believe me, my way is much easier."

"I don't like this," said Pegeen. "You didn't tell me I would have to leave my car, you didn't tell me we'd have a chaperone. I didn't think it would be like this."

"Donny's not a chaperone. He's here to—facilitate things."

"What does that mean?" Pegeen glanced at the highway, hoping to see Meisner miraculously appear. She did not like the turn this was taking at all. It was not hard to feign Robin Sheehan's reluctance.

"It means get in the other car," Donny said. "Now."

"Please," said Spring. "Please, really. It will be so much easier."

"I don't think so. It makes me uncomfortable. Let's just talk right here. Maybe Donny could stretch his legs." She turned to face the man behind her. "You wouldn't mind that, would you? Just give us a few minutes alone?"

"Please, Robin," Spring said. He touched her arm and Pegeen instinctively pulled free.

"Fuck this," said Donny. He thrust his weapon in Pegeen's face. "Get your ass in the other car."

A .22 caliber Browning with a 6.75-inch barrel. A professional's gun. Pegeen felt the blood drain from her face. An assassin's weapon of choice.

Special Agent Vanhooven was dressed in an ancient overcoat, once camel-colored but now an indeterminate shade of filth. He wore a winter cap with the flaps down over his ears and on his hands were woolen gloves with the fingers cut off. His shoes were Keds sneakers without laces. He looked like the derelict of Spring's instructions and after walking and pushing the shopping cart with the bad front wheel for half a mile he was beginning to feel like one, too. It felt as if he'd lost a pound of sweat already. Even his shoes were filling up.

The shopping cart with the wonky wheel held five million dollars in fifties with only a few crumpled newspapers on top to disguise it. It was a considerable weight and Vanhooven had been working hard by the time the basketball courts and the surrounding crowd of black faces came into view. He had never felt so white in all his life.

Two hundred yards from the courts he stopped and waited. He did not know what, or rather whom, he was waiting for, but the instructions from Spring had been specific.

Vanhooven looked around him. He saw some of the agents he knew personally and realized that there were many more within sprinting distance. Becker's copter thrummed away in the air on the edge of the park. The call letters of a television station on the side of the vehicle might have fooled someone, but he doubted that Spring would be taken in. He was surrounded by help and wearing his vest, of course, but as he waited Vanhooven sweated even more from anxiety than the heat. The vest had done McArthur no good.

Defone and Tony stood up—another advantage of the top row of the bleachers—and leaned against the railing as they con-

torted themselves to get a better view of the approaching derelict with the shopping cart.

"Oh, honey," said Defone. "Look at that white son bitch. Ain't he a pretty thing."

"You sure that's him?"

"He be white, don' he? Homeless honky pushing a shopping cart, that's what Spring tol' 'em. Them FBIses follow directions good."

"They do some other things pretty good too. Probably got a microphone stuck up the asshole of half the people here. Probably got somebody with a telescope reading your lips right now."

"Can watch me all they wants," said Defone. "I ain't doing nothing but looking. Probably be in more trouble for keeping company with the likes of you than anything else."

"They see you with me your rating will go straight up."

The derelict had stopped walking and stood on a path two hundred yards away.

"Where are they?" Tony asked impatiently.

"They be there," said Defone, who was reasonably certain it was true.

"I don't see them."

Defone laughed. "You ever see them cowboy movies where the honkies are riding out to exploit the Indians and one of them says, 'I don't like it. It's quiet . . . too quiet.' "

"That supposed to be a white man's accent?"

"Next thing you know, the Indians pop up on the top of the hill. Ten squillion of them . . . and yeah, that a *good* honky accent. Don't you know what you people sound like?"

"Guess we sound like a spade with a mouthful of marbles."

"And here they come," said Defone, ignoring Tony as much as he could under the circumstances.

They sent the children in first. Unarmed, lacking any significant criminal records yet, they were impervious to most judicial assaults. Five boys, all ten or under, approached the shopping cart. With scarcely a glance at Vanhooven they removed the covering newspapers and took handfuls of the wrapped fifty-dollar bills and crammed the pockets of their oversized pants. One of them turned back to face Vanhooven as they walked away, and grabbed his crotch in a gesture of defiance. The others, following instructions more faithfully, never looked back. The group of five split and each made his own way out of the park.

"Let them go," Becker's voice said into the earpieces of the two dozen agents and undercover cops who were situated throughout the park.

"There goes about a hundred thousand," Vanhooven muttered, forgetting he was on an open radio.

"A contribution to the underprivileged," Becker said. "Five more approaching from your left."

The height of the chopper gave Becker a full view of the operation but the vibration made it difficult to see details. The binoculars slid in and out of focus with each bounce of air from the props. He could see the five men walking toward Vanhooven but their faces swam indistinguishably as if viewed through vapor.

The second wave, the decoys, each pushed a miniature shopping cart. Each was dressed in the garish gold-plated baggy-pants-ed untied-sneakers-ed uniform of a ghetto gang. Even pushing the shopping carts they managed to walk the walk and indeed there was no better time, for they were the cynosure of more eyes than they would ever attract again. By now half the spectators of the game were craning to watch them. They pranced toward Vanhooven as if on a fashion show's runway. Center stage and knowing it.

The five surrounded Vanhooven, drawing their carts in a circle around the larger one.

"Kiss off, motherfucker," one of the five said to Vanhooven. Vanhooven towered over the man by half a head.

"I got something you can kiss, asshole," Vanhooven replied.

The gangbanger made a move toward Vanhooven, a half-stride that still kept him from the bigger man's reach, a gesture of posturing rather than true intent. Another man put his hand on the aggressor's arm.

"*Spring* say move on," said the second man. "Spring say leave us to do our bidness in peace."

"Why don't you do your business in the gutter where you usually do it?"

"Vanhooven," Becker's voice barked crisply in his ear. "Do what they tell you."

"They want me to leave the money," Vanhooven said, watching the hovering men.

"Who he talking at?"

"So scared he lost his mind."

"*I* want you to leave the money," said Becker. "Get out of there so they can do what they're going to do."

"What they're going to do is take the money," said Vanhooven. "No mystery there."

"That's the idea," said Becker impatiently. "Now get your ass out of there."

The most aggressive of the five put his face under Vanhooven's nose. "You going to move your white ass or am I?"

"I'll see you boys soon," Vanhooven said, backing away slowly. He pointed at his latest antagonist. "I'll ask for you personally."

"Won't have to look for me, motherfucker. I be right in your face."

"I'll recognize you, scumbag. You'll be the one using an asshole for a mouth."

"Boldly said," Becker said in Vanhooven's ear. "Spoken like a man. Now turn and walk away. Give them room."

"Why don't we just grab them right now?" Vanhooven asked, dutifully walking away from the shopping cart.

"Did you think any of those men was Spring?"

"Those punks? No chance."

"Exactly," said Becker. "Everyone just stay put."

He watched from the helicopter as the five men filled garbage bags in their mini-carts and then walked away in five directions.

"Keep an eye on them but let them go," Becker said into his radio.

Two dozen pairs of eyes regarded the gang members as they pushed their carts toward the different edges of the park.

"Don't you think we ought to take them?" Vanhooven asked.

"It's too easy," Becker said. "There's got to be more to it than that. He knows he can't get away with that."

"They're doing it," Vanhooven said.

"Fifty yards from the west perimeter," said another voice anxiously. It was well understood that once in the city streets the money would be much harder to follow.

"Same on the east perimeter," said another agent.

"We just going to let them walk away with it?"

"Stay put," said Becker.

A familiar voice crackled suddenly in Becker's ear.

"Uh, John, John Becker, this is Associate Deputy Director Hatcher speaking."

"Get off the line," Becker said. "An operation is in progress."

"I've been monitoring that operation and I think I must advise you that you are at risk of losing the suspects *and* the money."

"Get off the fucking line, Hatcher."

"I will in a moment. I have no wish to interfere with your handling of the operation. Just let me stress to you that the subjects and the money are within yards of the perimeter."

"Do you want to run this? Because if you do, get your ass up here in the chopper and I'll go home to Connecticut."

"Twenty-five yards from perimeter east," said a voice.

"Two subjects approaching west perimeter," came another voice, slightly anxious.

Becker swung his binoculars to the exits from the park.

"Stay put," he said.

Hatcher's voice broke in again. "John, John, listen to me. I'm not going to tell you what to do . . ."

"Not on record, anyway. That way you can always say it was my idea."

"I don't want to interfere . . . but if we lose the subjects and the money . . ."

"It's too easy," Becker said. "There's more to it. He knows he can't just take the money and walk away."

"But that's exactly what he's doing," Hatcher said.

"Subjects *at* east perimeter," said an agent.

A roar went up as the basketball players came onto the court.

"Subjects twenty-five yards from west perimeter."

"Take them down, John," said Hatcher.

"Is that a direct order?"

"It's *your* operation."

"They're getting ready to run," said the voice from the east perimeter, now undeniably anxious.

Through his binoculars Becker watched the two men at the east edge of the park lift the garbage bags from the shopping carts.

"Take them down!" Hatcher yelled.

"Is that an order?"

"Take them down, John!"

"Is that an order?"

"Subjects are running," said the east perimeter.

"Subjects removing bags from the carts," said the west.

"Stop them, Becker! That's five million dollars!"

"If that isn't an order, shut the fuck up."

"It's an order," Hatcher snapped.

"Take them down by the order of Associate Deputy Director Hatcher, intervening in this operation." Becker said calmly. "And countermanding my express order to the contrary."

Fifteen agents and cops broke cover and ran in pursuit of the fleeing gang members.

And that's when the main assault force struck. Mobilizing on a barked command, one hundred young black men pulled away from the crowd at the fence surrounding the ball courts and converged on the shopping cart.

"Hoooo," Defone breathed delightedly. "Just like the movies. Here come that whole fucking tribe of Apaches over the hill."

"Looks more like a tribe of Zulus to me," said Tony, who was torn between his desire for his share of the money and ethnic issues.

With discipline, each gangbanger took only as many bills as he could fit into the pockets of his baggy pants. By the time the fifteen agents had run down the gangbangers with the garbage bags and discovered that the bags were filled with newspapers and rags, the hundred gang members with the cash had dispersed like seeds tossed in a high breeze, each with close to fifty thousand dollars of government money in his pockets. There were nine agents left to cope with them. And things were about to get more confused.

"They's free money!" Defone yelled, pointing toward the cart. The last of the departing gangbangers ripped open several of the wrappers and tossed the fifty-dollar bills in the air. The first of the spectators to sprint there found that the gang members, in another display of discipline, had left most of the bottom layer of bills in the shopping cart intact. The last of the sprinters had to settle for loose fifties scattered by the feeding frenzy.

"Lookit 'em, lookit 'em," Defone crowed from his perch in the bleachers. "Just like a meebles."

"What the fuck's a meebles?" Tony demanded. His mood was deteriorating rapidly as he saw his money vanishing into the pock-

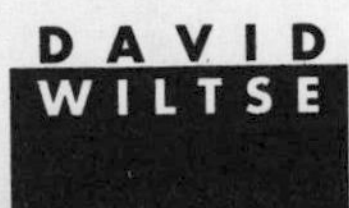

ets of a horde of blacks. It seemed that the only people in the park not taking a share were the players on the court. Five million was chump change to most of them, of course.

"Don't they teach you nothing in Guinea school 'cept tomato sauce? A meebles is that little squishy thing, goes all out and around and comes back together." Defone demonstrated with his hands, fingers wiggling like so many worms.

Tony looked at him with disdain. "This voodoo shit, or what?"

"Like a germ, only it's not," said Defone, giving up on higher education.

The agents stopped as many as they could, but it was like catching fish in your fingers.

"We lose a few thousand here and there," Defone said nonchalantly. "But shit, we can afford to. We lose a whole fucking million, so what. Still leaves two million for the gang, a million for me, a million for you." And since you be dead, I be having your share, too, Defone added in his head.

"How do you know we're ever going to see any of it?" said Tony, who had his own ideas about the split as well.

"They all come back together, just like a meebles . . ."

"Fuck the meebles."

". . . because they all just little pieces of the one big thing. They all members of the gang. What they gon' do, come back and say they *don't* gots the money? Rest of the gang know they be lying and kill they ass."

"What makes you so sure these meebles are going to give the money to *us*, asshole?"

"Shit, man, they just children. We be adults. We outsmart 'em."

CHAPTER 37

KAREN CRIST WOKE SUDDENLY, thinking at first that it must have been the pain that summoned her to consciousness, but the tingle in her limbs told her something else. She was afraid even though she did not know yet what had caused that fear. If there had been a nightmare she had no memory of it. Her head did not hurt her and had not done so for several days. She heard nothing in the stillness of her bedroom except her own breathing and no shapes moved in the darkness.

She sat up, moving carefully, and swung her legs over the edge of the bed, regretting even the rustle of her naked legs against the sheet. The central air-conditioning purred gently from the heating vent. Karen's service automatic was in the drawer of her night table. Unloaded, of course, but an intruder was not to know that.

She heard a stealthy footfall from outside her door, definitcly a footstep and a heavy one. It was not the house settling, it was not any of the usual, random, inexplicable noises any structure makes in the night. It was one footstep followed by another and then a third and then they stopped directly outside the bedroom door.

Karen could sense the man listening, she could feel him wondering if he had been too loud, if he had awakened her.

Too loud for your own good, you asshole, she said to herself with more bravado than she felt. She was no longer frightened now that she knew what had awakened her, but she could feel her heart leaping in her chest and knew that her breath was coming faster than it should. She was not frightened—but she had a healthy respect for her situation. She had endured worse, far worse, than anything lurking in the other room. Anger began to build in her, pushing the fear to the far recesses.

She slid open the drawer to the night table and winced at the noise. The weight of the automatic felt reassuring in her hand, even though the gun was never loaded while in the house.

"You're not going to shoot me, are you? I haven't been away *that* long," Becker said from the other side of the door.

Karen laughed with relief and sprang to the door.

"I should, just for scaring me," she said.

"I didn't want to wake you." He took her in his arms. "Besides, the gun isn't loaded."

She kissed him and after a moment moved his hands down to her naked legs.

"Which gun isn't loaded?" she asked.

He slid one hand under the oversized T-shirt in which she slept, and caressed her breasts. "I take it you're feeling better."

"You tell me."

He moved his hand slowly down her body to the moistness between her legs.

"Feeling even better than I remember," he said, "which I wouldn't have thought possible."

They made love, but not like a married couple.

After they had lain silently for a while she said, "I almost enjoyed it."

"Thanks a lot."

"No, I mean before. When I thought you were a burglar. When I was forced to take control of things. I remembered what it felt like to be in the middle of it, of the action, the danger. I remembered why I got into this business in the first place."

"That's your idea of fun?" Becker thought of telling her about his encounter with the hit man in the hotel room but decided against it. There would be a better time.

"Not fun. I said I *almost* enjoyed it. At least I wasn't feeling sorry for myself."

"Maybe you're ready to go back to work."

"Maybe."

"Because one of us needs to be working."

"Meaning?"

"I've been taken off the Spring case."

"By whom?"

"Officially it's Washington, but it's Hatcher, of course. He gave the order that screwed up the operation in Van Cortland Park, I called him on it publicly, he denied it and said it was *my* idea and is making charges of insubordination as well."

"He can't do that."

"Sure he can. That's what he's good at. You know that."

"Yes. The swine . . . Who's in charge now?"

"Denis King is flying in from California."

"Denis is a good man," she said.

Becker agreed. "Yes, he is, and Elise Ronning is coming from Massachusetts."

"That's a great team."

"Almost as good as we are. But it will take them a while to get up to speed. In the meanwhile, Hatcher is in command."

"There's a disaster waiting to happen."

"Well, he can't do much worse than I've done. His job will have

his own particular brand of deception and sleaze, but it might be just as effective as mine."

"Nobody could have done better," she said loyally, wondering if perhaps *she* might not have handled the case more effectively. Karen loved her husband and respected his abilities as an agent enormously—but they both acknowledged that his people skills were in need of constant attention.

"I lost a man," Becker said.

"It wasn't your fault."

Becker refused to be comforted. "I lost an agent. There's no one else to blame for that, I allowed myself to be suckered in. It's my responsibility."

"How about blaming Spring," Karen said. "He's the one who killed McArthur."

"I didn't prevent it. People around me . . . I talked to Gold about this . . . people around me get hurt. Now killed."

Karen shook her head, then realized that he could not see her gesture in the dark.

"We send you after men who kill people, John. We don't use John Becker on cases involving organized crime, or kidnapping, or mail fraud. We use John Becker when somebody is killing people and we want it stopped. People get hurt in the process—but the killing stops."

"Not this time," Becker said.

The phone rang and Karen lifted it from the night table. She said, "Hello," listened briefly, then handed it to her husband.

"Becker," he said by way of greeting. He listened for a moment, then asked when, and where, and how long.

"Did you report it to headquarters?"

"Sure," said Meisner. "And the New Jersey State Patrol. I heard about the mess in Van Cortland Park. I figure they got enough headaches, I'm not going to get their full attention on this."

"But you thought you'd get mine?"

"She was your partner, you worked with her before."

"I haven't been very good at catching this asshole so far," Becker said.

"She told me a hundred times that you're the best there is," said Meisner.

"You know that officially I'm removed from the case," Becker said.

"I heard. You still a private citizen?"

"They haven't deported me yet, so I guess so."

"Then what prevents you from driving to New Jersey?"

"I think I'll try New York instead," said Becker.

"I found the car. It's only a few miles from Fort Lee."

"She's not *in* the car, though, is she? I'm going to Jenksville, New York."

"What's there?"

"Someone I should have talked to several days ago. A man named Nels Kjelsen."

When Becker hung up Karen asked, "Pegeen?"

"She's disappeared. I didn't say her name. How did you know it was her?"

"Because you didn't say her name," Karen answered.

CHAPTER 38

THEY LEFT THE THRUWAY TWO EXITS after transferring cars and headed west across New Jersey through the town of Netcong, and then north through Pennsylvania, staying mostly on secondary roads. Spring talked incessantly, jabbering on at length on every conceivable topic, and it seemed to Pegeen that he had a slightly cockeyed view of each of them. He did not appear even to take breath until they reached the Poconos and then it was to ask Pegeen what she thought. The question had been preceded by such a welter of theories and lopsided assessments that Pegeen was not certain of even the present category, much less the specifics. She had tuned him out a long time ago, nodding and saying "Really," and "I never thought of it that way," and "That is so right" at intervals. Just like with a date, she thought. She was half turned toward him in the seat so that she could face him. He kept his eyes on the road, only turning to her now and then to emphasize a point, and Pegeen was always wide-eyed and attentive. It was pathetic to see how pleased he was each time she confirmed his genius with a little gasp of surprised appreciation or a "Really!" Hard to believe that this was a man who could have tied the city of New York and the Bureau into knots, much less a man responsible for the deaths of more than a dozen. She thought of Arendt's phrase "the banality of evil" and realized it applied in more than one circumstance.

She no longer had doubts that he was Spring, however. Donny's presence took care of that. If she listened to Spring's maunderings with half an ear, Donny had her full attention. He had not changed positions since they began driving. He was in the far corner of the back seat, an angle that gave him the clearest view of Pegeen. He held the pistol in his right hand, which was supported in his lap by his left hand. He could adjust fractionally and shoot from that position in less time than it would take for Pegeen to turn her head and face him. Far less than would be required for Pegeen to reach under her skirt for her weapon. She had strapped the Walther to the inside of her left thigh, the only place where the summer skirt and blouse would permit. She would not require much of an opportunity to get at it, but she would need *some* time. Donny's gaze was unwavering for more than an hour. That amount of self-discipline alone was enough to chill Pegeen. Such concentration was not easily come by, nor wasted on frivolity. It never occurred to Pegeen that he would not shoot. She did not doubt that he would do so without hesitation if she gave him any provocation.

"Robin? . . . What do you think?" Spring repeated.

"I'm sorry. It's all so new to me. I mean, you've thought about so many things . . ."

Spring nodded vigorously, smiling with self-approval.

". . . I need time to digest it all," she continued. "But I'd like to hear more, it's all so interesting."

"It is, isn't it?" Spring agreed.

Pegeen leaned closer and touched his arm. Spring tightened and the car swerved slightly.

"You startled me," he said.

"Sorry."

"I don't mind, though," he said, glancing coyly at her, then back to the windshield.

Pegeen lowered her voice as if there were any chance of not being overheard.

"I was wondering . . . does he have to keep that gun pointed at me?"

Spring seemed to ponder the question momentarily. "Yes, I think so," he said, and giggled nervously.

"Why?"

"I have enemies," Spring said. Pegeen detected a distinct note of pride.

"You don't think I'm one of them, do you?" She let her hand fall from his arm to the seat so that her fingers were in contact with his leg. He could take it as inadvertent if he wanted to. Pegeen's guess was that he couldn't believe his luck.

"Do you?" she asked again.

"No, I don't," Spring said. He giggled nervously again and shifted his weight so that his leg increased the pressure against her fingers. "But I'm not holding the gun."

"It frightens me," Pegeen said.

"You know what interests me, miss?" Donny asked, breaking a silence that had begun shortly after the trip began.

"What?"

"What interests me is how very *un*frightened you seem to be. If I was a girl out for a ride with my boyfriend and a man stuck a gun in *my* face, I believe I'd be screaming and hollering and crying my eyes out."

"How long ago were you a girl? We don't faint anymore just because we're scared, you know. Women stopped swooning a long time ago."

"Is that right?"

"But if it will make you put the gun away I'd be happy to cry for you. Are you the kind of man who likes to watch a woman cry?"

She allowed herself to stare directly in his face and wished she hadn't. He was frigid and blank behind the eyes. He would squeeze off a round as soon as blink. He was probably not the kind of man who liked to watch women cry, she realized, but he might very well like to see them die.

"Of *course* I'm scared," she said, turning away from Donny and toward Spring for commiseration. "Who wouldn't be scared?"

"Guns scare me, too," Spring admitted. "Although it doesn't bother me now because he's behind me and I can't see it. The thing is, if you're dealing with explosives, you're in charge. The chemicals can only do what you make them do. You can control your measurements, your ambient temperature, your voltage—all of it. You don't like the results you're getting? You can experiment, adjust a little. You can fine-tune an explosive, Robin. There's an art to it. But with a gun—you're dealing with *people* then. There's no telling what a man is going to do from one minute to the next. People are nuts. People are scary."

"Maybe you'd better take me back to my car," Pegeen said.

"Oh, I didn't mean Donny. There's no reason to be afraid of Donny. He's my friend, aren't you, Donny?"

"More than you know," said Donny. Conversation had not loosened him up. Pegeen noted that neither he nor the pistol had moved an inch.

By the time they entered the western reach of New York State and arrived at Binghamton Pegeen knew that Becker's search for Spring's hole-in-the-ground had not extended far enough. They were well over two hours from New York and showing no sign of slowing down. The farther they got from New York, the more her spirits sank. They were not only past the FBI net, they were even beyond the area of search. Meisner would not seek her here. Becker would never find her now.

CHAPTER 39

BECKER FLEW TO BINGHAMTON, then rented a car and drove to Oswego, where he turned north, following the signs toward Ithaca. He stopped in a village called Candor, where he made one phone call, then left the highway and took to the back roads. He had been in farm country since leaving Oswego. Half-grown fields of corn backed up to people's rear doors. Cattle and hogs could be seen in pastures and feedlots close to the road. They were small farms, owner-operated tracts of land that had long since lost the battle against agribusiness and were worked now by families too proud or too desperate or too stubborn to leave. The area had none of the rawboned, parched, dust bowl despair of the classical overwhelmed farms of Depression photographs—the land was too green and lush for that—but poverty poked through at the elbows, at every collapsing fence and outmoded tractor, nonetheless. Rural New York State was perennially and chronically impoverished.

Off the highway Becker became aware of the steepness of the terrain. Large hills jutted abruptly upward like burial mounds of giants and the road twisted and turned trying to avoid them. The hills only made the land harder to farm, of course.

He crossed Catatonk Creek and turned off at a sign announcing Jenksville five miles away. Abandoning the county road, Becker followed a long and winding dirt path whose entrance was marked only by the mailbox sitting atop a pole made of chain link welded into immobility. At the end of the road was a farmhouse, as aging and careworn as the rest of the region, and standing by the door was a man with shoulders so wide he looked as if he'd have to turn sideways to get in and out.

If Ichabod Crane had been a basketball player instead of a schoolteacher he would have looked like this, Becker thought. Very tall, lean and gangly, with an Adam's apple that protruded as if a turkey neck were stuck in his throat. His skin was brown from working in the sun and he wore a wrist-length work shirt despite the heat.

"John Becker, FBI," Becker said, approaching with an outstretched hand.

"Nels Kjelsen," the farmer said. "No initials."

When he shook hands his cuff slid up his arm, exposing a disturbingly pale skin beneath the shirt.

"I've been expecting you for several days," Kjelsen said, "but I already told the people on the phone I don't know the man you're after."

"Sorry I took so long to get to you," Becker said. "I've been kind of busy."

Kjelsen nodded. "I know. I've been watching on the television while this guy blows up New York City. Terrible thing—mostly."

"Mostly?"

"Well, just plain terrible, of course. Loss of life and whatnot. Nobody wants to see that."

"But what?"

"You're a *federal* agent, not a city cop, isn't it?"

"That's right."

"Then you probably know that a lot of people aren't too fond of New York City. A lot of those people are in New York State, as a

matter of fact. A certain amount of blowing up seems to us like what the city could use. Seems like a kind of justice . . . Not that anyone *really* wants it to happen, you understand."

"I think I understand."

"It's just not like Oklahoma City. *Nobody* thought those folks deserved that explosion. Not in any way."

"But New York City folks might deserve it in some way?" Becker asked.

Kjelsen thought for a moment, twisted his nose as if to scratch it. "It's hard to care as much about 'em," he said with a shrug. "I mean, they mostly *choose* to live there, don't they?"

"Some of them anyway. Do you know anyone who'd like to put a bomb in the city?"

"Whoa." Kjelsen held up his palms. "I was just speaking theoretically. Nobody I know hates the place that much."

"I think maybe somebody does," said Becker, and he explained how a man who claimed to be Spring used the name Nels Kjelsen as a code name for his telephone calls.

"Must have been another Nels Kjelsen," the farmer said, after recovering from his astonishment.

"There don't seem to be that many of you," said Becker. "And you're the closest one to the city."

"I don't know anyone named Spring. I've been going through my memory ever since they told me you wanted to talk to me. I've heard of a Spring family somewhere, I know that much, but for the life of me I can't think where or when."

"How about a Jason Cole?" Becker asked. "Do you know anyone by that name?"

"How do you spell it?"

"C-O-L-E. But anything that sounds like it is good enough."

"He's got you really buffaloed, doesn't he?"

Becker detected a note of glee in the farmer's voice. Was it anti-Washington bias? Or just a tendency to root for the underdog?

What the man didn't appreciate was that right now Becker was the underdog—and getting badly licked, too.

"Got us plain stumped," Becker admitted, trying to sound as folksy as he could. "That's why I need your help."

"Can't do it . . . I knew a Kroll once, that's as close as I can come. Runs the luncheonette in Candor. About seventy, nice guy. That your man?"

"I don't think so. This man would be about thirty-five, kind of frail, you might know him with a ponytail and glasses although he might do without both. Sometimes wears an old army fatigue jacket. Probably keeps pretty much to himself. He might have been a teacher."

"You think he lives somewhere around *here?* What's he do, bomb New York City on the weekends?"

"No, that seems to be his full-time job," Becker said wryly. What he might do is come up here every now and then. Maybe he owns an abandoned farm, or has access to one anyway."

"He comes up *here* on the weekends? Mr. Becker, you've got the wrong idea for certain." Kjelsen laughed, a mean sound from the back of his throat. "As far as I know, *I'm* the only man who came *back* in the last twenty years. Everybody with any sense is going the other way. You can't make a living working a farm this size anymore. You can *survive* but that's about it."

"Why did you come back?"

Kjelsen shrugged, a major undertaking with shoulders as broad as his. "My father died, left me the farm. I guess I was tired of trying to teach kids who didn't want to learn. I tell you, it's a hard thing when you teach a subject that *you* think is not only interesting but *basic* to an understanding of life—and know that it's the least popular course in school. You just can't explain to kids why they should want to know about it."

"Where did you teach?"

"Ithaca High School."

"What was the subject?"

"Chemistry."

"Chemistry? You taught chemistry?"

"I know. You hated it too, right? Everybody did. Makes you feel unwanted after a while."

"Mr. Kjelsen, my guess is you had at least one student who was paying very close attention . . . You wouldn't have a fax machine by any chance, would you?"

"Of course I've got a fax. Do you think this is the backwoods or something?"

From the high school in Ithaca they acquired a list of all the students whom Kjelsen had taught over a ten-year period and their grades in the chemistry class. Becker started with those who had received A's. He read the names aloud and then had Kjelsen look at them on paper to see if his memory was jogged either way.

For most of them Kjelsen waggled his head sorrowfully from side to side. "Blurs, most of them," he said. "Even the good ones. That's sad, isn't it? I recognize some of the names because they're distinctive, but the faces, the personalities—they're all trying so hard at that age to look and act just alike."

"John Christopher Schrag," Becker intoned slowly. Kjelsen stared blankly. "Maybe Johnnie Schrag, Jack Schrag. Chris Schrag?"

"A tall kid," Kjelsen said tentatively. "Glasses. I remember him because he had a couple of brothers who went through school before him. Seemed like I had a Schrag the whole time I was teaching. John was the best of them, though. Smarter. Taller."

"Was he white?"

Kjelsen blinked as if he didn't understand the question. "Extremely," he said at last.

"How tall?" Becker asked.

Kjelsen shrugged. "He could look me in the eye. Six three, maybe?"

"No, too big." The drunken cop who had spied Spring by the warehouse was certain his height was less than six feet.

"Wait a minute, I may have misspoken. Maybe it was the first one who was the best of them. Stephen, I think it was."

"He apparently didn't get an A. He's not on this list."

"He had other qualities . . . Well now, to be honest, I don't remember which of them was better."

"Maybe the middle one."

Kjelsen shook his head. "No, he didn't amount to much. I remember wondering how one woman could have three such different children."

"She a student too?" Becker asked impatiently.

"Who's that?"

"The mother of the Schrag boys."

"No, but a fine-looking woman. Funny, too. And sharp as a tack. We had a few meetings about the middle boy, I've forgotten his name . . . Sorry, I know this isn't relevant, but you're asking me to go down memory lane here."

"It's okay, take your time. The more you remember, the better. Next on the list is Charles Taylor."

"Don't remember him at all."

"Robert D. Gibson."

Kjelsen hesitated, squinting his eyes to aid his memory.

"Bob Gibson? Rob? Robbie?" Becker prompted.

"Oh, yeah. He got an A? I always suspected him of cheating but couldn't prove it. Lousy in quizzes, great in the tests. He was probably stealing the tests ahead of time some way."

"What did he look like?"

"Like most of them. He was an athlete, I think."

"White?"

Kjelsen nodded.

"Height?"

"Height? Six feet, a little less. I don't really remember."

Becker put a check beside the name. He would come back later to those with a check because they had not been eliminated as possibilities due to size or race or sex. So far there were only three with checks.

At a town called Weltonville Cole pulled into the parking lot of a gas station that doubled as a convenience store. He bumped against the cement curbing with a loud scrape.

"Careful of the car," said Donny. Jason's driving on the open road was tolerable but in close quarters Donny became very nervous. He sent Cole in to buy groceries and a newspaper and stayed in the back seat, the gun still trained on Pegeen.

"Put it out of your mind," he said to Pegeen.

"What?"

"Jumping out of the car and screaming help, help, there's a nasty man with a gun."

"I wasn't thinking about that."

"I've seen better liars, but I've seen a lot worse, too."

"Do you think of yourself as a nasty man? That's very sad."

"I think of myself as a hero in my life story."

"Because I don't think of you as nasty," said Pegeen. She had already dismissed the idea of escape before he mentioned it. There was nowhere to hide except in the store and then she would be exposing civilians to danger without greatly enhancing her own chances. What she needed was ten seconds when his eyes weren't on her. To have any chance she would need the gun in her hand and ready to fire *before* he knew it. "I just think you've misjudged me. Jason hasn't. But you have."

"Jason is an innocent. He believes certain things because he wants to, not because they're true."

"That's a wonderful trait."

"I didn't say it wasn't."

"What do *you* believe in? Your gun?"

He smiled for the first time since Pegeen had met him. "Is that a sexist remark?" he asked. Pegeen decided she would rather have him glower than smile at her. The smile looked much crueler.

"You know what I keep asking myself?" Donny continued. "Where do I know you from?"

"You don't know me."

"I seen you somewhere."

"I would remember you, I promise. Not that many men point a gun at me first thing."

"I'll think of it."

"I guess I'll just wait. I don't have anything else to do."

"What are you here for?" Donny asked.

"Because *he* invited me."

"What are you here for?" he repeated.

Pegeen paused. What did he want to hear? What would he accept? She looked away as if overcome by shyness. Finally she said, "It's exciting."

Donny stared at her, demanding more.

"Right now he's the most important man in the country. He has more power, he's better known than anyone. And he chose *me* out of everyone he could have had. He could have picked any girl in New York, but he wanted *me*."

Donny scoffed. "He doesn't have the first idea what to do with a woman."

"He doesn't have to *do* anything, not everything is sex, you know."

"No, I didn't know that."

"Just being with him is enough."

"Yeah, he's so fucking interesting. Your eyes have been glazed over for the last two hours."

"I can't follow all of it," said Pegeen. "It's all new to me."

"You mean you haven't heard such a crock since high school."

"You don't seem to like your friend very much," said Pegeen.

"That'd be my business, wouldn't it? What I want to know is what *you* see in him. It's not his conversation, it's not his smooth way with a woman."

Pegeen hesitated, to give herself time to work up the proper emotion. She knew how to cry when she needed to, a trick she had used to her advantage more than once. Although still afraid, she was no longer paralyzed by her fear and she was long past the moment of despair she had felt when she realized that no one else was going to be able to help her. That had been followed by a period of shame and embarrassment for letting herself feel so dependent upon a couple of men. She was a trained agent and it was past time that she acted like one. So she started silently weeping, letting the tears well up without any of the vocal histrionics of sobbing or sniffing.

"Have you ever been alone, Mr. . . . Donny?" She shifted slightly so that she was facing him directly. The tears did no good unless he could see them. "For years? . . . I'm no prize. I know that. I'm too dull for the men I want—and I don't want those who are dull enough for me. My job is tedious. I have a cat and my family lives fifteen hundred miles away. I'm tired of going out on the weekends with girlfriends. That's not politically correct to say, but it's true. They're nice, but they're all as bad off as I am or they wouldn't be with me. The best thing I have to look forward to is two weeks in Mexico, where I'll let myself get picked up by some local man who specializes in that sort of thing—and even then I'll worry the whole time about disease."

One of the tears finally overflowed from her eye and made its precipitous way down her cheek. She did not wipe it away.

"Then a man pops into my life out of the blue. I didn't ask him to show up, he just came, like a miracle. *He* may not be exciting but what he's doing sure as hell is. Nobody who's doing that can be boring, I don't care how much he talks."

"You think you're going to be Bonnie and Clyde?" Donny mocked.

"Make fun of it if you want to." She sniffed once, bravely, but kept her face squared up to him. "It's something. It's *something*. I don't care if it's dangerous—fire is dangerous, but we all need to keep warm."

She had worked her hand up her skirt and her fingers were touching the handle of the pistol holstered to her inner thigh. The gun was held securely by a spring within the leather and would require a firm yank to clear it. She could not tease it out and her skirt was impeding the upward movement necessary to get it out and up and ready to fire. Fuck it, she thought. He's going to kill me anyway. Maybe he's not as good as he looks, maybe I can beat him, maybe the seat will protect me. She had been too tense, too nervous, too frightened for too long. Sense had little to do with it by now. Her eyes were now filling with more tears as she anticipated the results of her actions and she blinked to clear them. She was sweating, her upper lip was damp, and she could smell herself. Fuck it, fuck it, fuck it. She didn't need ten seconds. She needed two.

"Could I have my purse, please?" Donny had confiscated and searched it when she entered the car. The documents gave away nothing. They all confirmed her as Robin Sheehan.

Donny hesitated.

"I need a tissue."

Without once looking away from her Donny handed her the purse. She put it in her lap, fumbling through it with one hand while the other tightened its grip on the gun. I'm not going to make it, she suddenly realized with chilling conviction. I'll be shot before I even get it clear of the holster. She tensed her body, preparing for the move.

Cole opened the car door.

Startled, then flushed with relief, Pegeen smoothed her skirt down and blew her nose on a tissue as Cole deposited a bag of

groceries in the back seat next to Donny. A newspaper peeped out of the top of the bag.

"I got us some hero sandwiches," Cole announced happily. He winked at Pegeen as if offering food in a courtship ritual. "Meatball for you, Donny. They heated them up in their microwave."

"Great," said Pegeen.

"Are you all right? You look funny."

"I'm fine," she said. She tried to smile.

"Are you shivering?"

"I have to go to the bathroom," she said.

"There's one around the corner."

"No," said Donny.

"Donny, really . . ."

"No. We're almost there. Hold it."

"It's only about twenty minutes from here," Cole said. "But I know what that feels like. It's very uncomfortable. I'll go as fast as I can."

"Thank you." Pegeen thought she would need at least that much time to recover herself. Adrenaline she could not use had flooded her body, making her tremble as if she were freezing cold. She did have to go to the bathroom now with a terrible urgency and her nose and eyes continued to run. It was as if her whole system was breaking down after her brush with death. Pegeen had come close to being killed before, but never because a voluntary action of hers had triggered it. Never when she had time to contemplate the action and its consequences ahead of time. She was trained to react, quickly, decisively, almost instinctively, like a skilled counter-puncher. The Bureau gave no courses in deliberately planning to activate a hit man's trigger finger. The FBI did not encourage high-noon center-of-the-street fast-draw contests. Especially not when the other guy had already drawn.

I must have been out of my mind, she thought. Too scared too long. If she was to survive, she would have to think. *Think.*

CHAPTER 40

KJELSEN SIGHED WEARILY AND pushed the list of names away from him. They had narrowed it to two boys, both of whom would be the right age now, both of whom, if not exactly the right physical type, were at least not the *wrong* size, shape, and appearance.

"I don't know what else I can give you," Kjelsen said. "I can't imagine either one of them being a bomber. Not in my wildest dreams—or nightmares. And a teacher has some pretty serious nightmares, you know. Did I steer this kid the wrong way? Should I have done something to stop that one? I'm not talking just in the classroom now. Study halls, monitor duty, chaperoning at the dances—you see them determined to get themselves all fucked up and there's just not enough you can do to turn them around. Detention doesn't do it. Lectures—hell, they turn the switch and don't hear a word you say."

"Maybe he wasn't an A student," Becker conceded. "Maybe I've been wasting your time. But he did use your name—and he sure as hell knows his chemistry."

"If it was my name and not some other Nels Kjelsen . . . What was the other thing you said?"

"I've been wasting your time?"

"No, no. He sure as hell knows his chemistry. That's not the same as getting a good grade."

"It isn't?"

"Of course not. Chemistry isn't just a textbook course. You're graded on your lab work, too. You can know the answers on tests but you still have to behave in the laboratory, you have to turn in your assignments on time, you have to come to class. . . . Karl Atlee."

"Who is Karl Atlee?"

"I think he tried to blow me up."

Becker spoke very carefully, trying not to reveal his excitement lest Kjelsen get agitated and forget.

"How did that come about?"

"He was a bright kid but very opinionated. You know the kind who thinks he knows more than the teacher and is determined to prove it? And sneaky. Very sneaky. I'd give them a simple lab experiment—learning how to precipitate a solid from a liquid or how to use a reagent, something like that—and Atlee would be off in the corner, running some experiment of his own."

"What kind of experiment?"

"Oh, the kind of thing lots of kids try at that age. Mixing potash and sugar to see if he could make it explode. Trying to make a stink bomb. That kind of thing."

"Trying to impress the other kids? The girls?"

"No . . . that's where he was different. He didn't interact much with the others. I thought he was trying to impress *me*."

"And were you impressed?"

"I was, yes. Not that I would let him know it since he was doing it all against the rules, but by the end of the semester he had learned a lot, he was miles ahead of everybody else. Of course, learning a lot at that age doesn't mean you've learned enough. He thought he knew more than he did and started a fire by accident while doing one of his unauthorized experiments."

"What did you do?"

"Took him to the principal to discuss discipline—and that's where Atlee made his big mistake. Instead of admitting what he had done, he tried to blame me. He said I had told him to do the experiment, but had given him the wrong proportions or the wrong chemicals—I don't remember the details."

"He blamed the authorities," Becker said.

"Well, yes, you could put it that way. The principal didn't believe him, of course."

"What happened to him?"

"He was expelled—more for the attempt to blame me than the fire. But the next day I found a bomb in the lab. A simple thing, very crude, really. It looked as if it had been whipped up quickly and not thought through carefully. It didn't go off, it never would have gone off."

"But Atlee put it there?"

"There was no proof, but I'm sure of it."

"What did he look like?"

Kjelsen shrugged. "Not much, nothing special. Average height—five eight, nine, ten. Light brown hair, I think. Not sure, but I think so. Unremarkable-looking, really. But skinny. Sort of weedy-looking. I think he wore glasses. You know the kind of kid you're sure is going to be skinny and intense all his life? That was Karl Atlee."

"I don't suppose you have any idea what happened to him, do you?"

"Oh, he recovered. He got his high school diploma via the GED test. Went on to college, some small technical school, I've forgotten the name. Got a bachelor's in science, then got his master's in chemistry in New York. City College, I think."

"In chemistry?"

"There's the irony of it, isn't it? As badly as I screwed it up, he still proved me wrong. Like he's rubbing my nose in it."

"Maybe he's *still* proving you wrong, Mr. Kjelsen. How do you happen to know so much about what happened to him after high school?"

"I used to run into his father frequently after I quit teaching and moved back here."

"Here? He lives around here?"

"His father did. Lot of kids from here used to go to school in Ithaca. His dad farms about two hundred acres ten miles from here. That is, he used to. He died about five years ago. Karl doesn't live there, though. Nobody does. The place has been sitting there fallow since the old man died."

"The farm has been unused for five years? It hasn't been sold? Isn't that a little strange?"

"Not terribly. Who's idiot enough to start farming these days?"

"Wouldn't the land have been auctioned off by now?"

"Not if the taxes are paid," Kjelsen said.

"And who would be paying the taxes?" Becker asked. "Or should I ask, why would anyone pay the taxes if they don't use the land?"

"Makes no sense to *me*."

"It's beginning to, to me. Can you tell me how to get to the Atlee farm, Mr. Kjelsen?"

"Sure thing. I'll draw you a map. But the place is deserted, Mr. Becker. I drive by it occasionally. There's no one there."

Becker nodded. "That's exactly the way it should look," he said.

The Atlee farmhouse sat perched precariously atop a hill like a loose toupee atop a bald head. One tree was atop the hill too, a huge, ancient oak that towered over the house and stood some fifty yards from it, a lonely remnant of the virgin forest that had once covered the entire region.

Cole drove the blue VW up the long dirt drive leading to the farmhouse and stopped in front of a barn that was tilted dangerously to one side. While he opened the barn door to the accompaniment of angry squeals from rusted hinges, Pegeen got a look at a farm collapsed into disrepair. Everything was bent or broken or stove in, every wall met the ground at the wrong angle, every door and window was off plumb. Weeds abounded in the untilled fields and made their way to the concrete foundation of the house. Here and there the tops of discarded machinery could be seen above the rampant vegetation, encrusted with rust. Even the crowded woods in the distance looked better maintained than the man-made structures and spaces, more ordered, less forbidding.

The inside of the house was worse. Rodent droppings were in evidence on the floor, on kitchen countertops. Beer cans and empty whiskey bottles were in every room. The sprung windows offered access to birds and there were everywhere signs of their passing. The layer of dust on the bare wooden floors was deep enough to show their footprints.

In the kitchen an ancient refrigerator with a bulbous front and a freezer the size of two ice trays stood with the door open. A stain of something orange was in one back corner, and a larger green one in the other. The refrigerator's shelves lay on the floor.

"The fridge doesn't work, but the stove does," Cole said, depositing the bag of groceries on the Formica table in the center of the room. "It's electric. I've still got electricity."

By way of demonstration he flipped a wall switch and a bare bulb in the ceiling lighted. He smiled as if it were a personal achievement.

"How can you live this way?" Donny demanded.

"Actually, it's pretty comfortable." He bounced on a day bed in the living room to a groan of protesting springs. A cloud of dust sprang up around him. "The TV works too."

"Can I use the bathroom now?" Pegeen asked.

"Wait, wait, wait, there's something I want to show you first," Cole said enthusiastically.

"Jason, I really—"

He interrupted her with a flapping of the arms. "No, no, no. This won't take long. I've been wanting to do it all the way up here but I want to *watch* you while you read it."

He ran back toward the barn.

"You are going to let me go to the bathroom sometime, aren't you?" Pegeen asked. Donny had turned on the television and was adjusting the set with his eye still on Pegeen.

"Sit where I can see you," he said.

"What on earth do you think I'm going to do? We're in the middle of nowhere."

"Sit."

Pegeen regarded the daybed skeptically before sitting. She would have preferred the floor but she was not sure she could keep the skirt down far enough to hide the gun. She cursed herself yet again for choosing such a short garment, summer or no. Was she trying to show off her legs, for pity's sake?

"You ever been in the Scalded Cat?" Donny asked.

"What is it?"

"A place in the Village. A bar."

"I've been to a lot of bars. Maybe that's where you saw me."

Donny shook his head. "You went to The Cat you'd remember it."

"I suppose I could just pee on this," said Pegeen. "I don't know that it would make much difference."

A picture came on the screen, obscured by snow, accompanied by static. Donny toyed with the dials as Cole scurried back in holding a paper bag. He placed it proudly on Pegeen's lap. Pegeen withdrew a scrapbook overflowing with yellowing pieces of newsprint.

"Is this it?" she asked.

He nodded, his eyes beaming.

"Wonderful. I'm looking forward to reading it. . . . Could I just go to the bathroom first?"

"No, no, read it. Read it now."

"Jason, I'm not sure I can concentrate properly . . ."

"Just the first one, then. Just read the first one."

"I want to read it all. But just let me go to the bathroom first."

"You're always like that!" Cole exclaimed. He was suddenly as angry as a thwarted child. "You've always got something more important to do! You never pay attention to *me* first! I want you to read it! I want you to read it!"

Pegeen opened the book and began to read. After a moment Cole sat down beside her in a small puff of dust and read looking over her shoulder. He made little noises as he read, like a pianist moaning some version of the tune to his piano.

"Uh-huh," he muttered, in agreement with his thoughts on paper. "Uh-huh."

Donny the Snake had found a semivisible news show on the television set and stood next to it, his eyes still watching Pegeen. He held the pistol loosely at his side now, still at the ready but no longer pointing directly at her.

"Jason, it's wonderful," Pegeen breathed, turning the first clipping facedown.

"It's an early one. I got better."

"You are such a good writer. Your thoughts are so clear and original." He grinned and looked at her and looked away and looked at her once more.

"Read another one," he said.

"Jason, I have to use the bathroom first."

"Just one more, just one more. I want to know how you like the next one."

"Jason . . ."

He shook his head, his voice dropping to a whisper. "You don't have to call me Jason. My real name's Karl. He doesn't know." He indicated Donny with a quick, furtive roll of his eyes.

"Why?"

"It's not good to have everybody know your real name," he said. "Jason Cole's name was still on the mailbox when I moved into the building so I just left it there. I liked one of the magazines he was getting. I wasn't expecting any mail of my own anyway so I figured, why bother to change?"

"For years?"

"Why not? Whenever I needed a name and didn't want to tell them my real one, I had Jason Cole already there." He indicated Donny with body language again. "He got my name off the mailbox too. He thinks I'm Jason Cole so I just let him keep thinking that way." To her amazement he winked at her. "It's our secret from Donny."

"I understand," Pegeen said in hushed tones. "Thank you for telling me."

"I like you," said Cole. "Read another one."

When she had read a paragraph, he took the clipping from her hand and turned it facedown.

"Not that one. Read the next one."

Donny turned up the volume on the news. Pegeen caught snatches of a story about another bombing.

"Do you think I can get it published?" Cole asked. "It's good, isn't it? What do you think? Will a publisher want it?"

"It's very good," Pegeen said, her eyes on Donny. For the first time he had turned his gaze from her and was staring at the snowy television set. "I'm sure someone will want it."

"I have some that weren't run in the papers that are even better. The editors were too afraid of them . . ."

"You dirty little fuck," Donny said. He strode toward the daybed, raising the pistol to shoulder level.

"Not now," Cole said. "We're working."

"You dirty little fuck," Donny repeated. He sounded more astonished than angry.

"Not now, Donny . . ."

Donny knocked the scrapbook from Pegeen's lap. With a squeal Cole went after it. Donny ripped it from his hands, then kicked it into the center of the room. The clippings settled like birds amid the dust.

"You killed those men in the garbage truck," Donny said. Cole rose to gather his clippings but Donny placed the barrel of the gun on his forehead, forcing him back onto the daybed. "You blew up those poor bastards who gave us a ride."

Cole shrugged.

"My cousin sent us those men. My *cousin*."

"Did it close the tunnel?"

"Yes, it closed the fucking tunnel, you maniac."

Cole clapped his hands once and looked triumphantly toward Pegeen.

"You were carrying a fucking *bomb* in that truck with me? With *me?* Bouncing around like that?"

"Bouncing had nothing to do with it. These things are *controllable—*"

"Control this, you crazy fuck!" Donny waved the gun in front of Cole's face. "I don't want that stuff near me, I told you that. I don't want it anywhere around me. That's why we left it in the warehouse."

Cole smiled. "This whole house is a bomb, Donny. You don't mind about that, do you?"

Donny looked about him wildly, as if expecting to see ticking timers and airplane bombs with fins.

"What do you mean?"

"You can't see it. It's in the foundation, in the walls instead of insulation, under the floors. There's some in the chimney." He

giggled and looked at Pegeen as if he expected her to appreciate this particular embellishment.

"It's under my *feet?*" Donny said, aghast.

"Some of it. Some over your head, too."

"Is it rigged to go off?"

"It's interconnected. I can set it off anywhere and it will all go up but it will be more efficient to do it from the cellar first."

"Why? Why would you bomb your own house, you crazy little fuck?"

"I had to store it somewhere. Did you want me to just throw a tarp over it and leave it in the yard? How about putting it in the kitchen so that every teenager with nothing to do can take some when he drops by to drink beer and fuck his girlfriend—pardon my French, Robin."

"Why didn't you keep it in New York?"

"Do you know how much ANFO you need to blow up the George Washington Bridge? I don't mean just stopping traffic, I mean knocking it into the river? Tons."

"You got that much shit *here?* Ready to go? And I'm *standing* on it?"

"I fooled you, you never would have guessed."

"Don't you know what could happen? You could blow us all up!"

"Never happen."

"The place could catch on fire. I mean, look at it, anything could happen. Some kid could light a fire in the fireplace."

Cole shrugged. "The house could burn down and it wouldn't explode. It takes a blasting device to set it off."

"How do you know?"

"I'm an expert. I know as much about explosives as anybody. More."

"Maybe you read one of the books wrong, you can't be sure about all this."

"I am absolutely sure."

"You never made a mistake in your life?"

"One. A long time ago."

"Do other experts stick this stuff in their chimneys?"

Cole turned to Pegeen. "You see how people defer to authority? He won't believe I'm an expert until he sees my name on an explosives manual." He turned back to Donny, savagely. "Do you seriously think the Roosevelt Island tramway, the Holland Tunnel, and the Triborough Bridge were just *luck?* The only thing that will turn this house into a bomb, no matter how much ANFO I stuff it with, is a blasting device."

"You're sure?"

"I'm positive. . . . I've only got a couple installed."

"Holy shit!"

"Not where anyone could set them off by accident. I needed them in case of emergency."

"What kind of emergency would make you blow up your house?" Donny grabbed Cole by the shirt and yanked him to his feet. He pressed the gun against his temple. "Disarm this shit! Now!"

"I'm not sure it can withstand the impact of a bullet, though. I never considered that."

"You think I need a bullet to kill you? There are a hundred different ways to kill you. If you don't disarm this place right now, I'll show you about six of them."

"I think you have a phobia, frankly. You might consider talking to someone about it. They're only chemicals, you know. I'm in complete control of them at all times."

Donny wheeled him around, raised the pistol over Cole's head, then stopped abruptly, looking out the window.

"There's someone out there," he said. His voice had come down from the level of hysteria to a near whisper.

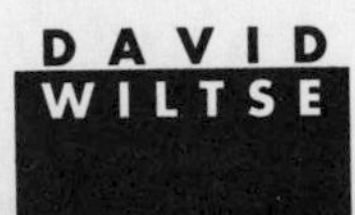

Now, Pegeen thought. Get your weapon *now.*

Before she could move, Donny took one step in her direction, swung the butt of the gun into her temple, and simultaneously grabbed her by the hair with his free hand. Disoriented and injured, Pegeen clawed at his hand. Later she realized that she should have gone for her pistol right then, when Donny was agitated and trying to haul her across the floor. Later, of course, was too late.

Donny manhandled her across the kitchen and thrust her into the empty refrigerator and slammed the door.

"I don't think she can breathe in there," Cole said.

"No shit. She can't warn anybody, either."

"Why would she warn anybody?"

Donny strode to the front window and looked out, pointing. Light from the setting sun flashed off glass two hundred yards away amid a copse of trees that bordered the drive.

"Who the fuck do you think is out there?" Donny demanded. "A neighbor come for a cup of tea? One of your teenagers?"

"Maybe."

"Then why hide the car in the trees? Why walk that far? And where the fuck is he? Do you see him? That's because he's checking the place out before he comes in."

"He? I don't . . . Donny, you don't mean Becker! Not Becker! Don't let him get me. Oh, God, Donny, you mustn't let him get me."

Cole clung to Donny's arm. He looked like a child awaiting some awful punishment from his parent.

"No one's going to get you," said Donny softly. "I told you I'd take care of you, and I will—even if you act like an asshole some of the time."

"It's him, isn't it! It's him."

"The fuck do I know who it is?"

"It's him, I know it is. I can feel him out there."

"Even if it is, he doesn't know exactly what you look like. Nobody knows exactly. That means it's going to take a couple seconds before he's sure and takes any action."

"What good are a couple of seconds?"

"How long do you think I need? I don't intend to introduce myself. Now just sit down, sit right there and wait. When he comes, be polite, say hello, talk to him."

"I can't talk to him, I'm *afraid* of him. Why don't you understand that? I told you that when I saw him on TV. He scares me. You said you were going to take care of it . . ."

"I'm going to take care of it now."

"You said you were going to take care of it then. You told me, you promised me—I don't want him near me, Donny!"

"I'm going to take care of him now. Now just sit there and read your scrapbook until he comes."

"Where will you be?"

Donny paused. "Better you don't know. I don't want you looking at me when he comes. I'll be close."

"How close?"

"Close enough to smell him when he dies."

CHAPTER

BECKER LOOKED FIRST FOR A TREE line standing against the lower level of the cleared fields. When he located it he moved stealthily toward the woods, keeping the setting sun over his shoulder so that the nearly horizontal rays would discourage anyone from looking in his direction. He could just see the upper story of the house in the distance—which meant that anyone in one of the upper windows could also see him. If they were looking. He might appear as no more than a black dot against the sun, but he would be moving, he would be detectable if someone was squinting into the light.

The ravine lay within the tree line like a gash cut with a saw. Erosion had long since defeated nature's attempts at soil building and the underlying rocks lay exposed like a picture in a geology text, twisted and bent and molded into contours unlike those in which they were originally laid down. Becker clambered down the steep side of the ravine and found himself in shadow at the bottom where a small stream hurried past as if frightened of the dark.

It was surprisingly cool at the bottom of the gouge in the earth. And very beautiful in the way that nature's tortured scenes are, arresting and stark. Becker walked carefully through the ravine, avoiding the stream and studying the walls of rock. Much of it was jagged and abrupt, and without the trained eye of a geologist he was not certain which slice or hack could have been made by man and which by the planet's epochal but incessant restless twisting upheavals.

He came at last to a rent in the earth different from the others. A hillock of scree led up to a vertical scoop in the rock that looked like a recess for a giant funerary urn, and some of the standing stone was blackened as if burned. Becker clambered to the top of the talus and reached his arm toward the dark smudges. He could not reach them and could not have done so with a six-foot torch. There was no way a man could have set fire to the side of a slab of stone that high off the ground. He scanned the trees along the top of both sides of the ravine. It did not look possible that lightning would have hit the hillside but missed the trees, even given the quixotic nature of thunderbolts. A man-made planted charge could have done it, however. He was standing in Spring's laboratory.

If the ravine was the lab, the house was the logical storehouse. Becker climbed to the top of the ravine and looked toward the dwelling. From his position he could see only the chimney and, fifty yards to one side, the upper branches of the canopy of the old oak that rose above the house and shared its hilltop. There were another twenty minutes or so before the sun would be below the horizon. Allow another half hour after that for the final glow to be gone from the sky and for night to descend on the farm. Becker found a comfortable position against a tree trunk and settled in to wait.

After he had made his plan of attack, he tried to empty his mind and let his spirit prepare for the necessary work ahead, just as he let his eyes adjust to the waning light. Spring had eluded him in the way no other quarry ever had—not on the ground but in his mind. Becker understood serial killers, men who killed because of the

rewards—sexual, emotional, psychological—that it provided them. To his enormous shame and at a serious cost to his spirit, Becker also knew those secret, lethal pleasures. He had struggled against their lure all his life—and he had failed because it was just that understanding that allowed him to be so extraordinarily successful in tracking the others who succumbed. In schoolyard parlance, it took one to know one, and Becker qualified. As a reformed alcoholic feels forever the unquenchable thirst no matter the length of his sobriety, Becker could never fully repress his own haunting urge. The Bureau, and his targets, made his *actions* legal, even laudable. But the urge . . . the *urge* . . .

Spring was different. If Becker had had so much trouble catching his scent in the air, it was because Spring was not a kindred spirit. He did not kill for the pleasure of killing. He was not concerned about the deaths of other people one way or the other. They were incidental to his true joy. Becker was not certain yet that he could name that joy. But his strongest instinct was not to understand Spring. It was first to find him . . . And then to deal with him.

Cole sat on the daybed, facing the front door, his hands folded in his lap, waiting like a child who has been promised punishment when Father comes home. Donny had turned down the sound but left the snowy picture on the television set and Cole saw images of the debacle in Van Cortland Park captured by a film crew that had been shooting a documentary on the basketball tournament. He smiled to himself, grateful that Donny was not there to see it. He had not told Donny about the ransom payoff for the same reason he had not informed him of the bomb in the garbage truck—he would not have approved. Donny would have wanted to partake in the millions. Like everyone else, Donny still thought it was about the money, no matter how often Cole told him otherwise. The ransom was just another way to make the city bleed. Just one more injury to be administered in the name of justice. It was of no interest to Cole who ultimately ended up with the five million—as long as it wasn't the city of New York.

When Donny discovered what had happened in Van Cortland Park, he would have to be dealt with, of course. Cole understand that the man's motives for helping him were mixed and had something to do with friendship and maybe something to do with sexual appetites, and seemingly something to do with honor and obligation as well, but all of them were hedged round and united by greed for the money. Remove the money from the equation and it was like withdrawing the buffers from a charge—what was stable suddenly became volatile. And dangerous. When the time came Cole would be forced to deal with Donny as he had dealt with Defone—he was, after all, only a more sophisticated, more professional version of Defone when all was said and done. In the meantime, the man still had his uses, and getting rid of Becker was the primary one.

Becker was out there, Cole was sure of it. He could sense his presence like a great lowering cloud looming just below the horizon. Cole had no illusions about what destiny Becker intended for him. He had seen those eyes staring at him for hours, frozen on the VCR; he had heard him describe Cole's fate in unmistakable terms. "You are not forgiven," he had said, and Cole knew exactly what he meant, just as if he had been in the same room when he said it. Cole did not fear the rest of the establishment. They were hemmed in by laws, by social policy, by a psychology that wanted to *understand* Cole as much as they wanted to stop him. How can he hate us so much? they would ask. Where have we gone wrong? they would demand. And when Cole explained, they would understand. And when they understood, they would forgive him.

But Becker would not. Becker had said so. He had looked into Cole's eyes and had seen into Cole's soul and he had understood it

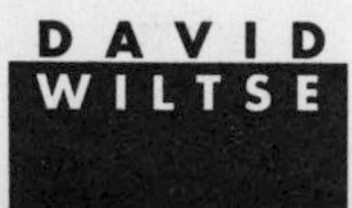

all and forgiven nothing. Becker was not the establishment. He was its wrath.

Just beyond the television the sun was setting in the corner of Cole's eye. With a chill he sensed something moving against the background of the glowing orb and glanced and winced and perceived only a black dot, now there, now gone. And now his eyes were filled with dancing burning shapes as if fiery embers of the sun had blown free of the great fire and implanted themselves on his pupil. He rubbed his eyes with the backs of his hands and smeared the red and green blobs further. When he was able to look again, shielding his eyes this time by peering through a slit between his fingers, he saw nothing backlit by the sunlight. No dark figures streaking toward Armageddon, no scepter-wielding death's-head rider coming at the house. But still he was out there. Cole *knew.*

Cole held a hand over the eye closest to the window, blocking the sun entirely until his vision cleared. He kept his gaze on the door and waited. The television had left the news and now he was annoyed by the inane figures of a game show that were mouthing and gesticulating on the screen. He wanted to turn off the set but was afraid to get closer to the door lest Becker suddenly come through it. If he rose he would leave his back exposed, a prospect as unthinkable as in a nightmare.

He waited, paralyzed by his growing terror. He wanted to call out Donny's name, he wanted the tall thin man to take him in his arms the way he had done that night when they first met back in Cole's apartment on West Eighty-seventh Street. But if Donny were in the house, holding Cole in his arms, he could not be wherever he was now, hidden, protecting him from Becker.

He thought briefly of Robin. He could open the refrigerator and let her hold him and make the furies vanish the way his mother had done when he was troubled in the night. Robin would do it, she liked him, he could tell. But then she might turn on him as his mother always had, comforting with one hand, punishing with the other, promising so much, delivering so little, praising with the sarcastic bite that cut to the bone—then expressing bewilderment and innocence when he cried. It was better not to trust her, not to trust anyone, than to be betrayed. He believed what she had said about his writings—they *were* brilliant, he knew it—but still she might change and admit to doubts, hint at criticisms, imply faults. Ultimately she was not to be trusted either. No one was. It was always safer to leave them before they left you. Do unto others, but sooner.

But for now, to have her comfort him when he was so frightened—maybe she would be different, maybe she wouldn't make him feel safe, then call him a baby, maybe she wouldn't taunt him for his bed-wetting or his fear of the dark or . . . But the thought of crossing all the way to the kitchen, of exposing himself for all that distance when Becker might be lurking in any shadow . . . no, no, no. He wrapped his arms around himself and squirmed backward so that his back was pressed hard against the daybed cushion, and that against the wall. The hands of evil could not reach through the wall *and* the cushion.

Shadows lengthened across the room and the sun was no longer heating the side of his face. Darkness grew from the floor up until all the light was gone in the house except the fuzzy glow of the television. It had been less than an hour since Donny had noticed the glint of light from the car's windshield but to Cole it seemed like days before he heard the tread upon the porch.

It sounded to Cole like the knell of doom. Becker had come, he had evaded Donny, and now he was going to look at Cole with those eyes that could bore into his soul. Those loathing, unforgiving eyes. Cole squeezed his own eyes shut. Whatever was going to happen to him he did not want to see. He thought his heart would leap through his chest or simply explode and kill him where he sat.

Another step. A pause. A knock on the door.

"Hello? . . . Anybody home?"

Cole held his breath, his eyes squeezed so tightly shut his head shook from the effort.

Another knock. Another questioning "Hello." The sound of the doorknob turning, the door easing open with a squeal. Cole's eyes flew open involuntarily.

A dark form filled the doorway, staring directly at him.

"Well, hello, asshole. Imagine meeting you here." The form stepped into the room and another shape appeared behind him, a taller, thinner shadow that lifted a gun and fired into the first form's head with a *pffff.* Cole squealed with delight.

Donny stood over the fallen body and fired twice more into the head while Cole cheered and applauded.

"Stop that," Donny snapped. "This ain't no ball game. Quit acting like a kid."

"But you did it, you killed him!"

"Yeah, I killed him." With his toe, Donny rolled the body onto its back. "You don't want to look at this, it ain't pretty."

But Cole hurried to see, as excited as a child at the scene of an accident.

"It's not him," he gasped.

"It's him," Donny said. "It just ain't Becker."

"Who is it?"

"A cop. Name's Meisner."

"How do you know?"

Donny shrugged. "He's a friend of a friend. I see him around. Simple as that."

"You didn't kill Becker," Cole said dully. He was already losing interest in the corpse on the floor. "You said you were going to but you didn't."

"Not yet."

"You said you would!"

"Shut the fuck up!" Donny lifted his hand to strike Cole, who cowered and scurried back to his position on the daybed.

"You said."

"Don't tell me what I said."

"You lied to me. You lie to me and you lie to me, you say you'll do something and you don't, you *promise* and you never do it, and I just can't trust you at all—"

"Be quiet and calm down."

"You are not to be trusted. You're an old queer and I can't believe you about anything."

Donny looked darkly at Cole and Cole could see traces of Becker in his eyes.

"I've had about enough of you," Donny whispered.

"What does that mean?"

"When I get back, we're going to reexamine the nature of this relationship. I don't think you quite get the picture."

"I know I can't trust you, I know that much. You never ever keep your promises. You say you'll give me things but you don't, you just say it to make me hope so you can hurt me later."

"What are we talking about, a new sled for Christmas? You want a present? Here's one, a dead cop. Stay here and I'll bring you another one."

"Where are you going?"

"This guy works with Becker, he's part of his unit. You think he came up here on his own? You think he's smart enough to find you by himself? He doesn't even have jurisdiction here. He couldn't arrest you if he wanted to. If he's here, Becker's here."

"He *is* here," said Cole with horror.

"Well, I wouldn't worry about it. So am I."

Donny started out the door again.

"Don't leave me again! What am I supposed to do?"

"Move around a little bit, make some noise, let him see you, let

him hear you. When he comes for you I'll take him." Donny turned up the volume on the television set and stepped into the darkness to the accompaniment of a sitcom theme song.

"Don't go! Don't, don't!" Cole followed after Donny as far as the door, then stopped at the wall of darkness. Donny had already vanished.

Cole retreated into the relative security of the house, beside himself with fear. He had seen the specter of the demon flash behind Donny's eyes when he looked at him. If Becker didn't come through the door to devour him, then Donny would. He was once more without friends or protection in a hostile world. He could rely only on himself. He would do what he knew how to do. He would do what he did well.

CHAPTER 42

PEGEEN HAD BEEN HURLED INTO the refrigerator with her knees pressed against her chest and her head lower than her feet. Her first chores were to right herself and to fight against the sense of claustrophobia that threatened to unhinge her. Working inch by inch, using her shoulders and toes for leverage, she finally achieved something resembling a sitting position. She was still wedged together like a fetus, but at least her head was on top, the blood was flowing where it should. It took several more painful minutes of maneuvering to raise her right elbow high enough to attain the proper angle for getting her pistol out of the holster.

Her primary concern was oxygen. She did not know how much of an air supply she had or how long it would last, but she was certain that eventually it must be exhausted, and she had to find a way to free herself, or at least breathe, before then.

There was no way to undo the latch from the inside and she was not even certain where it was. The door met the walls without knob or protrusion except for a strip of corded insulating material that ran the length of the seam. She tore it off easily enough and knew no more than she had before. Leaning her ear against the join, she tried to feel the existence of air coming into her box even though she knew it was futile. If removal of the insulating seal let in air it would also let in light and the refrigerator was as dark as a coffin underground.

Feeling as far as she could reach with her hand and then with her shoes and finally with her elbow, she could detect the bumps of the metallic screws that had been hidden under the insulating seal. She quickly learned that loosening them with her fingers was impossible.

She hesitated to try to shoot her way out for several reasons. First, she did not know what to shoot at. The catch was thick metal inserted into the very frame of the fridge, it was not like blowing a key lock out of a wooden door, and she didn't know exactly where the lock was in the first place. Second, if she fired her weapon, Donny would know she was armed. She would lose the element of surprise and have as much chance of getting out alive as a stationary target in a shooting gallery. Finally, and most frightening to Pegeen, was the possibility that the bullet would not penetrate the metal door at all but stay inside the refrigerator, ricocheting back and forth in the few square feet of the box as if in a pinball machine. She could kill herself several times with one bullet.

Fate had given her several options of how to die and she did not like any of them.

Donny the Snake Sabela left the house and sat on the upper step of the porch, looking straight ahead into the darkness in the direction of the car hidden amid the trees by the road. He waited until his eyes adjusted and sat perfectly still, watching for any sign of movement. He did not really expect Becker to come straight at the front of the house but it did no harm to check. He heard the noise of the television set behind him, and now and then little squawks, not quite words, as Jason vocalized his fears and indignations. The man had lived alone too long, talking to himself like that. Too much solitude made a man unfit for the company of others. Donny had been *single* all his life, but that wasn't the same as being constantly alone. Talking to a bed partner now and then was all you needed. It was enough to keep you sane, at least. Not that Jason would know anything about bed partners. Wouldn't know what to do if he found one under the covers, buck naked and ready to go. The man was not even enough in touch with himself to realize that he was gay. Thought he was straight. A straight man of thirty-five who had never slept with a woman. Uh-huh, sure. Now *that* was pathetic.

After he had killed Becker he would have to figure out what to do with Jason. He was beginning to look as if he wasn't worth the five million dollars, or worth the effort in any other department, either. Donny could abandon him. He could kill him. He could turn him in for the reward . . . No, that was not an honorable thing to do, under the circumstances. Easier just to kill him.

When he had sat stock-still for long enough so that anyone watching would begin to think he was a fixture of the house and not deserving of surveillance, Donny fell in one swift motion to his hands and knees behind the overgrown shrubs that fronted the porch. Using the hedges as cover, he crawled to the side of the house and paused for a moment under the window. He could hear Jason muttering in a rising tone, like a petulant child in argument.

A large shade tree sat atop a rise between the house and the barn on the highest point on the farm. It afforded a view of all approaches to the house except the one coming straight up the driveway, the one least likely to be used. Once there Donny could see anything that moved larger than a mouse. He worked his way toward the tree on his belly, keeping himself well below the cover of the weeds. The noises of the television—punctuated by the occasional squawk from Jason—would cover any sounds he made.

He took his time. Haste would only make him more likely to be discovered. Fifteen yards away from the tree he paused to rest,

listening to the sounds of the night audible over his own labored breathing and the noises from the house. Crickets, locusts, and frogs were all giving voice somewhere and a mosquito emitted a high-pitched warning whine close to his ear. He waved it away with his hand. A breeze had sprung up and it rustled the leaves of the tree just ahead of him. He heard one branch swish against another and rolled onto his back to look up at the canopy that stretched across the sky like a cloud. He had not been aware of the size of the tree. It was huge; the trunk was broad enough to hide two men. A perfect spot for him.

Donny crawled the rest of the way to the tree, then carefully stood up, rising as slowly as he could force his muscles to move, his back against the trunk so that his shape would meld seamlessly with the tree. When he was fully upright at last, he took a deep, quiet breath and felt the arm slide around his throat and tighten.

"Federal agent. You're under arrest," a voice hissed in his ear.

The arm tightened and Donny was lifted off the ground, up toward the canopy. Choking and gasping for breath, he clawed for the gun in the holster under his armpit. He lifted it to fire blindly above him but a hand grabbed his wrist and forced the gun away, into the dark. The .22 coughed discreetly once and shot at the stars.

Hurriedly making his preparations in the upstairs bedroom, Cole looked outside at a sudden spark in the darkness. Disbelieving, he saw giant forms writhe in the night. Donny, his feet kicking in midair, was clawing at his throat with one hand while the other pointed at the sky and sparked again. The second form was harder to discern, harder still to believe. A man hung upside down from the lower branches of the ancient oak like a catcher in a trapeze act and he had Donny by the neck, holding him in the air so that he danced like a marionette.

Becker! Of course it was Becker. No longer abstract, no longer just *out there* somewhere. Cole watched with horrified fascination as if at one serpent swallowing another. Death grappling with death.

With a squeal he yanked himself away from the spectacle and raced to finish his job. Hands shaking, fingers stiff as stones, he tried to slide the detonator into place. Sweat had burst forth on his brow and on his upper lip under the weedy mustache that Donny had demanded he cultivate. He blinked and blinked. His vision seemed to be failing him. He wished he had his glasses with him but Donny had made him jettison those, too. Everything looked blurry to him now and he forced himself to stop and concentrate. Concentrate. This was not the time to make a mistake, but how could he do it with his nerves screaming at him? He had no time. To hurry would cause mishaps, but he had no time. *No* time. No time!

The detonator fell from his hands and rolled under the bed. Muttering with fear and weeping now, he crawled after it. It was too dark under the bed! He couldn't see without his glasses! What did she expect of him! What was he supposed to do when he couldn't see and it was too dark and there was a monster devouring a monster in the tree. It wasn't his fault, none of it was his fault . . . His groping fingers found the detonator.

Growing light-headed, Pegeen found herself giggling at her predicament. A sure sign of oxygen deprivation, she told herself. You should not be laughing. You should be *acting* and now, while you still can. There was no point in any further thinking, she had thought it all through. All she needed to do was act. She selected the angle that she had calculated would not put the caroming bullet into her body on the first ricochet. By the second or third it would hit her, there was nowhere else for it to go.

She felt as if she were putting the gun to her own temple but her air was gone, she had no choice. Closing her eyes even though she was totally blind in the utter dark of the refrigerator, she squeezed the trigger.

Becker had underestimated his adversary. Donny was stronger than he thought, his will to survive more tenacious, his struggles more draining of Becker's energy. His grip on Donny's windpipe was not complete and the man was still getting air. Not much, but enough to keep him twisting in the air and trying to pull his gun hand free, and every gyration drained a bit more of Becker's strength.

It had become a test of endurance and the gains were incremental, but Becker felt himself being slowly worn down. He knew it and, worse, the man he was trying to overcome knew it. Activated by his sweat, the scent of cologne rose pungently from Donny's neck and face, and even in the midst of the battle Becker thought of the irony of the situation. Donny had made a mistake in their first encounter and Becker had made one this time. Donny's error had not proven fatal—Becker's might.

Too old for the job, Becker thought grimly as the other man began to slip away. Too old and not going to get much older.

Donny was free. He fell to the ground, gasping, as Becker hauled himself up into the branches. Donny fired once while rolling on his back and missed everything. Scrambling to his feet, he shot again and the bullet sank into the tree trunk.

Taking his time now, he located Becker's moving shadow amongst the limbs and held the gun as steadily as he could with both hands. He centered the gun on Becker's chest and night became day, the house turned into the sun and the giant oak began to fall. Donny was smashed to the ground with the force of the shock wave and he lay there, immobilized, as the mighty tree was bent sideways, its limbs and leaves acting like a sail, then snapping under the force. The trunk cracked with a noise that was lost in the deafening roar of the explosion, roots buried for centuries tore from the earth, and the ancient oak collapsed onto Donny the Snake and drove him deeply into the ground.

Becker was saved from the blast by the shelter of the trunk and when the tree fell he fell with it, but to the side so that the huge bulk of the oak missed him. He hit the ground with a shelter of limbs around him, still shielding him as debris of the house clattered down like the fallout of an artillery attack. Bricks from the chimney struck the tree trunk; nails, furniture, and shattered lumber tore through the foliage around him; shrapnel of metal and plastic, wood and mortar tattooed the earth. Becker lay beside the huge bole of the oak like a man in a bunker as a whirlwind of deadly debris sizzled and hissed and ripped over his head.

The wind suddenly reversed as air rushed in to fill the vacuum caused by the explosion. A tormented, roiling cloud boiled over the space where once the house had stood, rising slowly into the night sky, a balloon and pennant of destruction. Wind sucked and moaned as it raced through the foliage over Becker's head and joined the rising column of grit and ash and heat.

Becker lay motionless for a long time, thinking he had been deafened by the blast. His body was sore and a lesser branch had lashed him painfully on the shin but, miraculously, he was intact. Eventually he made his way to his feet, pulling himself up through a weave of bent and broken branches.

A full moon had risen as if summoned to see what calamity had struck the earth, and the night was startlingly bright. The tree was fifty yards from the house and every foot of the distance was littered with debris. Becker's hideout had been subjected only to the relatively small stuff; the items grew heavier the closer to the house they lay. Entire chunks of the foundation had been gouged out of the earth and Becker realized that much of the explosion had been underground. The old barn had been toppled like a house of straw and a Volkswagen lay on its back amidst the rubble, wheels up, a beetle on its back.

There was nothing left of the house but a hole in the ground. A refrigerator lay facedown in the hole, still rocking from side to side, and portions of the staircase and the furnace had been driven straight downward into the earthen floor of the basement where they sat, curiously intact, like the vanguards of some strange city emerging from the soil. Water had begun to seep into the excavation from subterranean springs but everything else was hot to the touch. Becker lowered himself into the hole. He would need daylight and a team of searchers to comb the surrounding area but at least he could give a cursory look to the remnants of the house by moonlight.

There was an eerie sound that seemed to emanate from everything on the site as if a giant tuning fork had been set to vibrating. Becker was not sure if things were still resonating in some way, or if the sound was in his ears, part of his deafness. There had been a workshop in the basement; some of its relics had been driven sideways rather than up and Becker recognized smashed bits of tools and printed wrappers from chemical supplies. There was so much broken glass underfoot that it was like walking on crusted snow.

In the sterile light of the moon he worked his way around the perimeter of the hole where most of the material lay. Some had been blown straight up and had cascaded back down but most of what remained had been forced into the foundations, or what remained of them. Whatever had been aboveground to begin with was now in pieces in the huge target circle stretching for yards around the house.

He could tell by the sheared pipe ends where the kitchen and the bathrooms must have been. The refrigerator had been tossed the length of the house and was still gently oscillating on its face at the opposite end of the basement. He found one leg of an old-fashioned stove but the rest was nowhere in sight. A toilet had fallen bowl down not far from the refrigerator.

In a corner was an ancient manual typewriter, its normal boxy shape made oblong by contact with the wall. Underneath it, stubs of fingers curled as delicately as if cradling a butterfly, was a human hand. The tips of the fingers had been severed at the first knuckle by flying debris as if with a butcher knife. The letter *s* of the typewriter, severed from its armature, lay in the palm, a freakishly demure deposit of the blast.

There was no other sign of Spring in the hole and Becker realized that it was possible that only bones would ever be found. He kicked the toilet to its side and sat down on it, feeling inexpressibly weary. The little prick had killed himself. Whether by design or accident, he had blown himself into little pieces, showered himself on the countryside. Although the bomber's demise was appropriate, Becker felt disappointed. He had wanted him for himself. The assassin with the .22 was just a sideshow. Becker had not obsessed on him, hunted him, tried to worm his way into his psyche. He had not hungered for his blood the way he had with Spring. He had wanted Spring to die, but not by his own hand. Not from the same chemicals with which he had caused such destruction in New York.

Stunned by the blast and the gale winds it caused, nature had been silenced for several minutes, but now it came back, resuming its nighttime symphony of peeps and scrapes and cheeps. To his astonishment Becker heard it and realized that he was not deaf. Not deaf, not dead, not even seriously injured. Just tired. Very lucky, very tired. He could have died as a result of his own stupidity and incompetence, killed by a thug whom he would have dealt with in past years with one hand. He was spared that death only by the explosion that could have killed him as easily as it did the assassin and Spring.

It was time to quit. Quit completely this time, just give it all up

and walk away from it. Find something else to do. Learn to love gardening and try to figure out the mysteries of cyberspace. Take courses. Take care of his wife.

He heard the shifting crunch of glass and noticed the refrigerator still moving gently. To his amazement he realized that it was not residual energy from the blast coupled with a miracle of balance that kept the appliance in motion. The refrigerator was not just rocking, it was moving with a pattern. It was sending code.

Squatting as low as he could get, Becker lifted and pushed. He prized the refrigerator up a couple of feet and pulled a loose chunk of concrete foundation under the appliance with his foot to hold it in place before squatting and pushing again, moving the big machine off of its door. Working the concrete chunk ever farther under the refrigerator and increasing the angle with every effort, he labored for several minutes until the machine collapsed with a thud onto its side.

He opened the door to find Pegeen pointing a gun in his face. She was laughing and crying at the same time.

"Thank God," he said.

"John . . ."

"I thought you were dead," he said.

"I was. I was," Pegeen blurted incoherently.

Before he could help her out she closed her eyes abruptly and for a moment he thought she had fainted. She broke her stillness with a sob and gasp for air so deep it racked her whole body.

She wept, her eyes squeezed shut, sucking in air in tortured spasms and exhaling with a sighing moan. Becker let her have her cry and when she came out of it she was giggling again.

"Guess what?" she asked.

"What?"

She laughed as if it were the silliest joke. "I shot myself twice with the same bullet. Isn't that stupid?"

When he got her out of the refrigerator he saw the bloody hole in one calf, a dark spot against her white flesh in the moonlight. The bullet was sticking out of the flesh of the other leg, so spent it could penetrate no farther. Becker plucked it out with his fingers. He felt the rest of her legs, searching for injuries.

"Like a dray horse," she said before she collapsed in his arms.

Becker put her on his back and carried her up and out of the hole. As he cleared a space amongst the debris with his foot and laid her gently on the ground he heard a siren wailing in the distance.

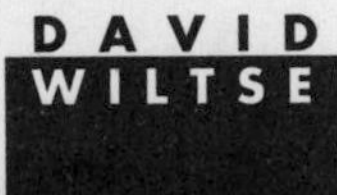

CHAPTER 43

DEFONE LEE AND TONY THE GOOD Buono marched single file through Central Park at precisely three minutes after the hour, just as the gangbangers had insisted. Defone walked slightly ahead of Tony, who poked him in the back every once in a while to remind him who had the gun.

"Don't have to keep doing that," Defone said, getting annoyed. "Ain't about to forget you back there."

"It makes me feel good," Tony replied.

"Poking me in the back make you feel good?"

"That's right."

"Should have been a massager. Get to jab peoples in the back all day long and get paid for it."

"I'm getting paid for this, too," Tony reminded him. They had left the last of Tony's people at the edge of the park—again at the gangbangers' insistence. A cluster of gang members had been there too, and Tony's toughs and the black boys were last seen scowling and posturing at each other. It was supposed to be a three man engagement in the park. Only Tony, Defone, and the spokesman for the gangs, an evil-looking punk called Latch, were allowed.

"Man's name is Latch?" Tony had snorted. "What is it with these people and the nicknames?"

"Tony the Good be asking me this?" Defone had stared at him as if he was crazy, but then that was Defone's reaction to just about everything Tony had done for the last twenty-four hours, since the ransom snatch in the Bronx. Tony thought it was time for Defone to have another baptism. Hold him in the vat for a real long time, see if he wouldn't get some religion that stuck for more than a day.

It was sundown and every sane person was leaving the park. Tony and Defone walked against the flow.

"In ten minutes I'll be the only white man left in the park," Tony said, feeling increasingly uneasy.

"You sure one racist whitey, ain't you?"

"I'm doing business with you, ain't I? How racist can I be?"

"I don't know. They got an outer limit to it?"

As they approached the Sheep Meadow the fading sunlight was directly in their eyes. Squinting behind his sunglasses, Tony could just make out the figure of Latch standing in the middle of the meadow, halfway up the long slope. Tony had been nervous about the rendezvous until Defone convinced him that the meadow was so large they would be able to be certain the meeting would be for just the three of them, or they could walk away.

Defone thought of cowboy movies again. This was the one where they had the shoot-out on Main Street and the smart one had the sun at his back.

Latch lifted a hand toward them, then casually sat on a small hillock. Other grass-covered mounds surrounded him and dotted the slope as the angle of the sun changed all perspective and produced shadows from even the smallest manifestations of topography. Looks like a graveyard, Defone thought. Boot hill at sundown.

Tony paused and surveyed the meadow. Latch was alone, as promised. The vastness of the park seemed to have become a play-

ground for just the three of them. Tony wondered if the muggers were already in the park, or if they filtered in later, hoping to catch the odd lover, tourist, or idiot after dark.

Tony poked Defone in the back.

"Let's go."

Least he didn't say giddyup, Defone thought. *Treats* me like a mule, though. Going to be an end to that real quick. *Real* quick. Get hold of that money, then come looking for Tony, show him what that bottom of a bathtub look like. Hold his Wop head underwater so long the grease come out.

Defone squinted up the hill at Latch. He liked his odds. If Latch gave them any trouble, Defone and Tony had him outnumbered. If Tony pulled any of his shit, Defone and Latch would have the upper hand, two brothers against the mob. Defone had it covered either way, and he knew sure as hell that the mob and the gangbangers weren't going to cooperate. If they were, Defone wouldn't have been brought along in the first place. He smiled secretly to himself. Defone had outsmarted them both.

Latch stood again as they approached. He had gold on every finger and thumb and enough chains around his neck to serve as a breastplate.

"Where's the money?" Tony demanded, looking around for a satchel or bag. He was still squinting hard into the sun and as he tried to change positions Latch moved with him, keeping the light in his eyes.

"I gots the money," Latch said. "Wouldn't worry about that, I was you."

"If I was *you,* I'd worry about this," Tony said, pulling the Glock from his jacket. "Now where is the money, asshole?"

Latch grinned.

"Something funny?" Tony demanded, waving the gun.

"White folks just naturally make me happy," said Latch. "They so comical."

"I'm about to give you a comical nine-millimeter hole in your dick," said Tony.

"Man is always worried about the black man's dick," Defone said.

"I know that," said Latch. "If he don't want to shoot it, he want to suck it."

"The money, asshole."

Latch smiled and lifted his arms toward the sky, mocking Tony and his single gun.

"Rise and shine," he said.

"What the hell does that mean?"

"It be code, motherfucker," said Latch, laughing.

Holy shit oh dear, thought Defone. All of a sudden they changed movies. This was the one where the cavalry rode through the empty desert and then quick as shit the sand moved and the desert came alive with these Apaches who had buried themselves until the horse soldiers had passed. Latch must have been watching the same movies as Defone, because first the mound right behind him and then all the other mounds that had been casting shadows *moved* and not just moved but rose up and about fifty gangbangers stood up and stepped away from the Astroturf carpets they'd been hiding under. Hard to believe these kids had planned it all, thought Defone. The sunlight blinding Tony, keeping him from telling phony grass from the real stuff, the precise timing, all of it.

"Son of a bitch," Tony muttered reverentially.

"I assume you ain't calling me that *now,*" Latch said.

Defone cheered as the ring of black youth closed in on Tony.

"We got him now, Home," Defone said.

Latch glared at him.

"Whatchoo mean *we,* nigga?" he asked.

CHAPTER 44

BECKER SAT ON A LAWN CHAIR ON the deck of his Clamden home, his feet up on another chair, his head tipped to catch the sun, a beatific smile on his face. Karen knelt in the flower bed that bordered the length of the deck, plucking out weeds and singing softly to herself. Karen had a lovely, gentle voice and seemed to know every song ever written prior to rap music but was needlessly shy about performing. When she sang to herself Becker assumed the role of happy eavesdropper, soaking in whatever she offered. He had learned that to compliment her about a song would only make her self-conscious and silence her for the rest of the day.

"I thought you were going to take up gardening," she said when she had finished the song.

"I've decided I'm better at pure sloth," he said. "I think I have a real knack for it."

"It's a good thing I'm healthy then, isn't it?"

"It certainly is. You can go back to supporting me in my idleness."

"How long do you plan to be idle?"

"A long time. Maybe forever. Why?"

"In that case, I'm happy I'm going back to work."

The telephone rang and Becker handed the portable phone to his wife.

"I'm not in, I'm not here, and I'm gone," he said.

"No matter who it is?"

"Well . . . if it's Sophia Loren I'll take the call. Otherwise, I've gone fishing."

"If it's Sophia Loren I won't give you the phone," she said. She answered the call and listened for a long time before she spoke. Alerted by her silence, Becker opened his eyes and sat upright.

"All right. Thank you for telling me. . . . I'll be in the office on Monday. . . . Yes, I'll be glad to get back to work too. . . . Thank you."

"Not Sophia," he said when she had finished.

"Pegeen Haddad," she said evenly.

"How's her leg?"

"She didn't say."

"I noticed you didn't inquire," he said.

"The lab has done DNA tests on the hand you found in the basement of the house," said Karen.

"Spring's hand. And?"

"They tested it against a blood sample that was taken after the explosion when you were in the apartment on West Eighty-seventh Street."

"I don't remember that we got a blood sample from Spring then."

"This was from the hospital where you and the others were taken. The DNA in the fingerless hand matches the DNA of Detective Arnold Meisner of the NYPD."

"Christ."

Karen nodded. "Apparently Meisner drove to Jenksville and called this man Kjelsen to find out where you had gone. He didn't

tell anyone in the department, so the police knew only that he was missing, not where he'd gone. They found his car abandoned in Bridgeport this morning . . ."

"Bridgeport?"

"In the parking lot of the train station."

"If he left it there how did he get to Jenksville? Is there a train . . . ?"

Karen shook her head. "They think Meisner drove to Jenksville, was killed in the blast, and that someone else drove his car from there to Bridgeport."

"The little shit," Becker said. "It's Spring, isn't it? He got out of there while I was dealing with his gunman, probably cut off the fingertips himself so it would take us a while to realize he wasn't dead, blew up the house, took the car . . ."

"Bridgeport is just over an hour from New York City by train," said Karen.

"He wouldn't go back there, would he? Why would he go back? Why wouldn't he just run away?"

"Unfinished business?"

"It could have been anyone who stole the car, a local kid, anybody. Have they dusted for prints yet?"

"I don't think it will make much difference what prints they find," Karen said. "Thirty minutes ago there was an explosion on the railroad bridge connecting Manhattan and the Bronx. . . . The bastard is still out there."

Becker sat in silence for several moments, watching a yellow cat stalk something in the bushes at the edge of his property. When he turned to Karen she was still on her knees in the dirt, watching him, waiting for him.

"I don't care," he said flatly.

She nodded as if it were her cue to start moving. "I understand. But *I* do." She stood and brushed the dirt from her pants and removed her gardening gloves. "I'll go into work tonight, I think, when the traffic is down."

"I'm out of it," Becker said. "I've had enough. I've *done* enough."

"Nobody's arguing with you," she said.

The yellow cat was preparing to pounce. It was belly down on the ground, its hindquarters quivering in anticipation.

"I mean it," Becker said. "I've had enough. Nobody cares, anyway. Ultimately nobody else gives a damn. They'll find somebody to take my place and they'll catch Spring and then somebody will come along to take *his* place."

"Look, you're right. If you don't want to track down one more lunatic, no one can find fault with that. Personally, I'm not finished. But if you are, so be it." She entered the house.

"I just don't *care,*" he called after her.

The yellow cat sprang forward, all of the quivering excitement unleashed in the form of lethal speed and power. Becker heard, or imagined that he heard, a quick piping squeal of alarm, and then the cat had a field mouse in its jaws. It walked from the bush into the center of the yard and began to play with its victim.

Becker watched as the cat toyed with the still-living mouse, tossing it, letting it move with the momentary illusion of freedom, then holding it in place with a paw while looking around the yard. It regarded Becker carefully for a moment as if fearing he might want the mouse for himself, then resumed its playful torture.

He heard Karen's sweet voice coming from within the house, singing again. Happy, he thought. She's happy to be going back to it.

He rose heavily from his chair and knelt in the flower bed, taking Karen's place. She had made some progress, plucking the earth clean of all but flowers for several yards of bare dirt. Beyond that the weeds took over, a few large ones and a multitude of little

ones, dozens, then hundreds—the closer he looked, the more he saw—of nascent weeds, tiny green sprouts poking from the soil. So many weeds. An endless, thankless chore of tweezing them out, one by one, over and over again. He remembered why he hated gardening.

When Karen finished her song he went into the house.